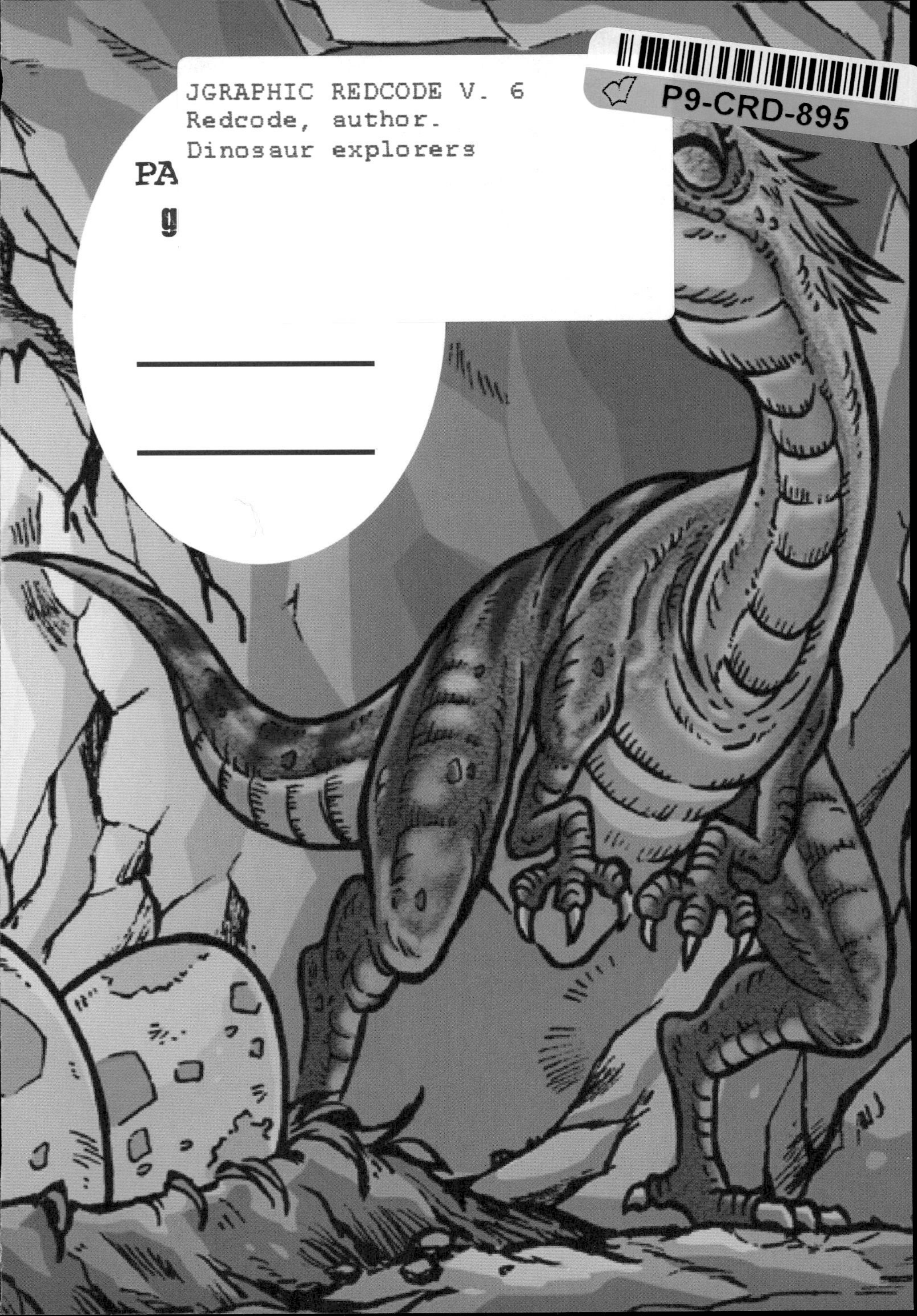
PA
g

DINOSAUR EXPLORERS

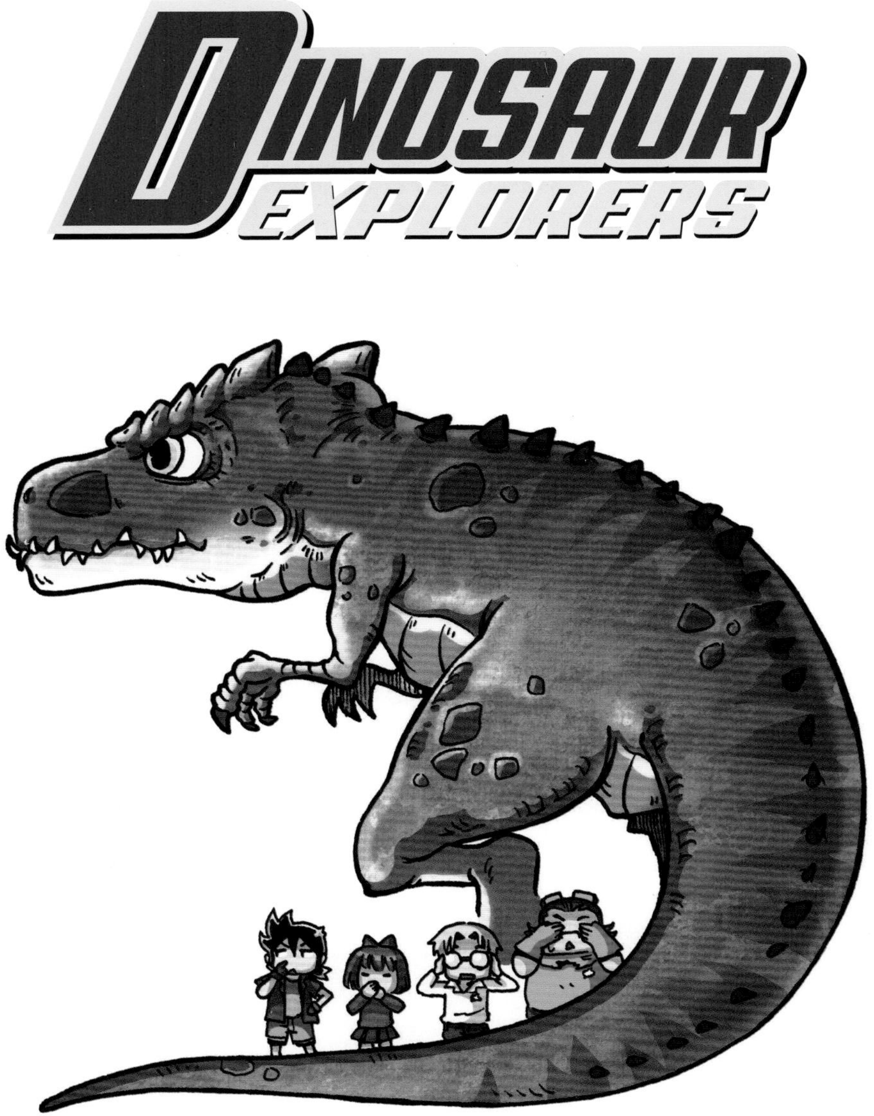

PAPERCUTZ

DINOSAUR EXPLORERS

#6 ESCAPING THE JURASSIC

Original Chinese edition published in 2012 by
KADOKAWA GEMPAK STARZ SDN. BHD., Malaysia.
English translation rights in United States
arranged with KADOKAWA GEMPAK STARZ SDN. BHD., Malaysia.

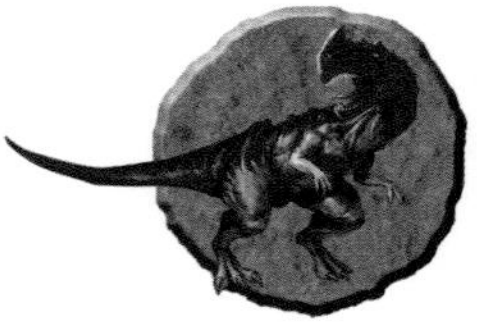

REDCODE & ALBBIE — Story
AIR TEAM — Art
REDCODE & SAMU — Cover Illustration
MAX — Cover Color
EVA, MAX, FUN, SENG HUI — Interior Color
KENNY CHUA & KIAONG — Art Direction
ROUSANG — Original Design
BALICAT & MVCTAR AVRELIVS — Translation
MARK McNABB — Production
ROSS BAUER — Original Editor
SPENSER NELLIS — Editor
JEFF WHITMAN — Managing Editor
JIM SALICRUP
Editor-in-Chief

Papercutz books may be purchased for business or promotional use.
For information on bulk purchase please contact Macmillan
Corporate and Premium Sales Department at (800) 221-7945 x5442

ISBN HC: 978-1-5458-0415-5
ISBN PB: 978-1-5458-0416-2

Printed in China
February 2020

Distributed by Macmillan
First Papercutz Printing

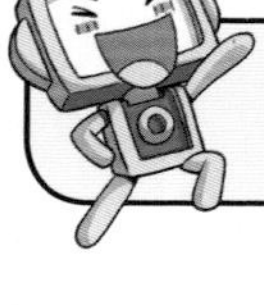

DINOSAUR EXPLORERS Reading Guide
And Lesson Planner available at:
http://papercutz.com/educator-resources-papercutz

DINOSAUR EXPLORERS

#6 ESCAPING THE JURASSIC

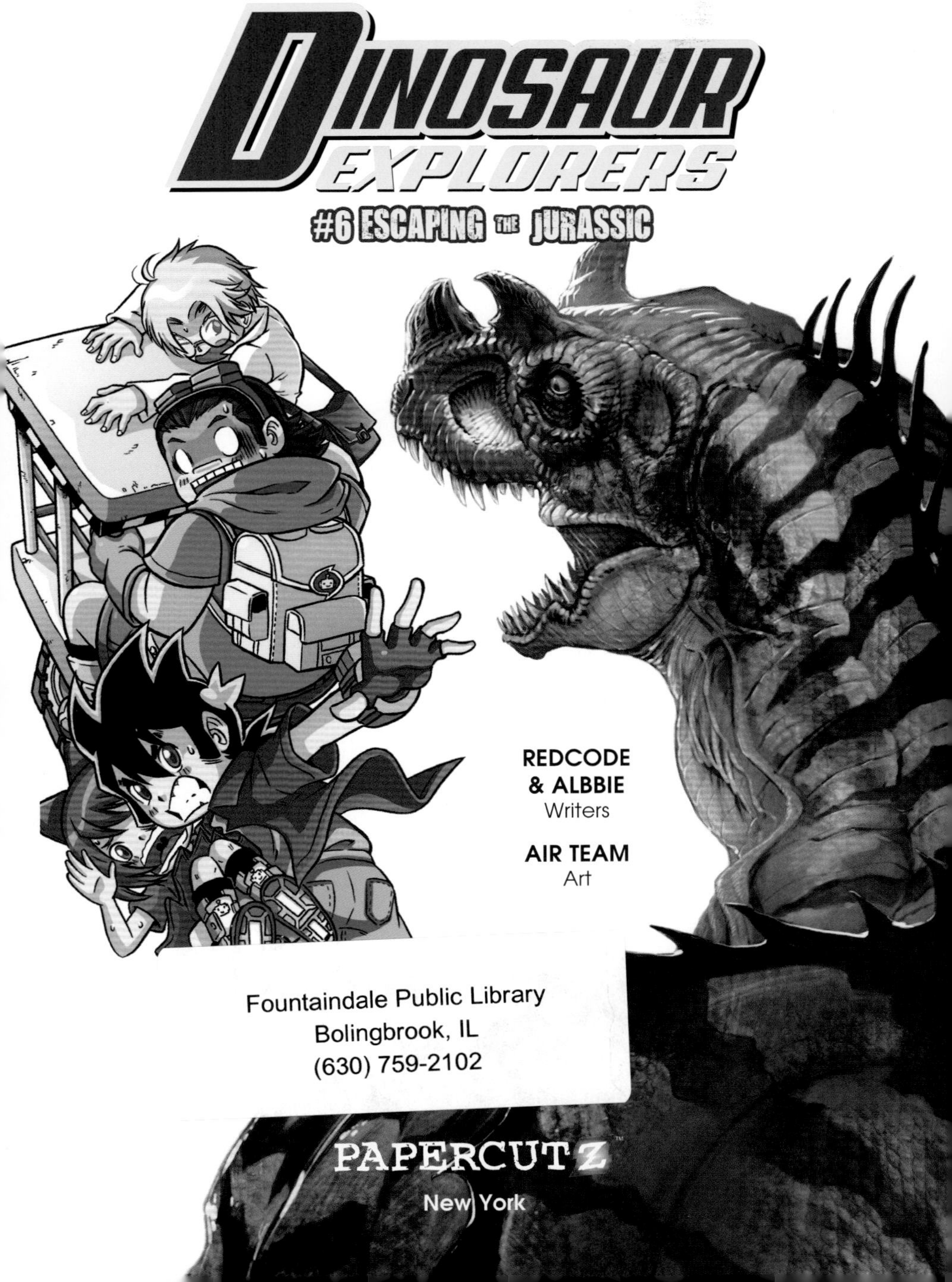

REDCODE & ALBBIE
Writers

AIR TEAM
Art

PAPERCUTZ™
New York

FOREWORD

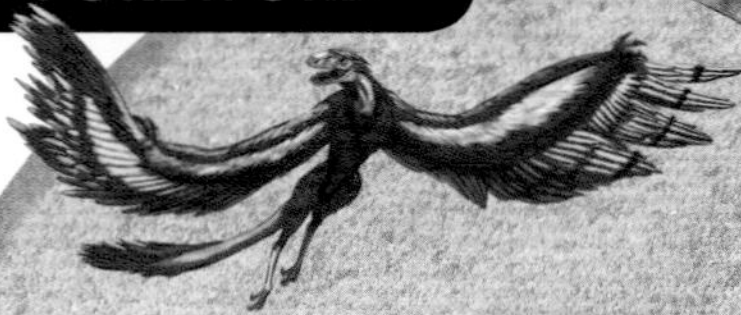

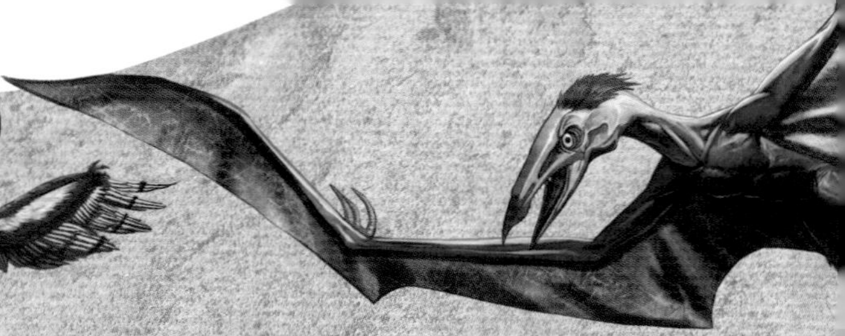

Our planet is more than 4.5 billion years old, but we have only been around for 2 million! What strange creatures inhabited the Earth before we did?

While the DINOSAUR EXPLORERS series does refer to dinosaurs, the first book focused on where they came from—and the creatures even dinosaurs would call prehistoric! This series contains as much fun as scientific information and you will see how our planet was transformed from a dry, barren ball of space rock into the haven it is today. See how the Earth's surface and seas formed, how single-celled microorganisms became complex multi-celled creatures, how bones evolved, and how we are not descended from monkeys, but fish!

Oh, yes, dinosaurs are the stars of the series, —from the magnificent pterosaurs, to the terrifying Tyrannosaurus rex, to the seafaring Icthhyosaurs; all mighty beasts of fact and legend. But even they had to start somewhere, and that is what we presented in the first two volumes of DINOSAUR EXPLORERS.

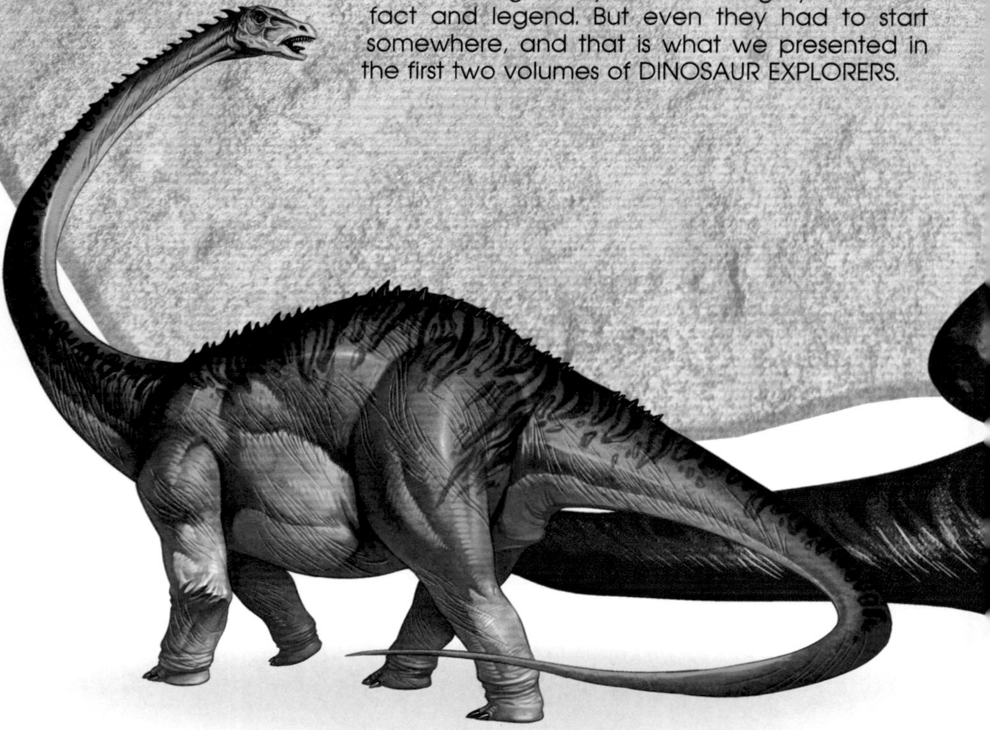

As our heroes try to make their way back to the present, they've been "Puttering in the Paleozoic" (in volume 2), "Playing in the Permian" (volume 3), "Trapped in the Triassic" (volume 4), "Lost in the Jurassic"(volume 5), and now that they've found their way, they're dead set on "Escaping the Jurassic"! Once they've escaped the Jurassic's dangerous dinosaurs, they'll come face-to-face with some "Cretaceous Craziness" (volume 7)!

With great stories and science that will wow your friends and teachers, this Papercutz graphic novel series is something not to be missed.

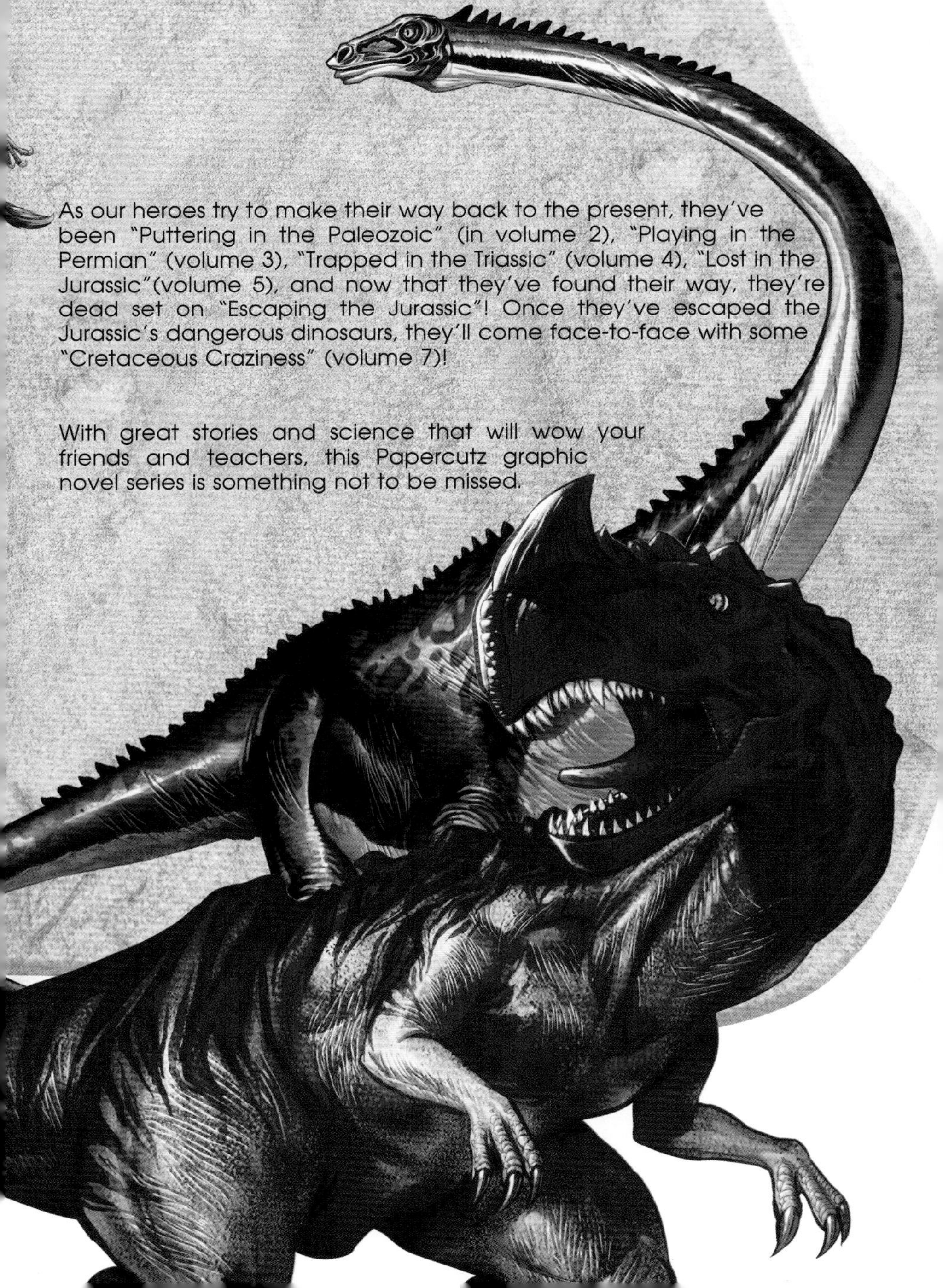

HOW THE EARTH WAS FORMED

We know the Earth is the third planet in the solar system, the densest planet, and so far, the only one capable of supporting life (although new evidence is emerging that Mars may also be able to support various forms of life). But how did that happen?

2 Formation of the Earth

As the Earth formed, its gravity grew stronger. Heavier molecules and atoms fell inward to the Earth's core, while lighter elements formed around it. The massive pressures from the external material heated up the Earth's interior to the point where it was all liquid (except for the core, which was under so much pressure it could not liquify). These settled down into the Earth's 3 layers: the crust, mantle, and core.

While we cannot say for sure just when these dust clouds solidified to form the Earth, nor when they came into being in the first place, we can tell that it took place more than 4.5 billion years ago.

The Sun's formation

Way, way back, there was a patch of space filled with cosmic dust and gases. Slowly, gravity (and a few nearby exploding stars) forced some of this dust and gases together into clumps—the gases formed into a massive, pressurized ball of heat which became the Sun, while the dust settled into planets, the Earth being one of them.

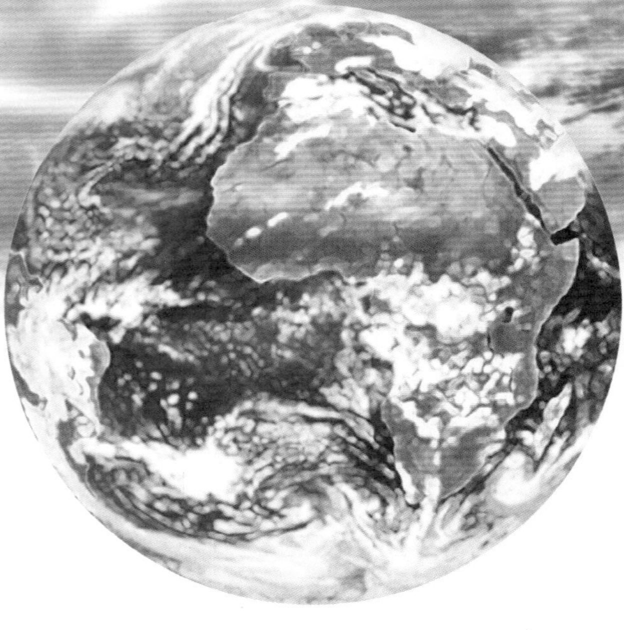

6 The Earth today

Even now, our Earth changes with time; its tectonic plates still move about on the lava bed of the mantle, pushing and pulling continents in all directions.

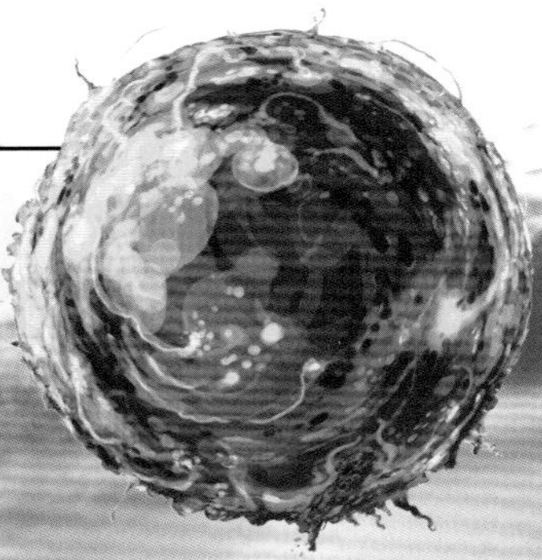

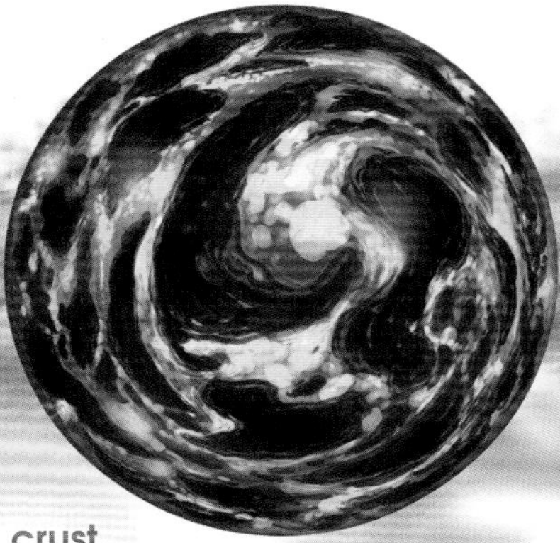

3 The crust

The crust was created around 4 billion years ago, as cooled, solid rock floating on the molten lithosphere merged. Even today, as the continental plates shift away from and against each other, some of this rock and molten material might still change place.

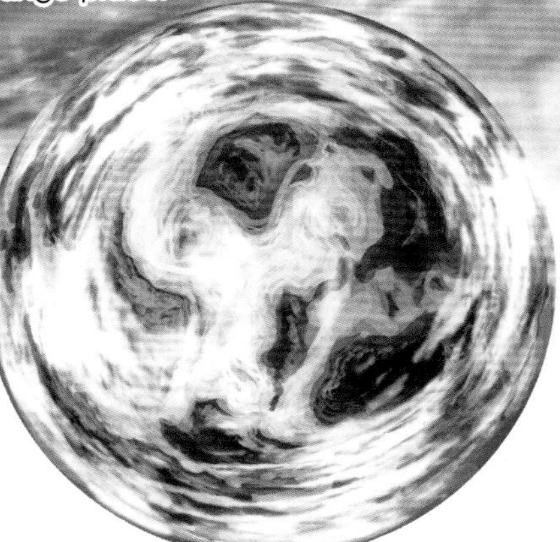

4 The formation of the atmosphere

After our crust solidified, volcanic gases formed our atmosphere. The cooling surface allowed the formation of water vapor and bodies of water.

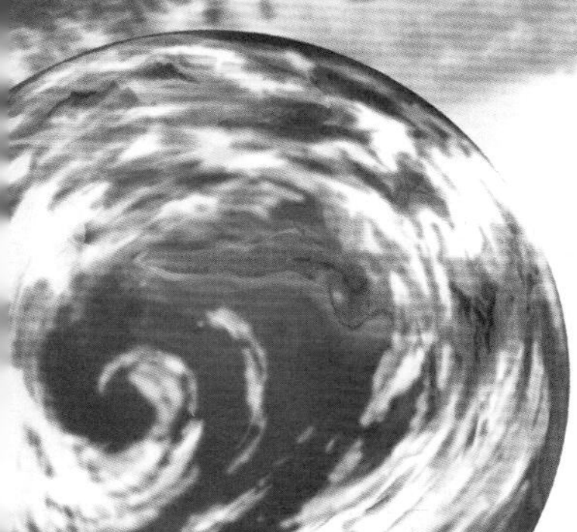

5 Land forms

Around 3.5 billion years ago, several land masses rose above the global ocean, giving rise to the continents we know today.

Geological Time Spiral

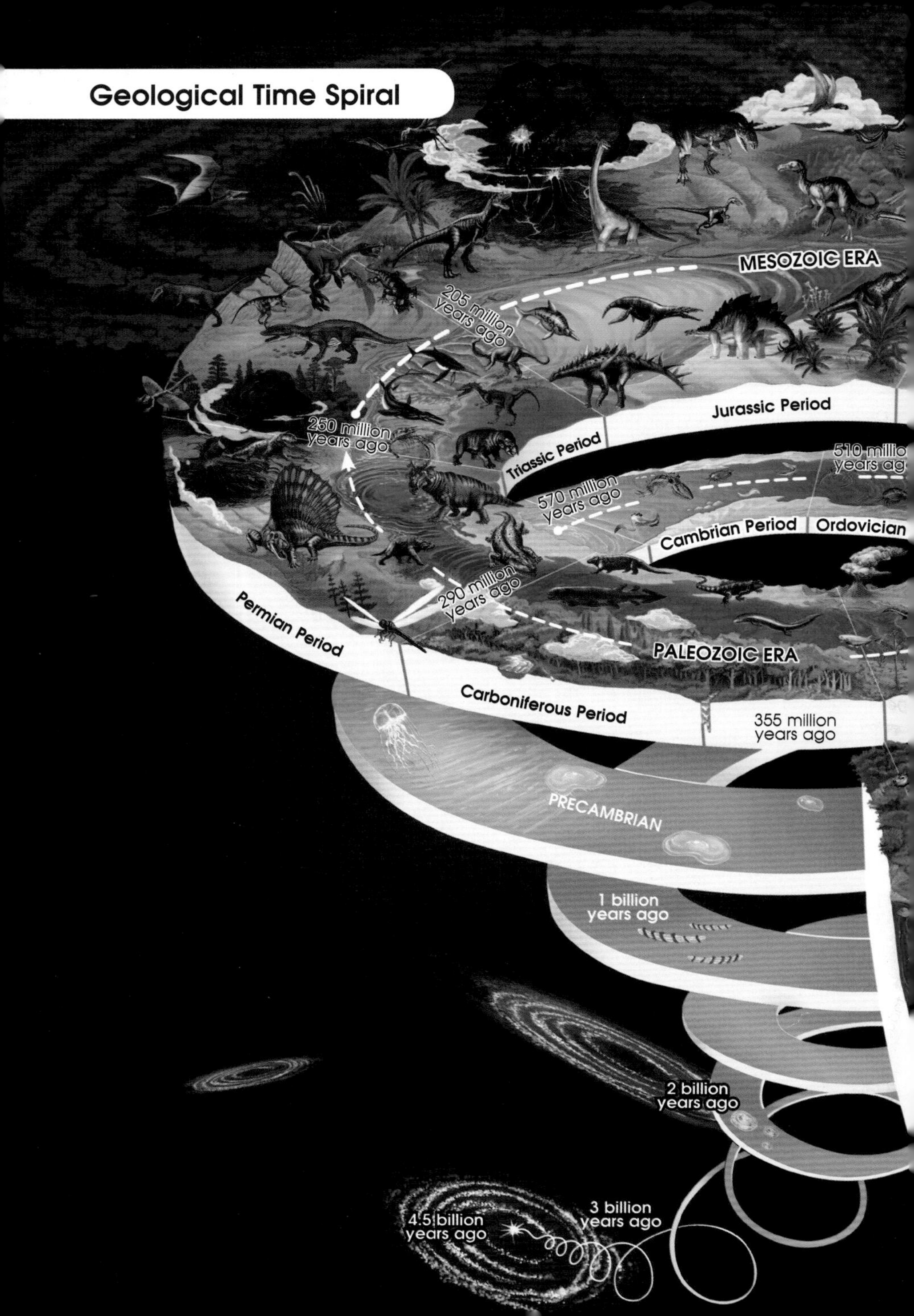

MESOZOIC ERA
205 million years ago
250 million years ago
Jurassic Period
Triassic Period
510 million years ago
570 million years ago
Cambrian Period
Ordovician
290 million years ago
Permian Period
PALEOZOIC ERA
Carboniferous Period
355 million years ago
PRECAMBRIAN
1 billion years ago
2 billion years ago
3 billion years ago
4.5 billion years ago

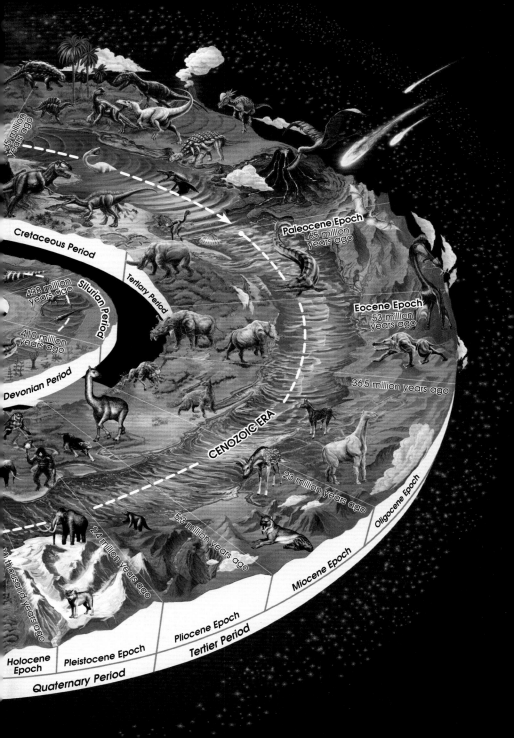

Cretaceous Period

Silurian Period

438 million years ago

410 million years ago

Devonian Period

Tertiary Period

Paleocene Epoch
65 million years ago

Eocene Epoch
53 million years ago

36.5 million years ago

CENOZOIC ERA

23 million years ago

5.3 million years ago

Oligocene Epoch

2.4 million years ago

10 thousand years ago

Holocene Epoch

Pleistocene Epoch

Pliocene Epoch

Tertier Period

Miocene Epoch

Quaternary Period

GEOLOGIC TIME SCALE

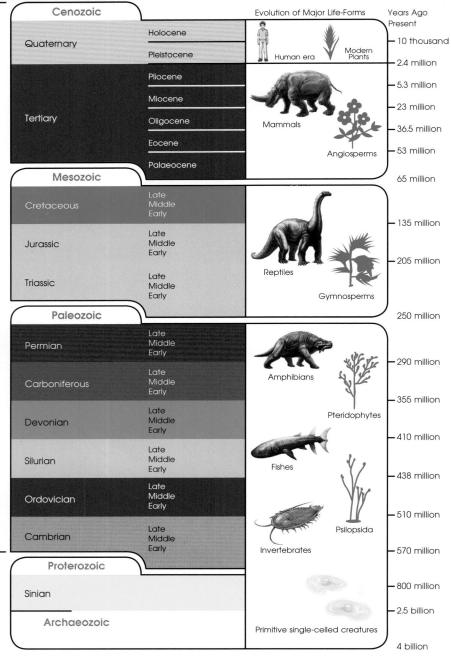

Evolution of Major Life-Forms

Years Ago

Cenozoic		
Quaternary	Holocene	Present
	Pleistocene	10 thousand
Tertiary	Pliocene	2.4 million
	Miocene	5.3 million
	Oligocene	23 million
	Eocene	36.5 million
	Palaeocene	53 million

Human era — Modern Plants

Mammals — Angiosperms

65 million

Mesozoic		
Cretaceous	Late / Middle / Early	135 million
Jurassic	Late / Middle / Early	205 million
Triassic	Late / Middle / Early	

Reptiles — Gymnosperms

250 million

Paleozoic		
Permian	Late / Middle / Early	290 million
Carboniferous	Late / Middle / Early	355 million
Devonian	Late / Middle / Early	410 million
Silurian	Late / Middle / Early	438 million
Ordovician	Late / Middle / Early	510 million
Cambrian	Late / Middle / Early	570 million

Amphibians — Pteridophytes

Fishes — Psilopsida

Invertebrates

Proterozoic	
Sinian	800 million
Archaeozoic	2.5 billion

Primitive single-celled creatures

4 billion

Phanerozoic

Proterozoic

Archaean | Proterozoic

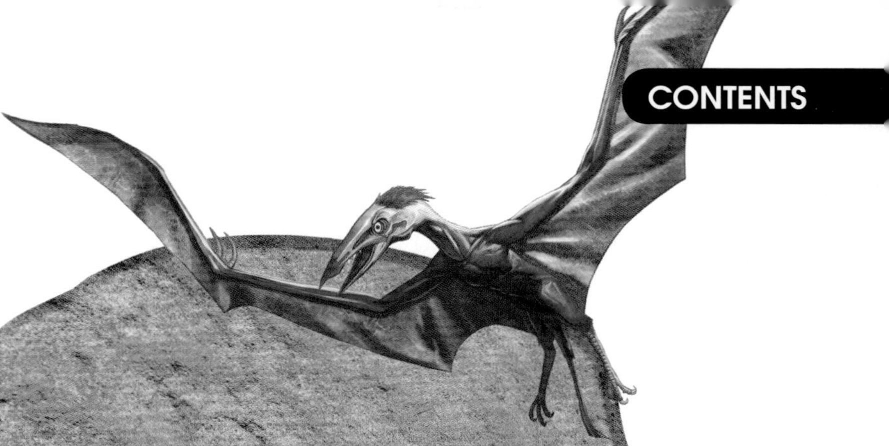

CONTENTS

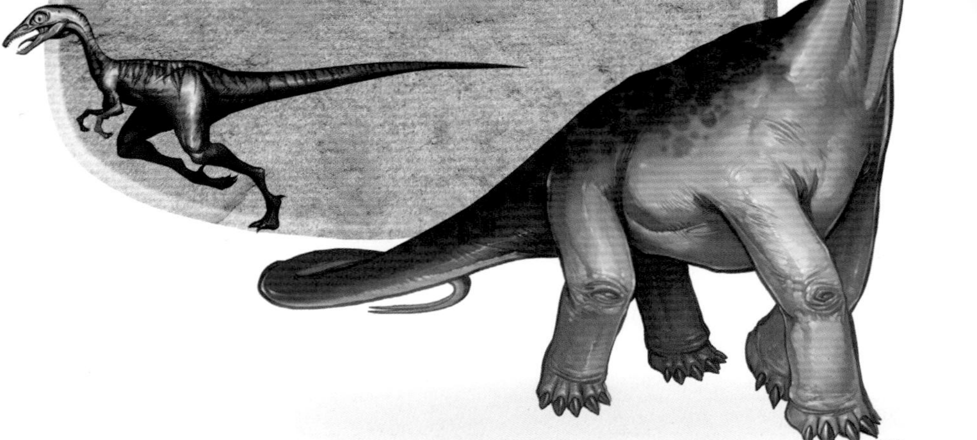

Cast

Sean (Age 13)
- Smart, calm, and a good analyst.
- Very articulate, but under-performs on rare occasions.
- Uses scientific knowledge and theory in thought and speech.

Stone (Age 15)
- Has tremendous strength, appetite, and size.
- A boy of few words but honest and reliable.
- An expert in repairs and maintenance.

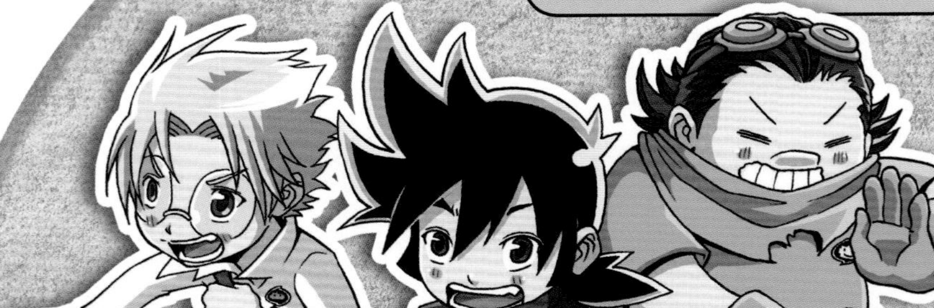

STARZ
- A tiny robot invented by the doctor, nicknamed Lil S.
- Multifunctional; able to scan, analyze, record, take images, communicate, and more.
- Able to change its form and appearance. It is a mobile supercomputer that can store huge amounts of information.

Rain (Age 13)
- Curious, plays to win, but sometimes misses the big picture.
- Brave, persevering, never gives up.
- Individualistic and loves to play the hero.

Dr. Da Vinci (Age 60)
- A professor at the National Scientific Research Institute.
- A genius inventor.
- Highly knowledgeable, loves adventure, but lazy by nature.

Diana (Age 30)
- Research-based Administrator, the Doctor's helpful assistant.
- A mature, beautiful, and capable lady.
- Good at problem solving.

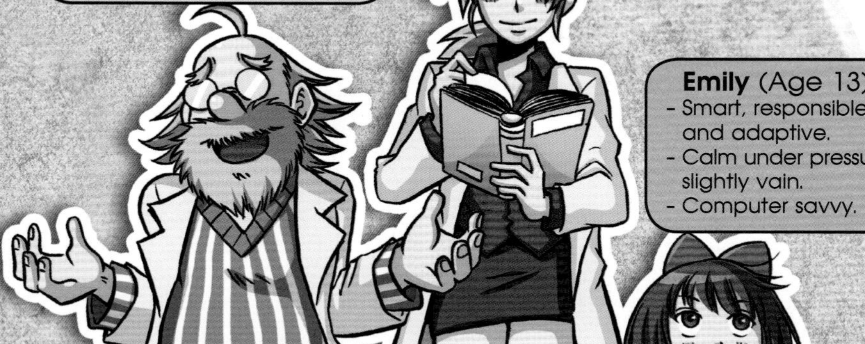

Emily (Age 13)
- Smart, responsible, and adaptive.
- Calm under pressure, slightly vain.
- Computer savvy.

Particle Transmitter
- One of Dr. Da Vinci's most important inventions.
- Able to teleport the team to any period of time and space to execute their missions.
- Able to send urgently needed items to the team at any time.

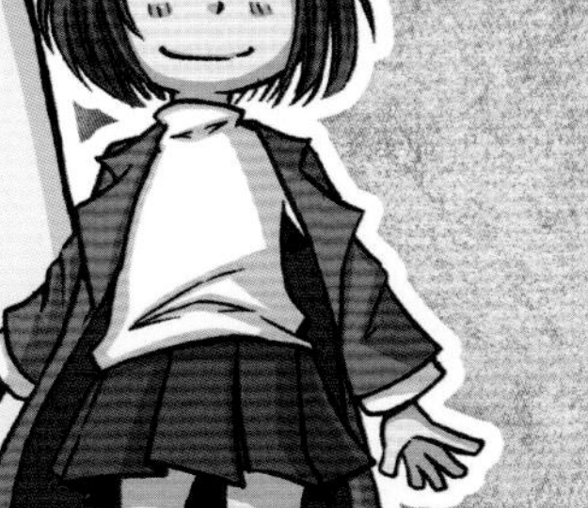

A massive earthquake sends the Dinosaur Explorers team millions of years into the past! Emerging in the Cambrian, they manage to jump away in time (literally!) to avoid sinister Silurian sea life, but find that their Particle Transmitter only allows them small jumps several million years at a time- and they're over 500 million years in the past!

Cambrian

Ordovician

Silurian

Devonian

Carboniferous

The Silurian sees their anxiety and despair results in in-fighting; Rain's behaviour angers Emily, who decides to set out with the Dinosaur Explorers to prove herself — and prove herself she does! Facing everything from giant squids to sand-burrowing sea scorpions with will and wherewithal!

Unfortunately,the team manages to step away from the Silurian, only to end up facing the Devonian's major maulers, the Icthyostega and Placodermi! Only a labload of luck and some fried fish enable a clean get away.

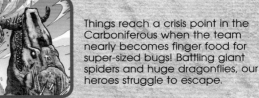

Things reach a crisis point in the Carboniferous when the team nearly becomes finger food for super-sized bugs! Battling giant spiders and huge dragonflies, our heroes struggle to escape.

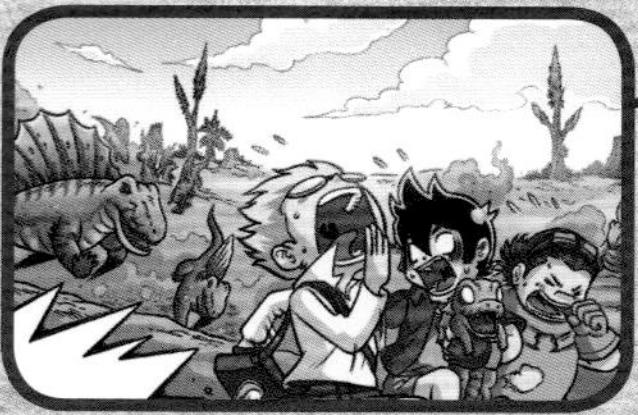

In the Permian, they're stuck with the proto-reptile great grandparents of the dinosaurs! Things get complicated when the team's forced to babysit! Thankfully, our heroes get the job done in time to jump... to the Triassic!

Permian

Triassic

Jurassic

Cretaceous

Tertiary

Quaternary

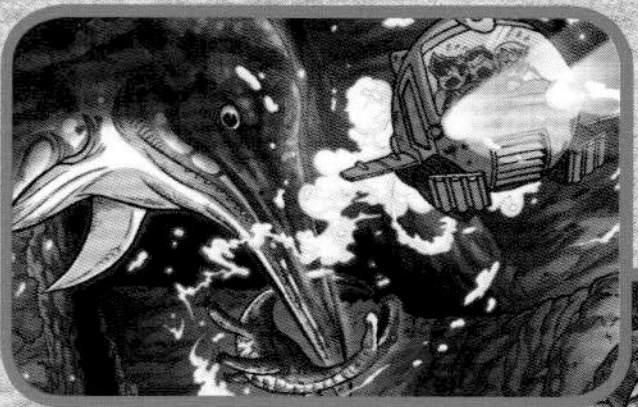

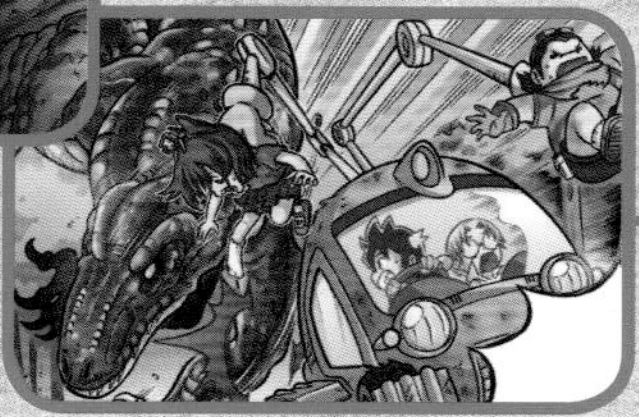

...where they face their greatest challenge yet — themselves! Tensions cause tempers to rise once again, but thankfully, they patch things up before they have to patch themselves up, eluding some of history's earliest predators!

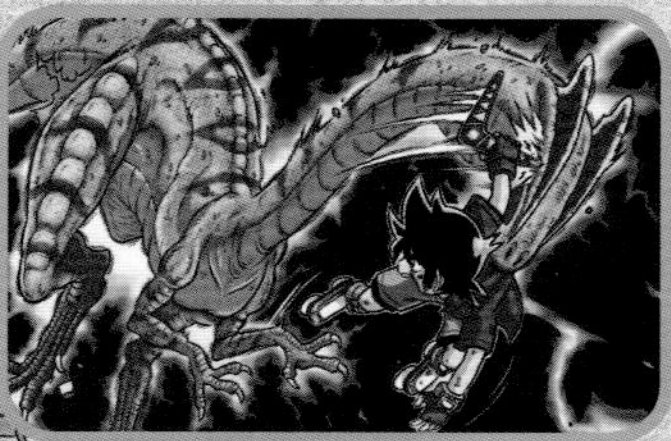

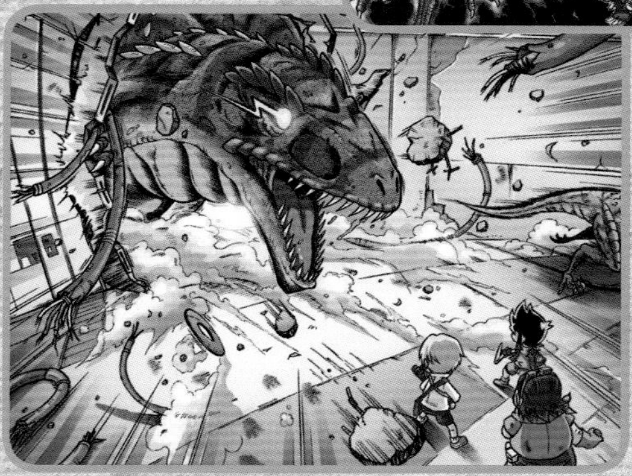

Its Sean out, Diana in during the Jurassic! Keeping a childhood promise sees their Jurassic jaunt begin well, before it all goes wrong, and Dinosaur Explorers labor to defend their lab from uninvited guests!

*The size of this graphic novel's critters are exaggerated, and do not really represent the true sizes of the creatures. Hey, it makes for a more visually exciting story!

CHAPTER 1

RUN OFF

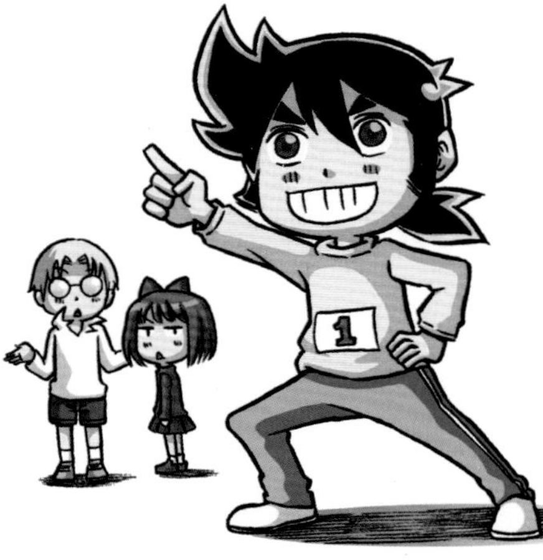

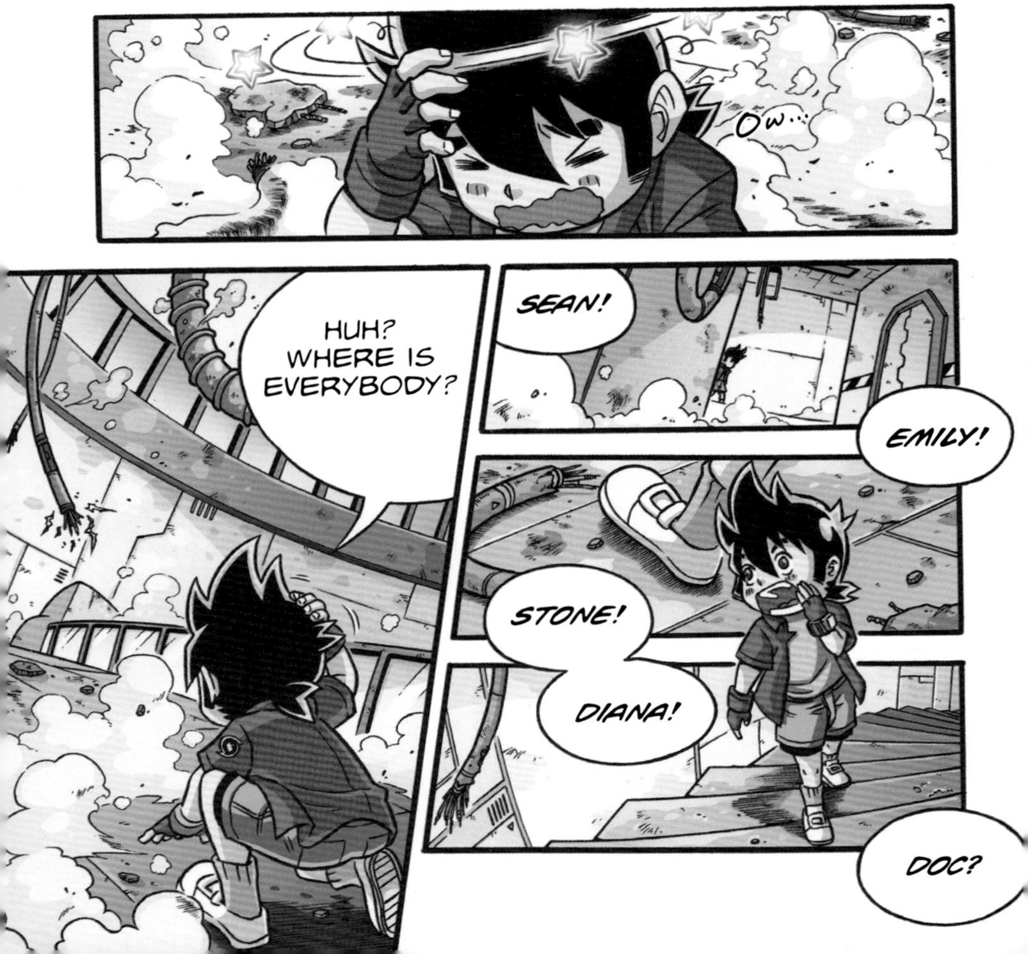
OW...
HUH? WHERE IS EVERYBODY?
SEAN!
EMILY!
STONE!
DIANA!
DOC?

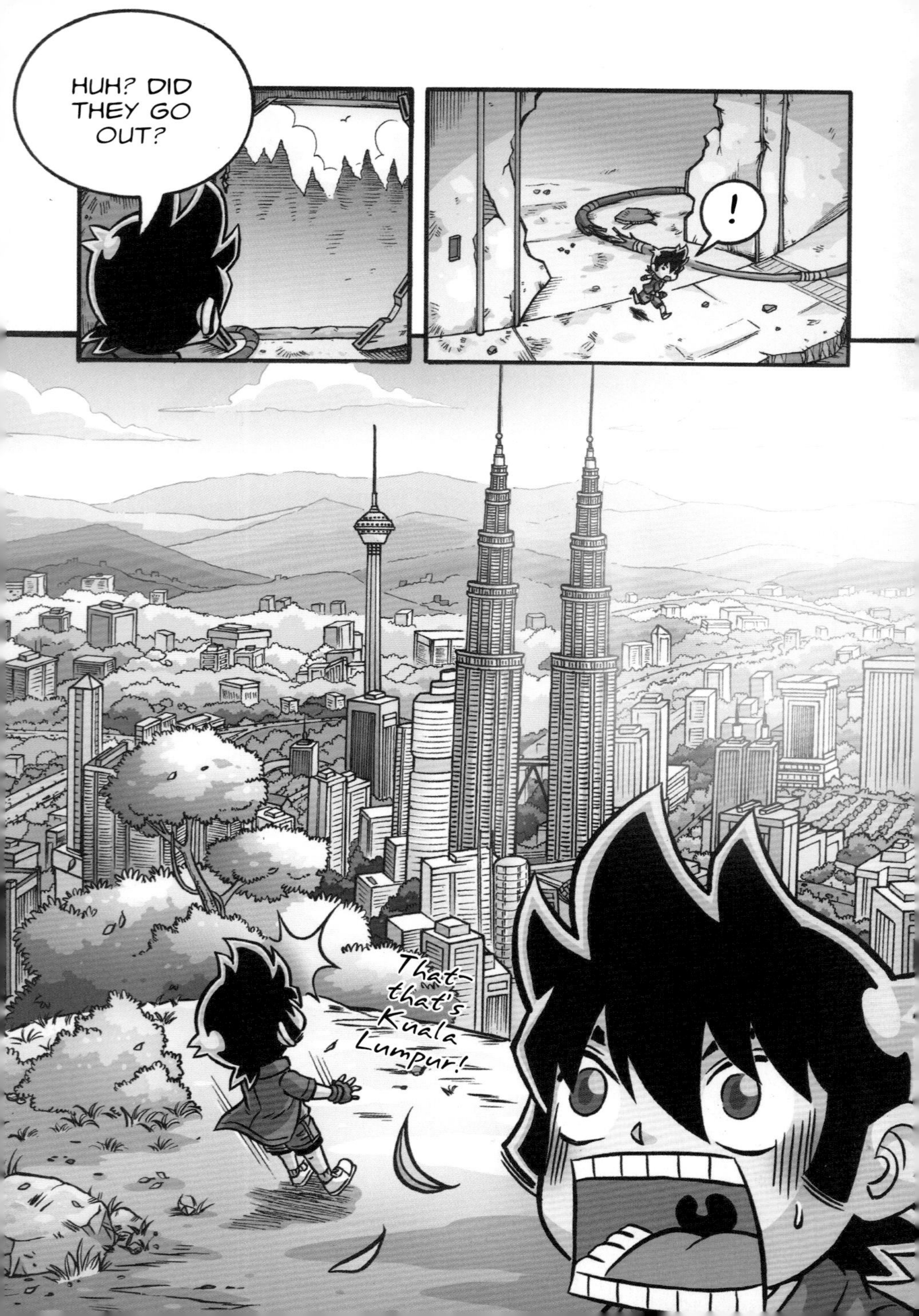
HUH? DID THEY GO OUT?
!
That-that's Kuala Lumpur!

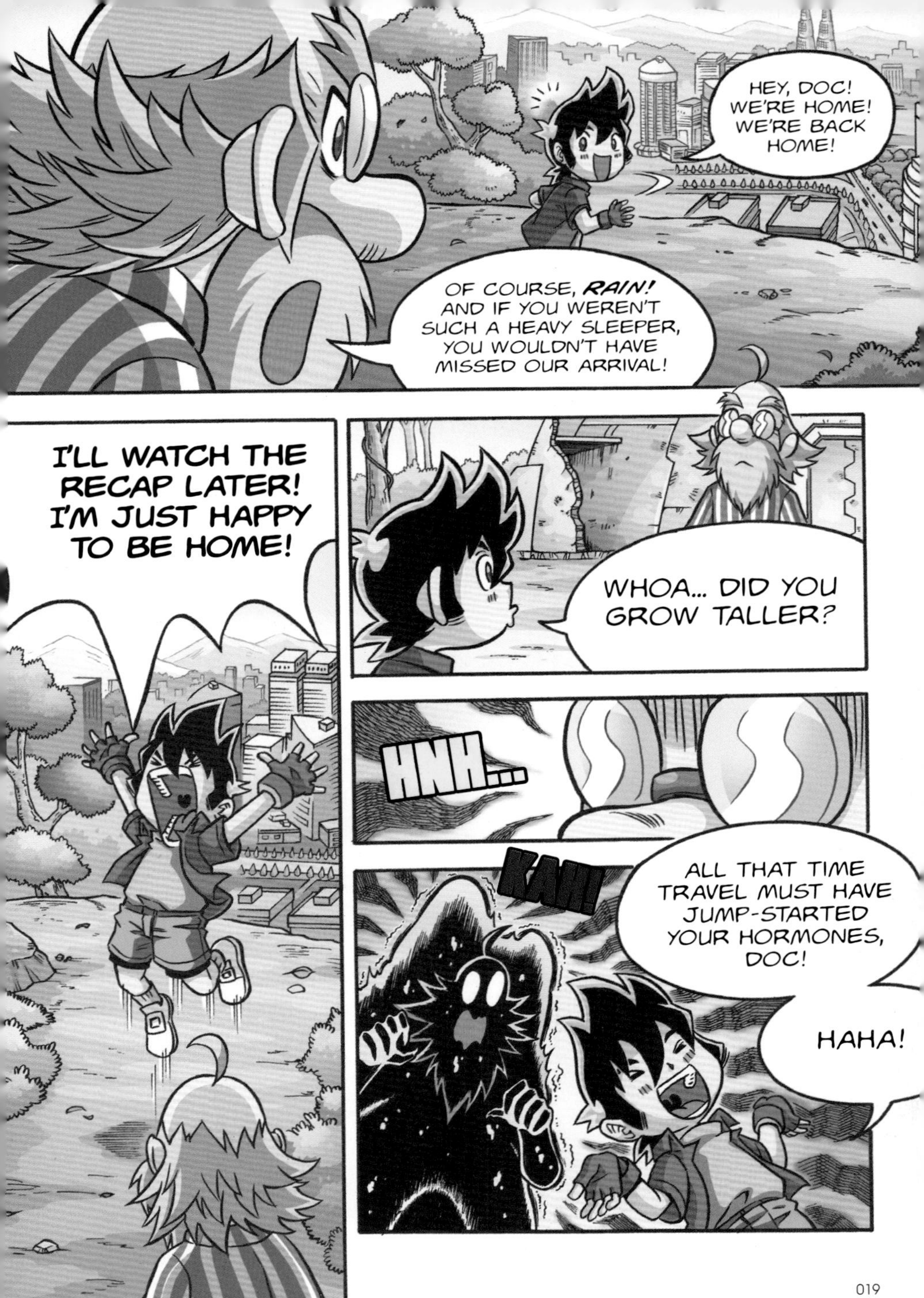
HEY, DOC! WE'RE HOME! WE'RE BACK HOME!
OF COURSE, ***RAIN!*** AND IF YOU WEREN'T SUCH A HEAVY SLEEPER, YOU WOULDN'T HAVE MISSED OUR ARRIVAL!
I'LL WATCH THE RECAP LATER! I'M JUST HAPPY TO BE HOME!
WHOA... DID YOU GROW TALLER?
HNH...
KAH!
ALL THAT TIME TRAVEL MUST HAVE JUMP-STARTED YOUR HORMONES, DOC!
HAHA!

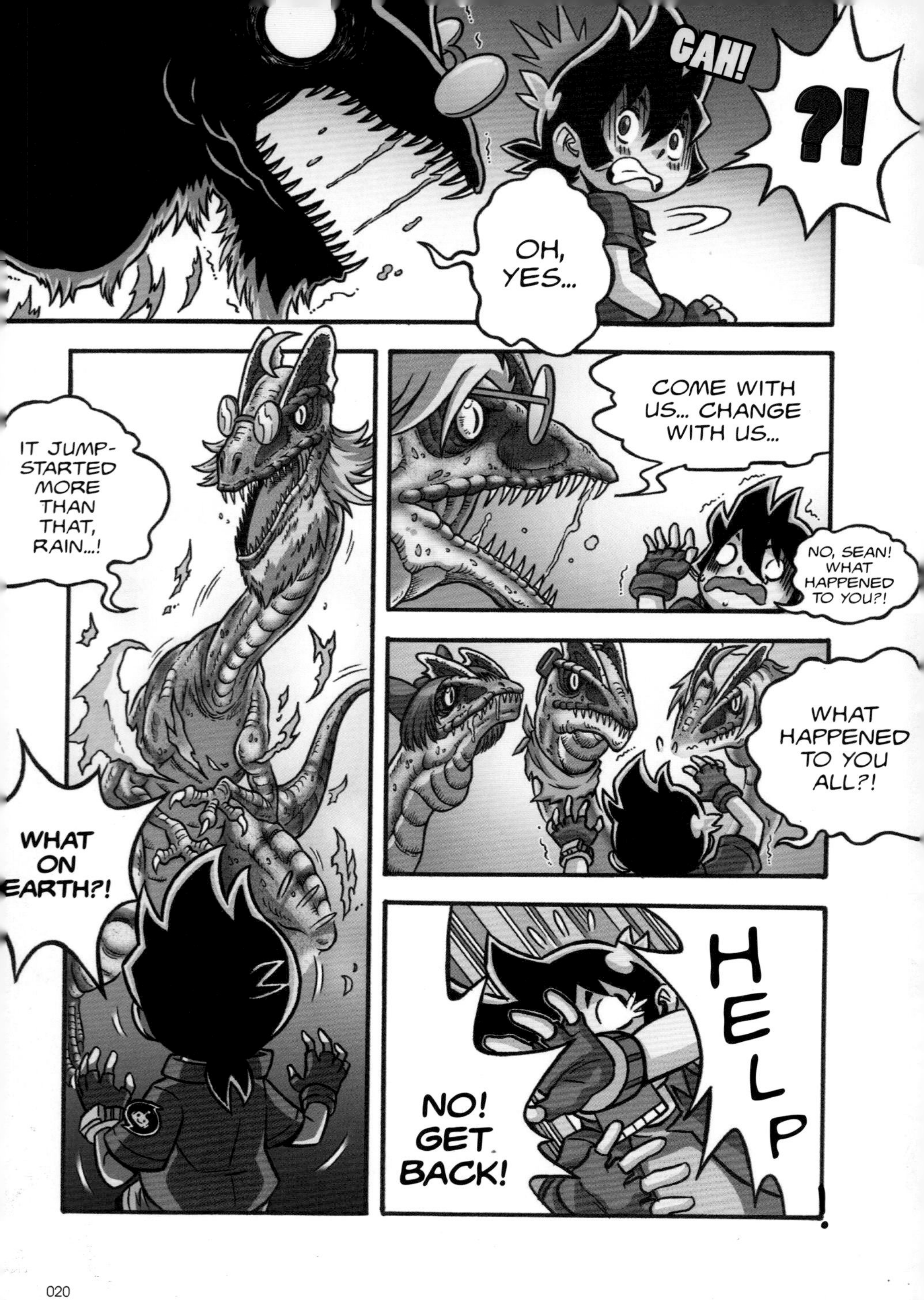
GAH!
?!
OH, YES...
IT JUMP-STARTED MORE THAN THAT, RAIN...!
WHAT ON EARTH?!
COME WITH US... CHANGE WITH US...
NO, SEAN! WHAT HAPPENED TO YOU?!
WHAT HAPPENED TO YOU ALL?!
HELP!
NO! GET BACK!

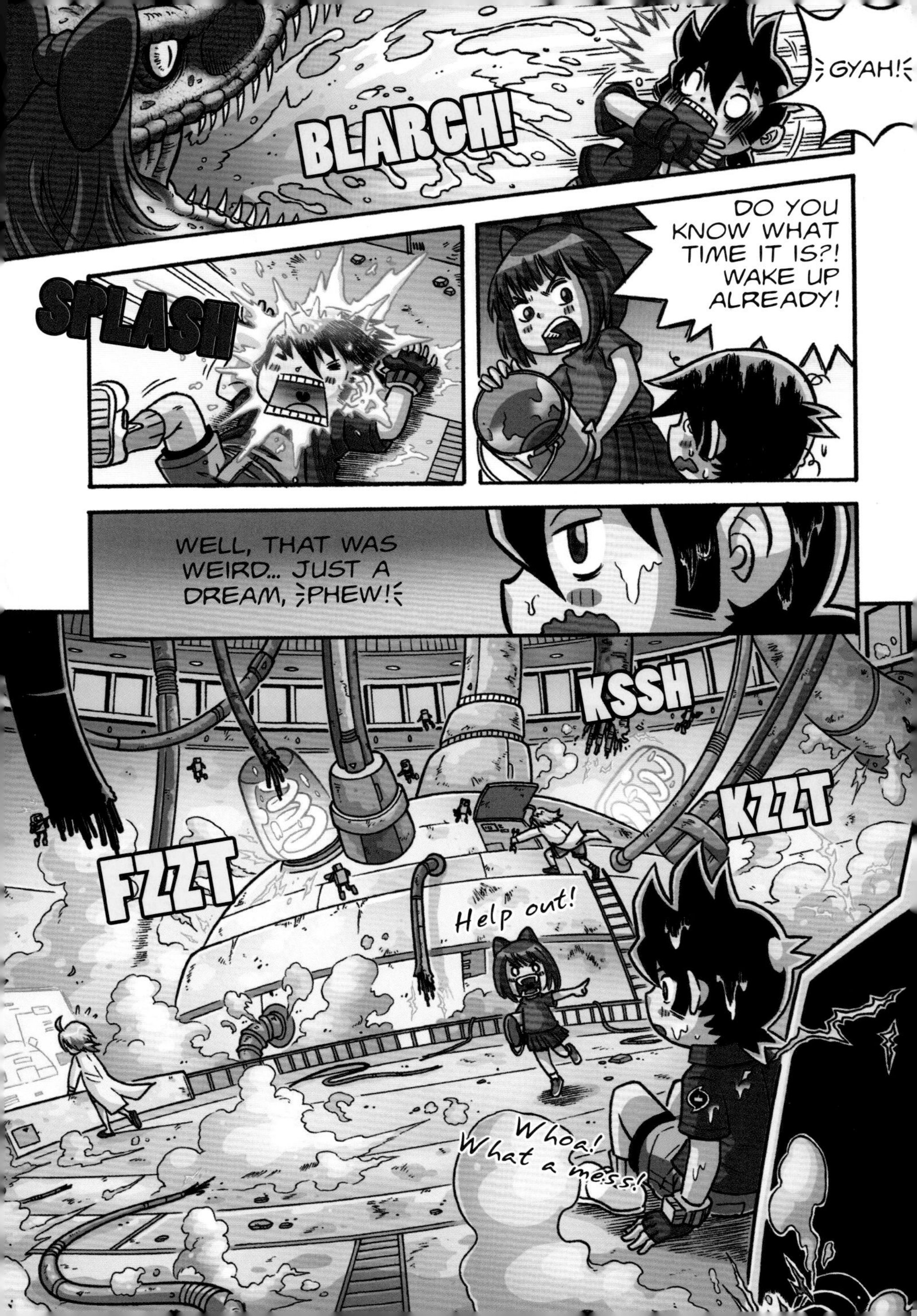
BLARCH!
GYAH!
SPLASH
DO YOU KNOW WHAT TIME IT IS?! WAKE UP ALREADY!
WELL, THAT WAS WEIRD... JUST A DREAM, PHEW!
KSSH
KZZT
FZZT
Help out!
Whoa! What a mess!

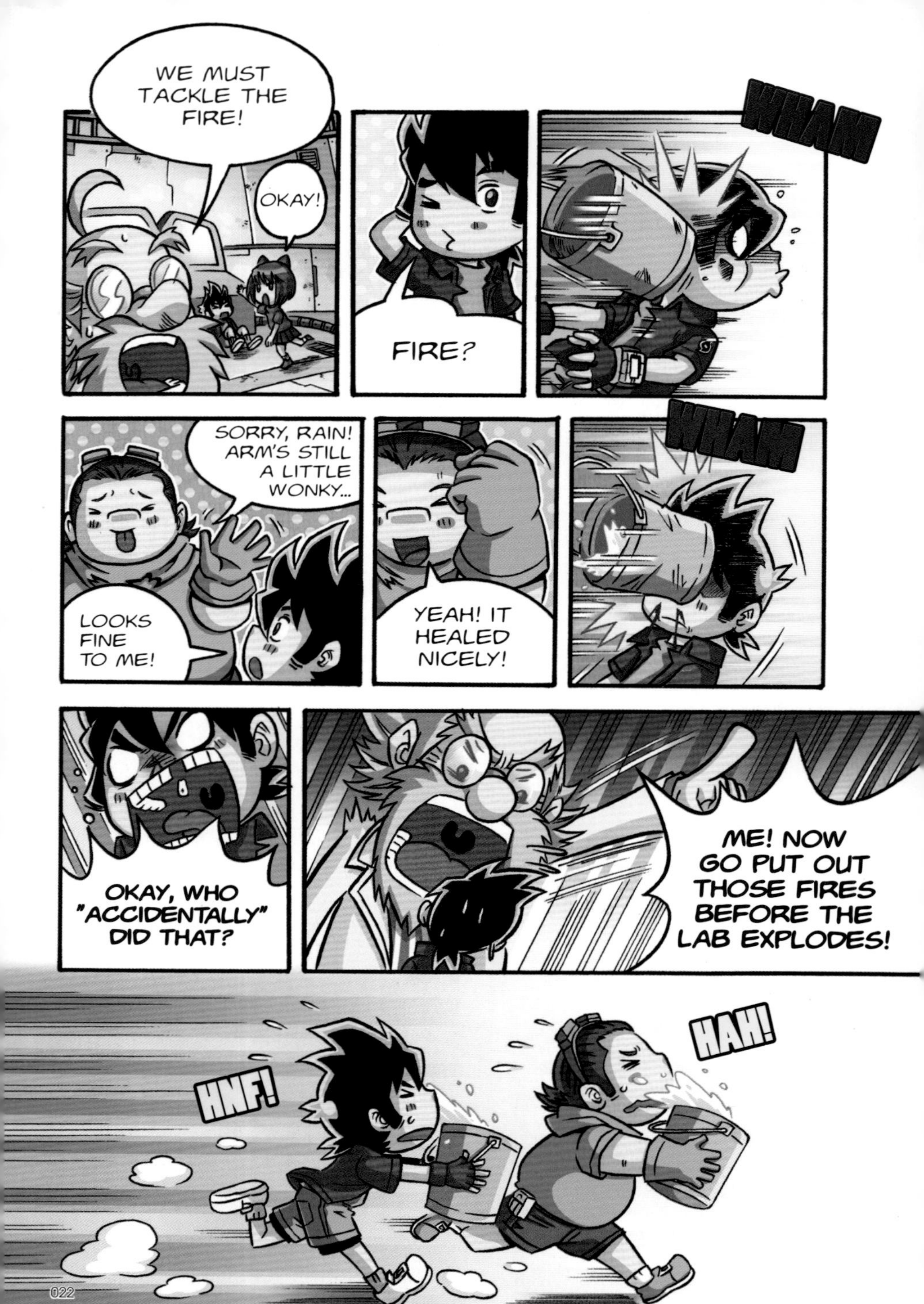
WE MUST TACKLE THE FIRE!
OKAY!
FIRE?
WHAM
SORRY, RAIN! ARM'S STILL A LITTLE WONKY...
LOOKS FINE TO ME!
YEAH! IT HEALED NICELY!
WHAM
OKAY, WHO "ACCIDENTALLY" DID THAT?
ME! NOW GO PUT OUT THOSE FIRES BEFORE THE LAB EXPLODES!
HAH!
HNF!

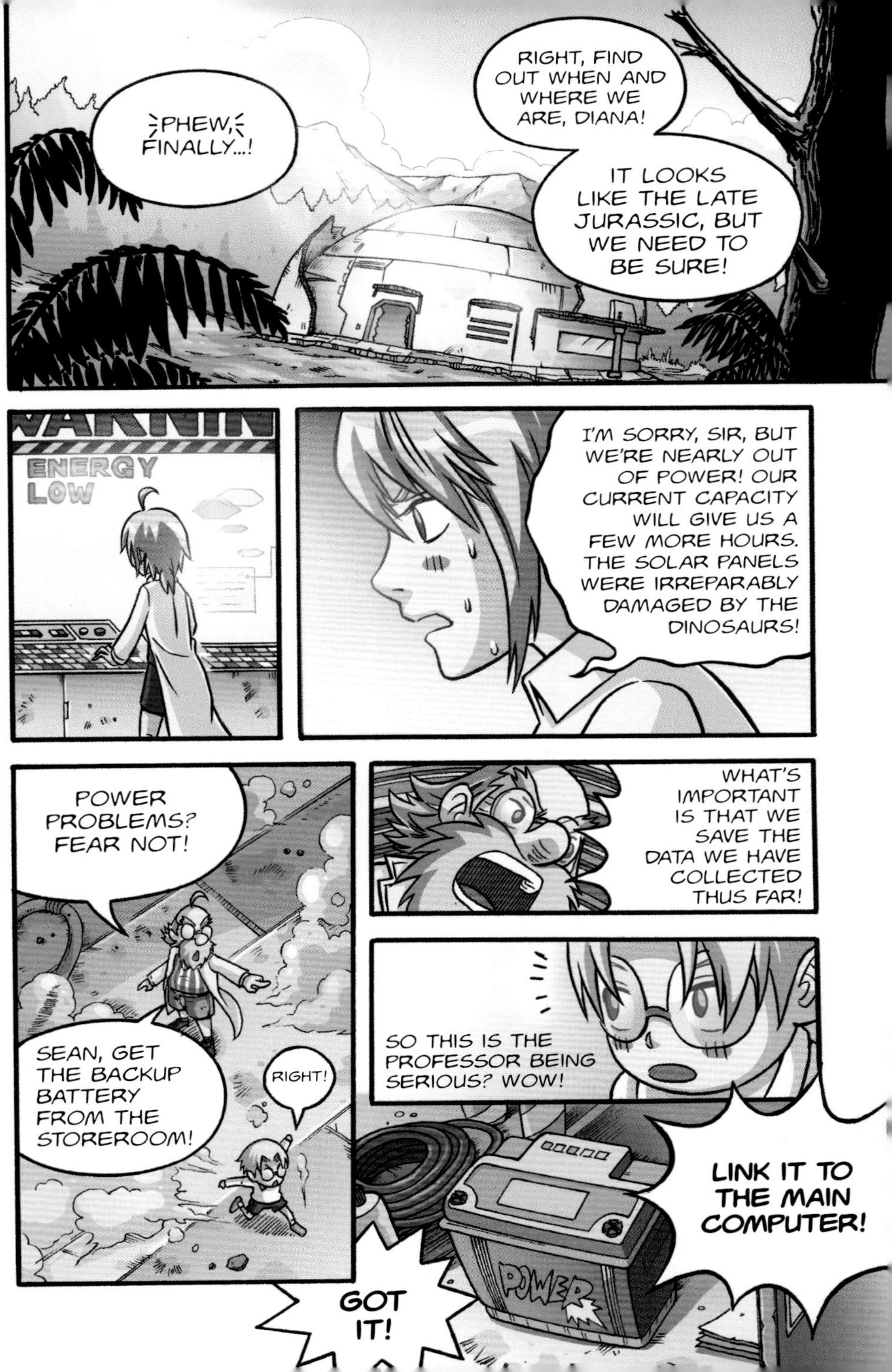
PHEW, FINALLY...!
RIGHT, FIND OUT WHEN AND WHERE WE ARE, DIANA!
IT LOOKS LIKE THE LATE JURASSIC, BUT WE NEED TO BE SURE!
WARNIN
ENERGY LOW
I'M SORRY, SIR, BUT WE'RE NEARLY OUT OF POWER! OUR CURRENT CAPACITY WILL GIVE US A FEW MORE HOURS. THE SOLAR PANELS WERE IRREPARABLY DAMAGED BY THE DINOSAURS!
POWER PROBLEMS? FEAR NOT!
WHAT'S IMPORTANT IS THAT WE SAVE THE DATA WE HAVE COLLECTED THUS FAR!
SO THIS IS THE PROFESSOR BEING SERIOUS? WOW!
SEAN, GET THE BACKUP BATTERY FROM THE STOREROOM!
RIGHT!
LINK IT TO THE MAIN COMPUTER!
GOT IT!
POWER

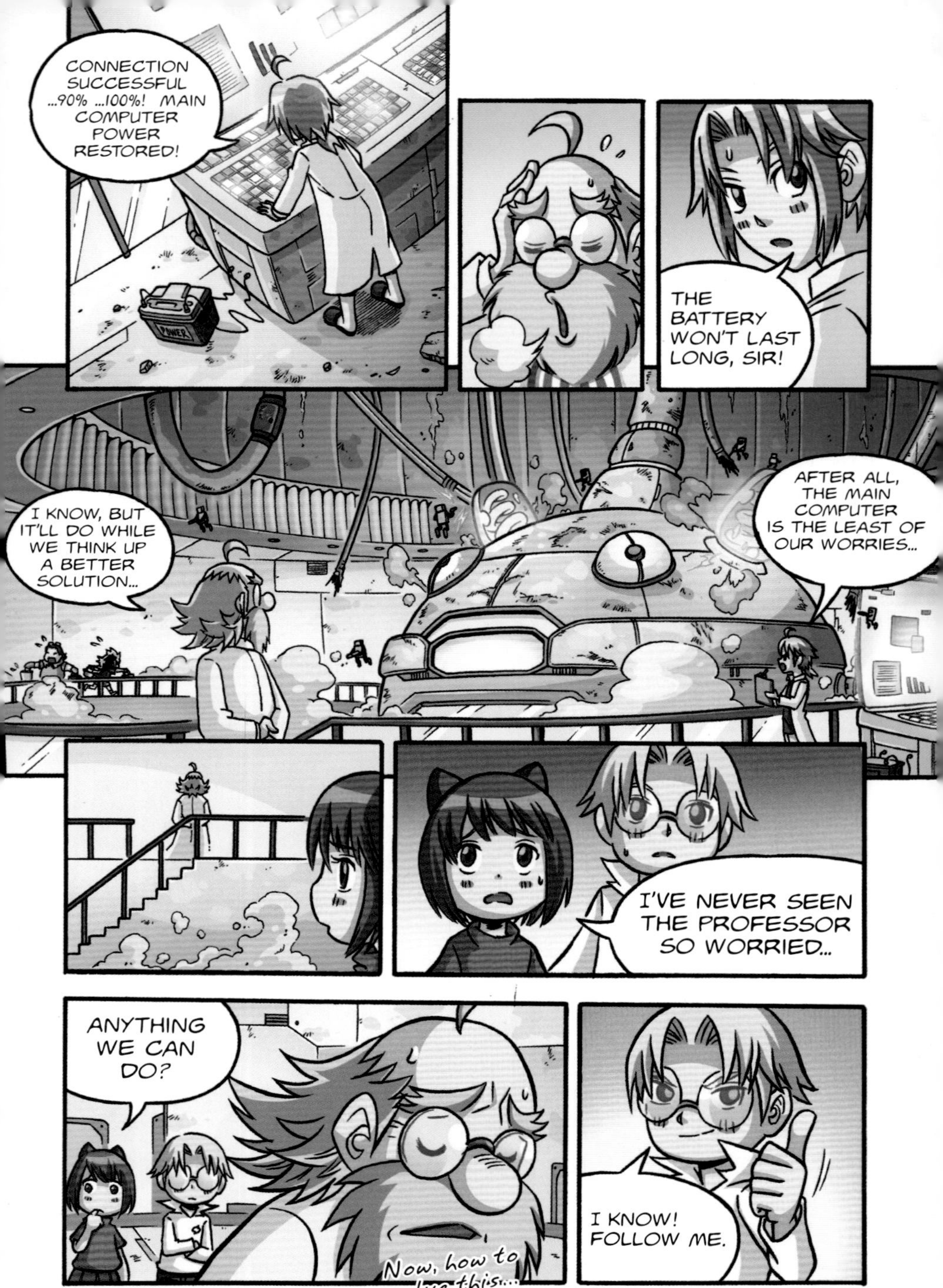
CONNECTION SUCCESSFUL ...90% ...100%! MAIN COMPUTER POWER RESTORED!
POWER
THE BATTERY WON'T LAST LONG, SIR!
I KNOW, BUT IT'LL DO WHILE WE THINK UP A BETTER SOLUTION...
AFTER ALL, THE MAIN COMPUTER IS THE LEAST OF OUR WORRIES...
I'VE NEVER SEEN THE PROFESSOR SO WORRIED...
ANYTHING WE CAN DO?
Now, how to solve this...
I KNOW! FOLLOW ME.

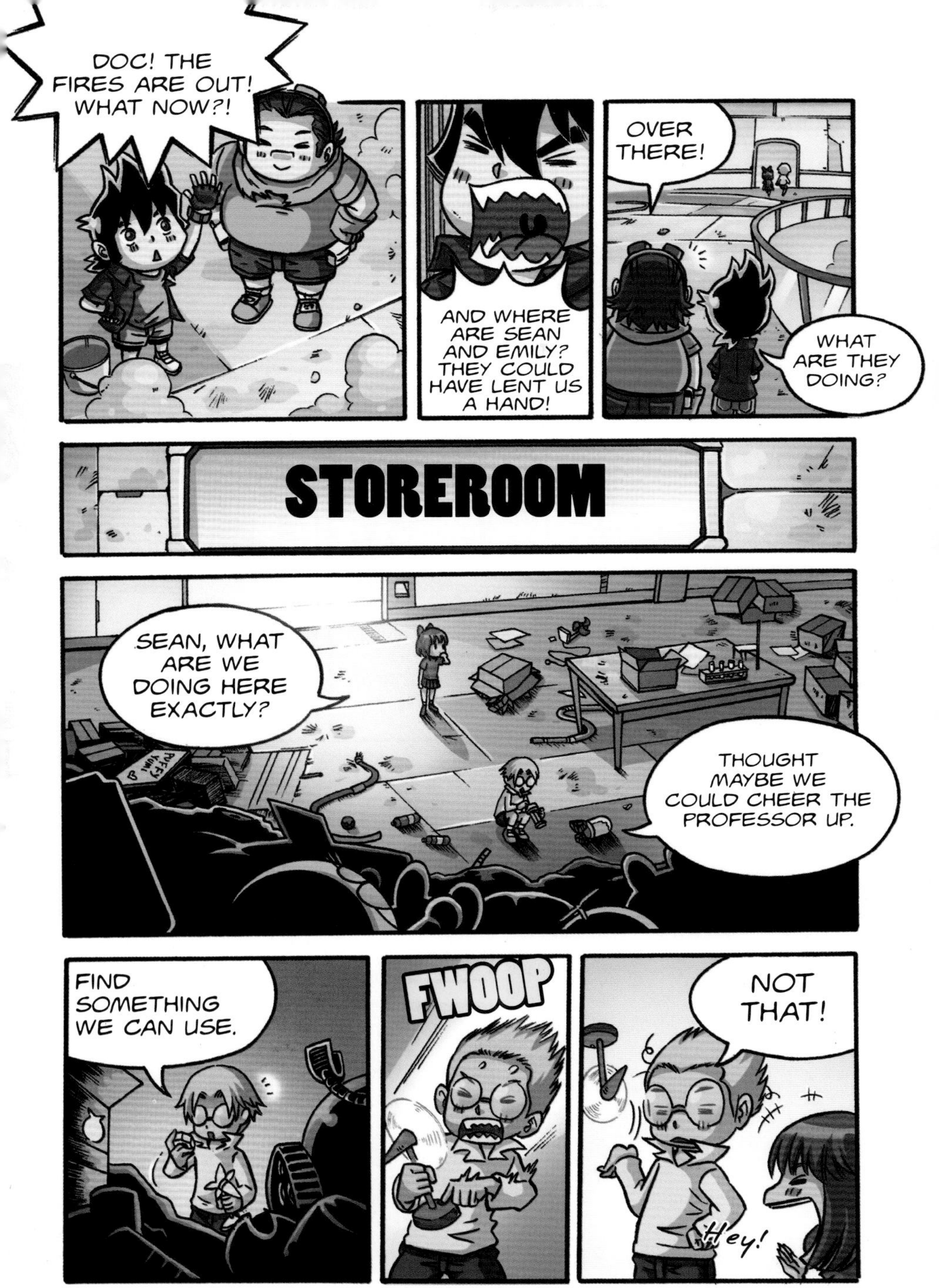
DOC! THE FIRES ARE OUT! WHAT NOW?!
AND WHERE ARE SEAN AND EMILY? THEY COULD HAVE LENT US A HAND!
OVER THERE!
WHAT ARE THEY DOING?
STOREROOM
SEAN, WHAT ARE WE DOING HERE EXACTLY?
THOUGHT MAYBE WE COULD CHEER THE PROFESSOR UP.
FIND SOMETHING WE CAN USE.
FWOOP
NOT THAT!
Hey!

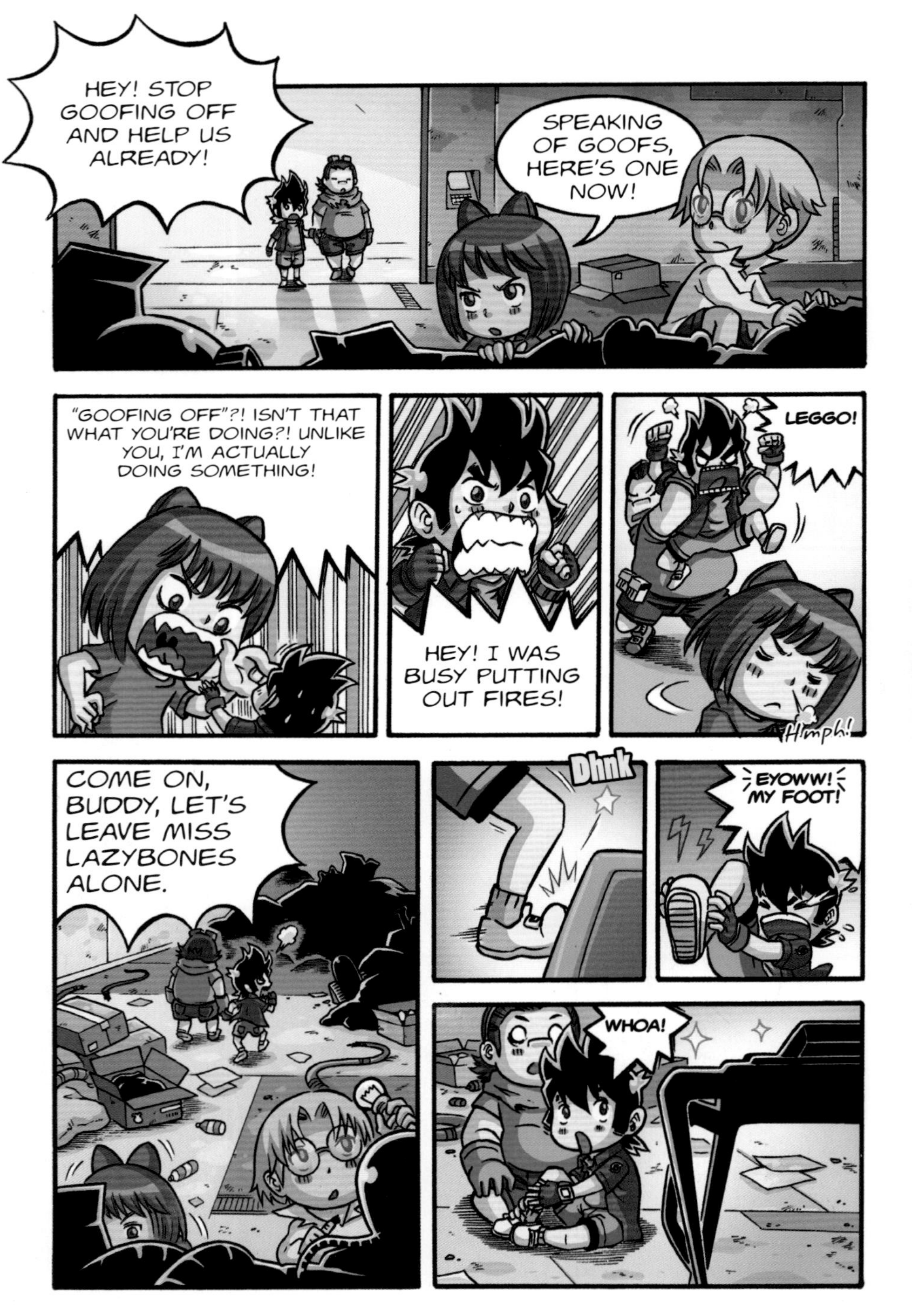
HEY! STOP GOOFING OFF AND HELP US ALREADY!
SPEAKING OF GOOFS, HERE'S ONE NOW!
"GOOFING OFF"?! ISN'T THAT WHAT YOU'RE DOING?! UNLIKE YOU, I'M ACTUALLY DOING SOMETHING!
HEY! I WAS BUSY PUTTING OUT FIRES!
LEGGO!
Hmph!
COME ON, BUDDY, LET'S LEAVE MISS LAZYBONES ALONE.
Dhnk
EYOWW! MY FOOT!
WHOA!

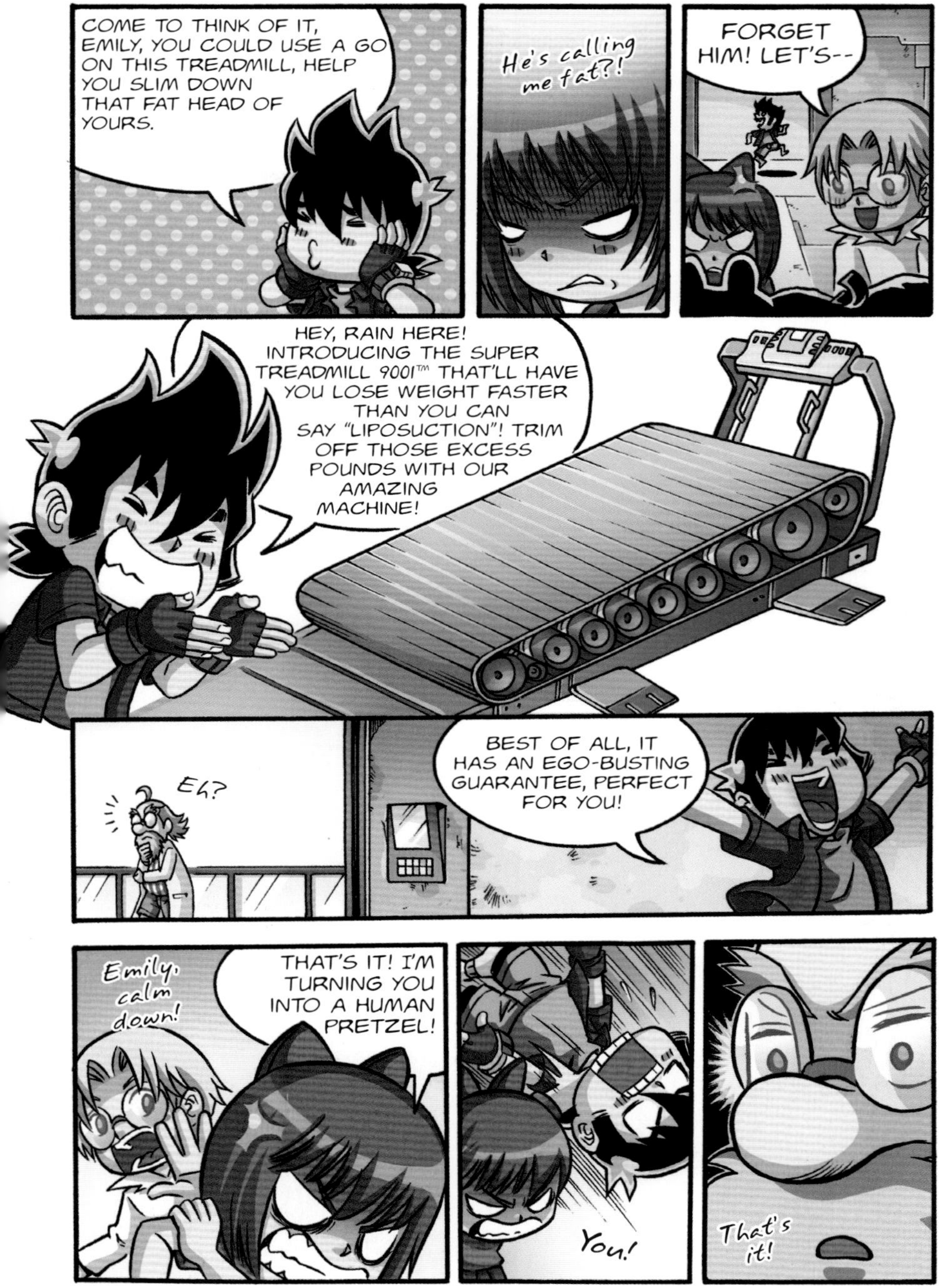

COME TO THINK OF IT, EMILY, YOU COULD USE A GO ON THIS TREADMILL, HELP YOU SLIM DOWN THAT FAT HEAD OF YOURS.
He's calling me fat?!
FORGET HIM! LET'S--
HEY, RAIN HERE! INTRODUCING THE SUPER TREADMILL 9001™ THAT'LL HAVE YOU LOSE WEIGHT FASTER THAN YOU CAN SAY "LIPOSUCTION"! TRIM OFF THOSE EXCESS POUNDS WITH OUR AMAZING MACHINE!
Eh?
BEST OF ALL, IT HAS AN EGO-BUSTING GUARANTEE, PERFECT FOR YOU!
THAT'S IT! I'M TURNING YOU INTO A HUMAN PRETZEL!
Emily, calm down!
You!
That's it!

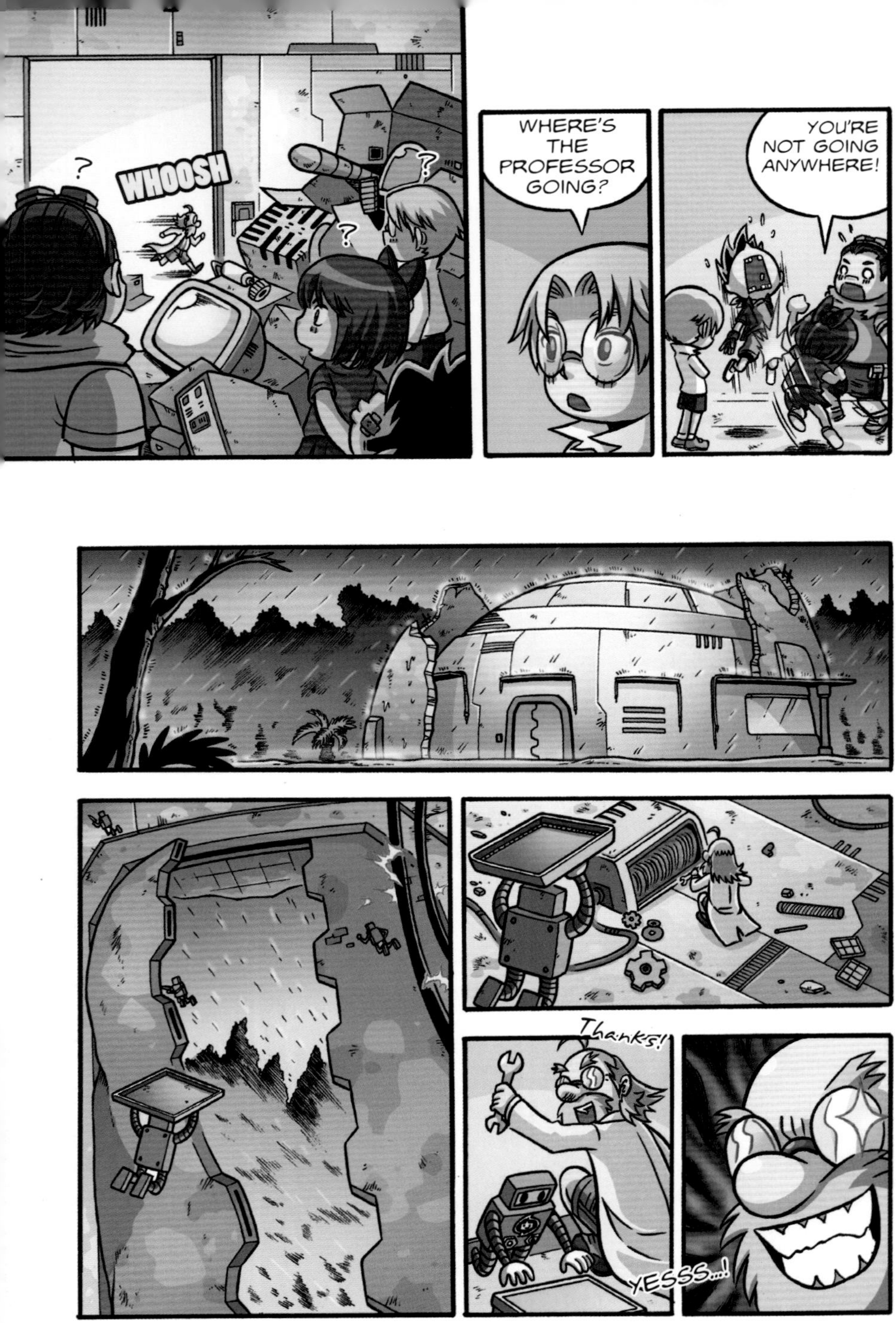

?
WHOOSH
?
?
WHERE'S THE PROFESSOR GOING?
YOU'RE NOT GOING ANYWHERE!
Thanks!
YESSS...!

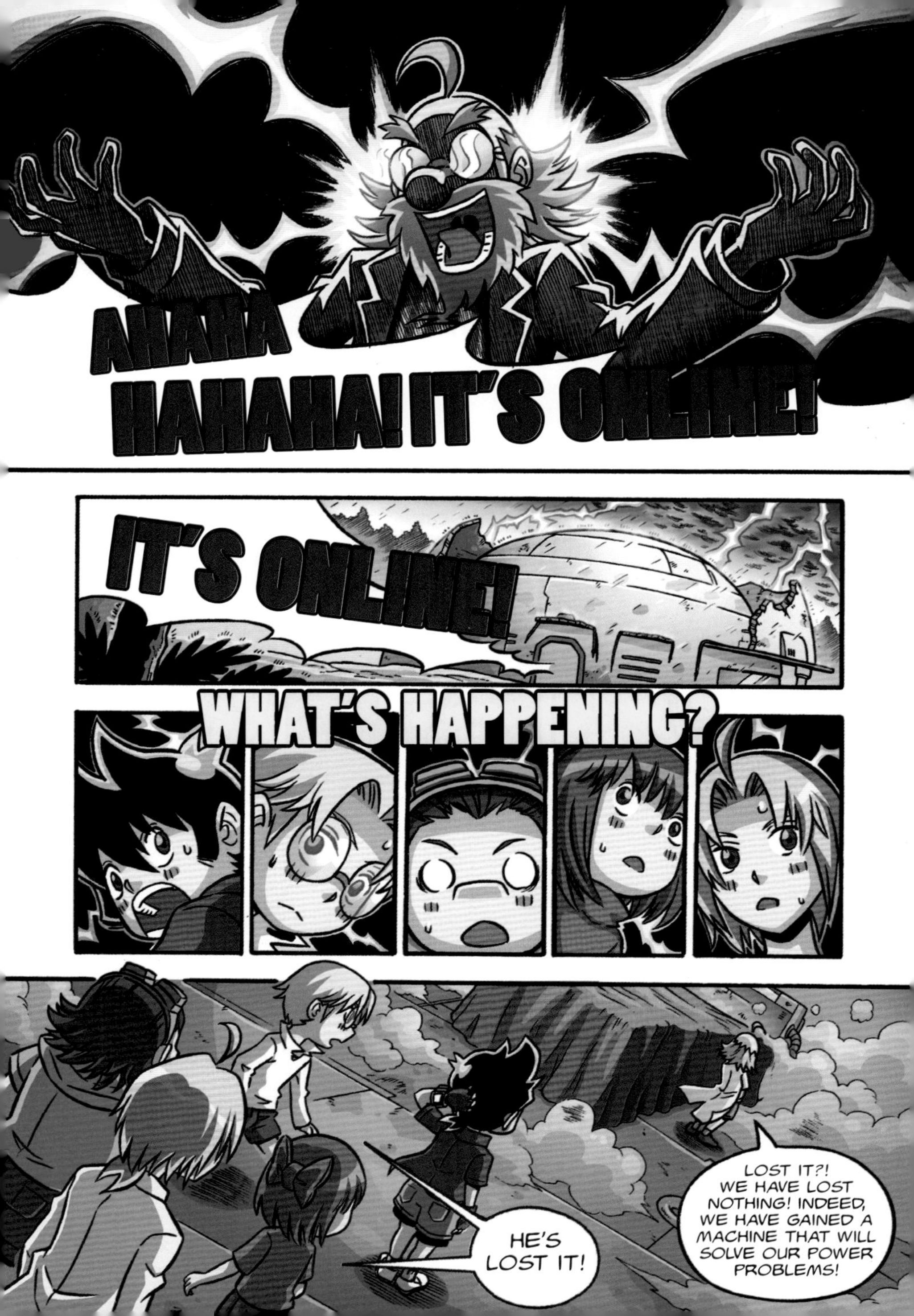
AHAHA HAHAHA! IT'S ONLINE!
IT'S ONLINE!
WHAT'S HAPPENING?
HE'S LOST IT!
LOST IT?! WE HAVE LOST NOTHING! INDEED, WE HAVE GAINED A MACHINE THAT WILL SOLVE OUR POWER PROBLEMS!

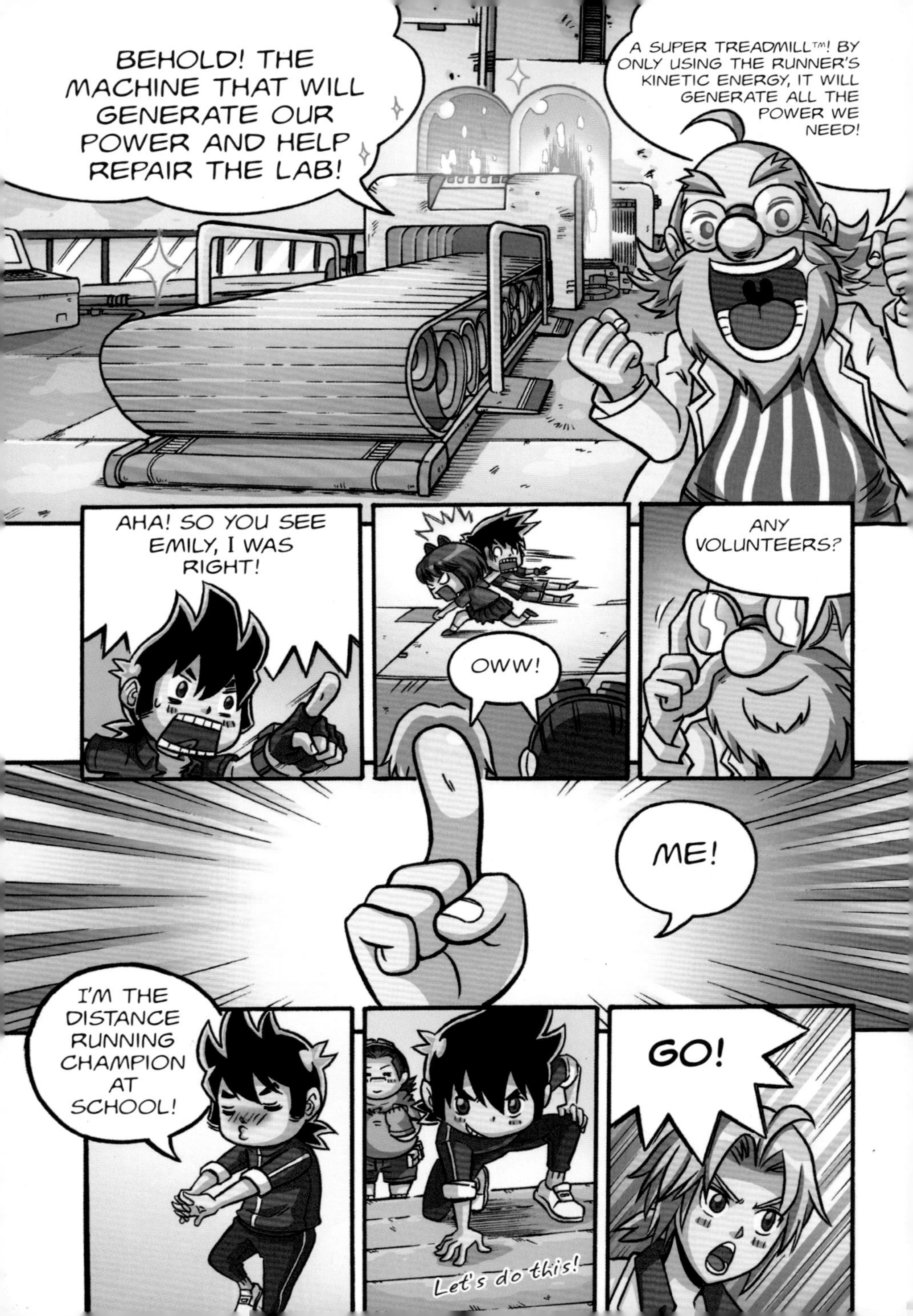

BEHOLD! THE MACHINE THAT WILL GENERATE OUR POWER AND HELP REPAIR THE LAB!
A SUPER TREADMILL™! BY ONLY USING THE RUNNER'S KINETIC ENERGY, IT WILL GENERATE ALL THE POWER WE NEED!
AHA! SO YOU SEE EMILY, I WAS RIGHT!
OWW!
ANY VOLUNTEERS?
ME!
I'M THE DISTANCE RUNNING CHAMPION AT SCHOOL!
Let's do this!
GO!

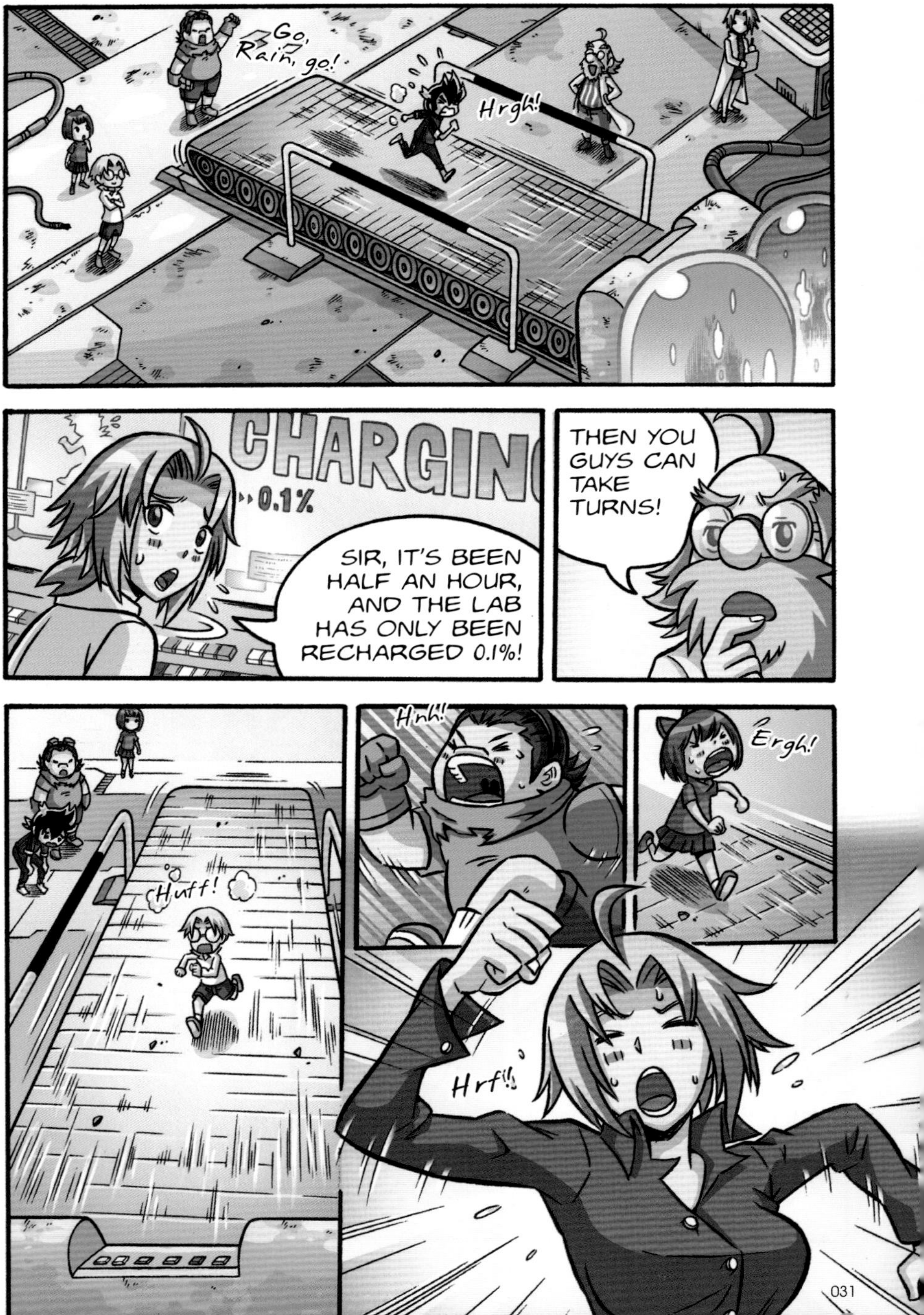
Go, Rain, go!
Hrgh!
CHARGING
0.1%
SIR, IT'S BEEN HALF AN HOUR, AND THE LAB HAS ONLY BEEN RECHARGED 0.1%!
THEN YOU GUYS CAN TAKE TURNS!
Huff!
Hnh!
Ergh!
Hrf!!

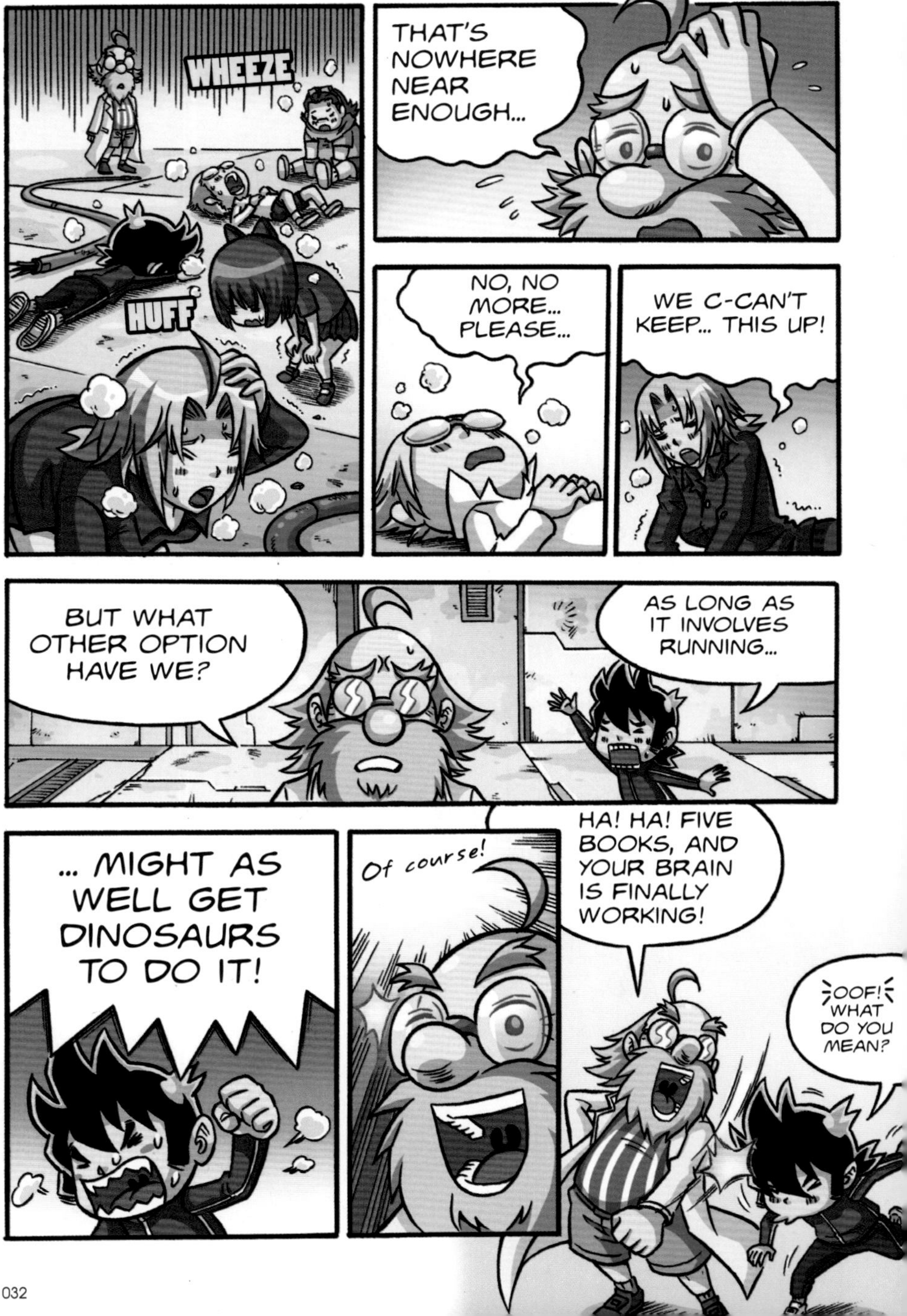
WHEEZE
HUFF
THAT'S NOWHERE NEAR ENOUGH...
NO, NO MORE... PLEASE...
WE C-CAN'T KEEP... THIS UP!
BUT WHAT OTHER OPTION HAVE WE?
AS LONG AS IT INVOLVES RUNNING...
... MIGHT AS WELL GET DINOSAURS TO DO IT!
Of course!
HA! HA! FIVE BOOKS, AND YOUR BRAIN IS FINALLY WORKING!
OOF! WHAT DO YOU MEAN?

Dinosaur teeth

Whether carnivore, herbivore, or omnivore, a dinosaur's teeth were essential, (dinosaurs needed their teeth to keep them alive) whether they were used for eating, or self defense. In terms of composition, their teeth were very much like our own, mostly calcium carbonate, with an inner layer of dentine and an outer layer of enamel. These materials not only ensured that dinosaur teeth were long-lasting but also enabled them to survive intact to the present age. The arrangement, function, and type of teeth also made it possible to identify dinosaur diets.

Dinosaur dentine differences

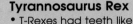

Tyrannosaurus Rex

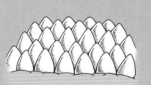

Which was harder a dinosaur's teeth or its bones? Teeth on a whole; it was especially important to carnivores as the inside of a victim's bones often had the most nutrition.

- T-Rexes had teeth like uneven knives.
- They were curved inwards and sawlike on the sides, with the largest tooth specimens to date being 8 inches in length.
- The root was up to three times longer than the crown so they would not fall out during a meal or a fight.
- New teeth were always waiting within the jawline, ready to replace any that broke off.

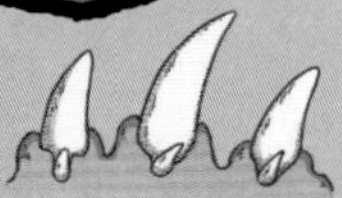

Plateosaurus

- Herbivore teeth varied dramatically, some resembled spoons, or screws, and the Plateosaurus had leaf-shaped teeth.
- The sides of its teeth were also saw-edged, but to slice though plants, not flesh.
- Where the T-Rex relied on long dental roots, the Plateosaurus had thick roots to secure its teeth.

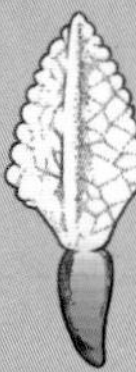

Hadrosaurus

- The Hadrosaurus had over 2000 closely packed teeth which ground its tough, fibrous food into a palatable paste.

Dino diets

A four ton elephant needs around 660 pounds of food a day, which means that a 32 ton dinosaur would need around 5,290 pounds of food daily, but as most dinosaurs were cold-blooded, they did not require that much energy; meaning that a 32 ton dinosaur would have needed no more food than the elephant would! Predators would have acted like modern anacondas and crocodiles, not needing to eat for up to a month after a good kill.

Dinosaur eating habits

We can find out what dinosaurs ate based on their teeth and their fossilized droppings and stomach contents. For example, examining a Hadrosaurus' teeth only showed that it was an herbivore, and it was only after examining other clues was it discovered that it ate fruits and pine needles. By a similiar process it was discovered that Stegosaurus liked young fern leaves and cycads, Diplodocus ate mature leaves, while Brachiosaurus preferred young shoots.

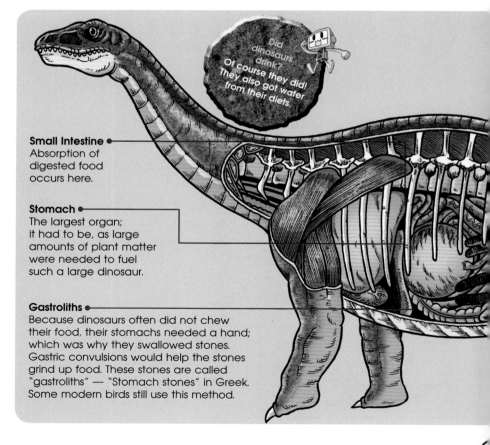

Did dinosaurs drink? Of course they did! They also got water from their diets.

Small Intestine
Absorption of digested food occurs here.

Stomach
The largest organ; it had to be, as large amounts of plant matter were needed to fuel such a large dinosaur.

Gastroliths
Because dinosaurs often did not chew their food, their stomachs needed a hand; which was why they swallowed stones. Gastric convulsions would help the stones grind up food. These stones are called "gastroliths" — "Stomach stones" in Greek. Some modern birds still use this method.

Carnivorous digestive systems

Carnivores often lacked the grinding teeth omnivores and herbivores had, and as such it is believed that they simply swallowed chunks of meat whole, hence their need for large stomachs. Some scientists believe that a few carnivores had birdlike digestive systems, allowing them to digest food in mere hours.

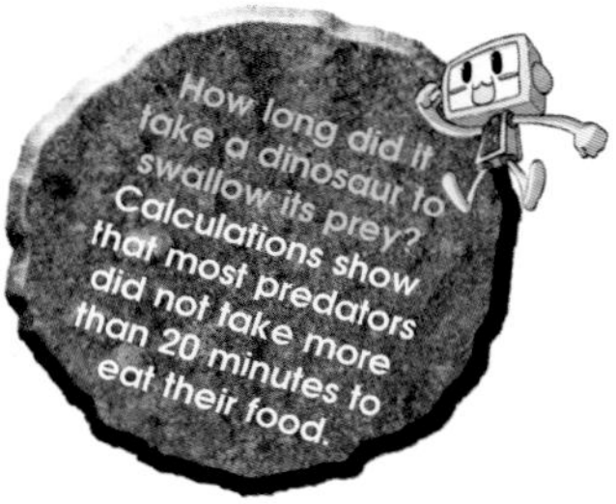
How long did it take a dinosaur to swallow its prey?
Calculations show that most predators did not take more than 20 minutes to eat their food.

Herbivorous digestive systems

Herbivores often did not sufficiently masticate their food; instead, they lightly chewed it before swallowing, letting their stomachs do most of the work.

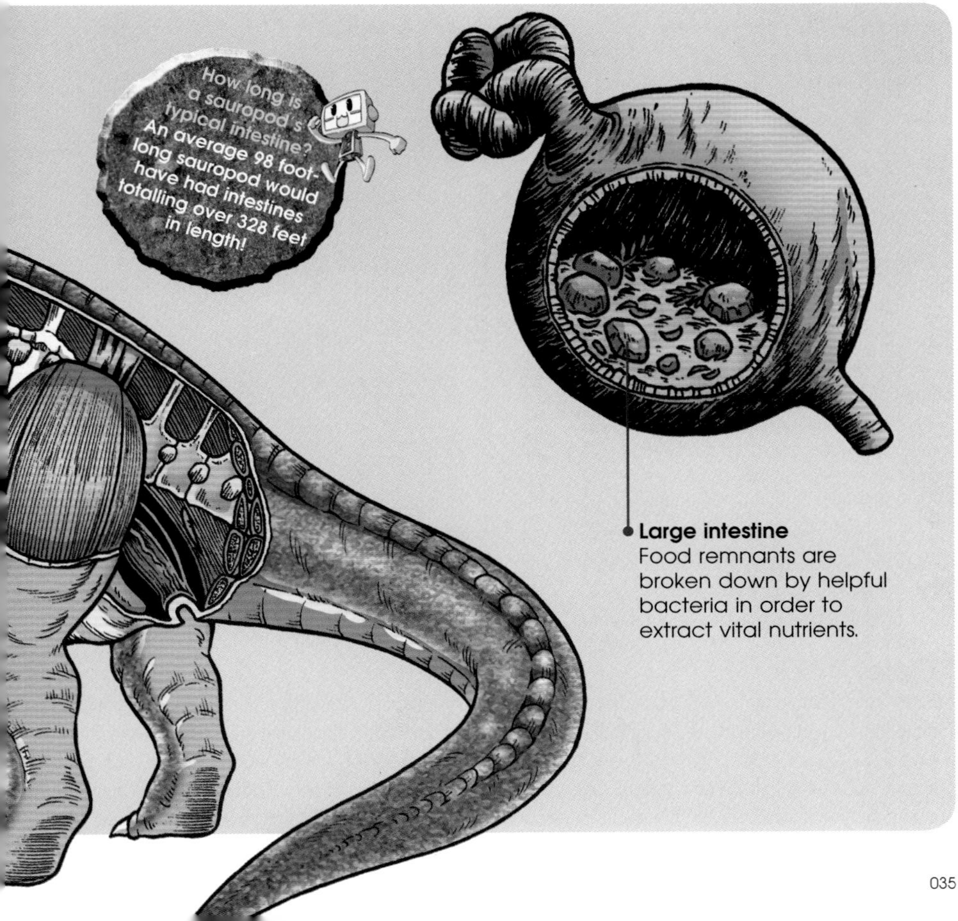
How long is a sauropod's typical intestine?
An average 98 foot-long sauropod would have had intestines totalling over 328 feet in length!
Large intestine
Food remnants are broken down by helpful bacteria in order to extract vital nutrients.

Dinosaur hide

Though some dinosaurs were protected by bony armor and/or spikes, skin in general was a great evolutionary step forward, protecting dinosaurs from heatstroke and parasites. Dinosaur hide might have also been brightly colored to attract potential mates, scare off predators or serve as camouflage.

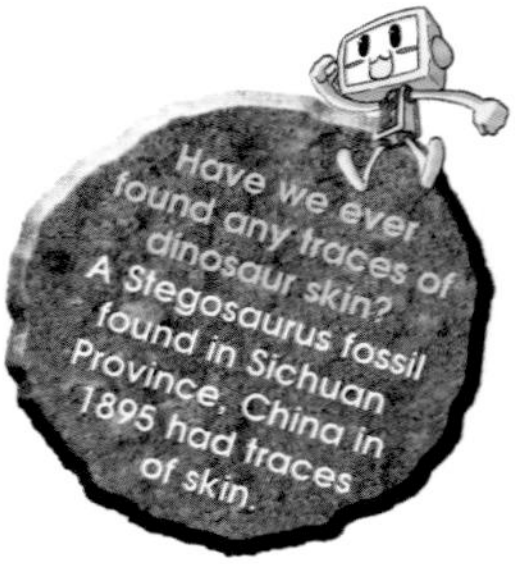
Have we ever found any traces of dinosaur skin? A Stegosaurus fossil found in Sichuan Province, China in 1895 had traces of skin.

Dinosaur colors

Even though there is a lot of debate about exactly what color dinosaurs were, the current belief is that while smaller dinosaurs and younger large dinosaurs might have been camouflaged, mature adult dinosaurs might have been brightly colored to attract mates. Most of the debate revolves around whether dinosaurs were dark or light-colored.

The argument for dark colors

Dark colors would suit larger creatures, crocodiles and elephants are just two modern examples. Those who believe that dinosaurs had dark colors say that even large creatures might have needed camouflage, and dark colors would support that theory.

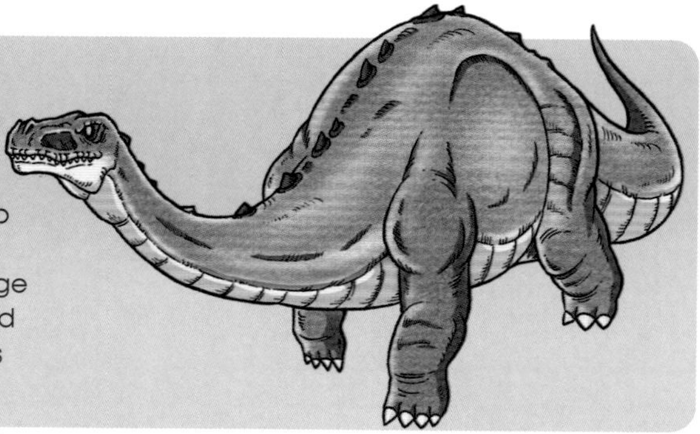

The argument for bright colours

Some have argued that a dinosaur's large size would have rendered camouflage useless, and as the largest dinosaurs were also the ancestors of modern, brightly colored birds, it stands to reason that they might have been brightly colored too.

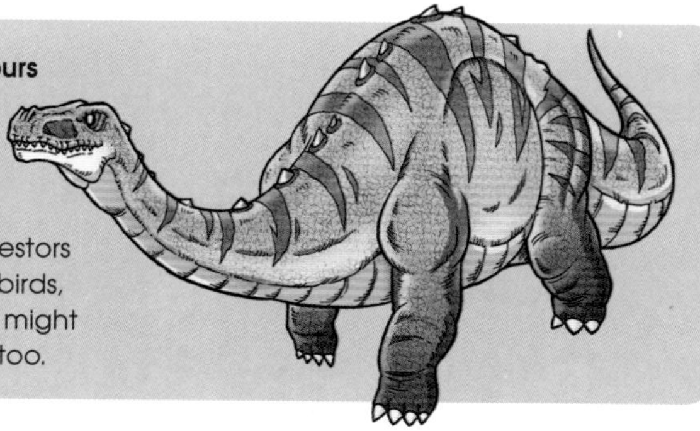

Color coded?

Birds are the only other species along with humans and primates that are not colorblind. If dinosaurs were as colorblind as other animals, then they would have no need for bright colors. If they were not colorblind, however, then bright coats would have been a big advantage. Some paleontologists believe the Hadrosaurus could change its colors during the mating season, or when defending its territory.

CHAPTER 2
RAINSTORMING

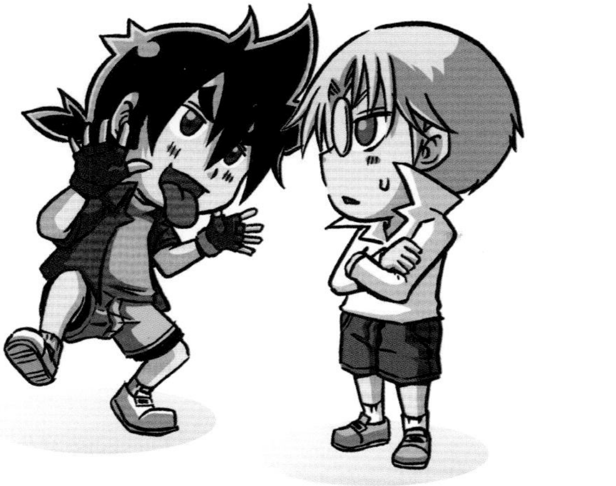

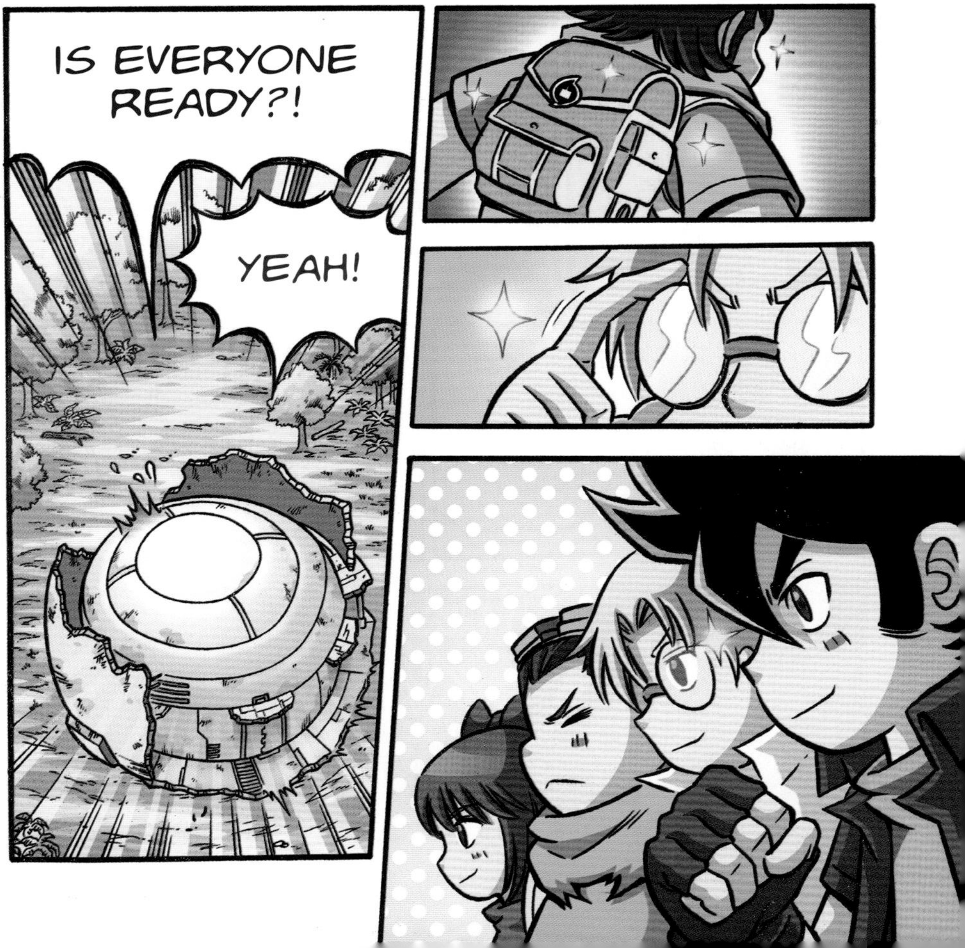
IS EVERYONE READY?!
YEAH!

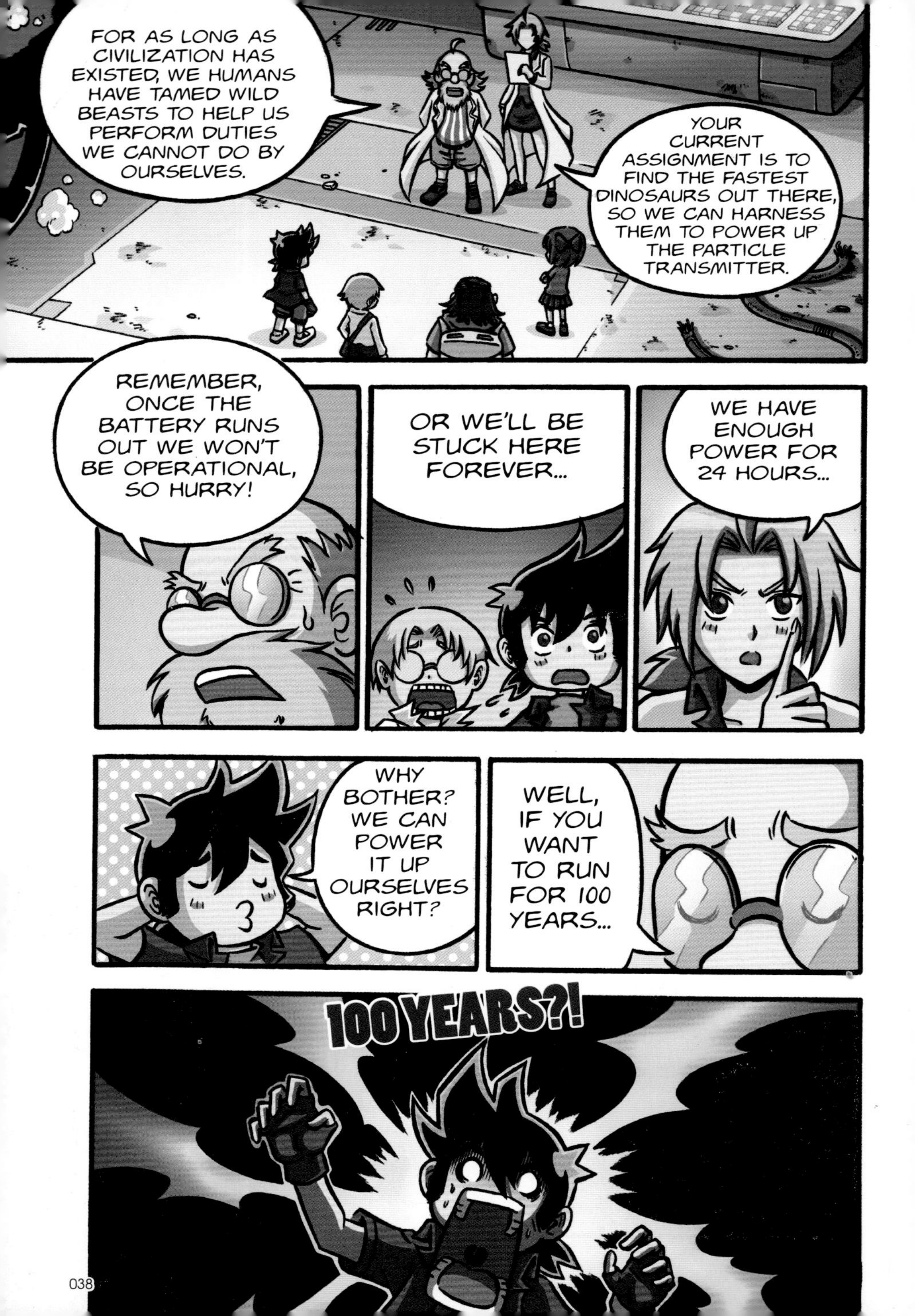
FOR AS LONG AS CIVILIZATION HAS EXISTED, WE HUMANS HAVE TAMED WILD BEASTS TO HELP US PERFORM DUTIES WE CANNOT DO BY OURSELVES.
YOUR CURRENT ASSIGNMENT IS TO FIND THE FASTEST DINOSAURS OUT THERE, SO WE CAN HARNESS THEM TO POWER UP THE PARTICLE TRANSMITTER.
REMEMBER, ONCE THE BATTERY RUNS OUT WE WON'T BE OPERATIONAL, SO HURRY!
OR WE'LL BE STUCK HERE FOREVER...
WE HAVE ENOUGH POWER FOR 24 HOURS...
WHY BOTHER? WE CAN POWER IT UP OURSELVES RIGHT?
WELL, IF YOU WANT TO RUN FOR 100 YEARS...
100 YEARS?!

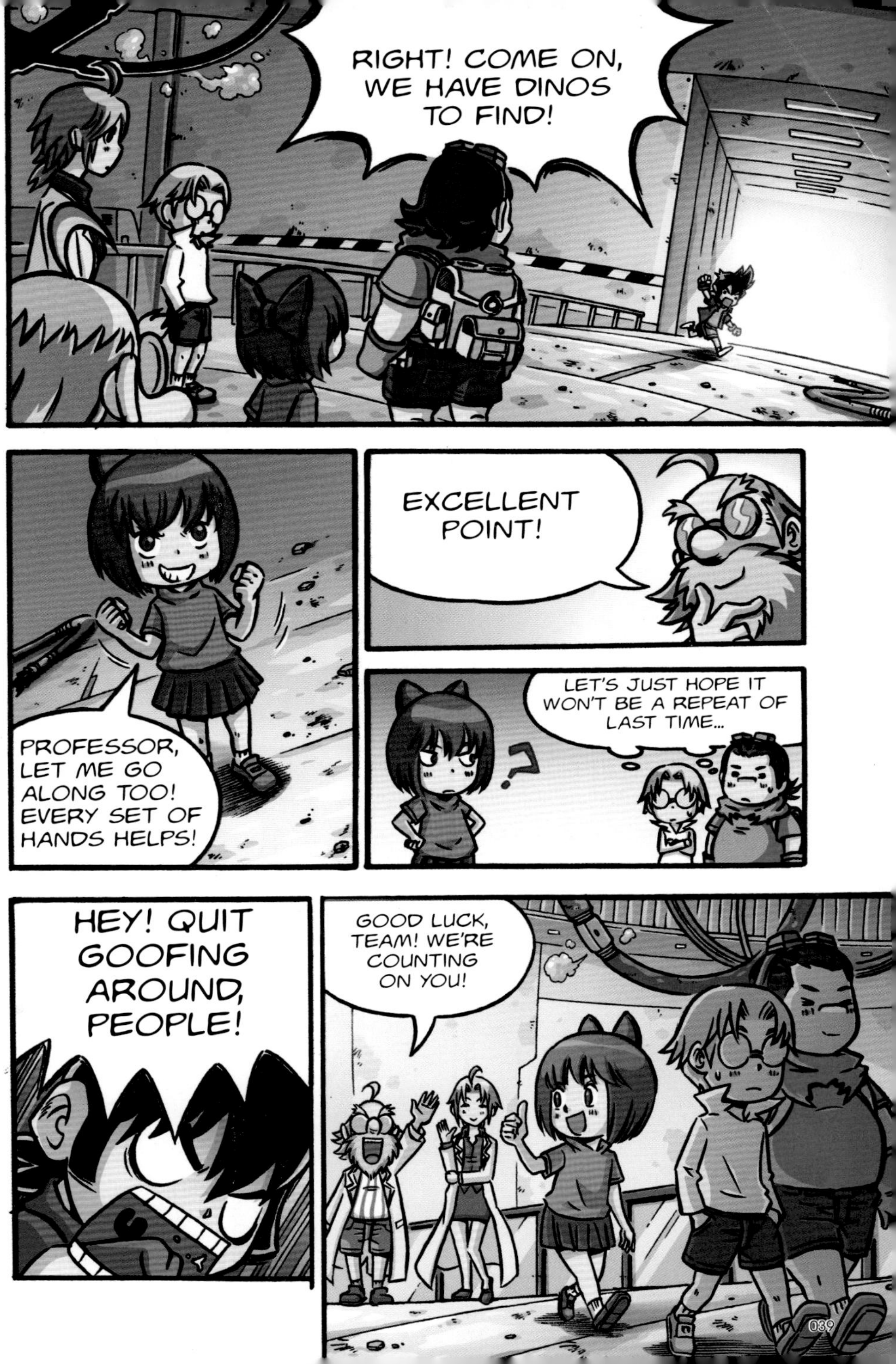
RIGHT! COME ON, WE HAVE DINOS TO FIND!
PROFESSOR, LET ME GO ALONG TOO! EVERY SET OF HANDS HELPS!
EXCELLENT POINT!
LET'S JUST HOPE IT WON'T BE A REPEAT OF LAST TIME...
HEY! QUIT GOOFING AROUND, PEOPLE!
GOOD LUCK, TEAM! WE'RE COUNTING ON YOU!

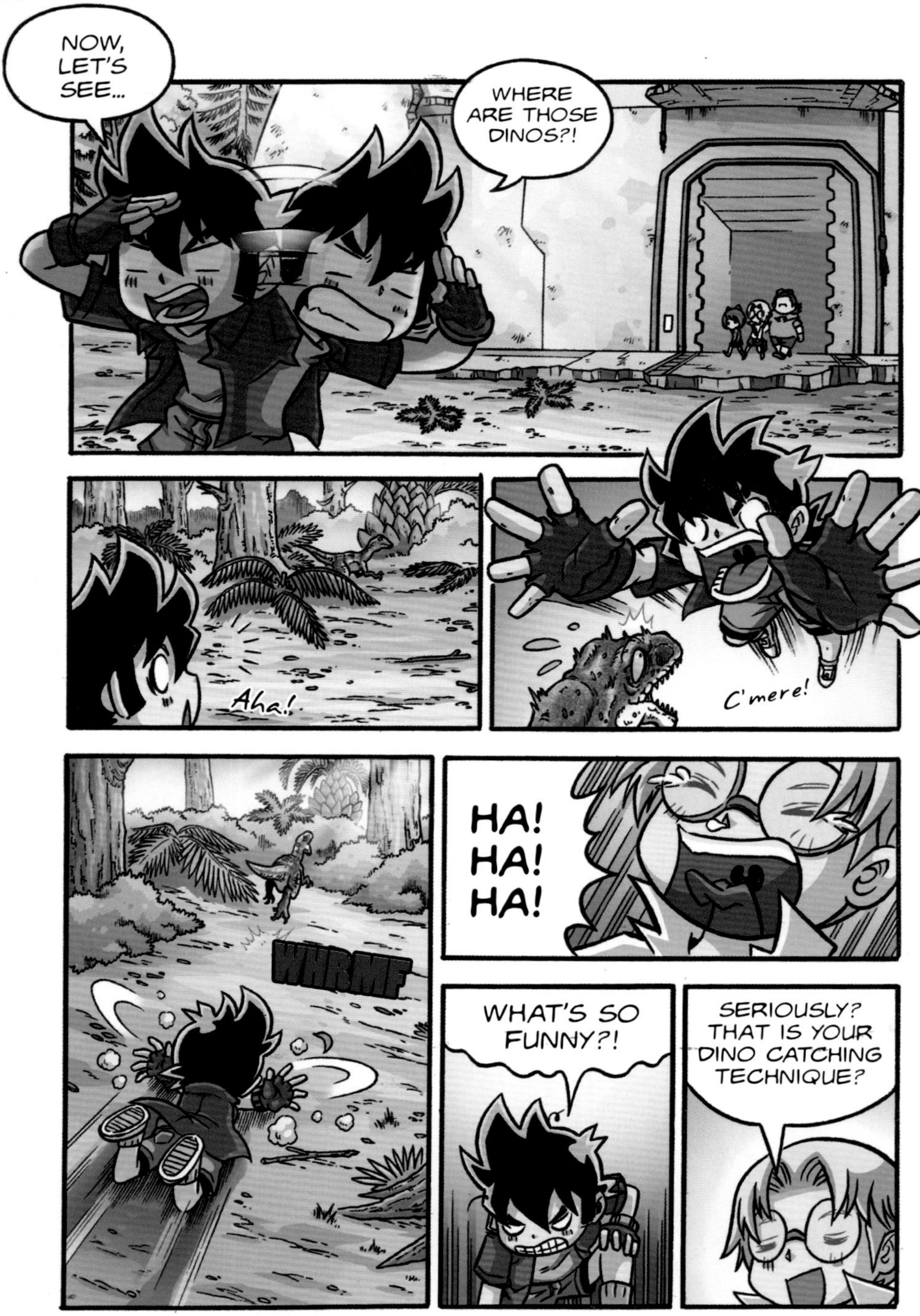
NOW, LET'S SEE...
WHERE ARE THOSE DINOS?!
Aha!
C'mere!
WHRMF
HA! HA! HA!
WHAT'S SO FUNNY?!
SERIOUSLY? THAT IS YOUR DINO CATCHING TECHNIQUE?

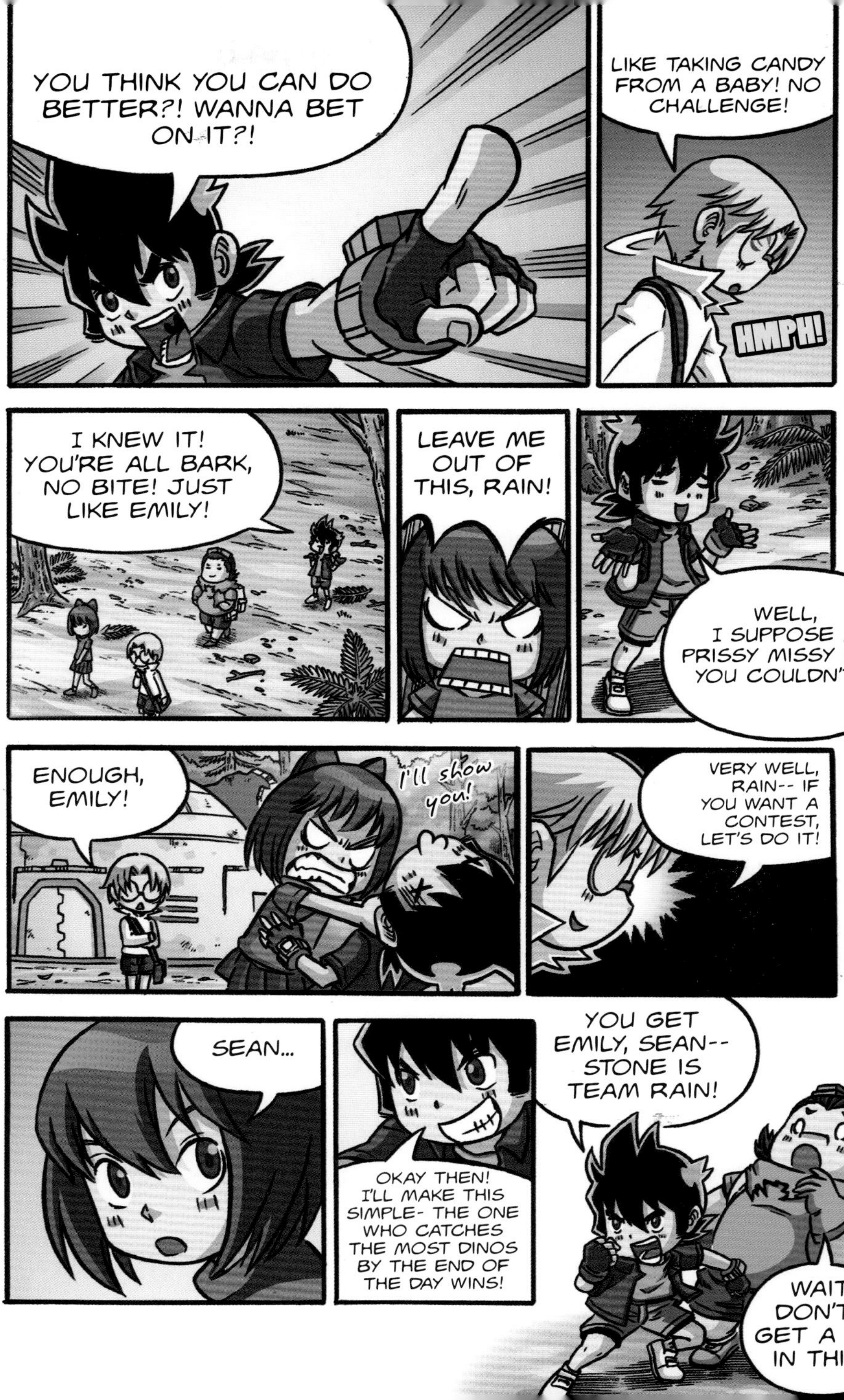
YOU THINK YOU CAN DO BETTER?! WANNA BET ON IT?!
LIKE TAKING CANDY FROM A BABY! NO CHALLENGE!
HMPH!
I KNEW IT! YOU'RE ALL BARK, NO BITE! JUST LIKE EMILY!
LEAVE ME OUT OF THIS, RAIN!
WELL, I SUPPOSE A PRISSY MISSY LIKE YOU COULDN'T--
ENOUGH, EMILY!
I'll show you!
VERY WELL, RAIN-- IF YOU WANT A CONTEST, LET'S DO IT!
SEAN...
OKAY THEN! I'LL MAKE THIS SIMPLE- THE ONE WHO CATCHES THE MOST DINOS BY THE END OF THE DAY WINS!
YOU GET EMILY, SEAN-- STONE IS TEAM RAIN!
WAIT! DON'T I GET A SAY IN THIS?

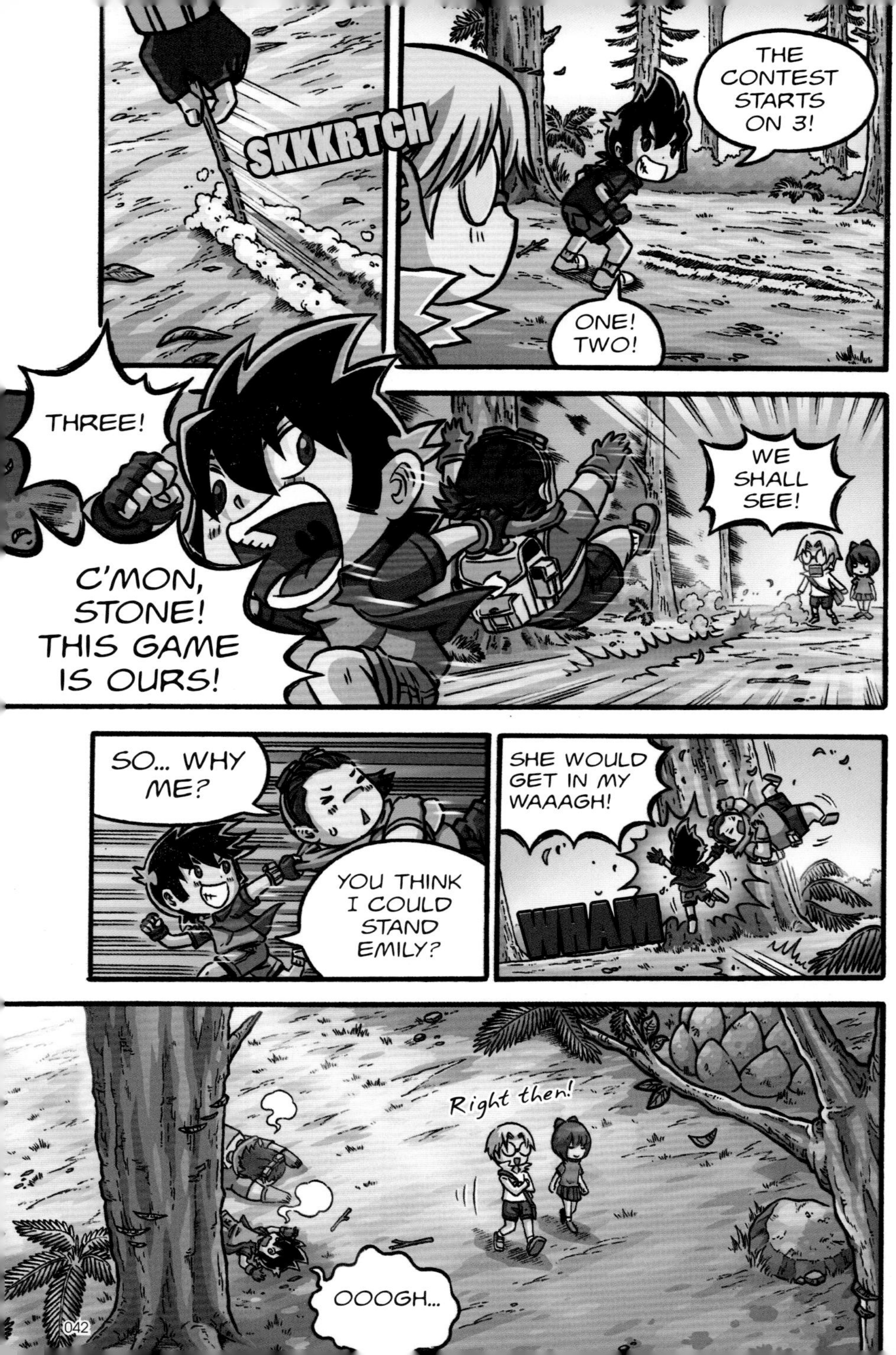

SKKKRTCH
THE CONTEST STARTS ON 3!
ONE! TWO!
THREE!
C'MON, STONE! THIS GAME IS OURS!
WE SHALL SEE!
SO... WHY ME?
YOU THINK I COULD STAND EMILY?
SHE WOULD GET IN MY WAAAGH!
WHAM
Right then!
OOOGH...

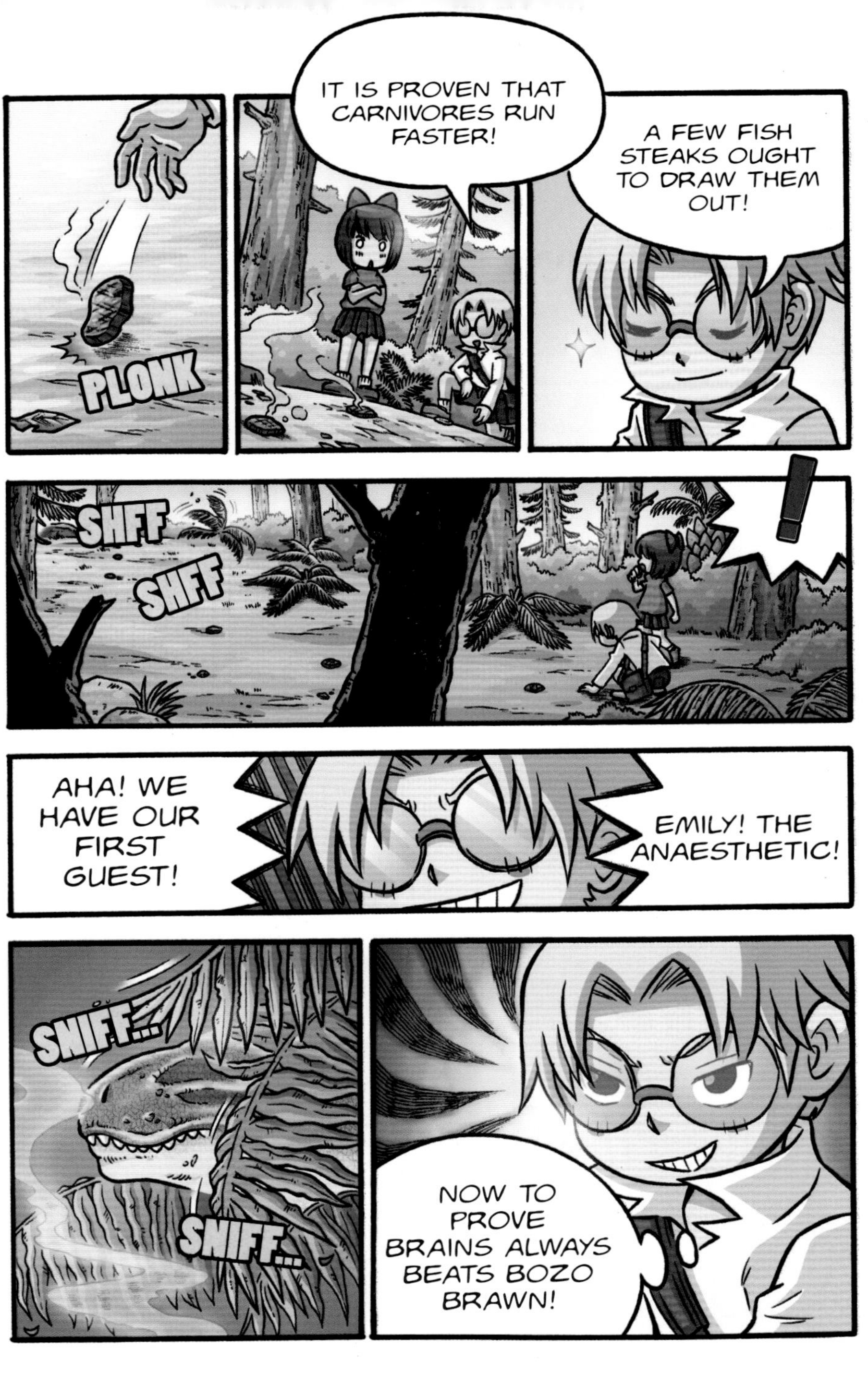
PLONK
IT IS PROVEN THAT CARNIVORES RUN FASTER!
A FEW FISH STEAKS OUGHT TO DRAW THEM OUT!
SHFF
SHFF
!
AHA! WE HAVE OUR FIRST GUEST!
EMILY! THE ANAESTHETIC!
SNIFF...
SNIFF...
NOW TO PROVE BRAINS ALWAYS BEATS BOZO BRAWN!

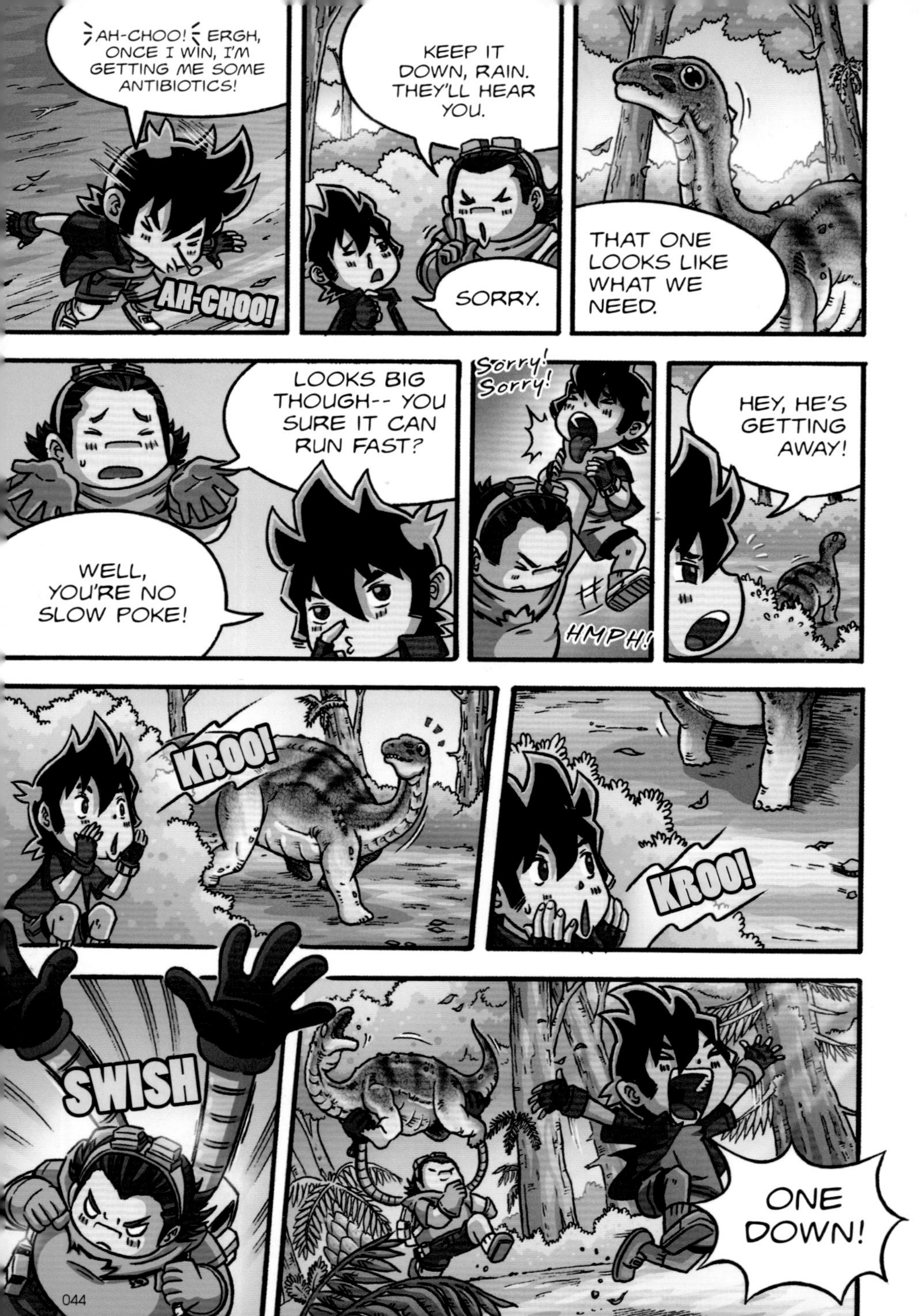
AH-CHOO! ERGH, ONCE I WIN, I'M GETTING ME SOME ANTIBIOTICS!
AH-CHOO!
KEEP IT DOWN, RAIN. THEY'LL HEAR YOU.
SORRY.
THAT ONE LOOKS LIKE WHAT WE NEED.
LOOKS BIG THOUGH-- YOU SURE IT CAN RUN FAST?
WELL, YOU'RE NO SLOW POKE!
Sorry! Sorry!
HMPH!
HEY, HE'S GETTING AWAY!
KROO!
KROO!
SWISH
ONE DOWN!

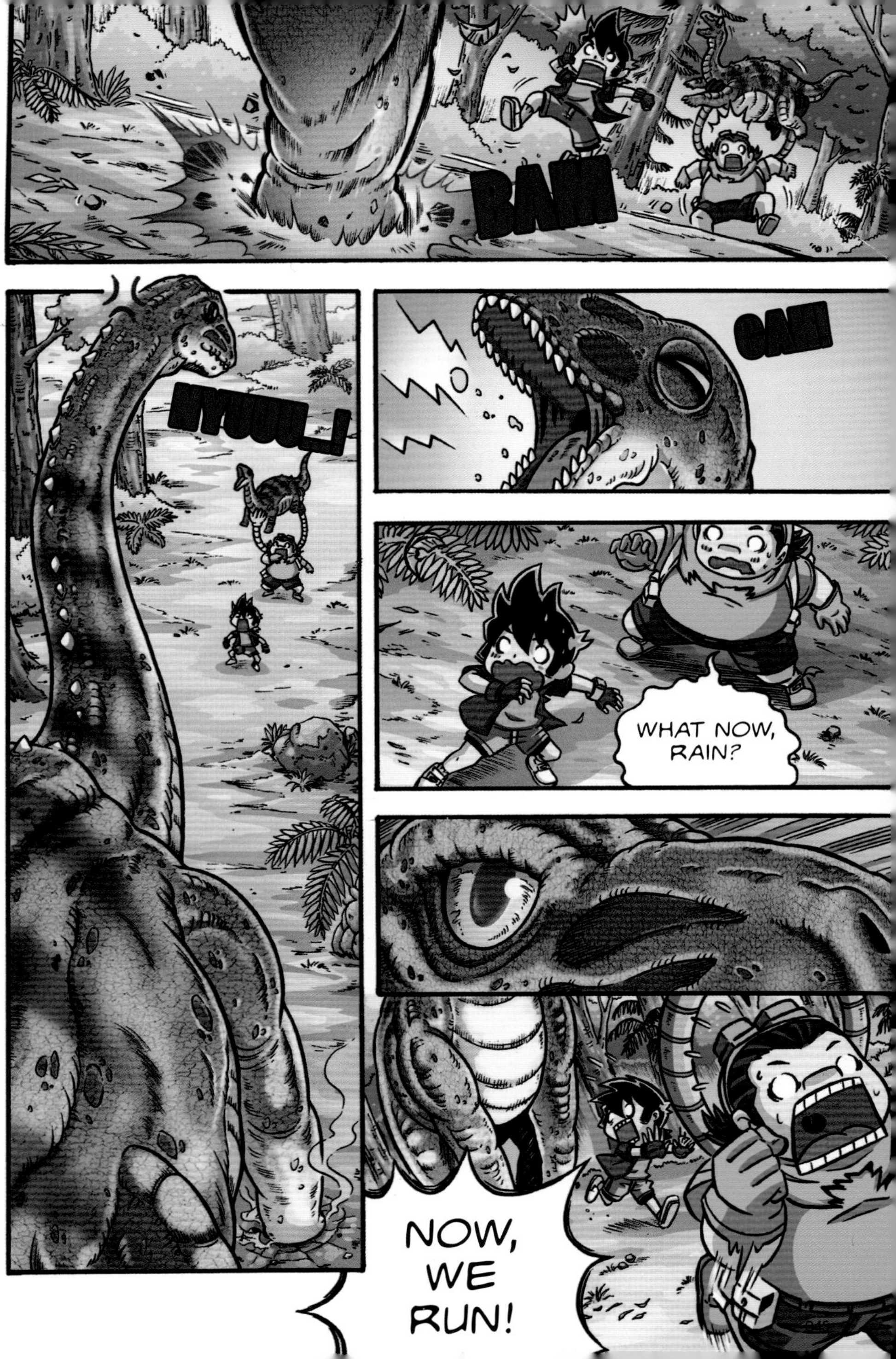
WHAT NOW, RAIN?
NOW, WE RUN!

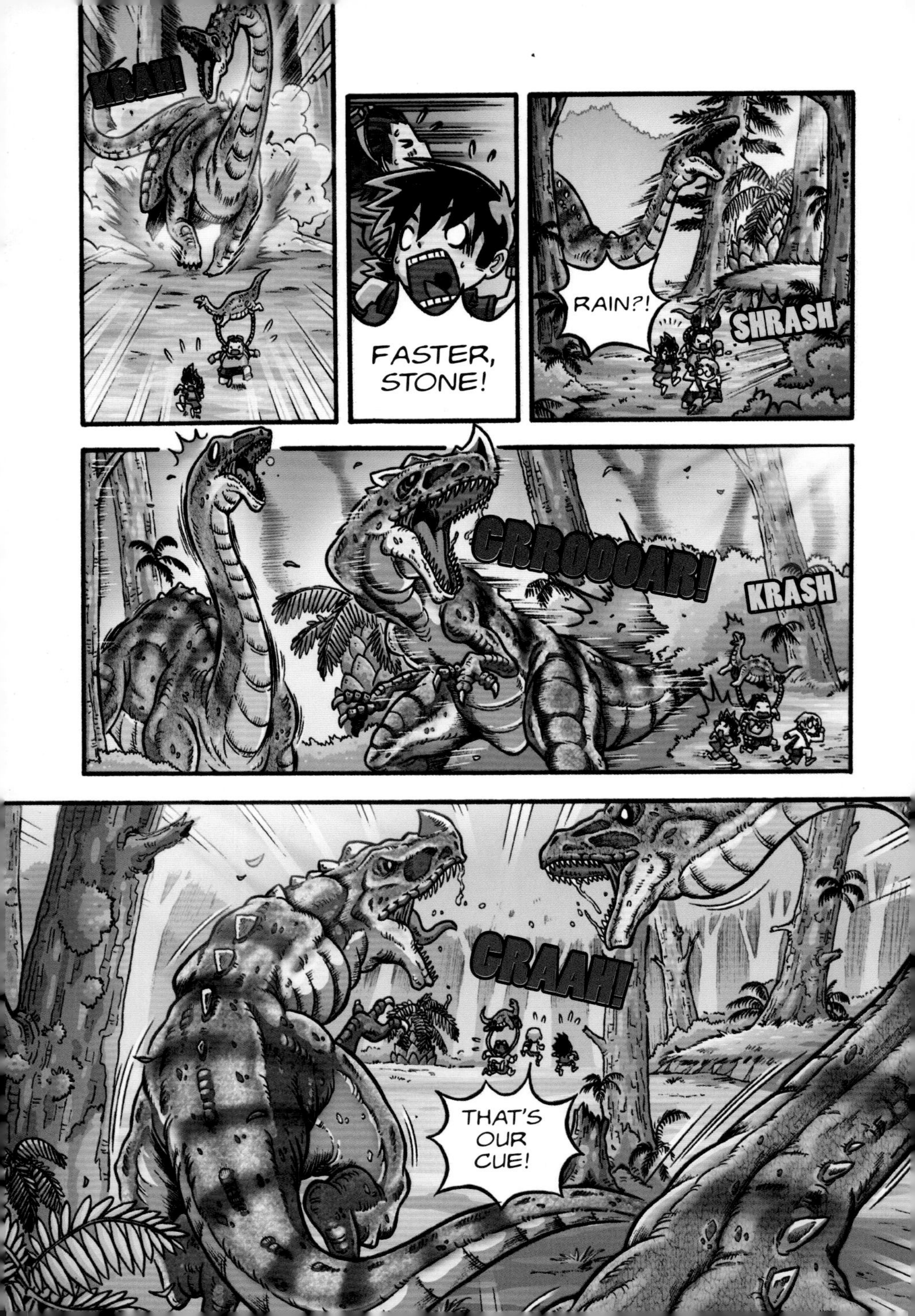
KRAH!
FASTER, STONE!
RAIN?!
SHRASH
CRROOOOAR!
KRASH
CRAAH!
THAT'S OUR CUE!

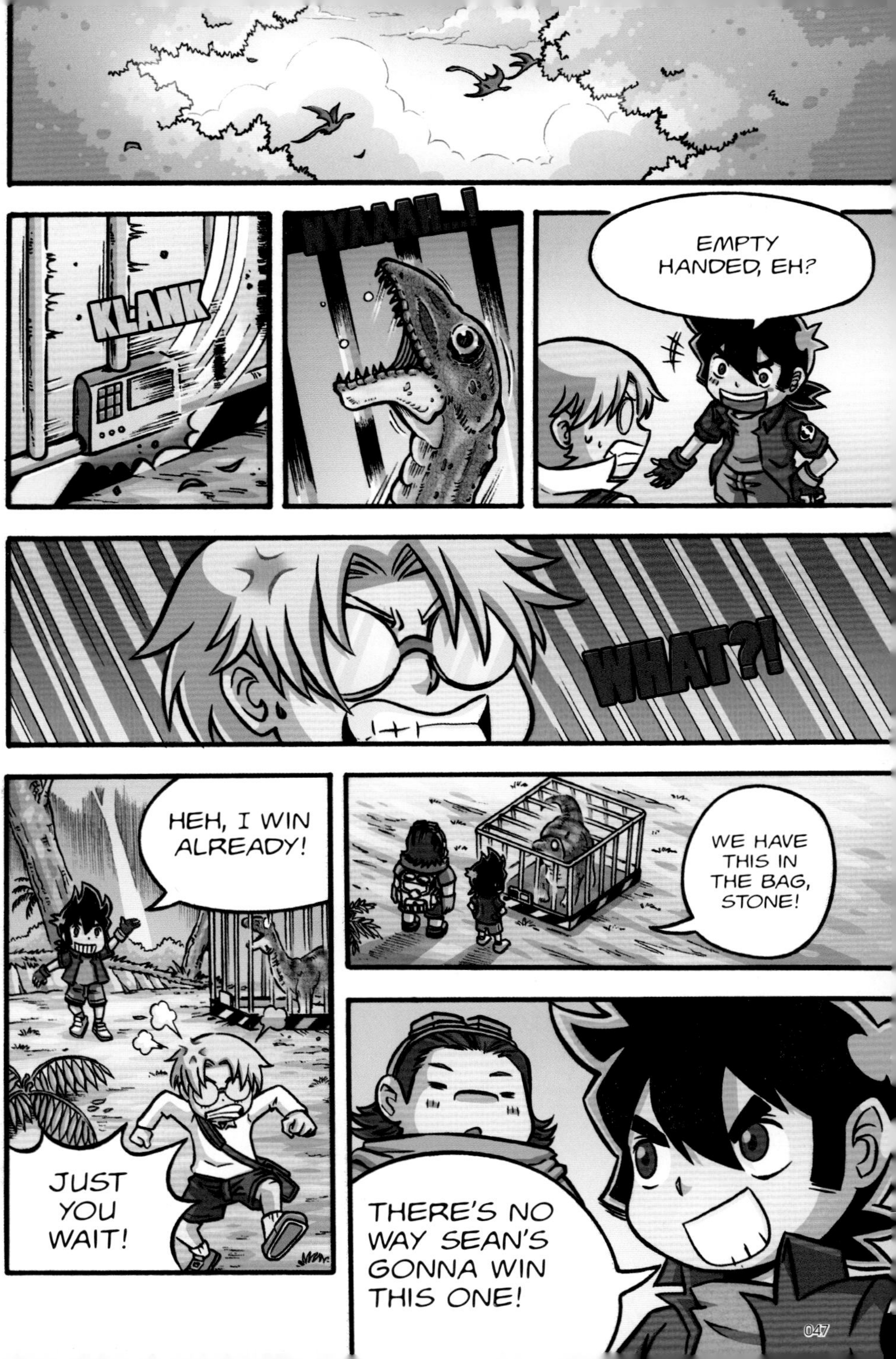
KLANK
NYAAAH...!
EMPTY HANDED, EH?
WHAT?!
HEH, I WIN ALREADY!
JUST YOU WAIT!
WE HAVE THIS IN THE BAG, STONE!
THERE'S NO WAY SEAN'S GONNA WIN THIS ONE!

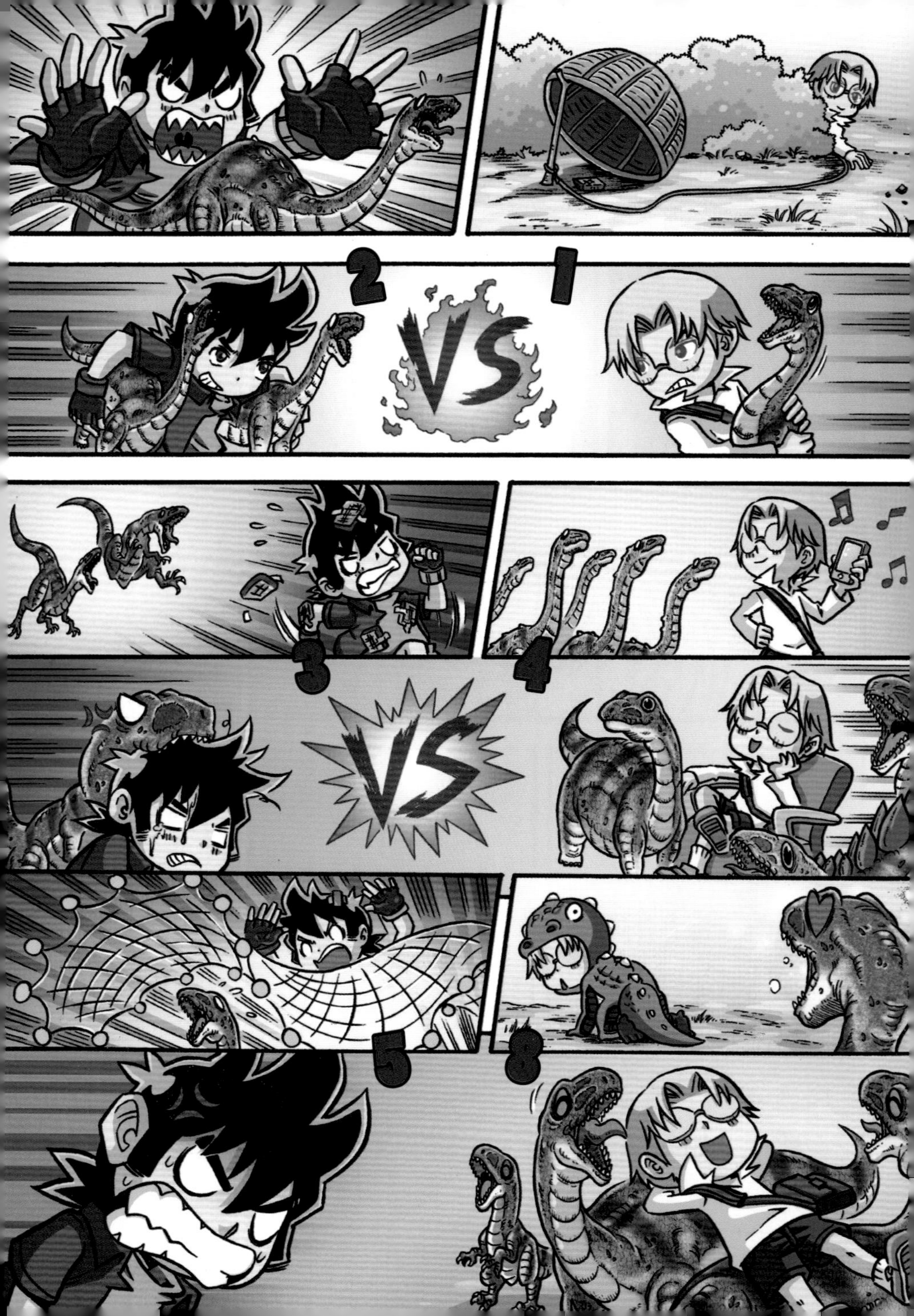
2
VS
1
3
VS
4
5
8

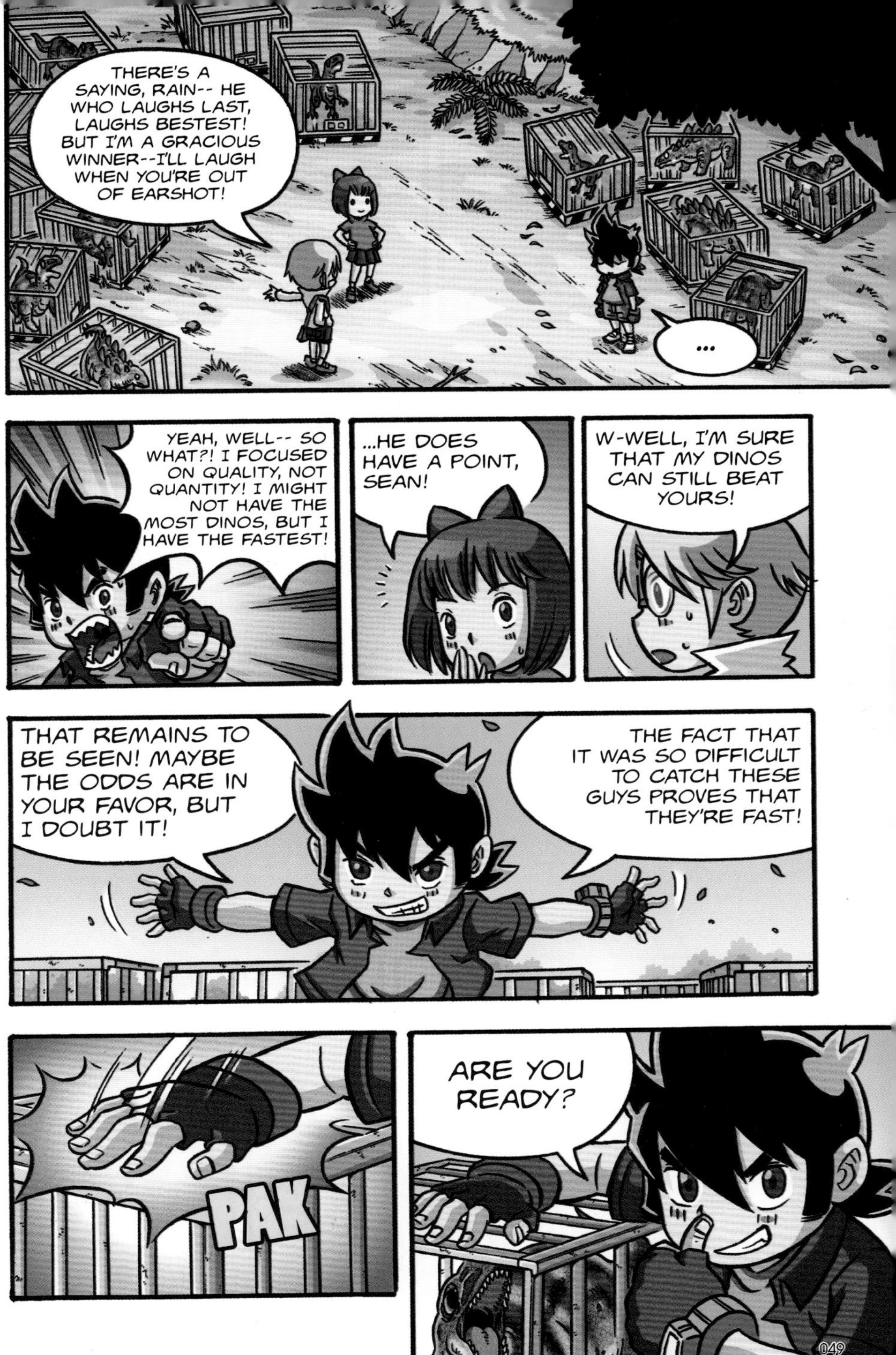
THERE'S A SAYING, RAIN-- HE WHO LAUGHS LAST, LAUGHS BESTEST! BUT I'M A GRACIOUS WINNER--I'LL LAUGH WHEN YOU'RE OUT OF EARSHOT!
...
YEAH, WELL-- SO WHAT?! I FOCUSED ON QUALITY, NOT QUANTITY! I MIGHT NOT HAVE THE MOST DINOS, BUT I HAVE THE FASTEST!
...HE DOES HAVE A POINT, SEAN!
W-WELL, I'M SURE THAT MY DINOS CAN STILL BEAT YOURS!
THAT REMAINS TO BE SEEN! MAYBE THE ODDS ARE IN YOUR FAVOR, BUT I DOUBT IT!
THE FACT THAT IT WAS SO DIFFICULT TO CATCH THESE GUYS PROVES THAT THEY'RE FAST!
PAK
ARE YOU READY?

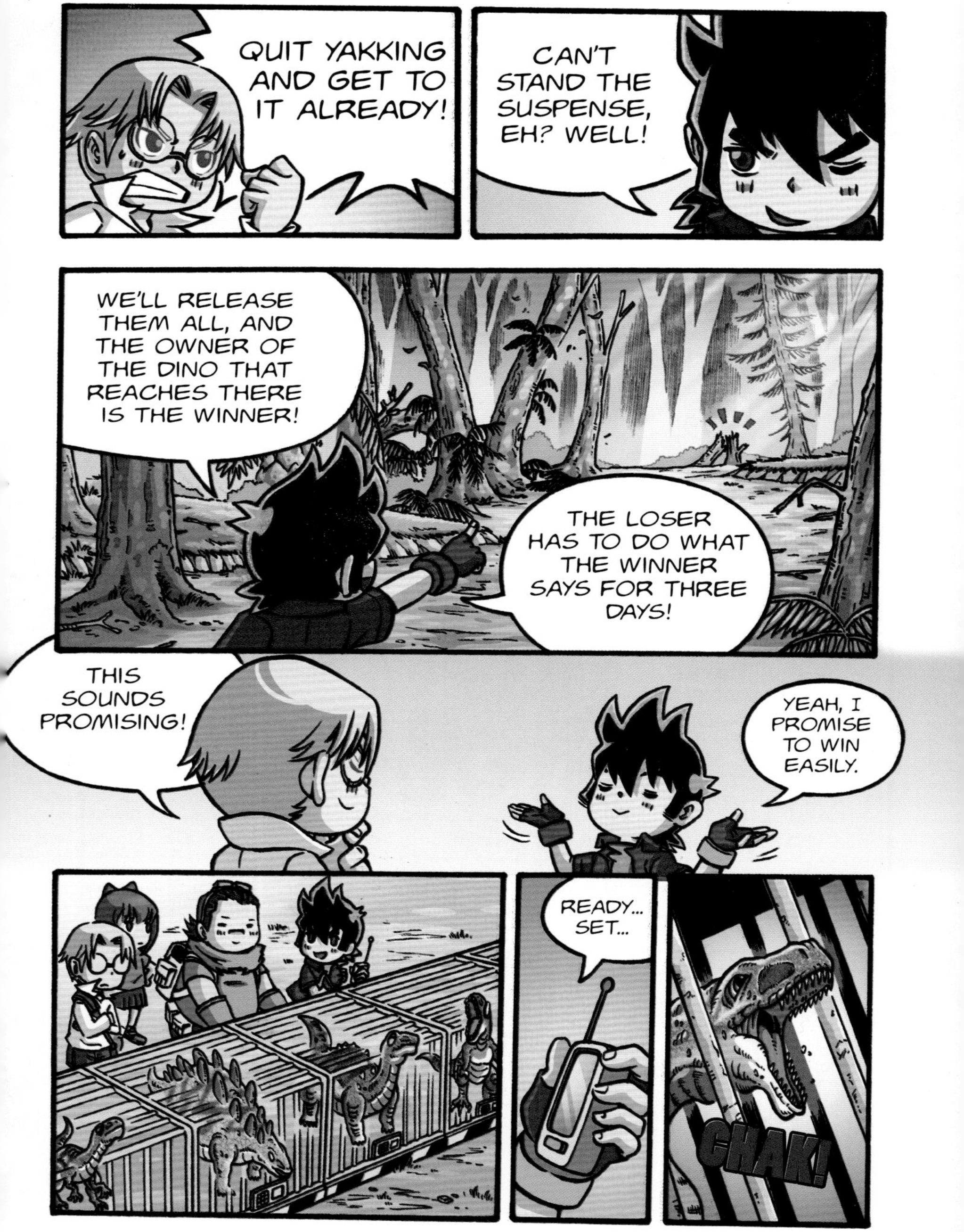
QUIT YAKKING AND GET TO IT ALREADY!
CAN'T STAND THE SUSPENSE, EH? WELL!
WE'LL RELEASE THEM ALL, AND THE OWNER OF THE DINO THAT REACHES THERE IS THE WINNER!
THE LOSER HAS TO DO WHAT THE WINNER SAYS FOR THREE DAYS!
THIS SOUNDS PROMISING!
YEAH, I PROMISE TO WIN EASILY.
READY... SET...
CHAK!

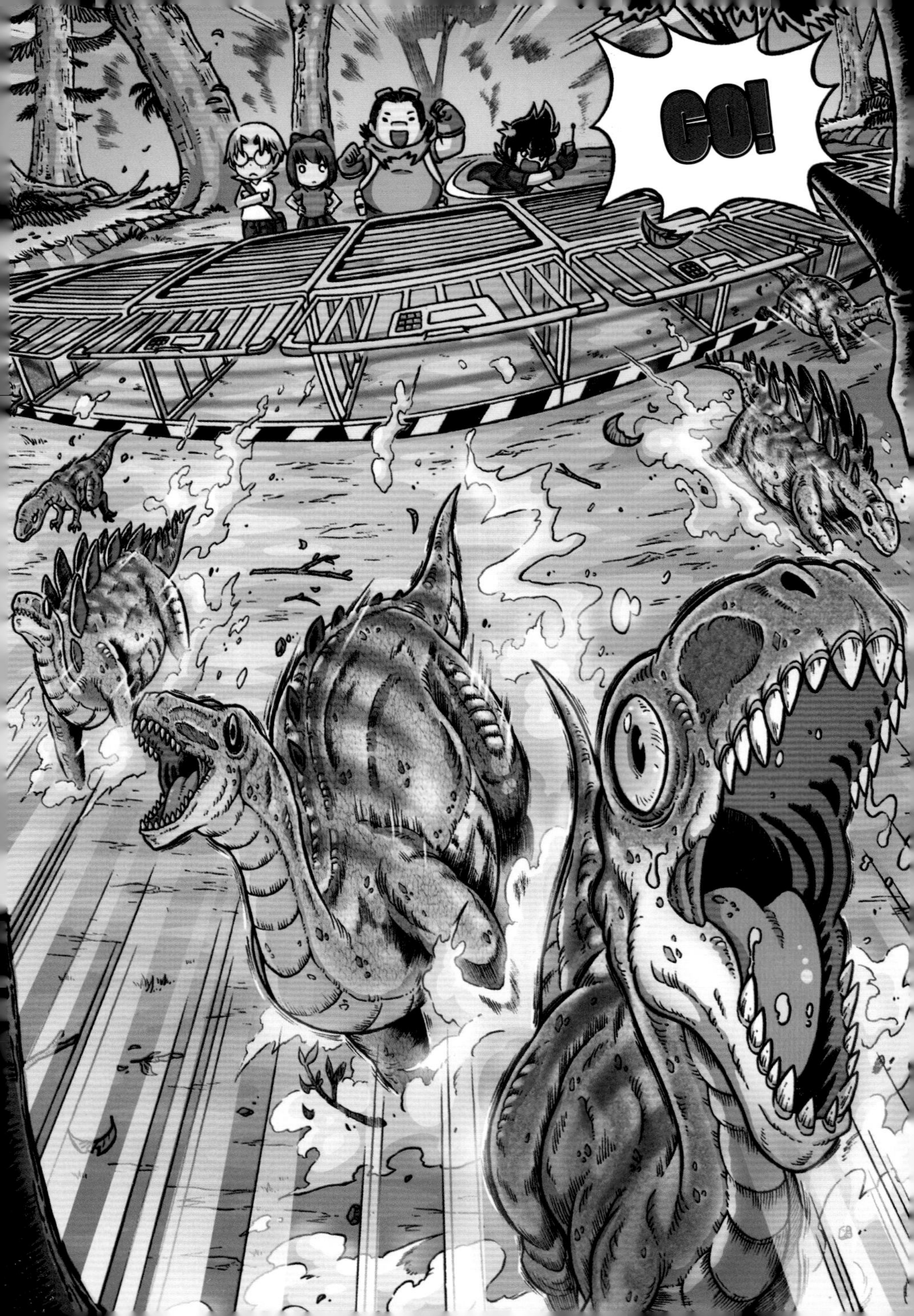
GO!

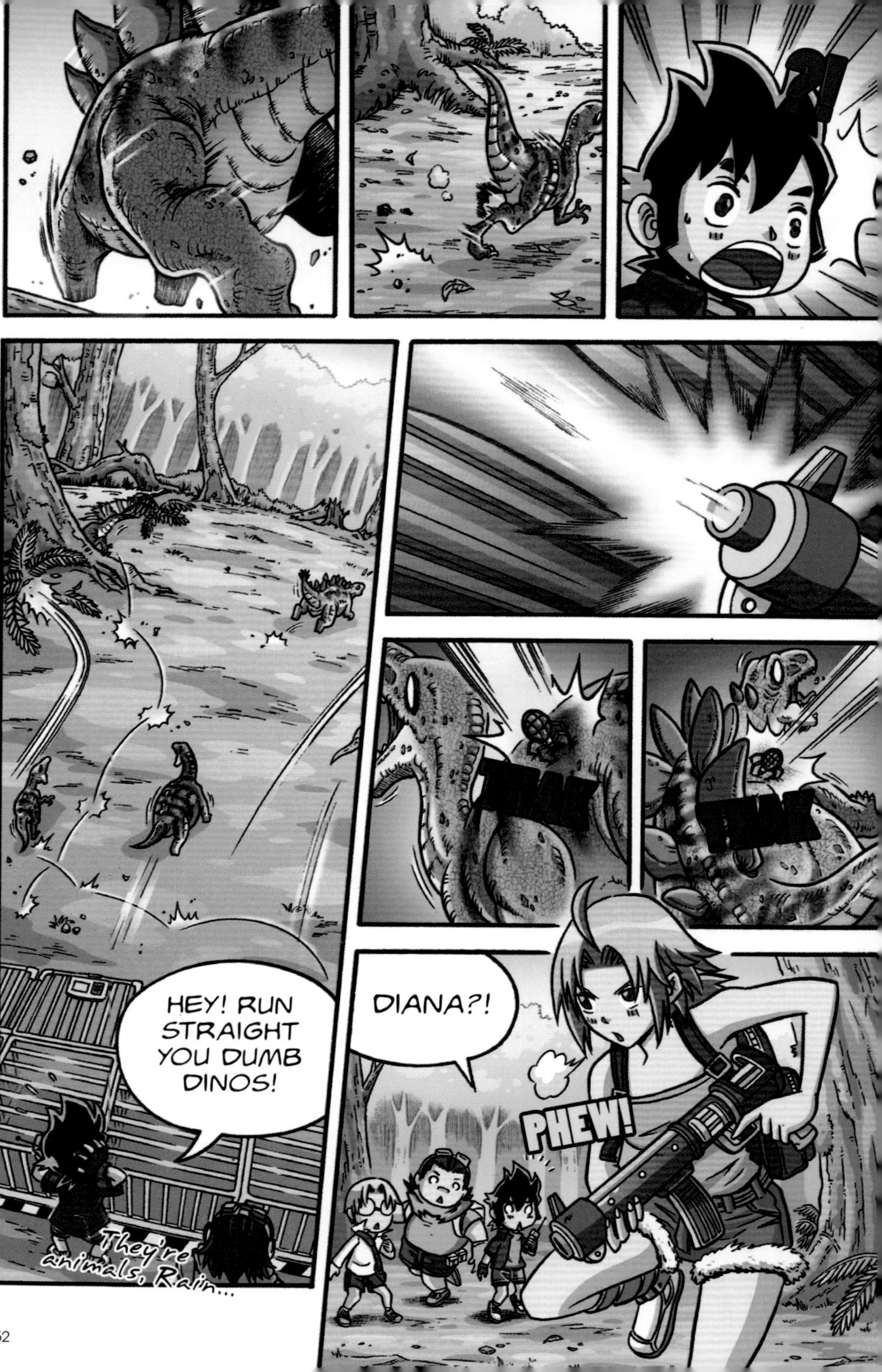

?!
HEY! RUN STRAIGHT YOU DUMB DINOS!
They're animals, Rain...
DIANA?!
PHEW!

JONESING FOR THE JURASSIC

Seismosaurus

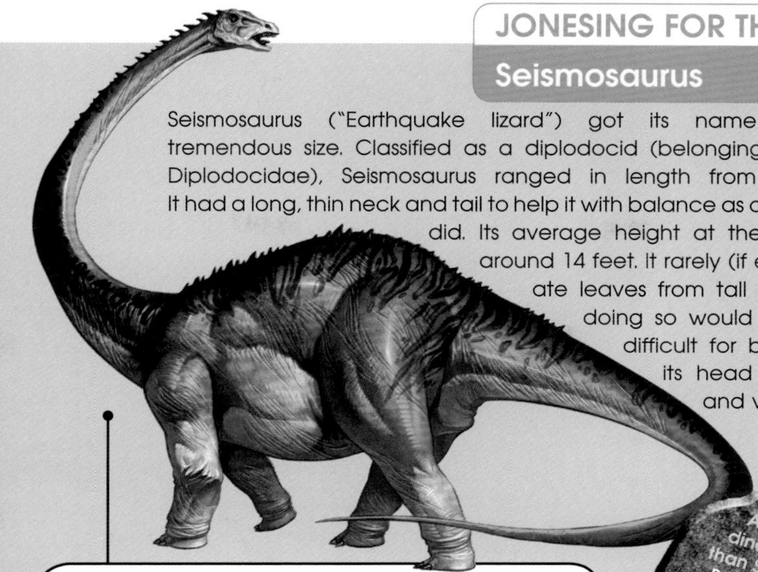

Seismosaurus ("Earthquake lizard") got its name due to its tremendous size. Classified as a diplodocid (belonging to the family Diplodocidae), Seismosaurus ranged in length from 137-170 feet. It had a long, thin neck and tail to help it with balance as other sauropods did. Its average height at the shoulder was around 14 feet. It rarely (if ever), however, ate leaves from tall trees; because doing so would have made it difficult for blood to reach its head from its body and vice versa.

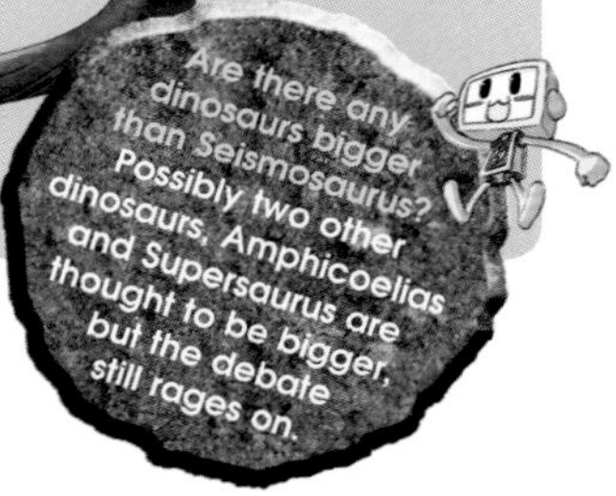
Are there any dinosaurs bigger than Seismosaurus? Possibly two other dinosaurs, Amphicoelias and Supersaurus are thought to be bigger, but the debate still rages on.

Scientific name: Seismosaurus
Length: 137 to 170 feet
Diet: Herbivore
Habitat: Woodlands and grassy areas
Discovered: North America
Era: Late Jurassic

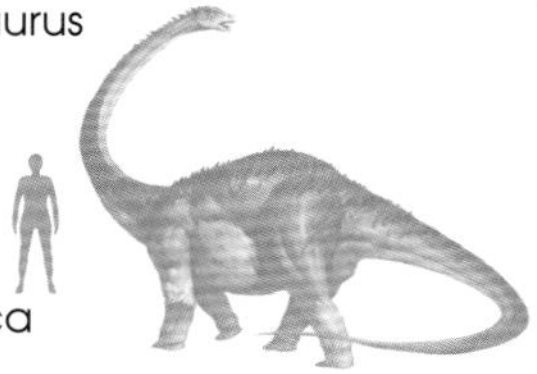

JONESING FOR THE JURASSIC

Diplodocus

When most people imagine a dinosaur with a large body, long neck and slim tail, it is usually the Diplodocus they picture. It got its name from unique bone structures at the base of its tail, a trait it shares with other dinosaurs in family Diplodiocidae. Diplodocus skeletons are among the most complete skeletons to be discovered so far. Indeed, some even consider Seismosaurus to be just a large Diplodocus.

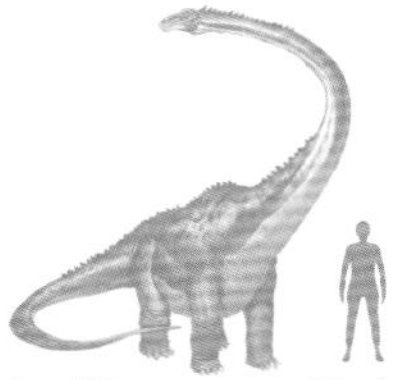

Scientific name: Diplodocus
Length: 88.5 feet
Diet: Herbivore
Habitat: Flatlands
Discovered: North America
Era: Late Jurassic

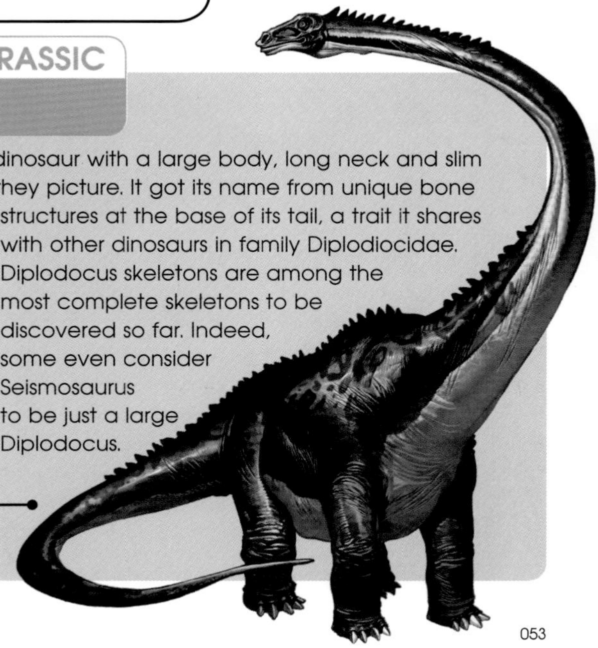

JONESING FOR THE JURASSIC

Camarasaurus

Camarasaurus was a small sauropod notable for its remarkably square skull. Nonetheless it had an excellent sense of smell, which probably helped it avoid danger. Its advanced tooth structure let it process and digest high-cellulose plants other herbivores could not.

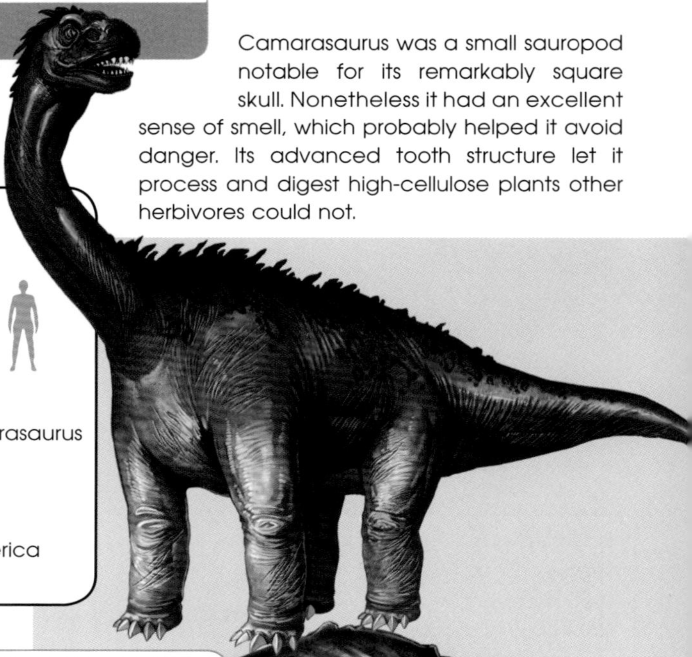

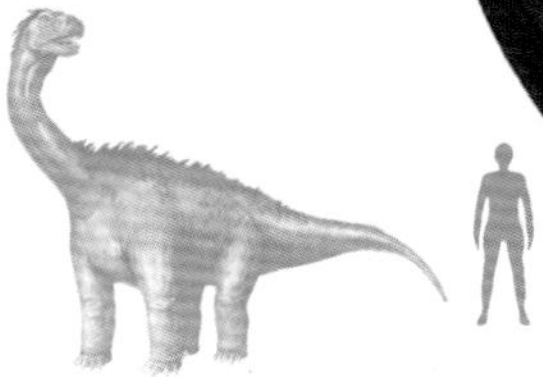

Scientific name: Camarasaurus
Length: 59 feet
Diet: Herbivore
Habitat: Flatlands
Discovered: North America
Era: Late Jurassic

JONESING FOR THE JURASSIC

Apatosaurus

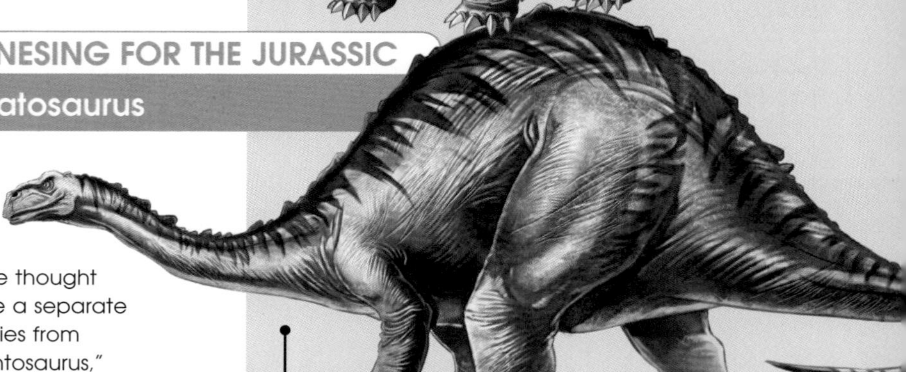

Once thought to be a separate species from "Brontosaurus," new discoveries have led archaeologists to believe them to be in the same species. Though not as long as other sauropods, it was immensely strong, and its clawed front legs and whiplike tail ensured it was not easy prey.

Scientific name: Apatosaurus
Length: 68 feet
Diet: Herbivore
Habitat: Woodlands
Discovered: North America
Era: Late Jurassic

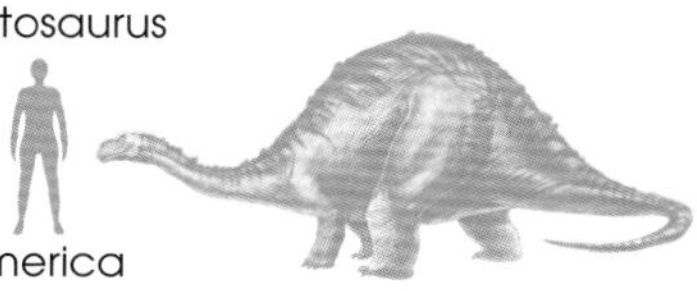

JONESING FOR THE JURASSIC

Brachiosaurus

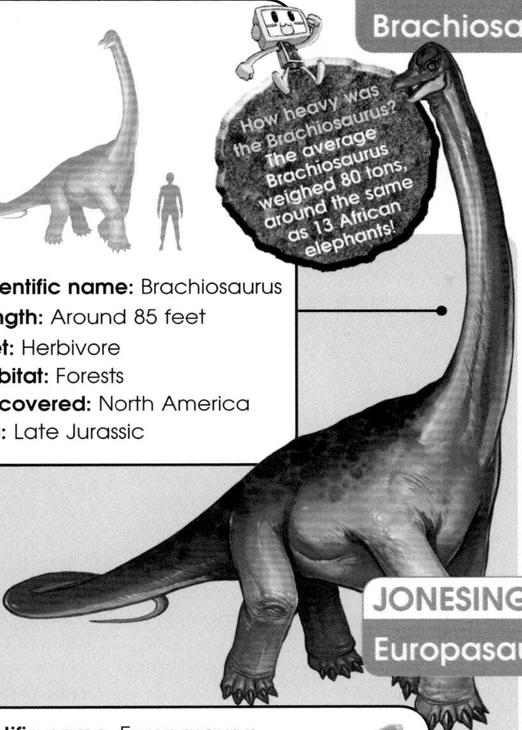
How heavy was the Brachiosaurus?
The average Brachiosaurus weighed 80 tons, around the same as 13 African elephants!

Scientific name: Brachiosaurus
Length: Around 85 feet
Diet: Herbivore
Habitat: Forests
Discovered: North America
Era: Late Jurassic

Brachiosaurus' longer forelegs gave it an almost diagonal skeletal structure, providing elevation which allowed it to have a wide field of vision. Its diet consisted of branches and young shoots, which its chisel-like teeth were well-adapted to chewing.

JONESING FOR THE JURASSIC

Europasaurus

Scientific name: Europasaurus
Length: 19 feet
Diet: Herbivore
Habitat: Forests
Discovered: Europe
Era: Late Jurassic

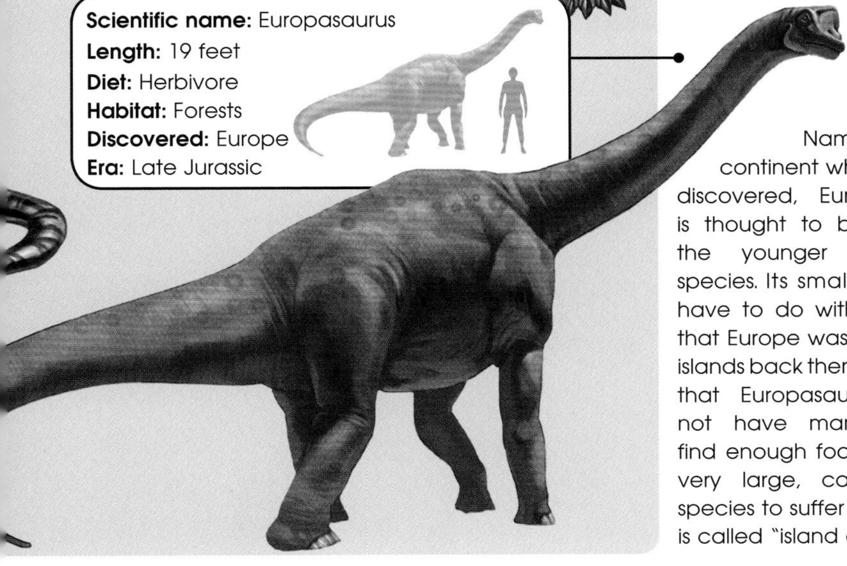

Named for the continent where it was discovered, Europasaurus is thought to be one of the younger sauropod species. Its small size may have to do with the fact that Europe was a mass of islands back then, meaning that Europasaurus might not have managed to find enough food to grow very large, causing the species to suffer from what is called "island dwarfism."

Sinornithosaurus

Another early bird, Sinornithosaurus shared physical similarities with its local cousin Sinosauropteryx; a bizarre blend of reptilian features and birdlike ones. Its head and shoulders had a lot more in common with birds than reptiles, and it definitely had feathers, though paleontologists remain undecided on whether it could fly.

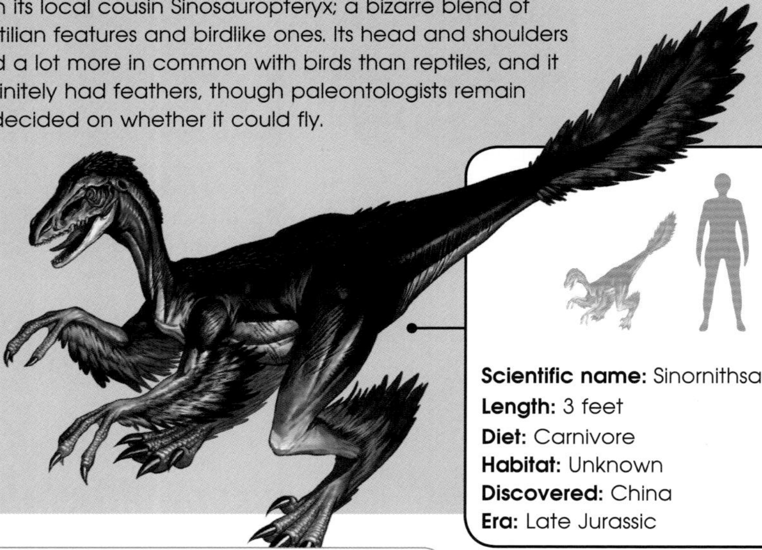

Scientific name: Sinornithsaurus
Length: 3 feet
Diet: Carnivore
Habitat: Unknown
Discovered: China
Era: Late Jurassic

Sinraptor

A genus of theropod, Sinraptor had a massive 3 feet long skull, a third of its height, which, when combined with its powerful jaws lined with sharp teeth, made it a terrifying predator. Sinraptor skeletons have been found with teeth marks from others of their kind, which might indicate it was a highly aggressive, possibly, even cannibalistic species.

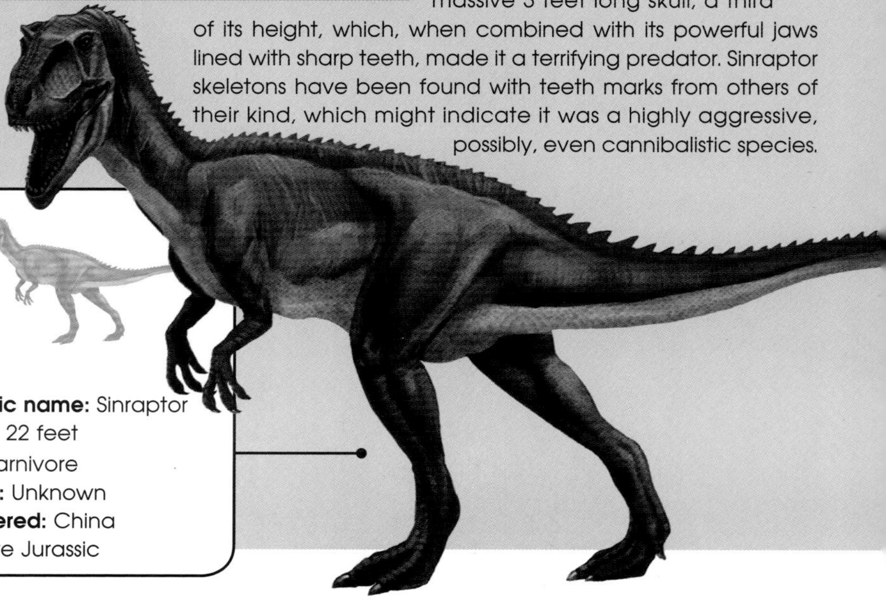

Scientific name: Sinraptor
Length: 22 feet
Diet: Carnivore
Habitat: Unknown
Discovered: China
Era: Late Jurassic

CHAPTER 3

EGGSTREME TARGETING ACTION!

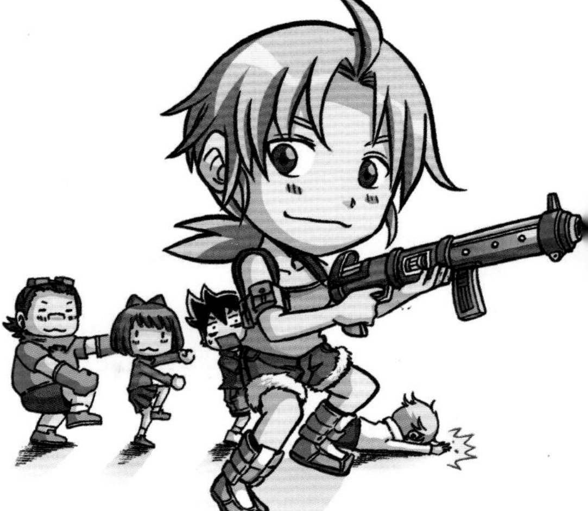

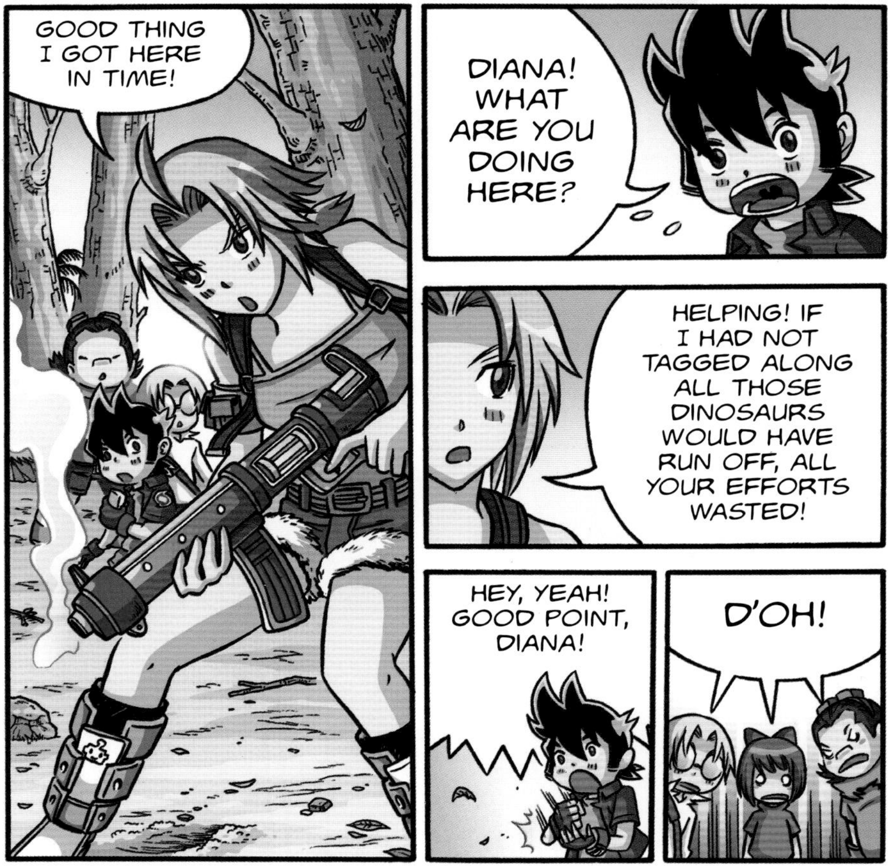
GOOD THING I GOT HERE IN TIME!
DIANA! WHAT ARE YOU DOING HERE?
HELPING! IF I HAD NOT TAGGED ALONG ALL THOSE DINOSAURS WOULD HAVE RUN OFF, ALL YOUR EFFORTS WASTED!
HEY, YEAH! GOOD POINT, DIANA!
D'OH!

SO THIS MEANS NEXT UP IS TRACK AND RECAPTURE?

KCHAK

THAT'S RIGHT! WE'RE ALSO GOING TO MEASURE ACCELERATION AND VITALS! AFTER ALL, WE NEED DINOSAURS THAT ARE NOT JUST FAST, BUT HAVE HIGH ENDURANCE!

SEARCHING...

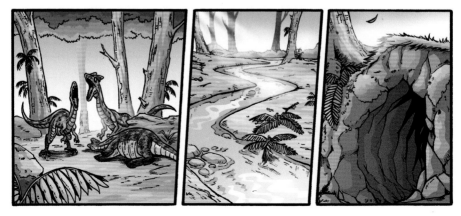

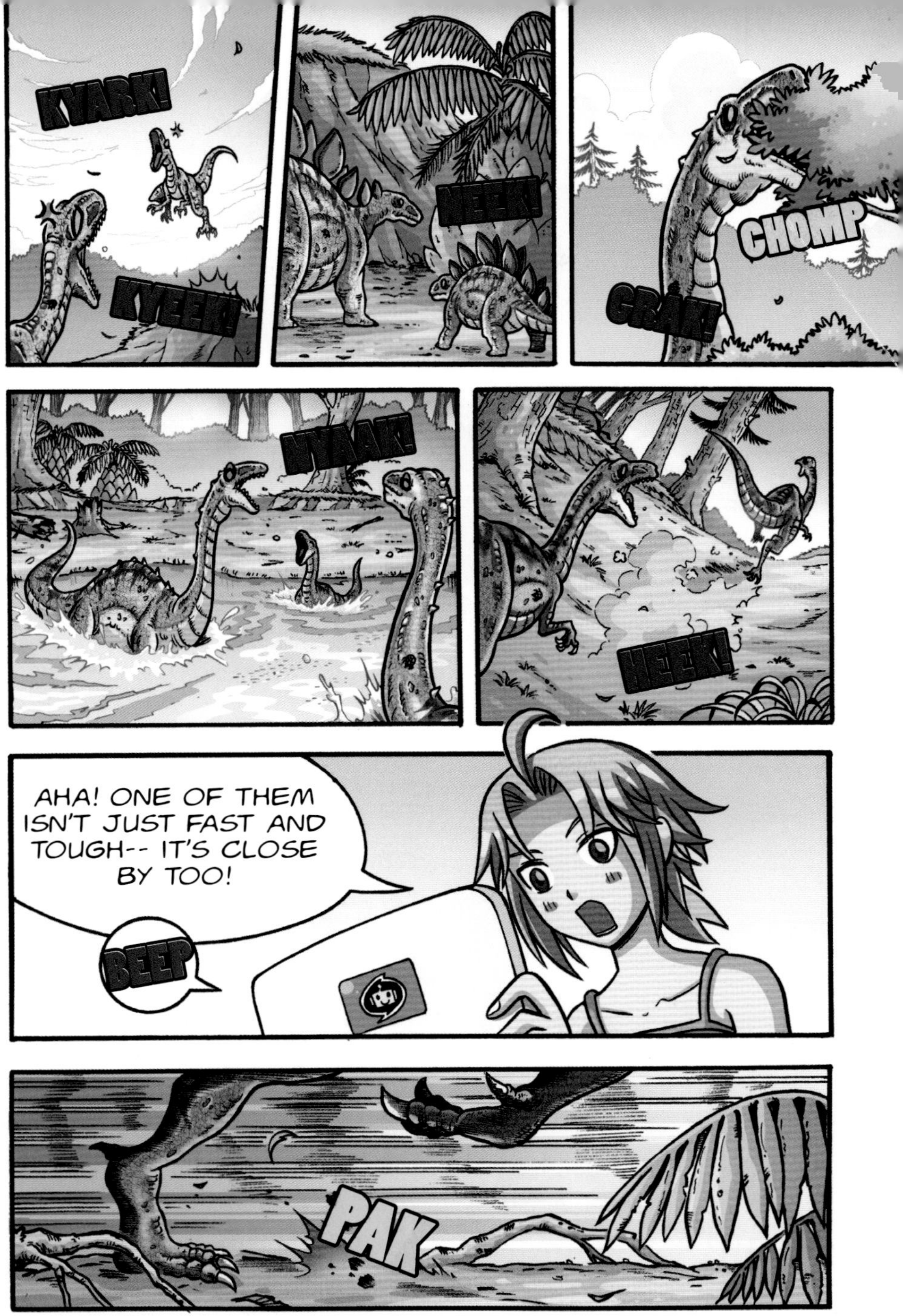
KYARK!
KYEEK!
NEEK!
CHOMP
CRAK!
NYAAK!
HEEK!
AHA! ONE OF THEM ISN'T JUST FAST AND TOUGH-- IT'S CLOSE BY TOO!
BEEP
PAK

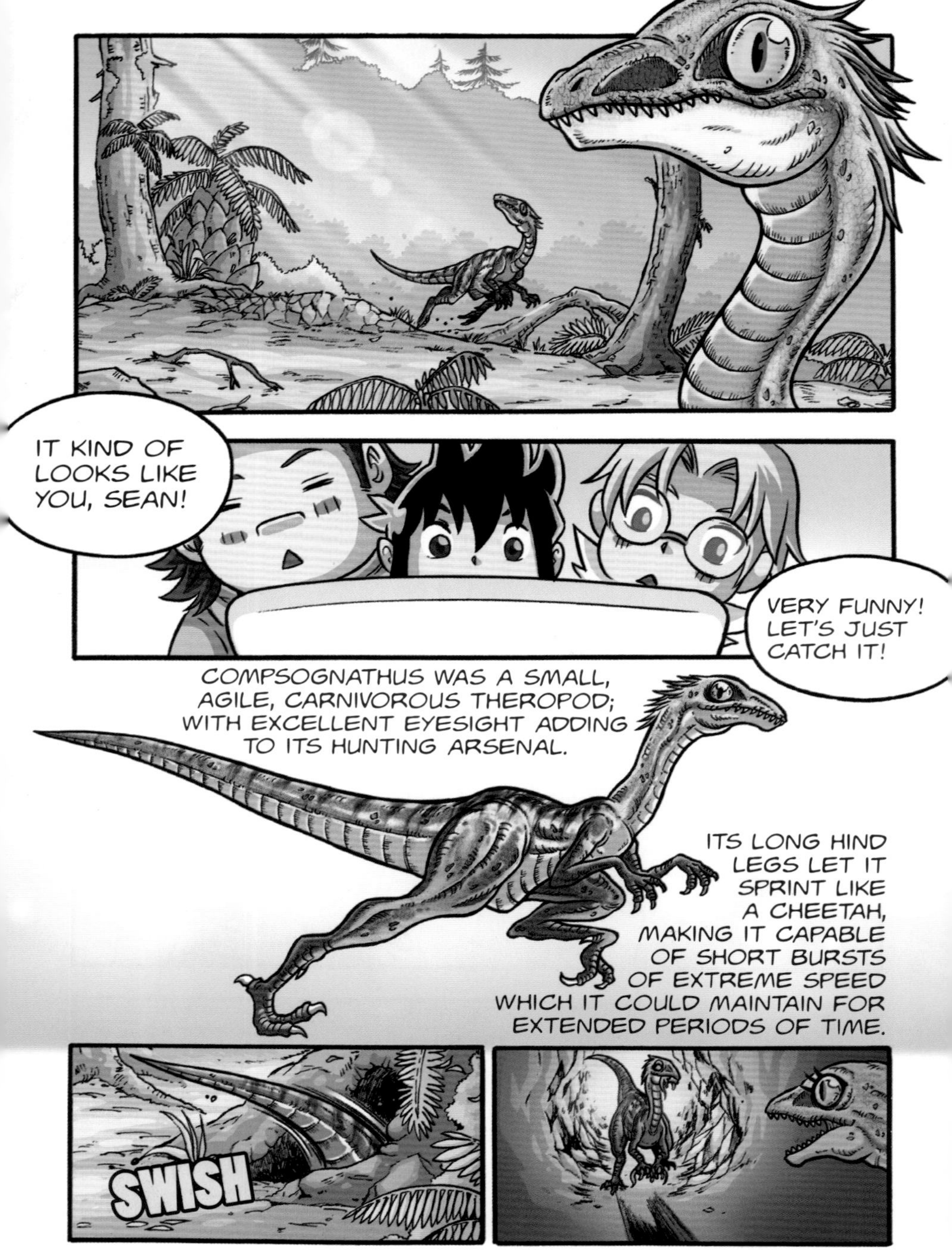
IT KIND OF LOOKS LIKE YOU, SEAN!
VERY FUNNY! LET'S JUST CATCH IT!
COMPSOGNATHUS WAS A SMALL, AGILE, CARNIVOROUS THEROPOD; WITH EXCELLENT EYESIGHT ADDING TO ITS HUNTING ARSENAL.
ITS LONG HIND LEGS LET IT SPRINT LIKE A CHEETAH, MAKING IT CAPABLE OF SHORT BURSTS OF EXTREME SPEED WHICH IT COULD MAINTAIN FOR EXTENDED PERIODS OF TIME.
SWISH

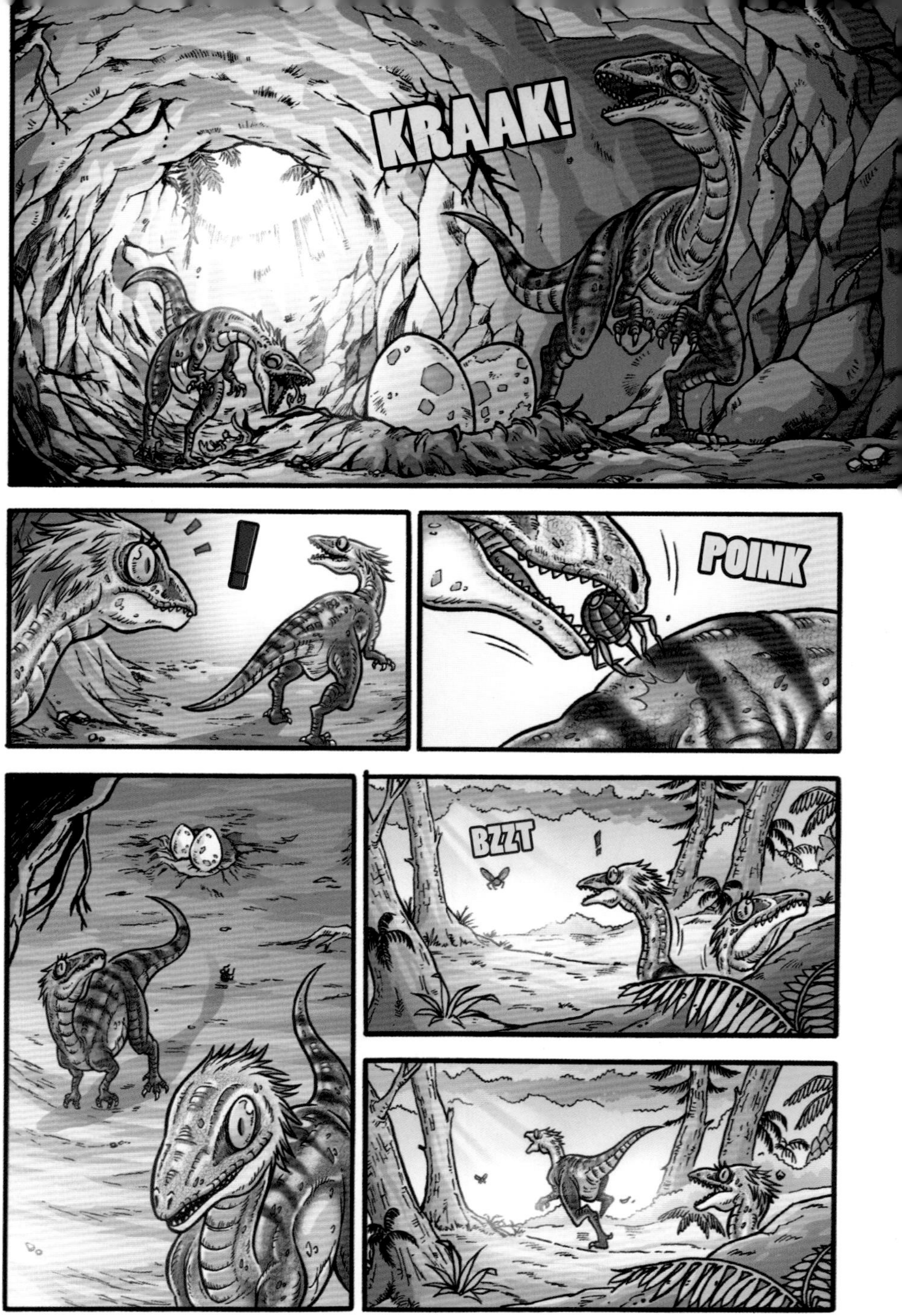
KRAAK!
!
POINK
BZZT
!

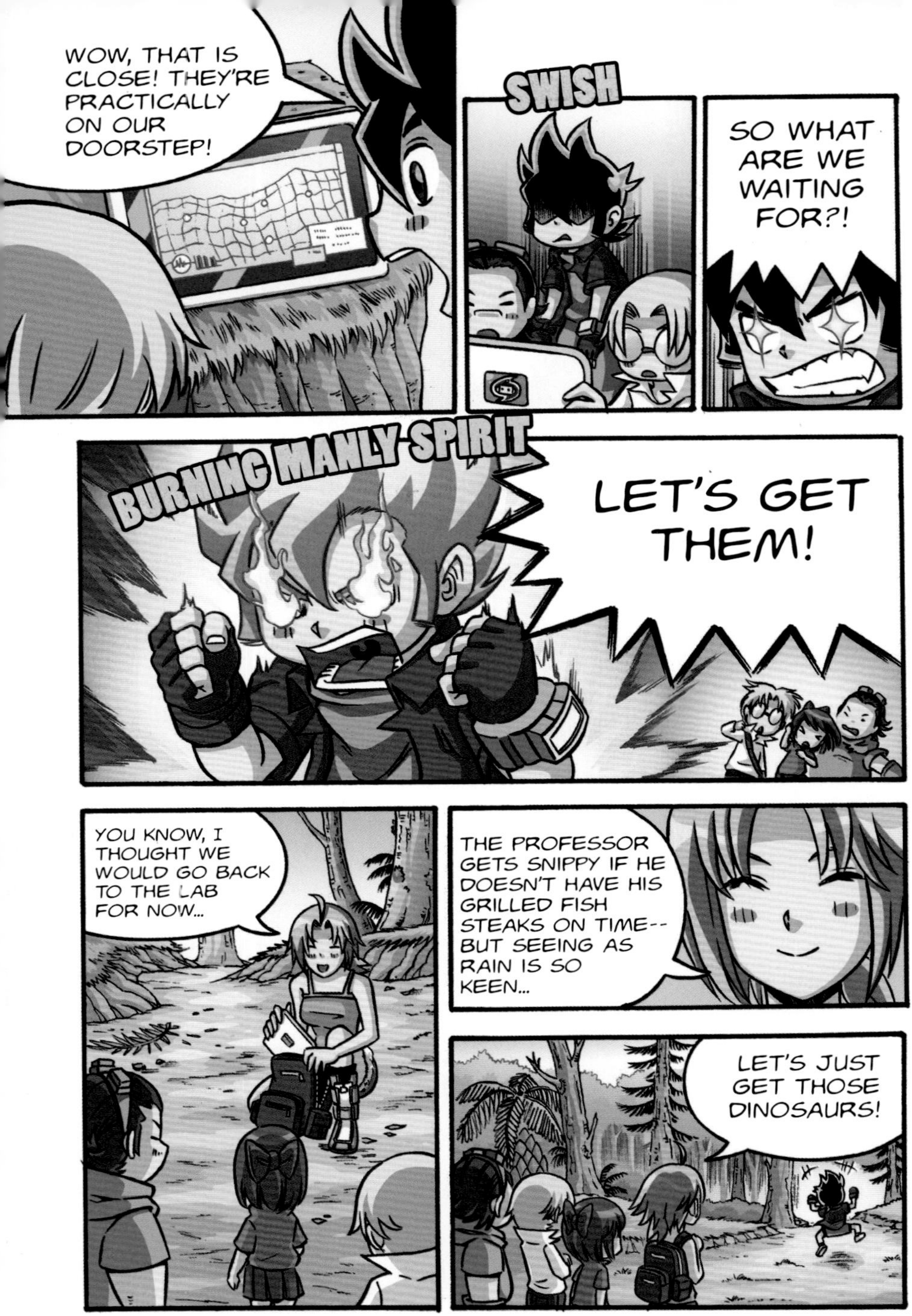

WOW, THAT IS CLOSE! THEY'RE PRACTICALLY ON OUR DOORSTEP!
SWISH
SO WHAT ARE WE WAITING FOR?!
BURNING MANLY SPIRIT
LET'S GET THEM!
YOU KNOW, I THOUGHT WE WOULD GO BACK TO THE LAB FOR NOW...
THE PROFESSOR GETS SNIPPY IF HE DOESN'T HAVE HIS GRILLED FISH STEAKS ON TIME-- BUT SEEING AS RAIN IS SO KEEN...
LET'S JUST GET THOSE DINOSAURS!

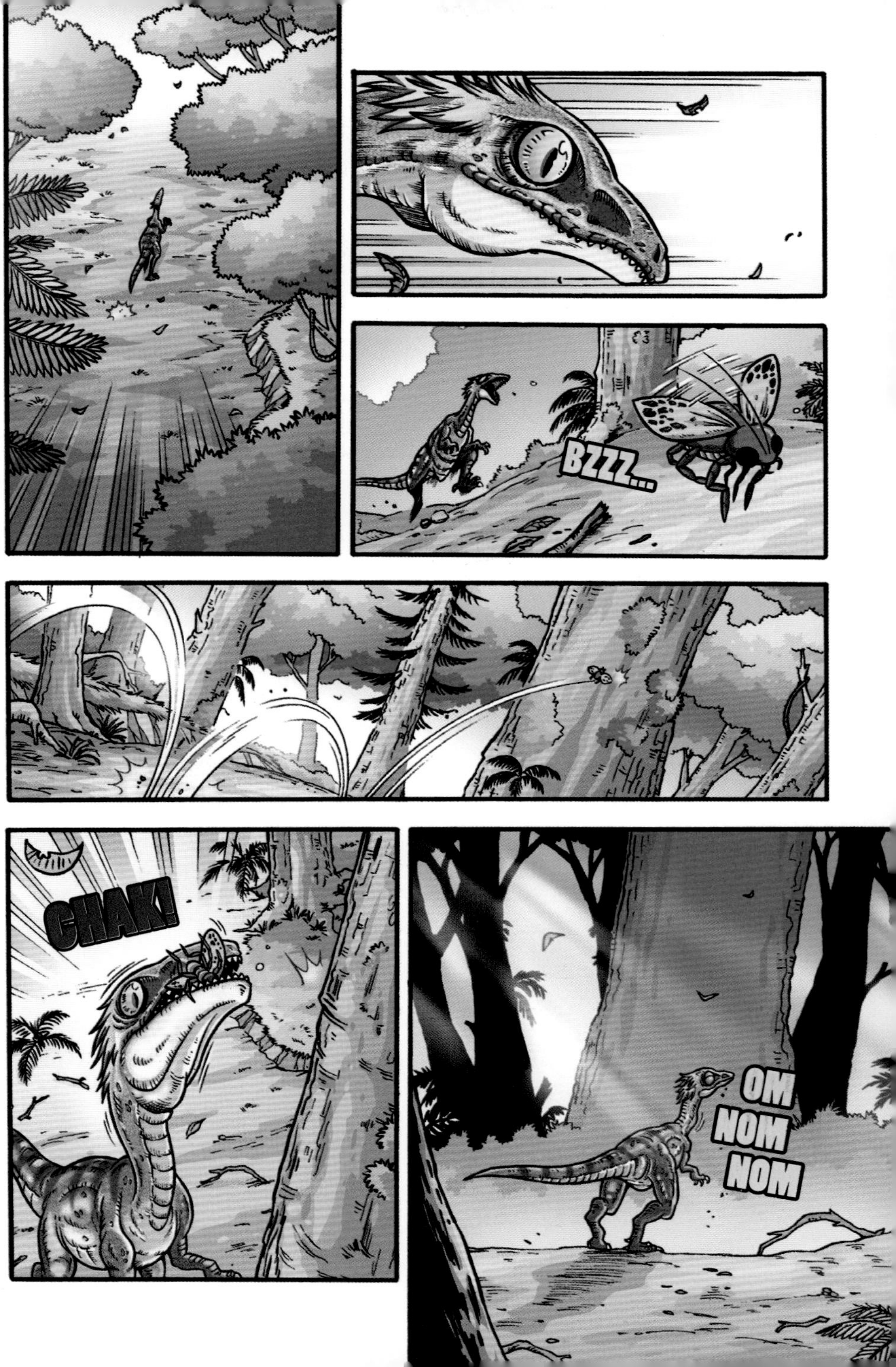
BZZZ...
CHAK!
OM
NOM
NOM

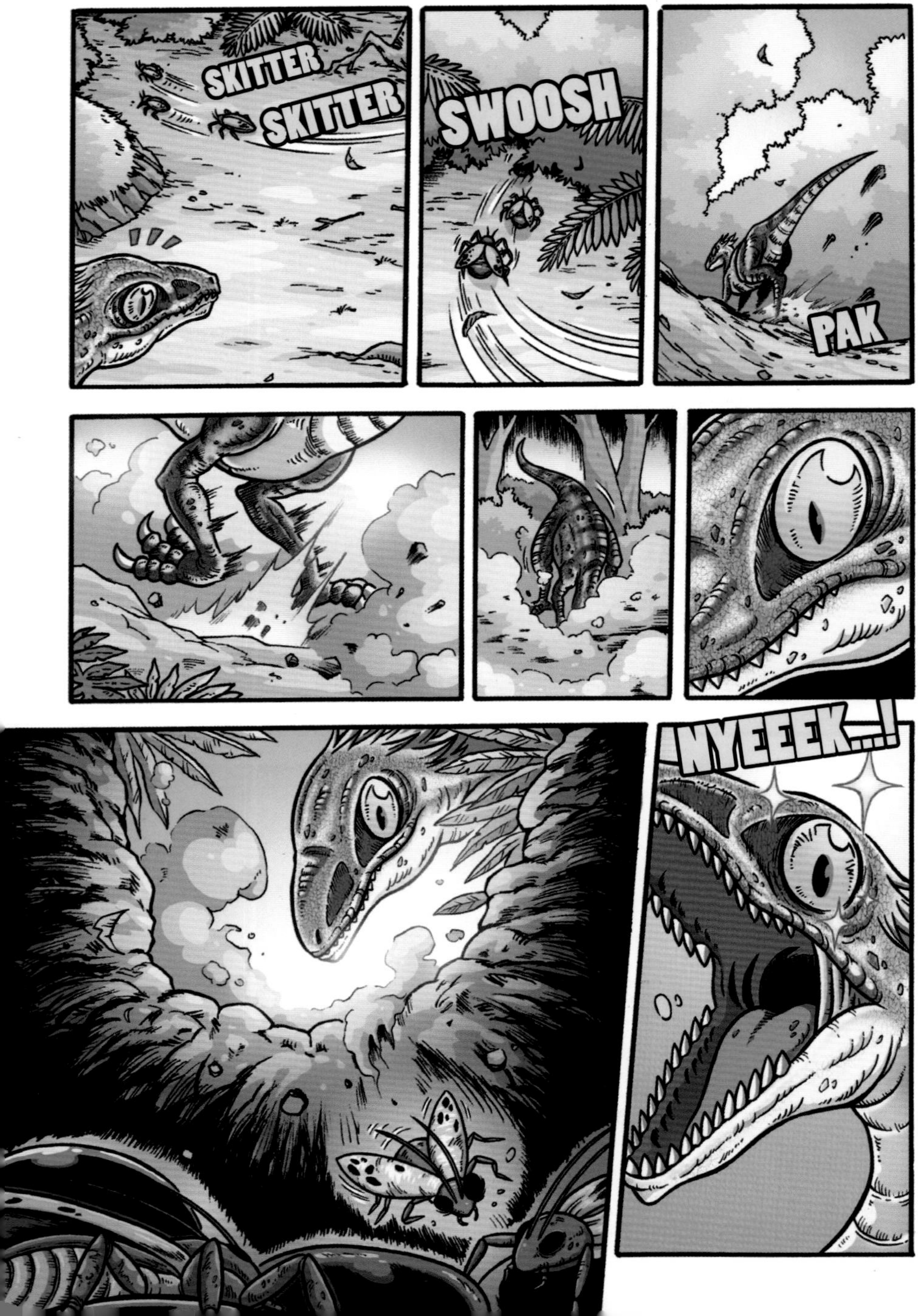
SKITTER
SKITTER
SWOOSH
PAK
NYEEEK...!

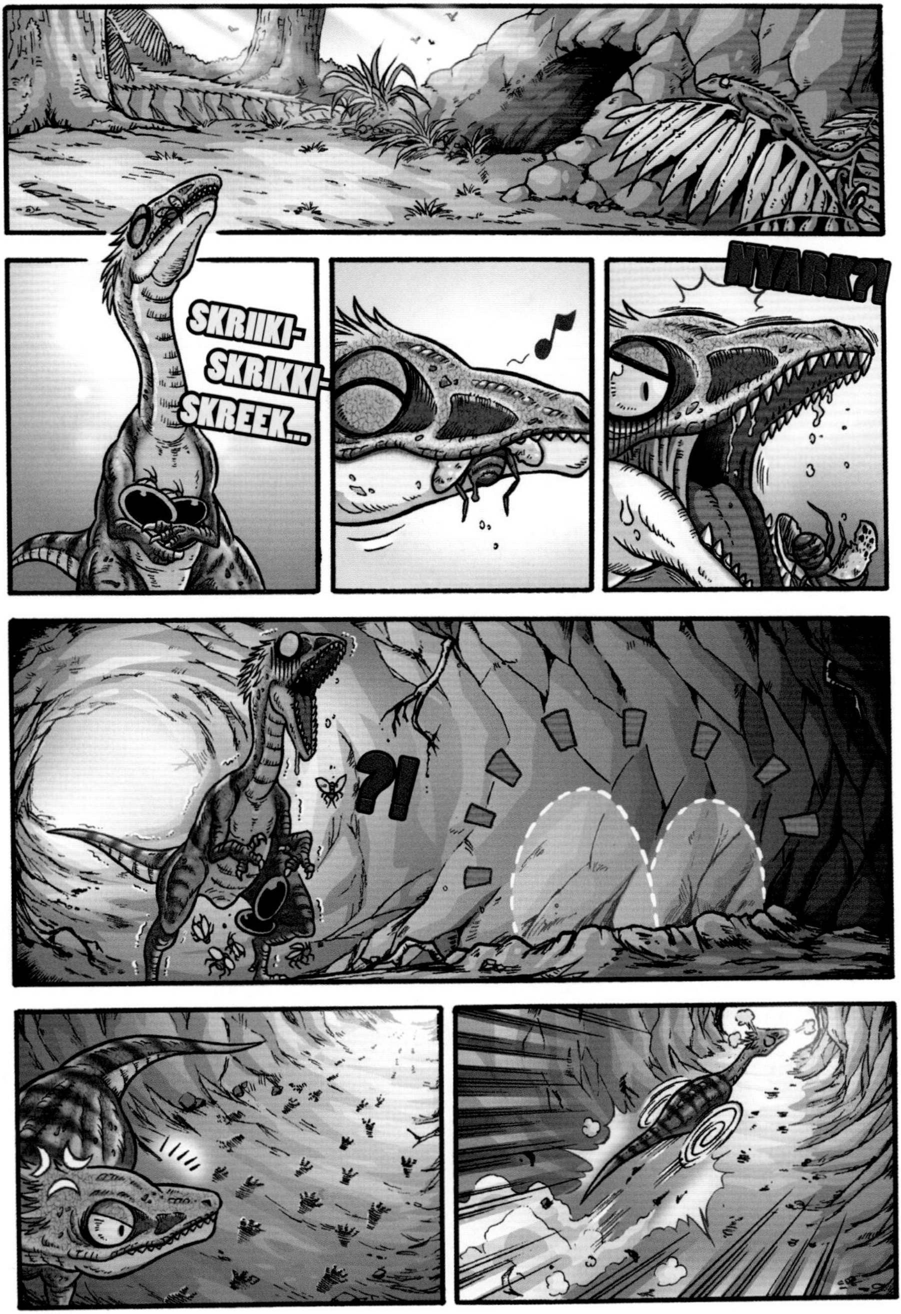
SKRIIKI-
SKRIKKI-
SKREEK...
NYARK?!
?!

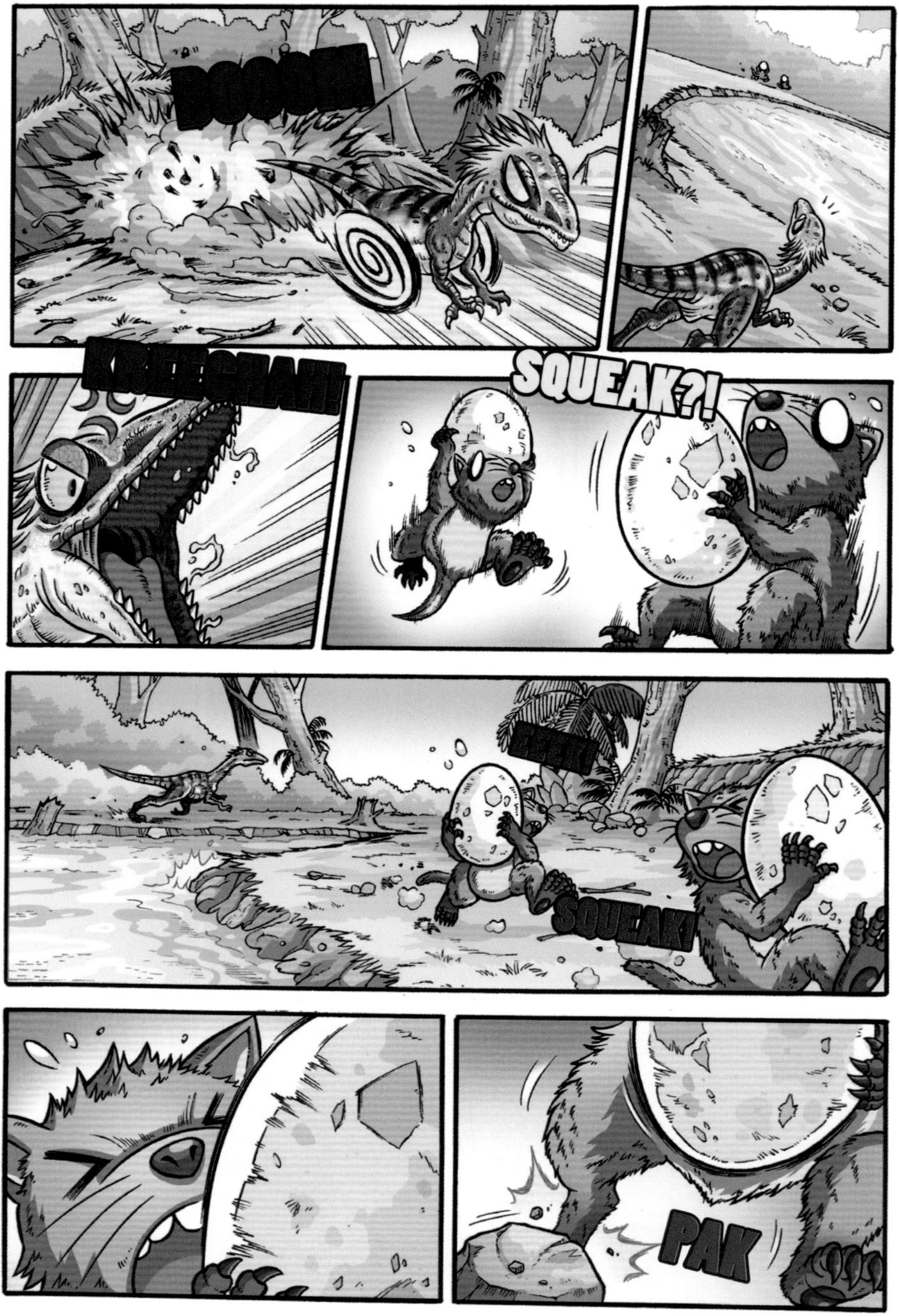

KREECHAH!
SQUEAK?!
SQUEAK!
PAK

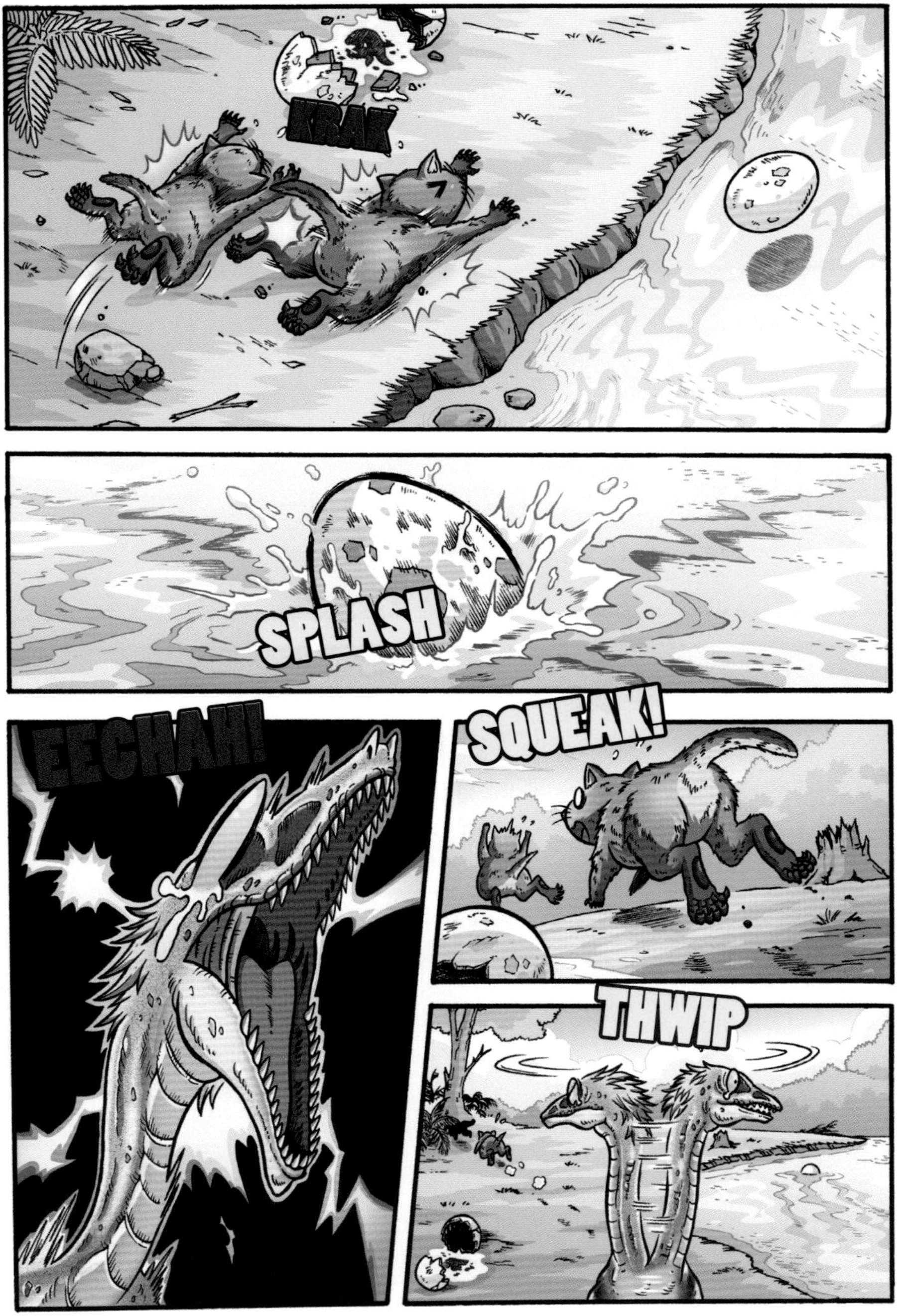
KRAK
SPLASH
EECHAH!
SQUEAK!
THWIP

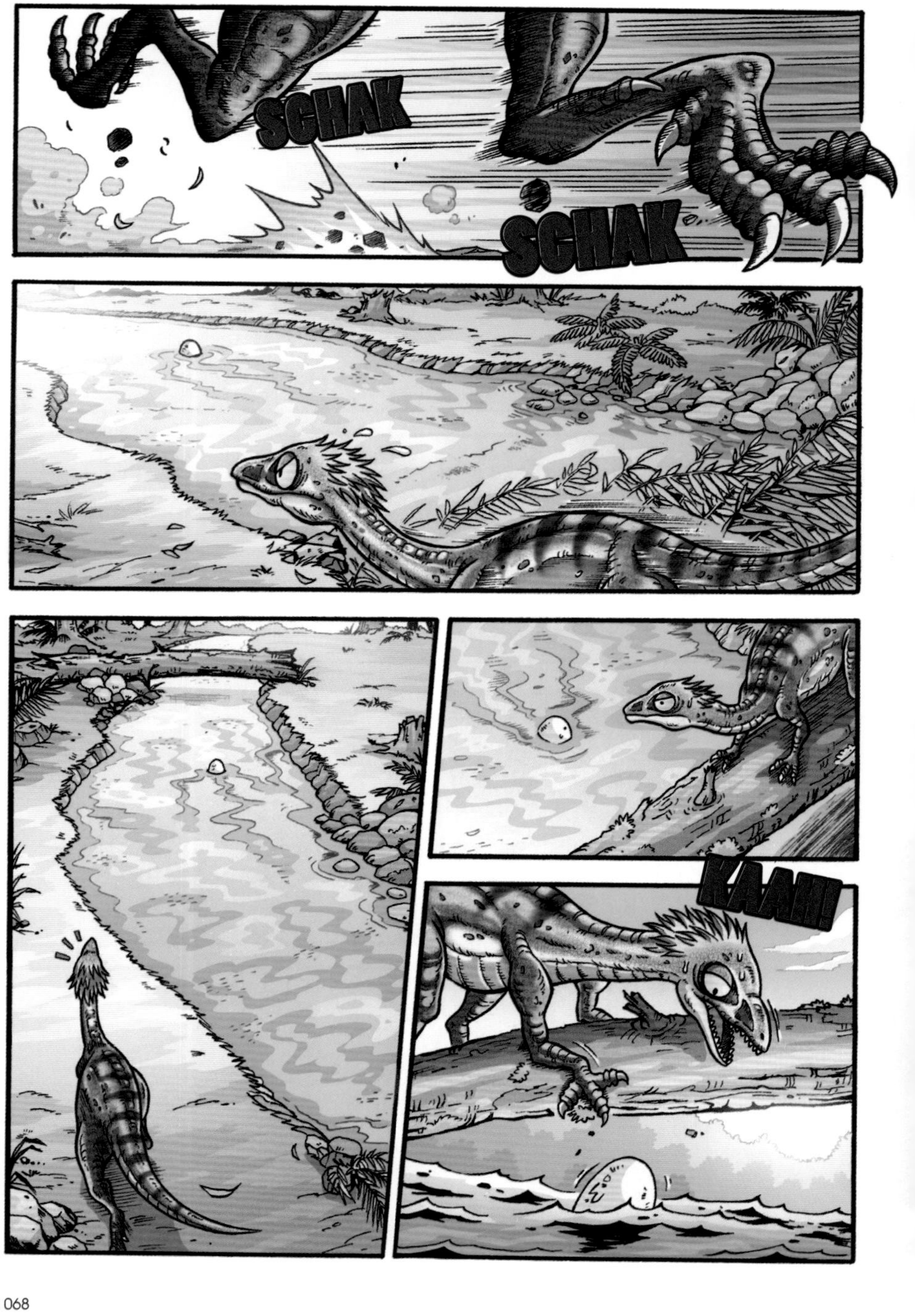
SCHAK
SCHAK
KAAH!

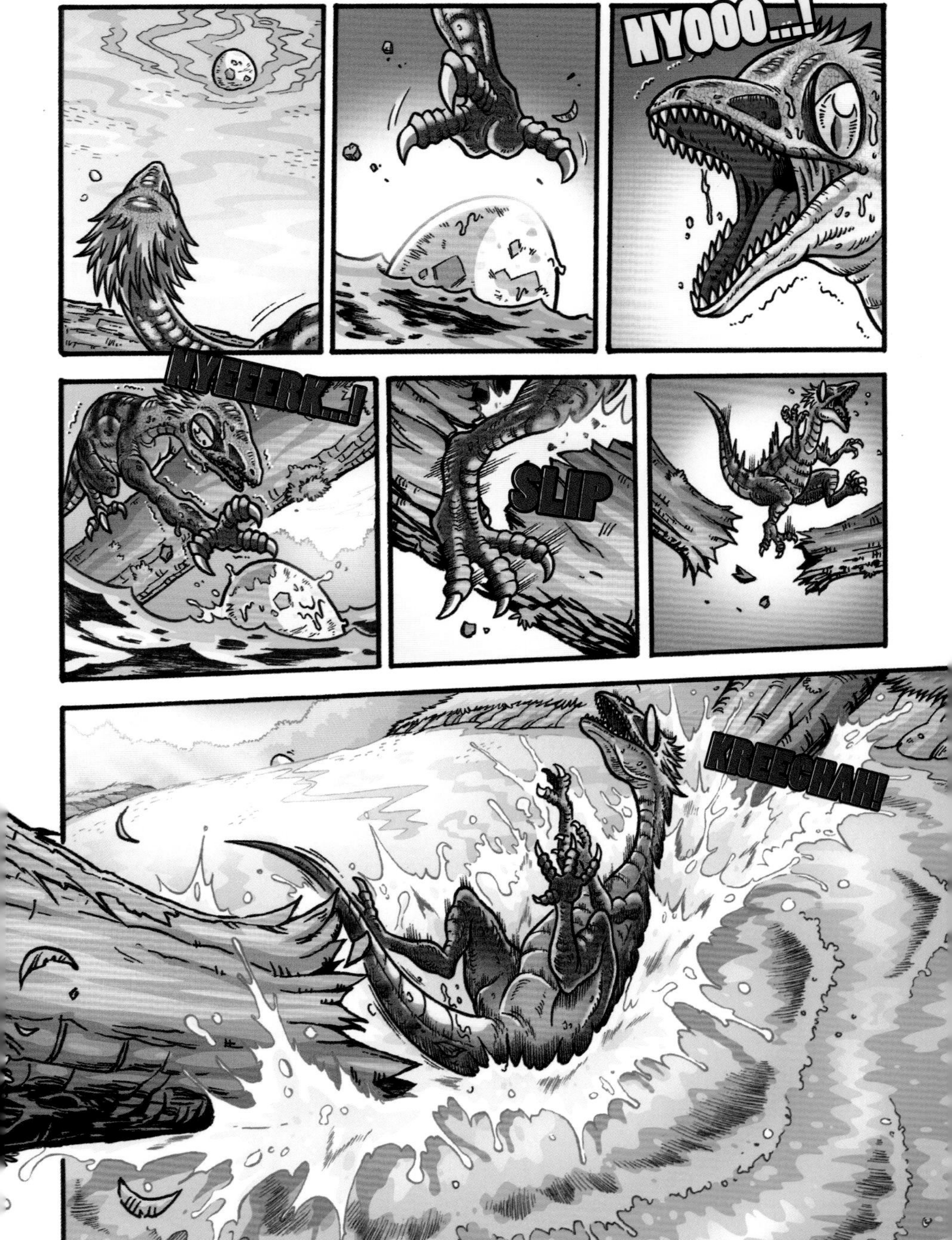
NYOOO...!
NYEEERK...!
SLIP
KREECHAH!

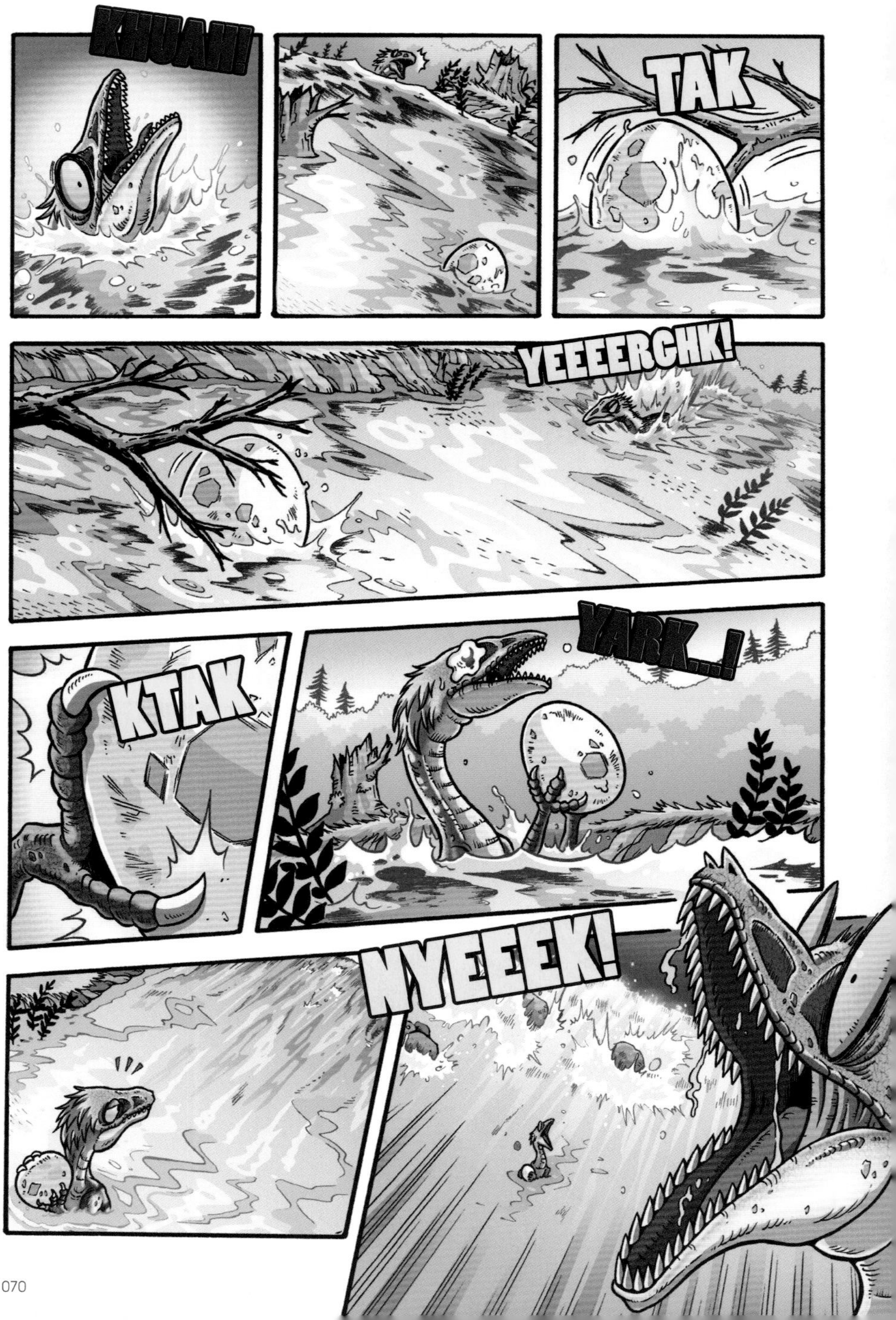
KHUAH!
TAK
YEEEERCHK!
KTAK
YARK...!
NYEEEK!

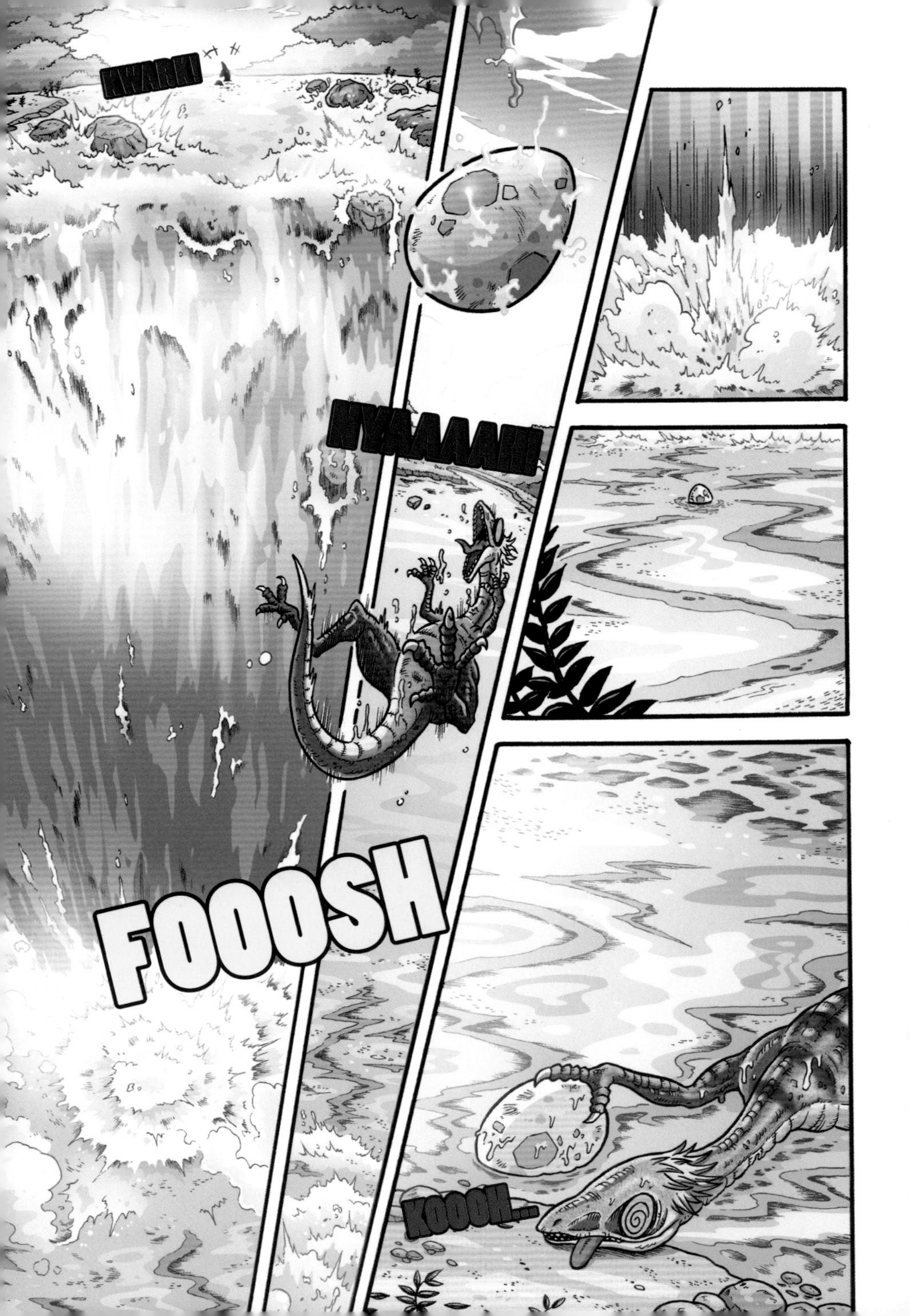
KWARK!
NYAAAAAH!
FOOOSH
KOOOH...

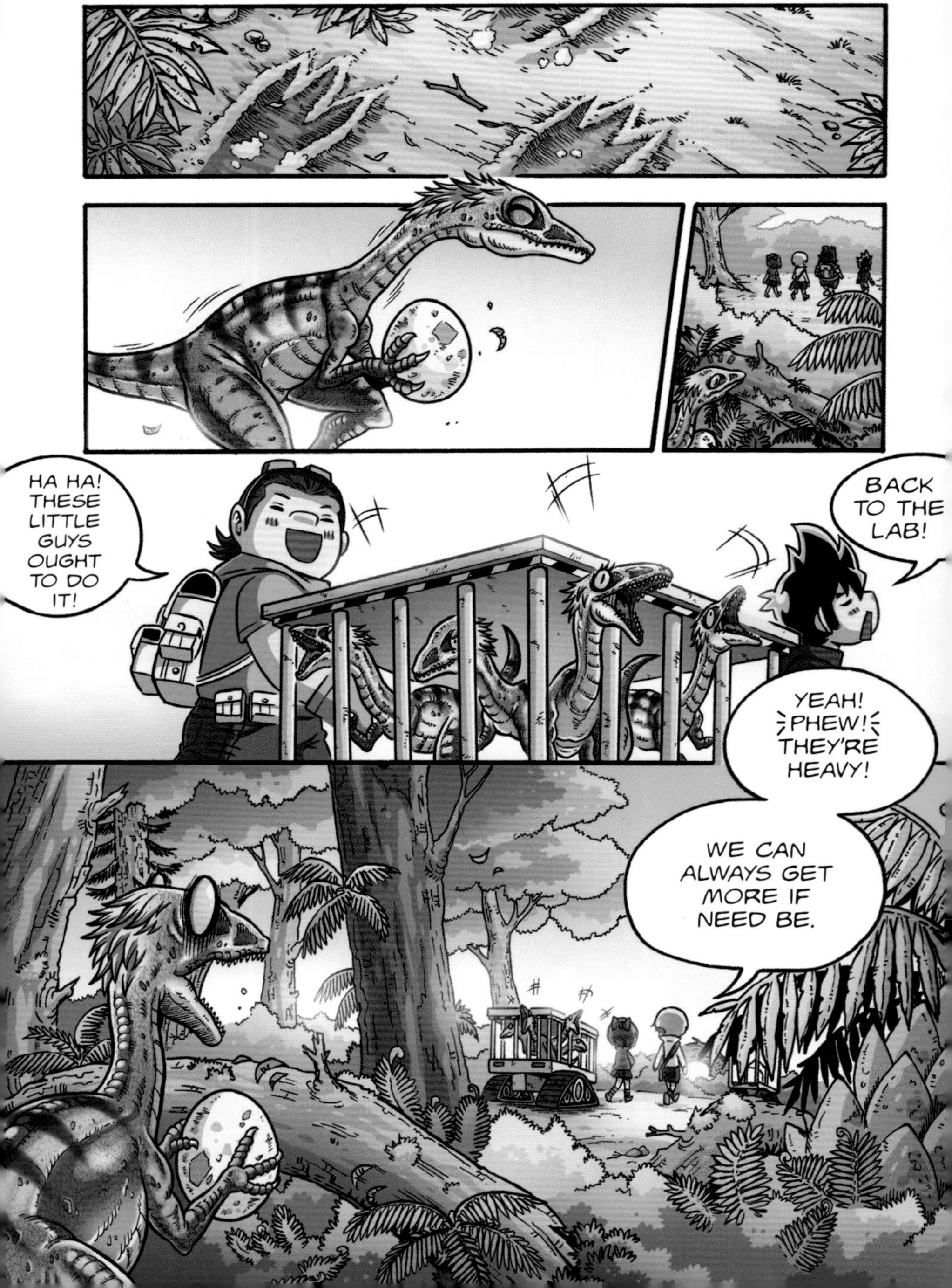
HA HA! THESE LITTLE GUYS OUGHT TO DO IT!
BACK TO THE LAB!
YEAH! PHEW! THEY'RE HEAVY!
WE CAN ALWAYS GET MORE IF NEED BE.

Compsognathus

A small, agile theropod, the chicken-sized Compsognathus might have been closely related to Archaeopteryx and Sinornithosaurus, though it is still debated as to whether the Compsognathus had feathers.

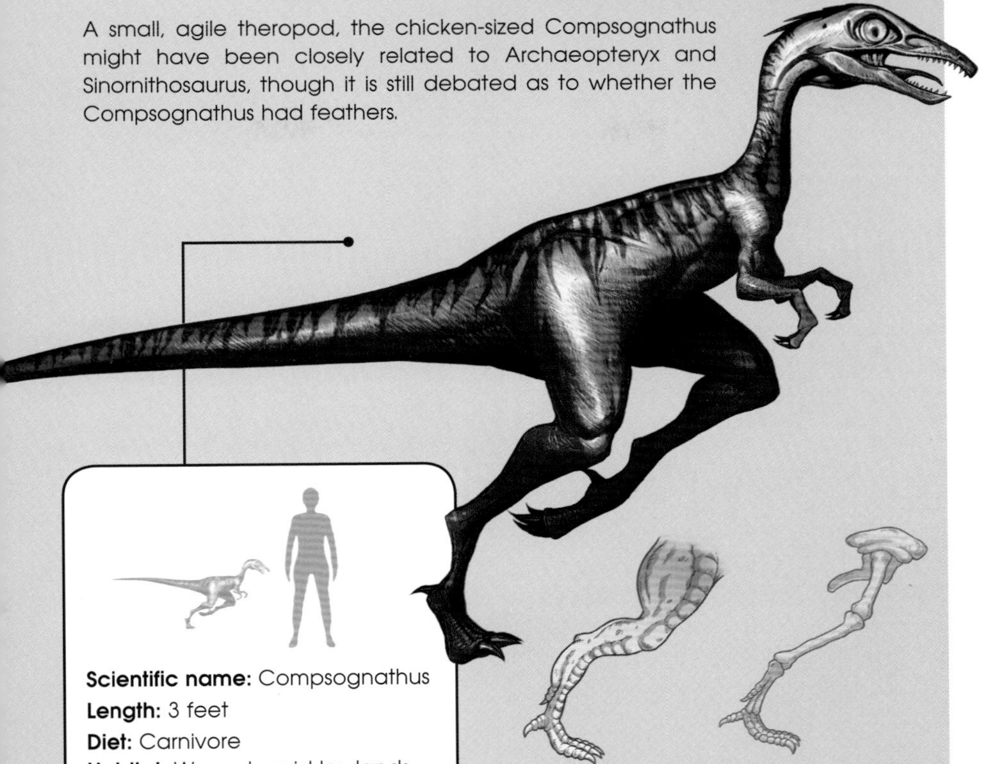

Scientific name: Compsognathus
Length: 3 feet
Diet: Carnivore
Habitat: Warm, humid lowlands
Discovered: North America
Era: Late Jurassic

Compsognathus had hollow bones; its tibia was longer than its femur, leading paleontologists to believe it was exceptionally fast, for its size.

Pedal power; comparison with modern speedsters.

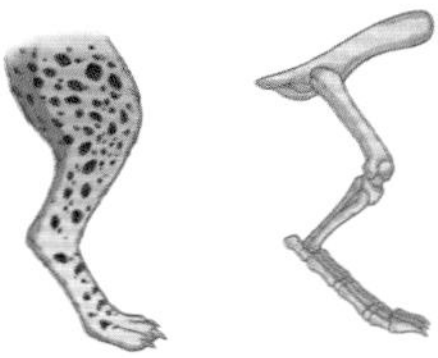

Cheetah
(68 mph)

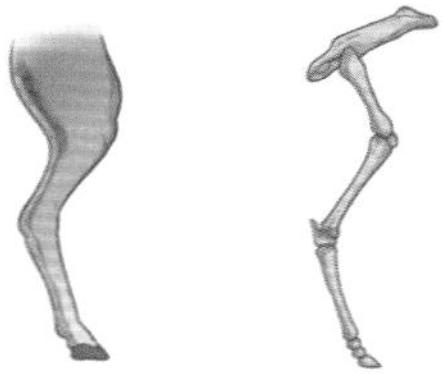

Antelope
(59 mph)

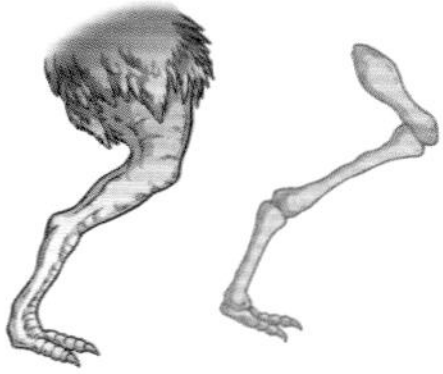

Ostrich
(40 mph)

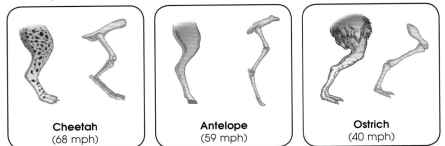

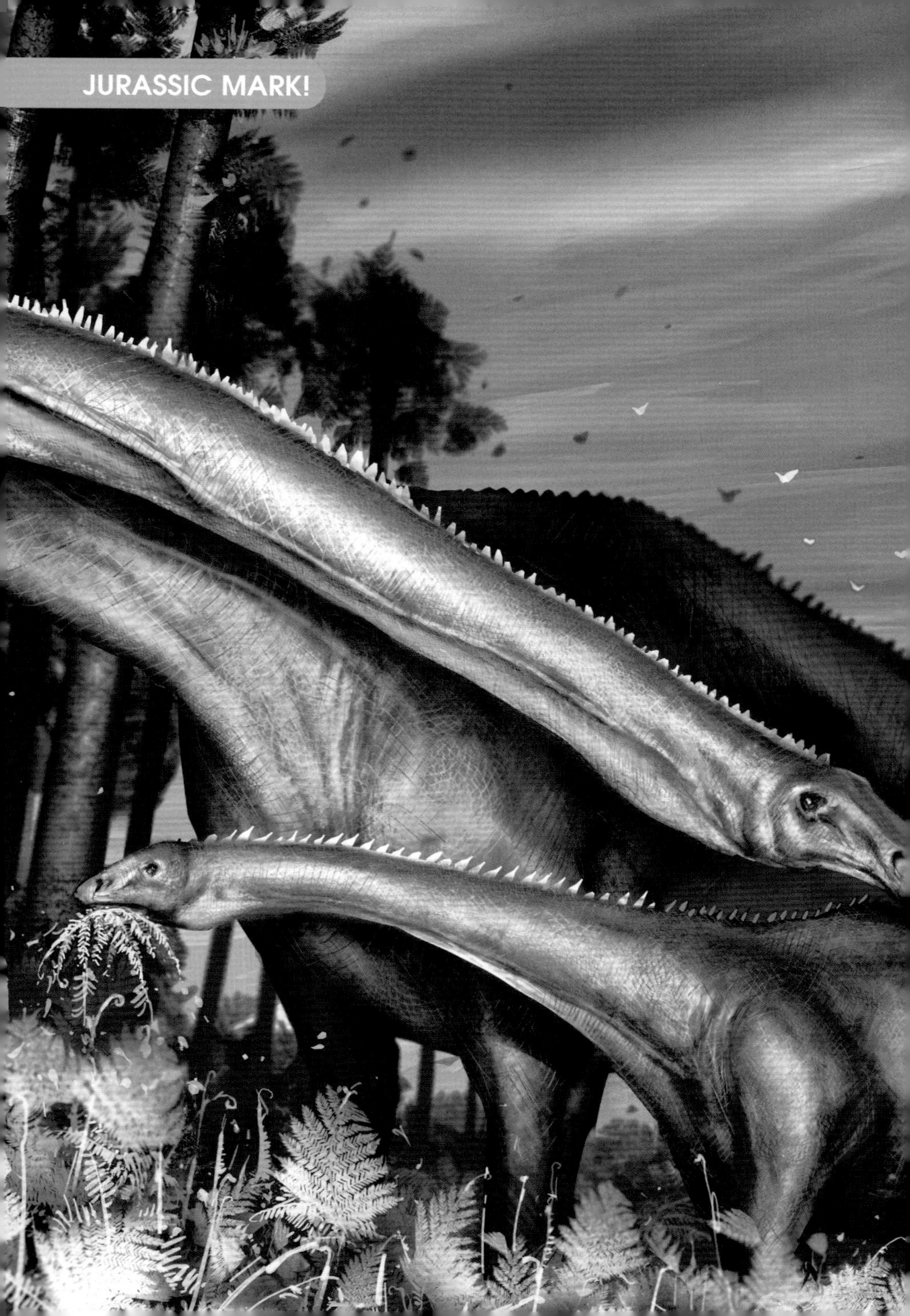

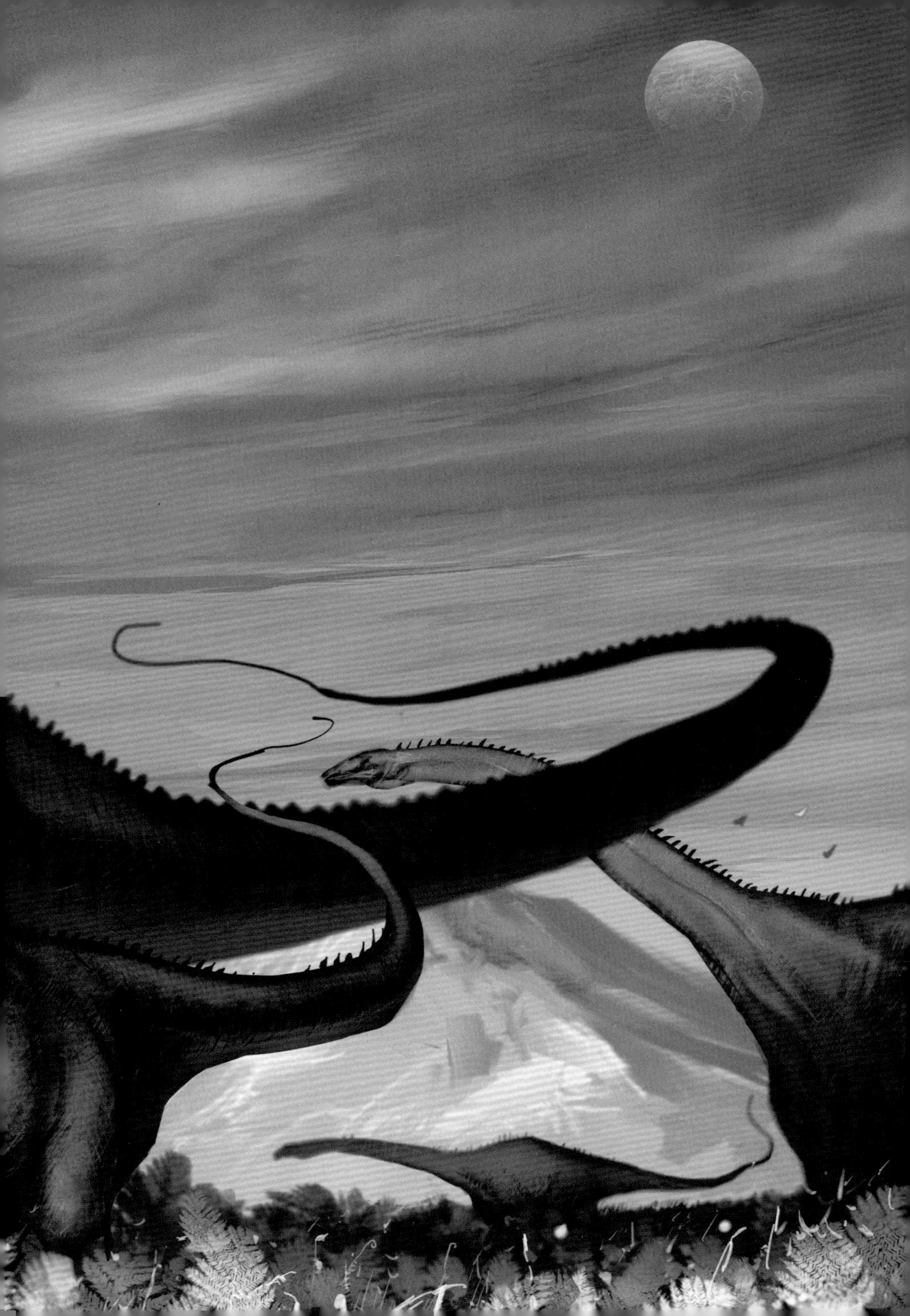

JONESING FOR THE JURASSIC

Dacentrurus

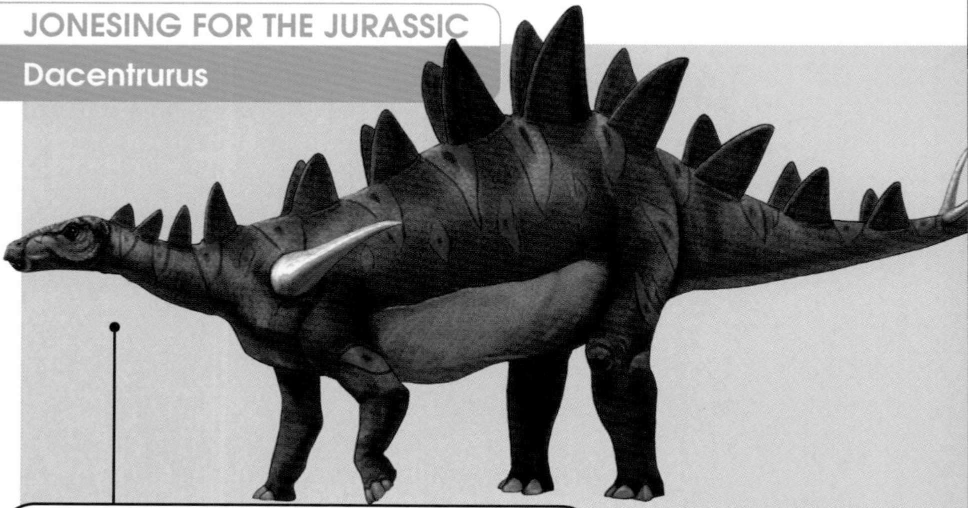

Scientific name: Dacentrurus
Length: 26 feet
Diet: Herbivore
Habitat: Woodlands
Discovered: Western Europe
Era: Late Jurassic

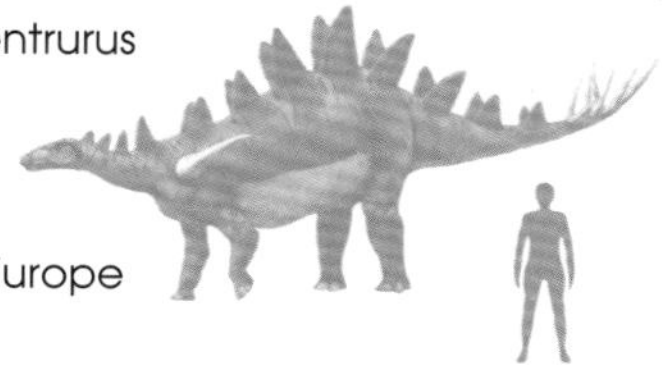

A large stegosaur, Dacentrurus' back plates and spines gave it both offensive and defensive capabilities. Although not the quickest, its defenses made it quite a challenge for any would-be predator.

JONESING FOR THE JURASSIC

Docodon

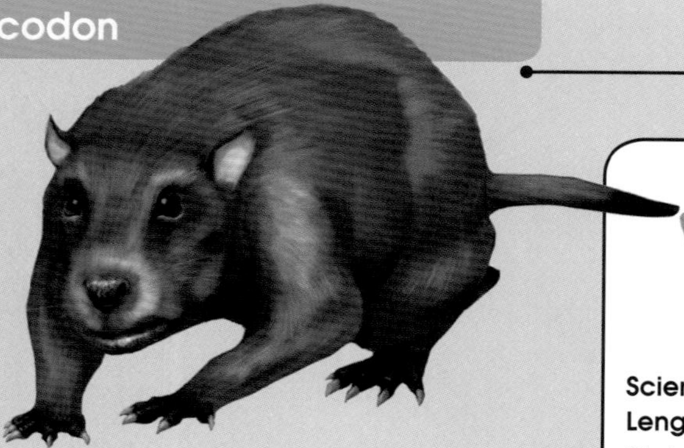

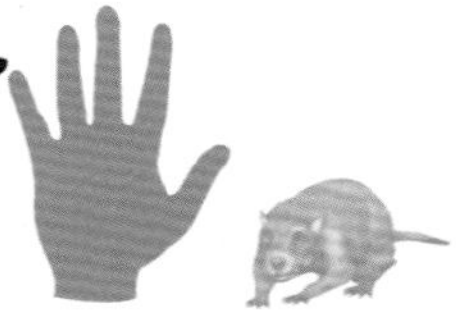

Scientific name: Docodon
Length: 3.9 inches
Diet: Omnivore
Habitat: Jungles
Discovered: North America
Era: Late Jurassic

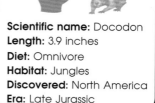

A small Jurassic mammal, paleontologists have deduced that it was an omnivore, due to its complex tooth structure.

CHAPTER 4
PURSUIT

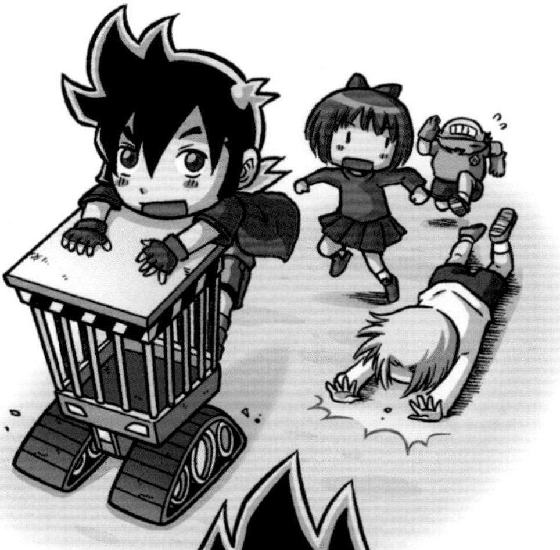

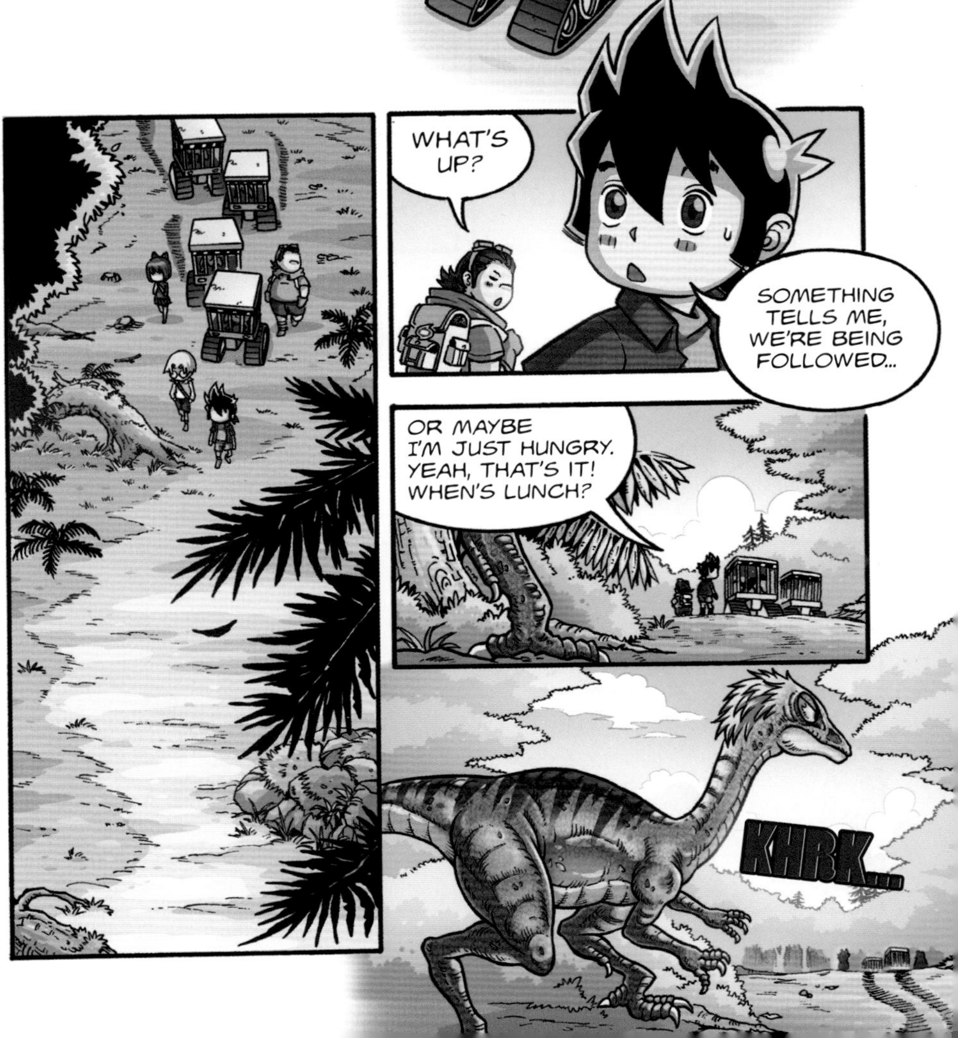
WHAT'S UP?
SOMETHING TELLS ME, WE'RE BEING FOLLOWED...
OR MAYBE I'M JUST HUNGRY. YEAH, THAT'S IT! WHEN'S LUNCH?
KHRK...

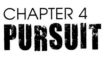

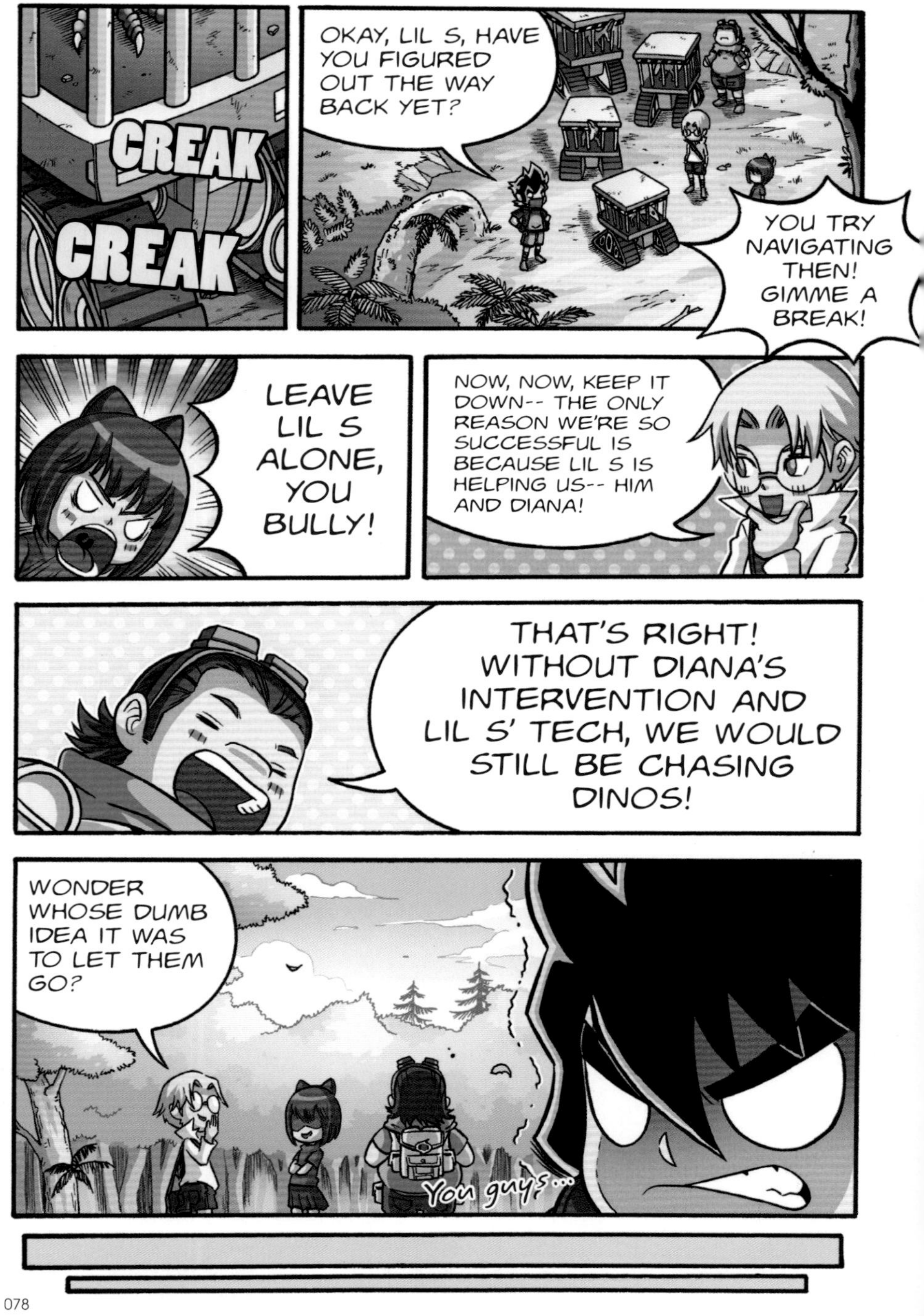
CREAK
CREAK
OKAY, LIL S, HAVE YOU FIGURED OUT THE WAY BACK YET?
YOU TRY NAVIGATING THEN! GIMME A BREAK!
LEAVE LIL S ALONE, YOU BULLY!
NOW, NOW, KEEP IT DOWN-- THE ONLY REASON WE'RE SO SUCCESSFUL IS BECAUSE LIL S IS HELPING US-- HIM AND DIANA!
THAT'S RIGHT! WITHOUT DIANA'S INTERVENTION AND LIL S' TECH, WE WOULD STILL BE CHASING DINOS!
WONDER WHOSE DUMB IDEA IT WAS TO LET THEM GO?
You guys...

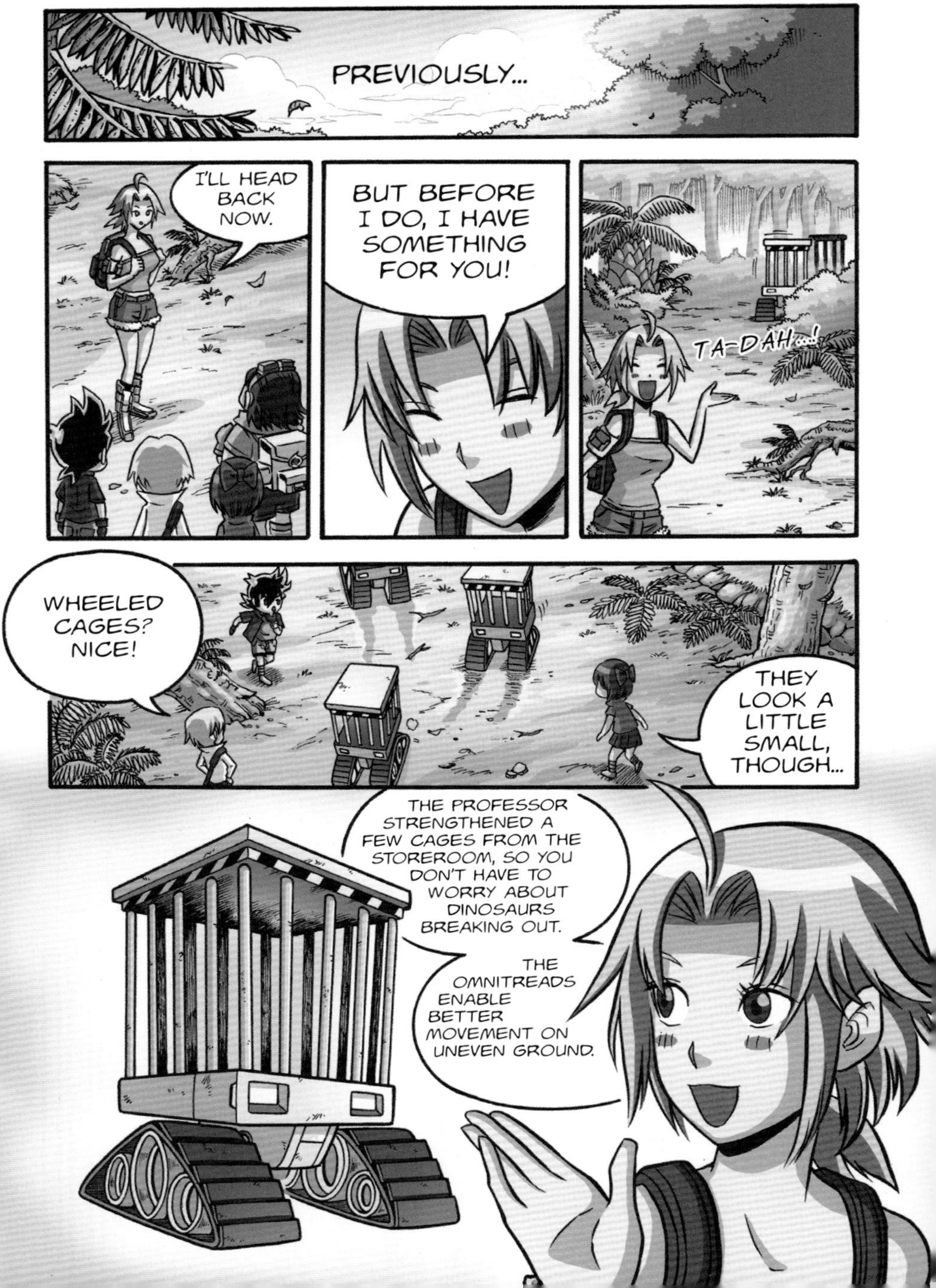

PREVIOUSLY...
I'LL HEAD BACK NOW.
BUT BEFORE I DO, I HAVE SOMETHING FOR YOU!
TA-DAH...!
WHEELED CAGES? NICE!
THEY LOOK A LITTLE SMALL, THOUGH...
THE PROFESSOR STRENGTHENED A FEW CAGES FROM THE STOREROOM, SO YOU DON'T HAVE TO WORRY ABOUT DINOSAURS BREAKING OUT.
THE OMNITREADS ENABLE BETTER MOVEMENT ON UNEVEN GROUND.

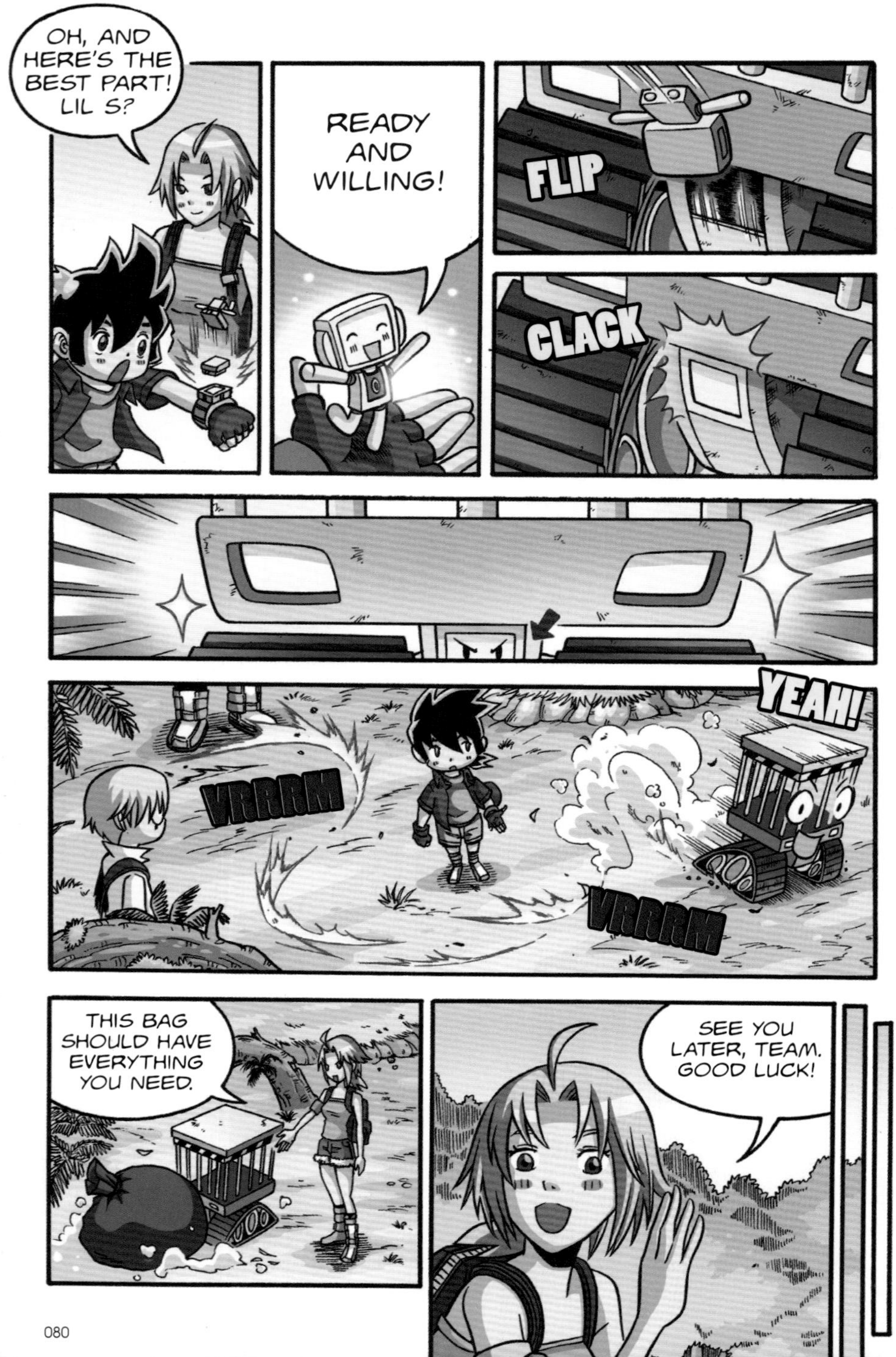
OH, AND HERE'S THE BEST PART! LIL S?
READY AND WILLING!
FLIP
CLACK
YEAH!
VRRRM
VRRRM
THIS BAG SHOULD HAVE EVERYTHING YOU NEED.
SEE YOU LATER, TEAM. GOOD LUCK!

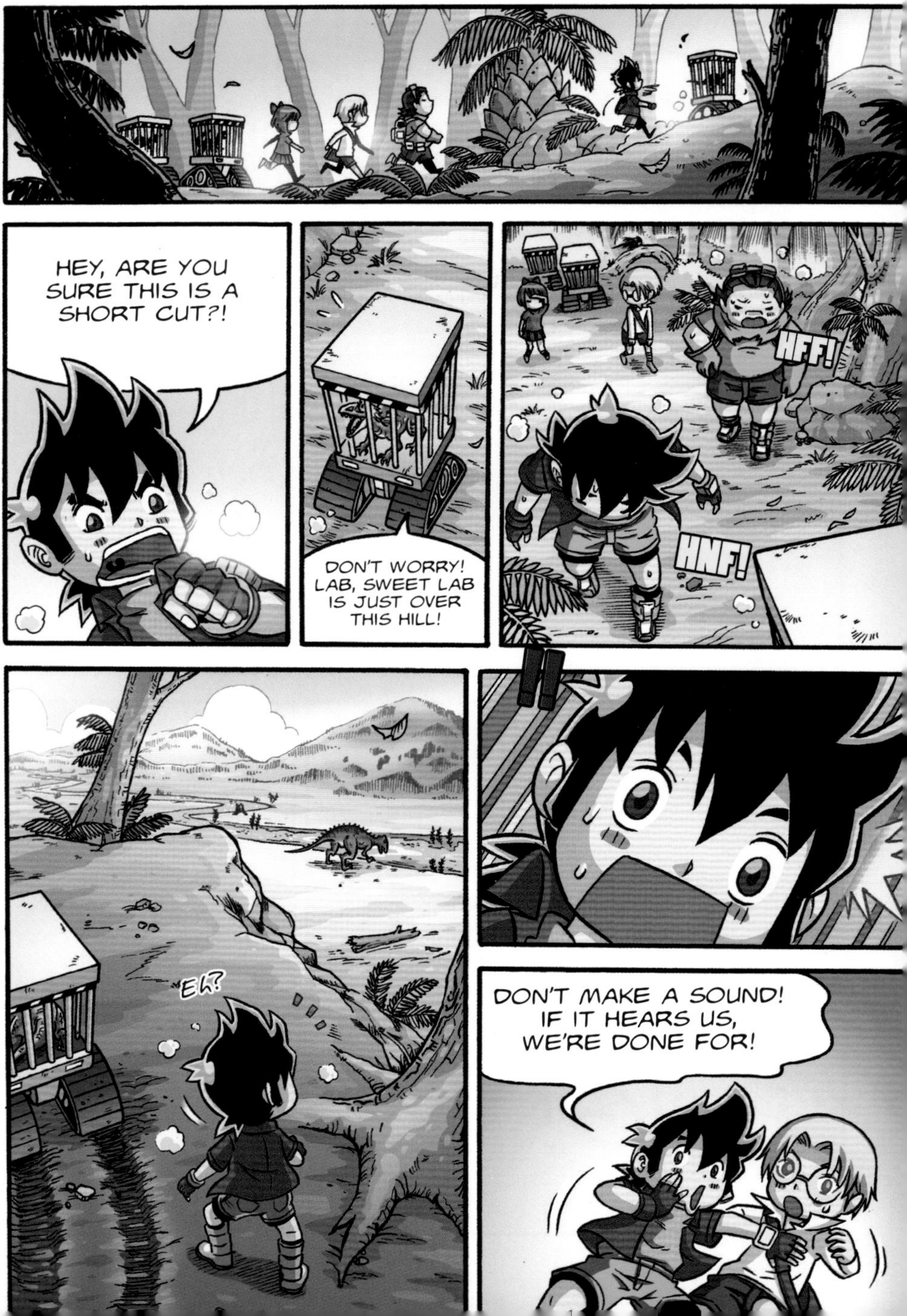
HEY, ARE YOU SURE THIS IS A SHORT CUT?!
DON'T WORRY! LAB, SWEET LAB IS JUST OVER THIS HILL!
HFF!
HNF!
EH?
DON'T MAKE A SOUND! IF IT HEARS US, WE'RE DONE FOR!

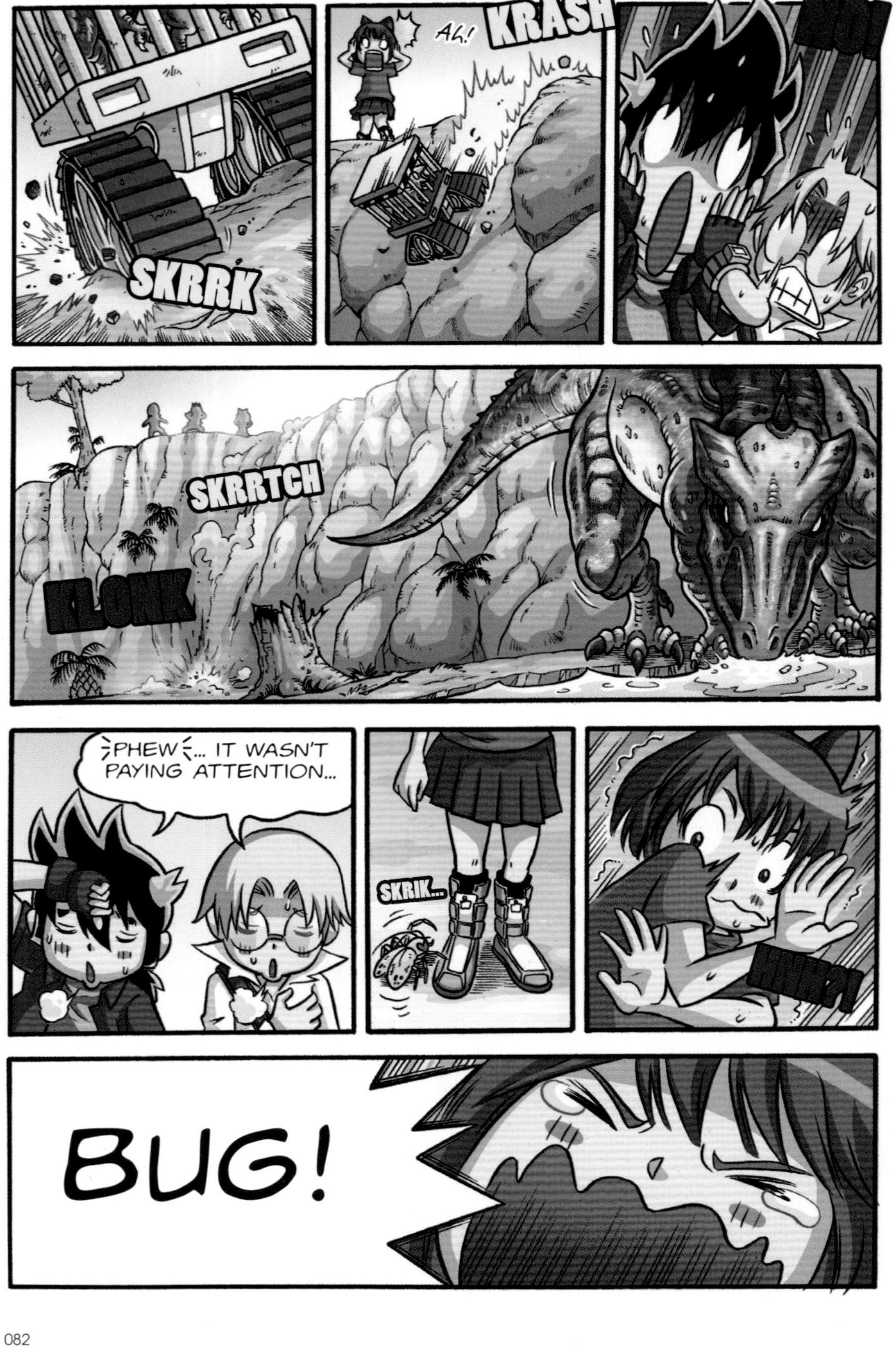
SKRRK
AH!
KRASH
SKRRTCH
KLONK
PHEW... IT WASN'T PAYING ATTENTION...
SKRIK...
BUG!

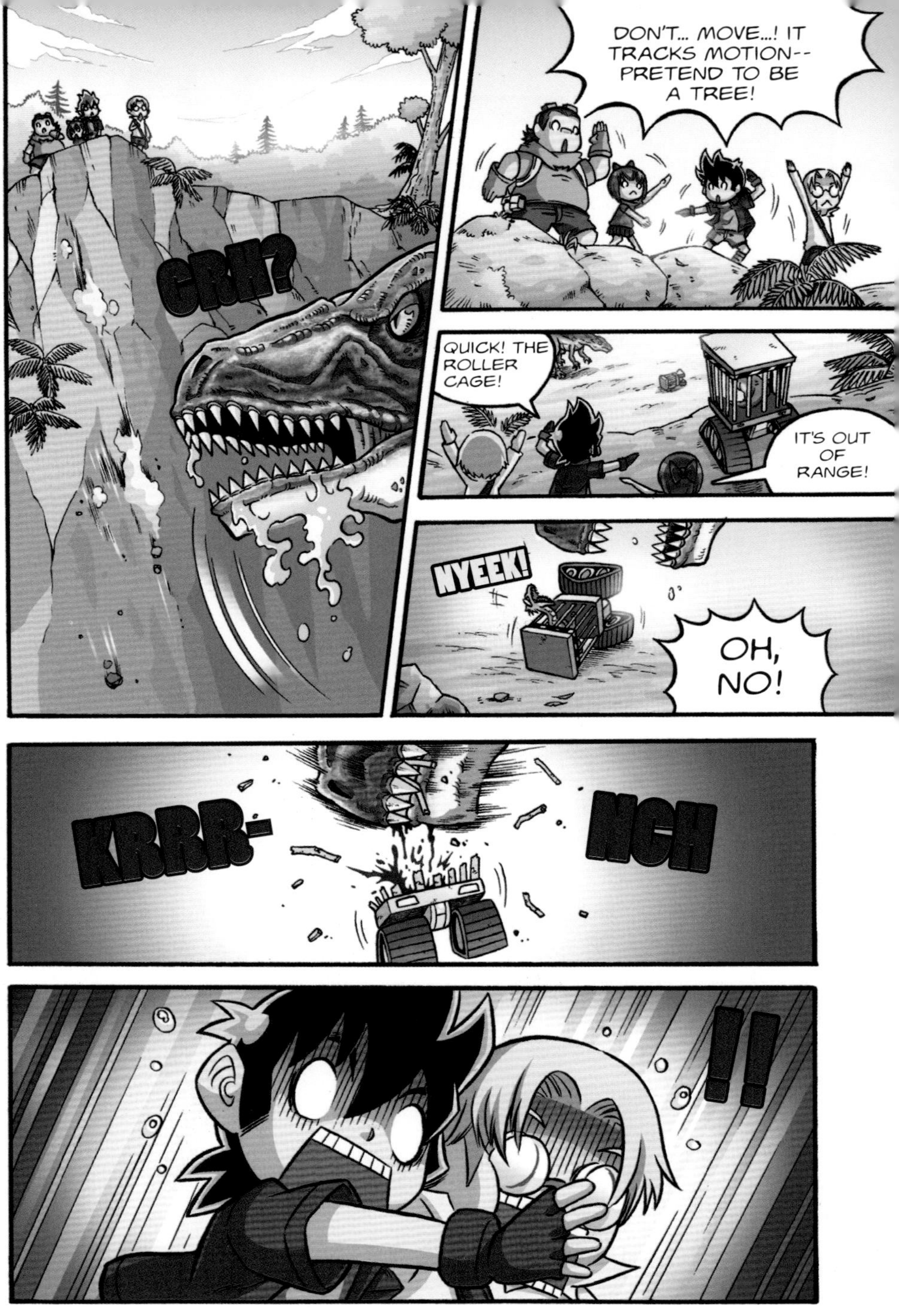
CRK?
DON'T... MOVE...! IT TRACKS MOTION-- PRETEND TO BE A TREE!
QUICK! THE ROLLER CAGE!
IT'S OUT OF RANGE!
NYEEK!
OH, NO!
KRRR-
NCH
!!

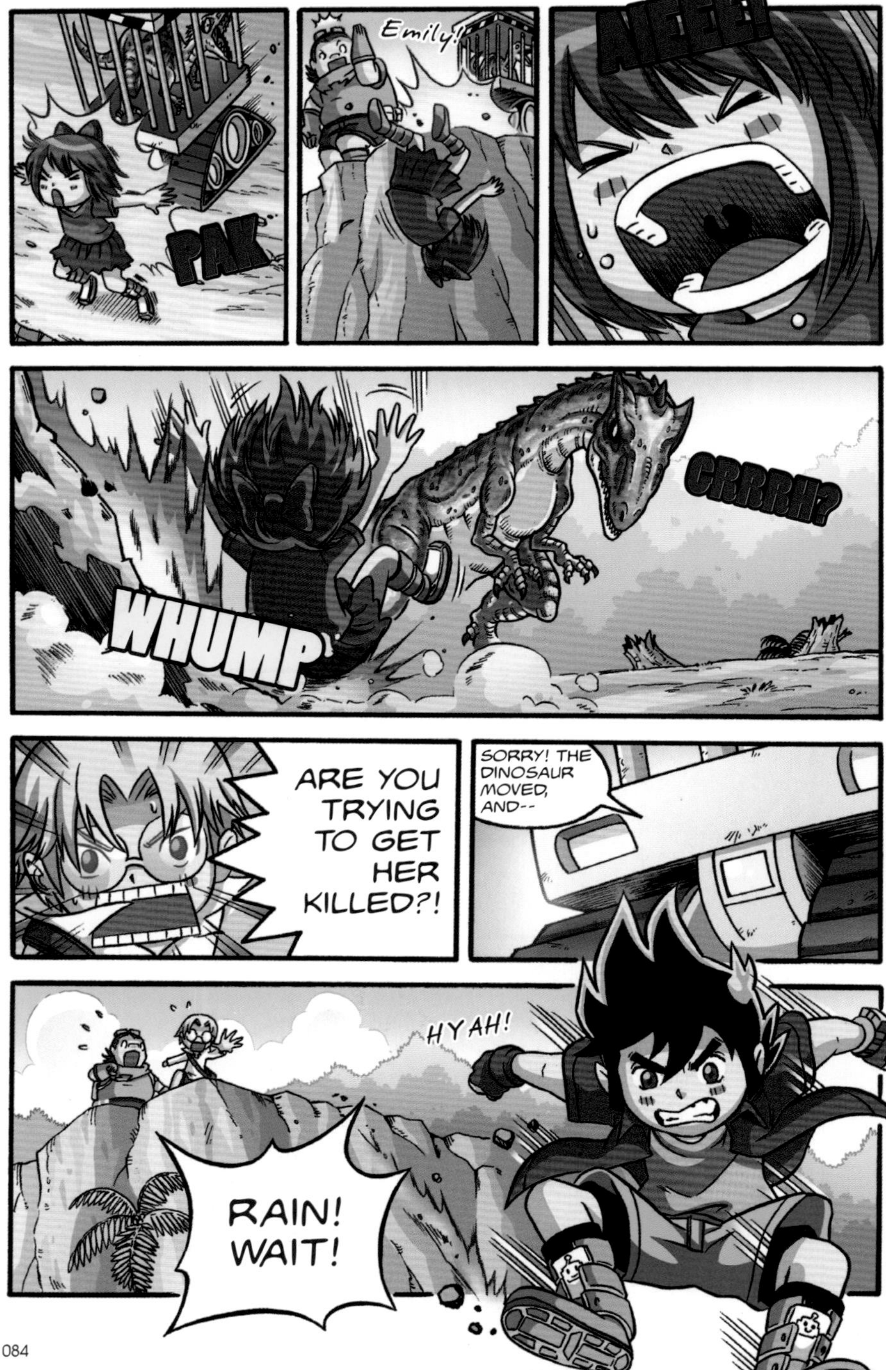
PAK
Emily!
AIEEE!
WHUMP
CRRRH?
ARE YOU TRYING TO GET HER KILLED?!
SORRY! THE DINOSAUR MOVED, AND--
HYAH!
RAIN! WAIT!

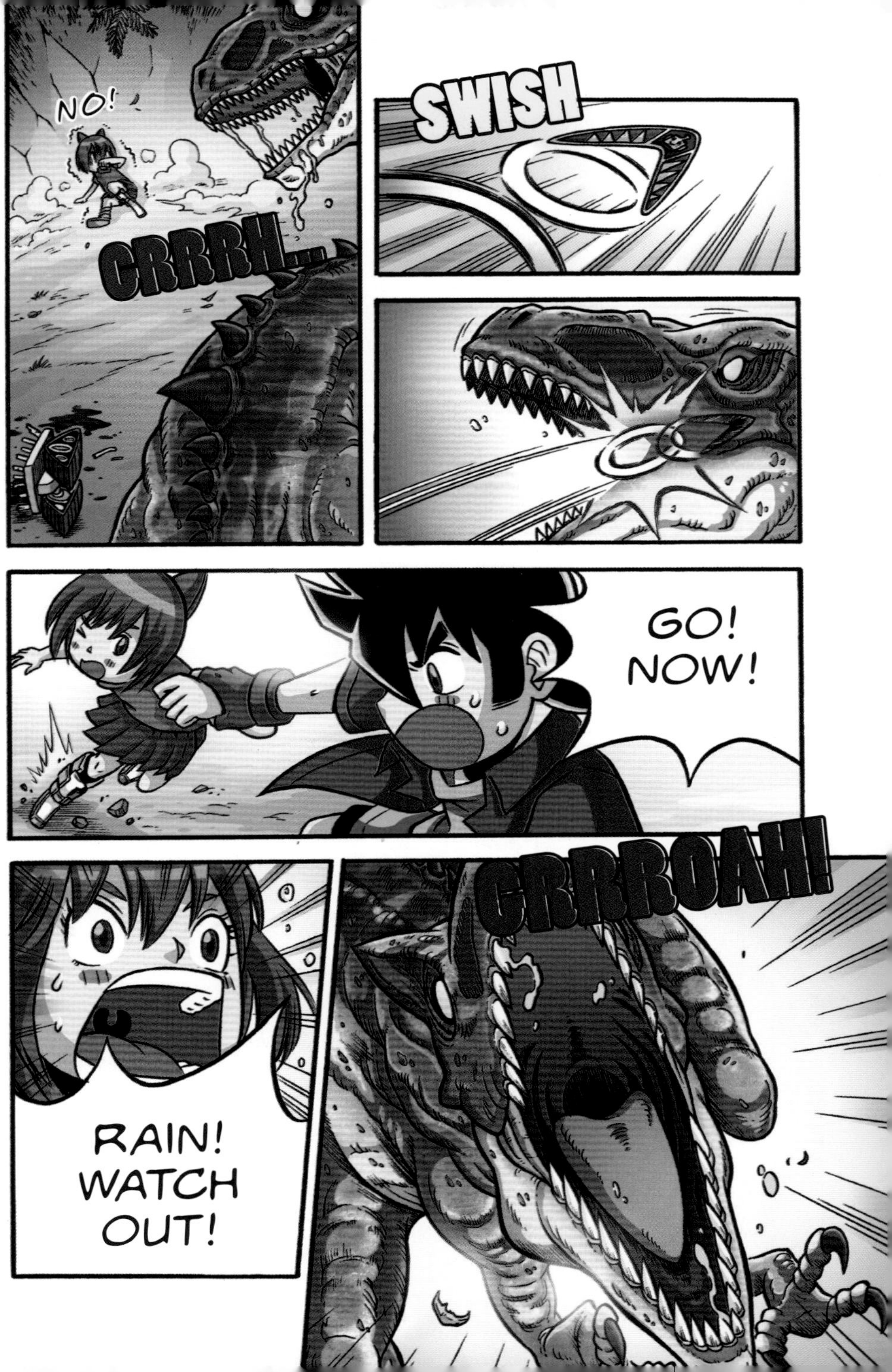
NO!
CRRRH...
SWISH
GO! NOW!
RAIN! WATCH OUT!
CRRROAH!

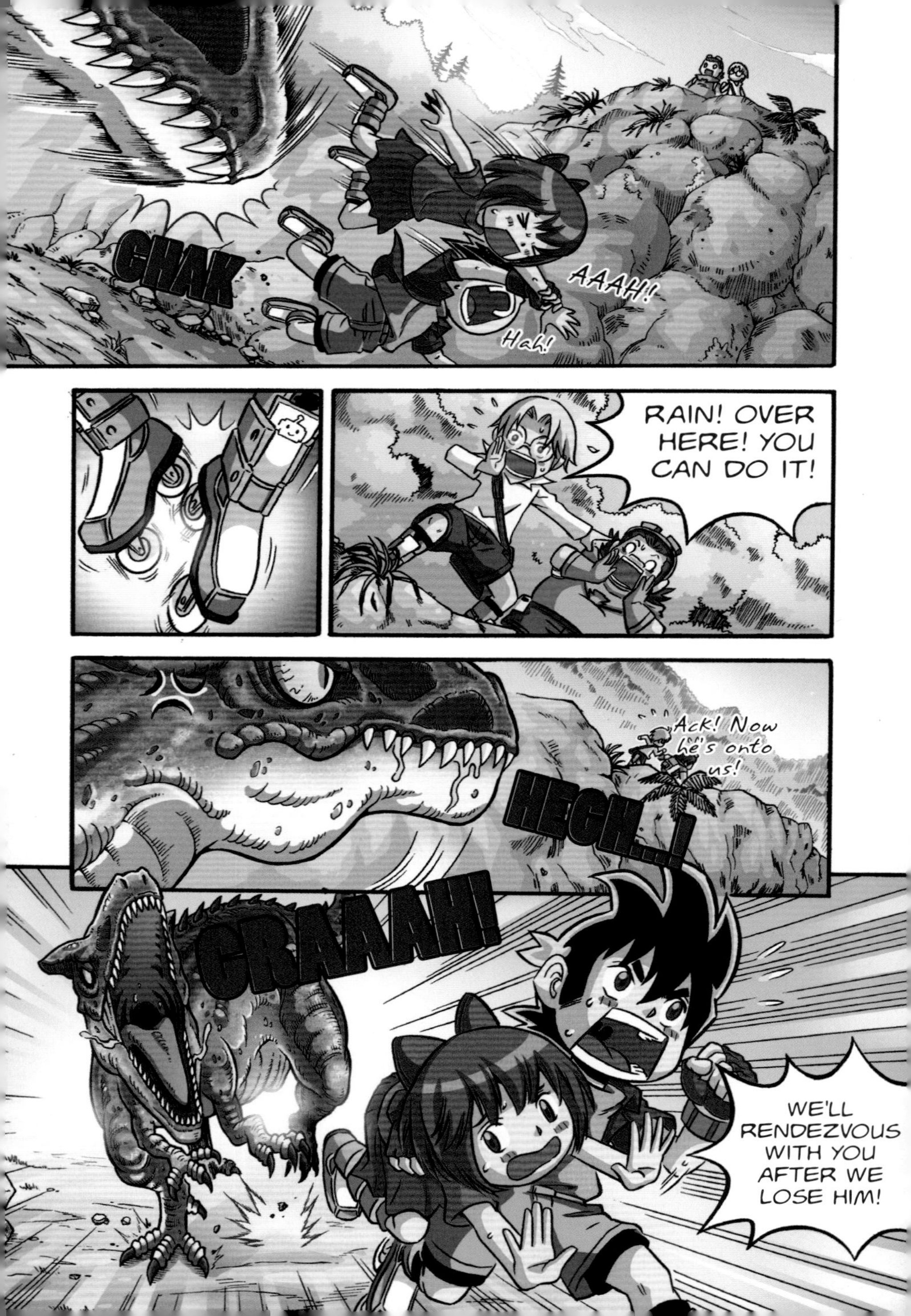
CHAK
AAAAH!
Hah!
RAIN! OVER HERE! YOU CAN DO IT!
Ack! Now he's onto us!
HECH...!
GRAAAAH!
WE'LL RENDEZVOUS WITH YOU AFTER WE LOSE HIM!

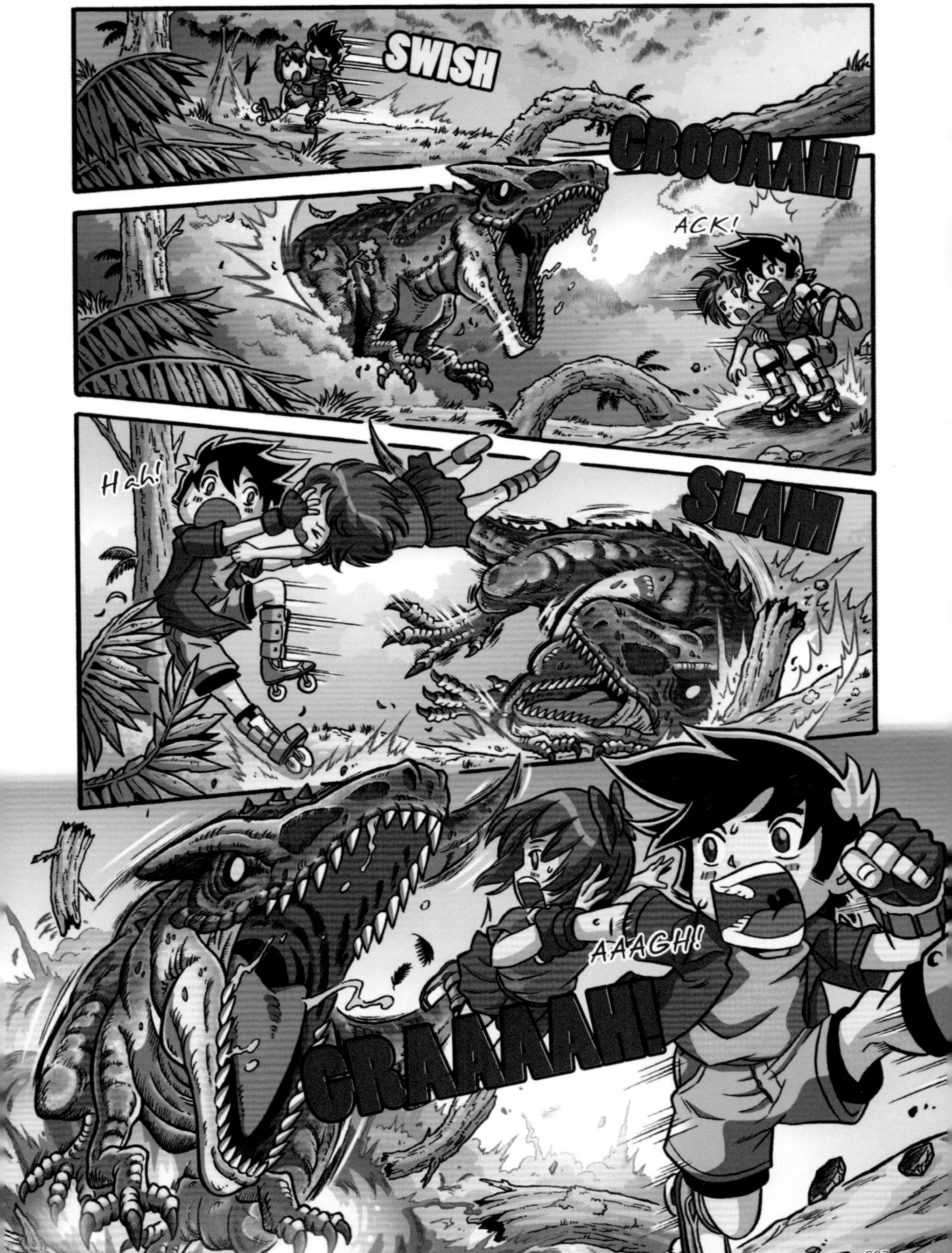
SWISH
CROOAAAH!
ACK!
Hah!
SLAM
AAAGH!
CRAAAAAH!

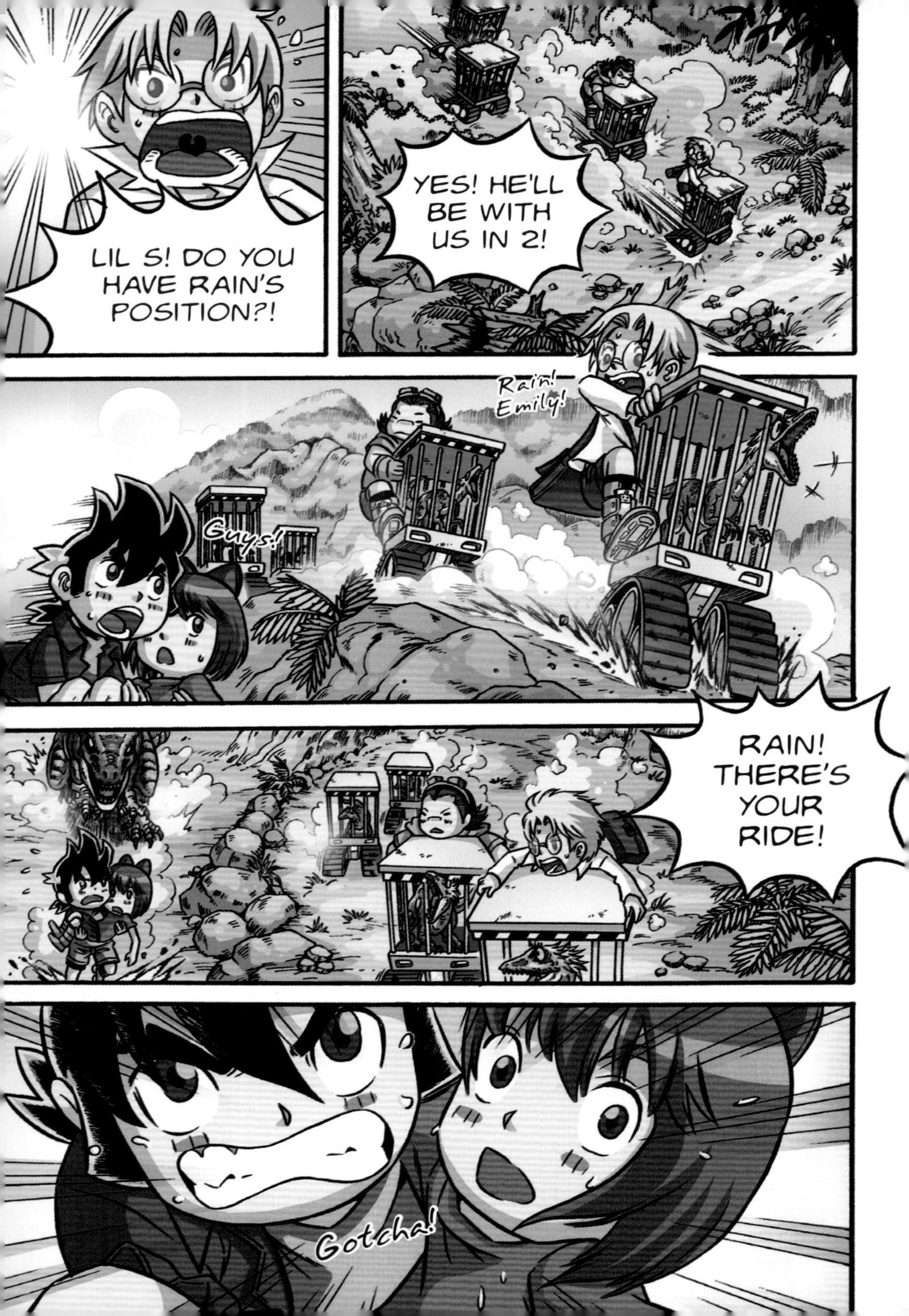
LIL S! DO YOU HAVE RAIN'S POSITION?!
YES! HE'LL BE WITH US IN 2!
Rain! Emily!
Guys!
RAIN! THERE'S YOUR RIDE!
Gotcha!

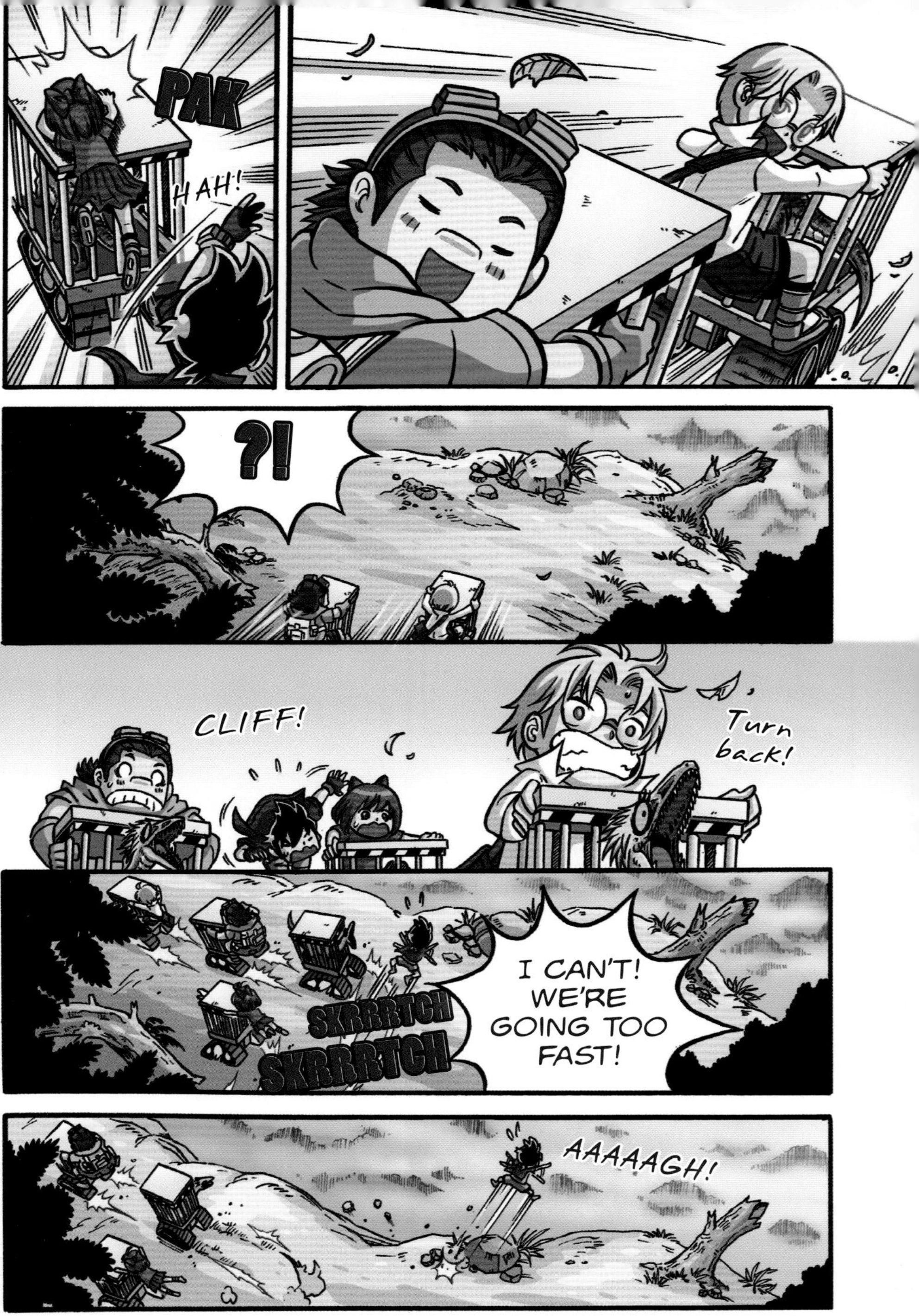
PAK
HAH!
?!
CLIFF!
Turn back!
I CAN'T! WE'RE GOING TOO FAST!
SKRRRTCH
SKRRRTCH
AAAAAGH!

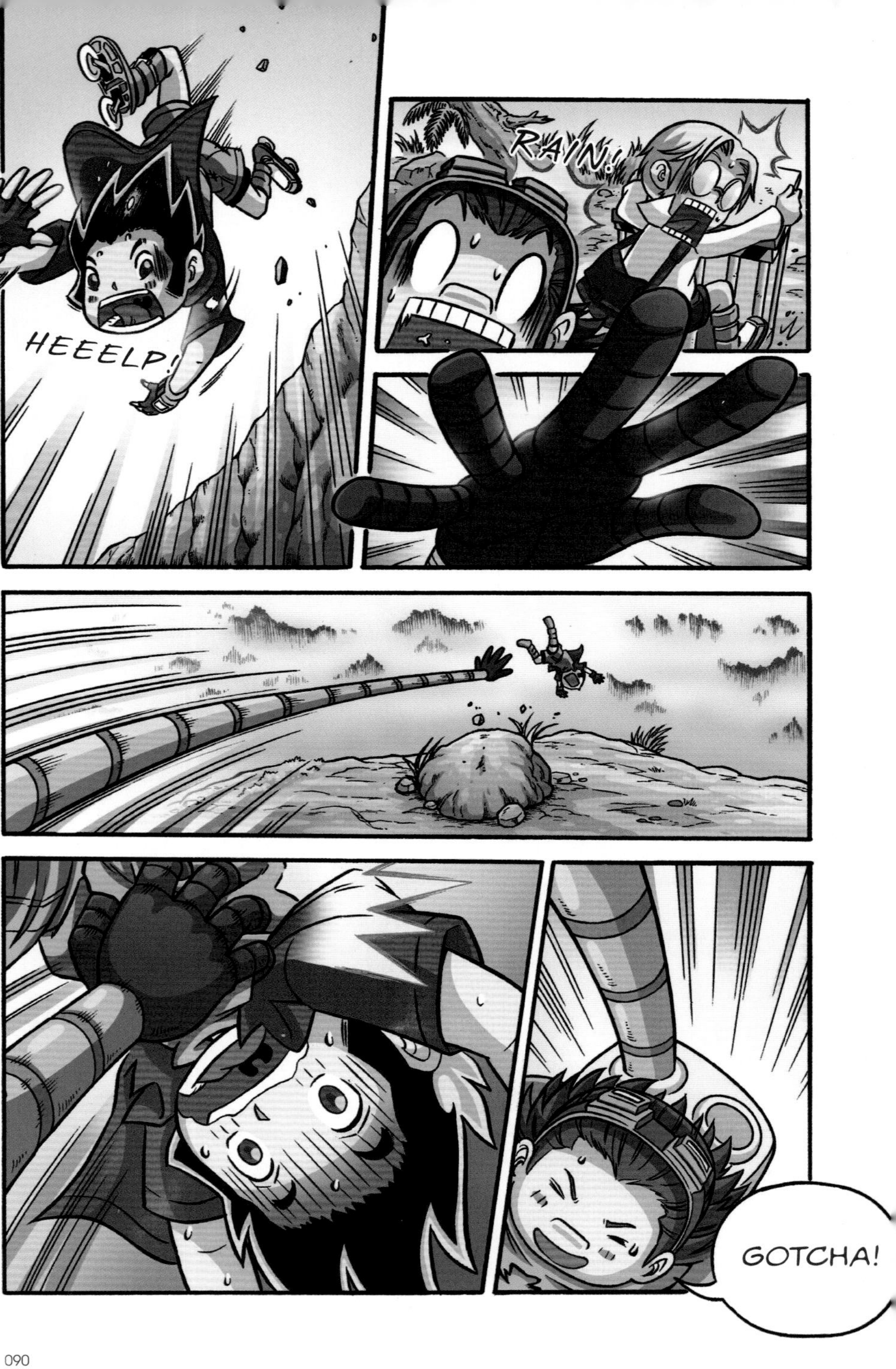
HEEEELP!
RAIN!
GOTCHA!

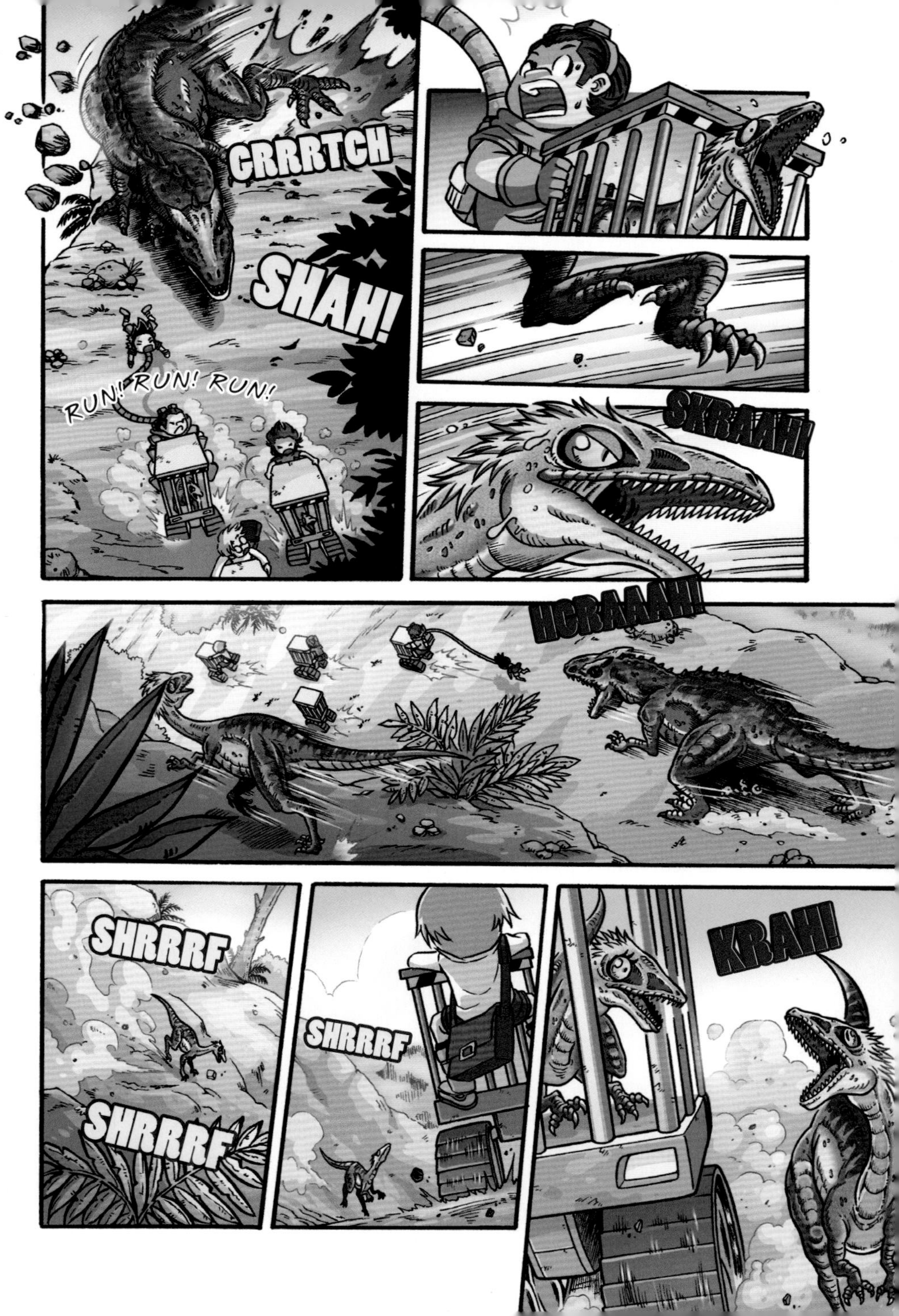

CRRRTCH
SHAH!
RUN! RUN! RUN!
SKRAAAH!
HCRAAAH!
SHRRRF
SHRRRF
SHRRRF
KRAH!

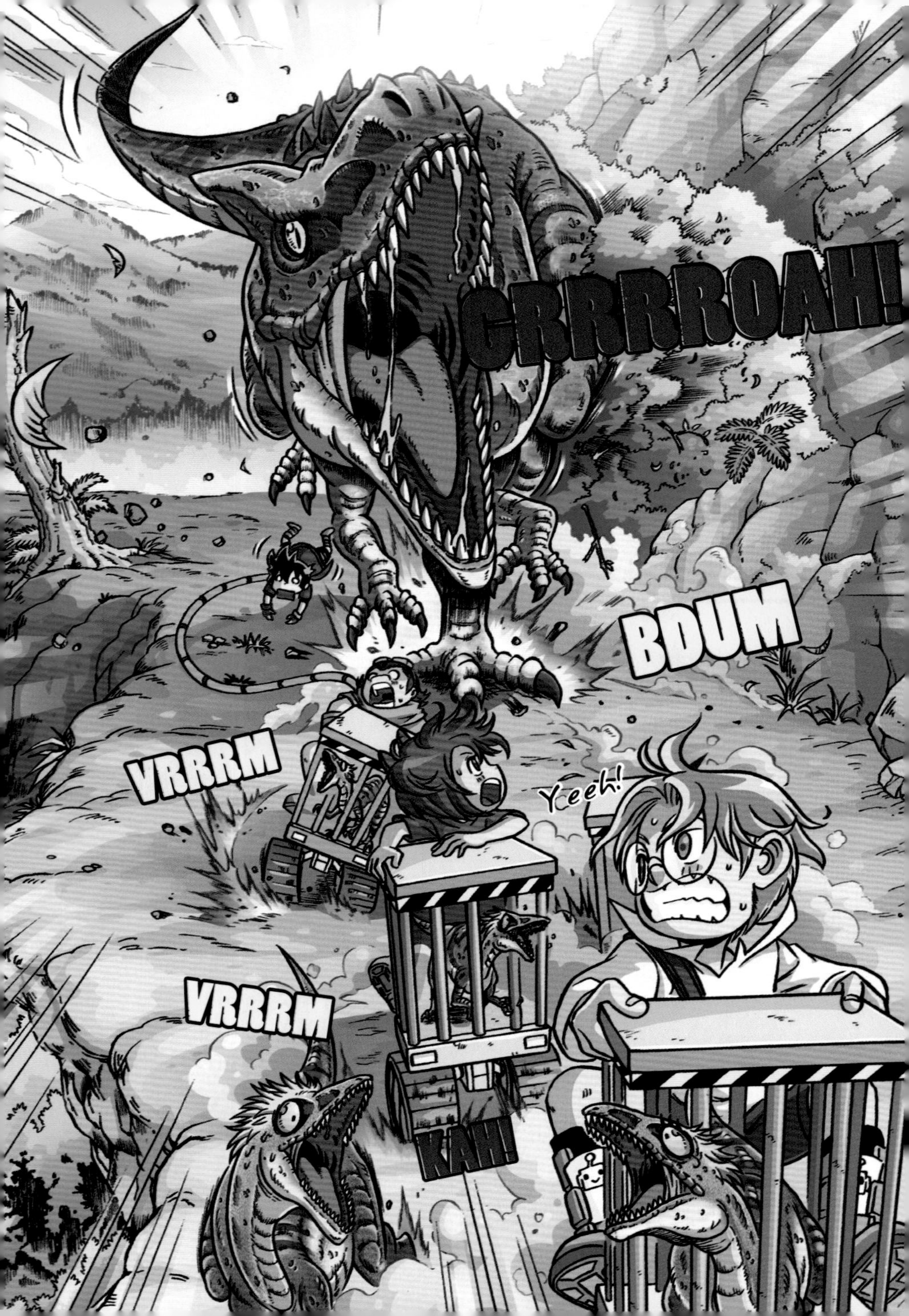

GRRRROAH!
BDUM
VRRRM
Yeeh!
VRRRM
KAH!

Allosaurus

A formidable predator, Allosaurus had dozens of large serrated teeth set along both sides of powerful jaws that would have granted a quick end to its victims. It also had more muscular legs and more dexterous three-fingered hands than the T-Rex, making the Allosaurus the apex predator of its time, Allosaurus hunted in packs. The horn-like ridges above and in front of its eyes facilitated recognition of its fossil remains.

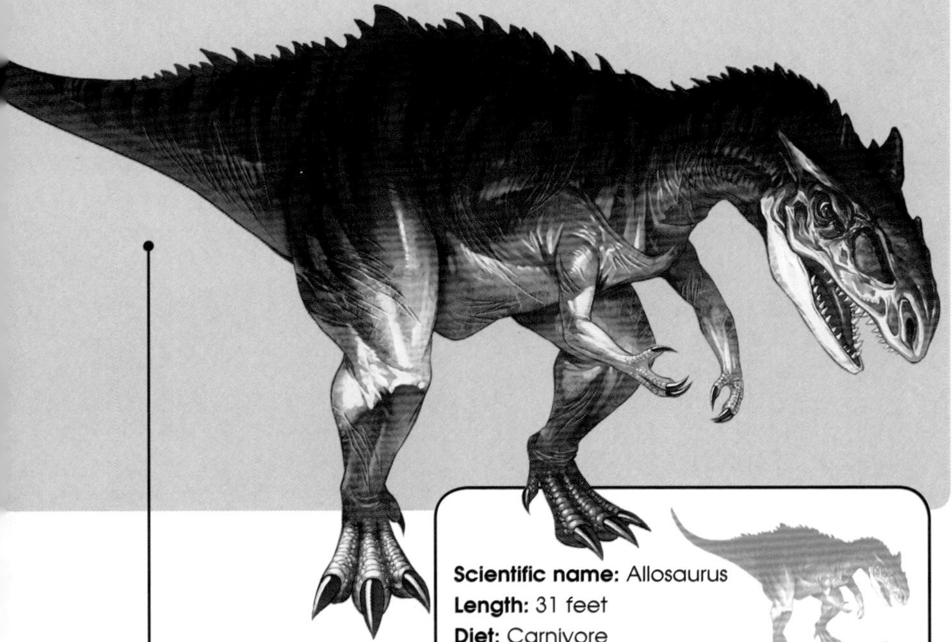

Scientific name: Allosaurus
Length: 31 feet
Diet: Carnivore
Habitat: Flatlands
Discovered: North America, Europe and East Africa
Era: Late Jurassic

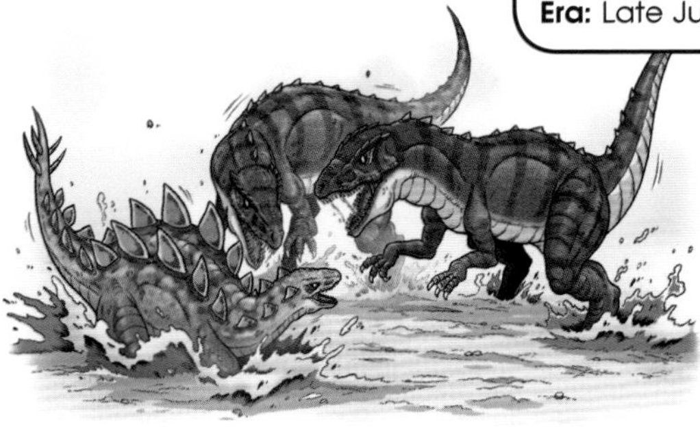

Lloyd's Quarry in North America contains many Allosaurus fossils, more than could reasonably be expected. As such, it is believed that these predators were attracted by the herbivores that were caught in the mudlands where the quarry is now.

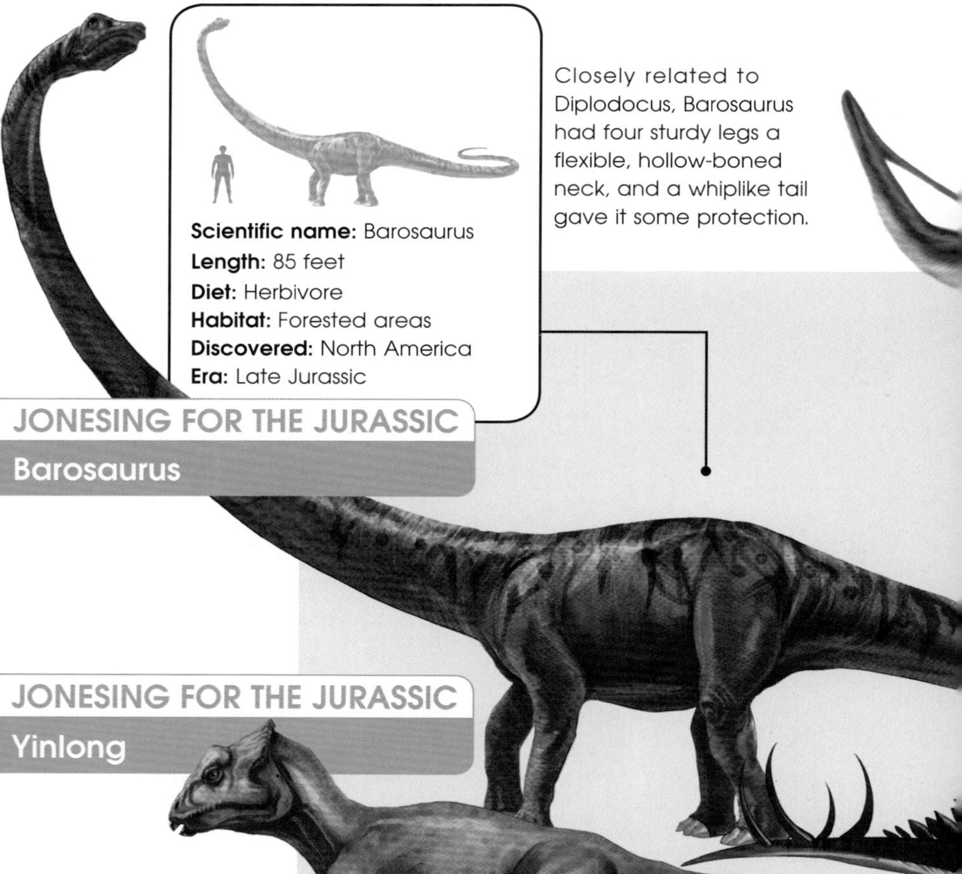

Scientific name: Barosaurus
Length: 85 feet
Diet: Herbivore
Habitat: Forested areas
Discovered: North America
Era: Late Jurassic

Closely related to Diplodocus, Barosaurus had four sturdy legs a flexible, hollow-boned neck, and a whiplike tail gave it some protection.

JONESING FOR THE JURASSIC

Barosaurus

JONESING FOR THE JURASSIC

Yinlong

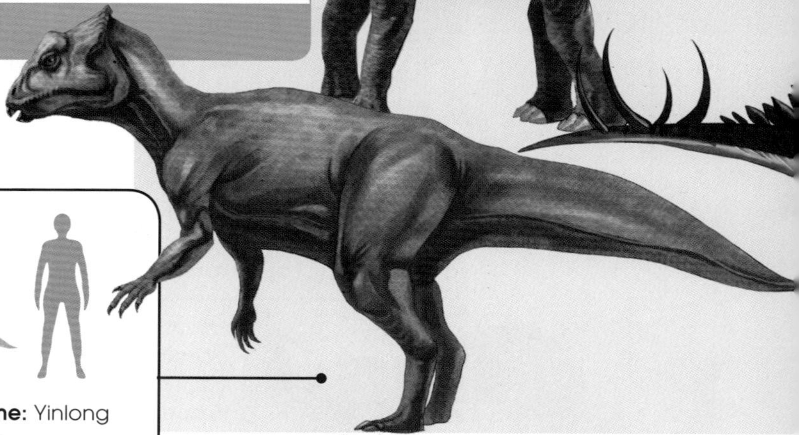

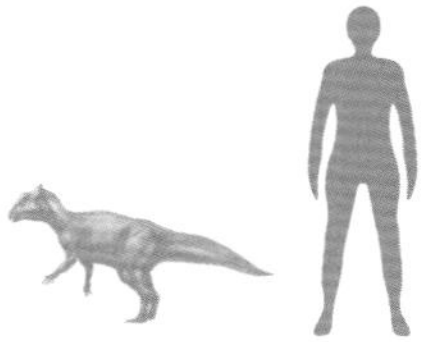

Scientific name: Yinlong
Length: 3 feet
Diet: Herbivore
Habitat: Unknown
Discovered: China
Era: Late Jurassic

A basal ceratopsian from the late Jurassic, it is one of the few dinosaurs with a non-Latin or Greek name (its name is derived from Mandarin). The raised bony protrusions at the back of its head bore resemblance to a Pachycephalosaur, while the rostral bone on its upper jaw identified it as a ceratopsian.

JONESING FOR THE JURASSIC

Falcarius

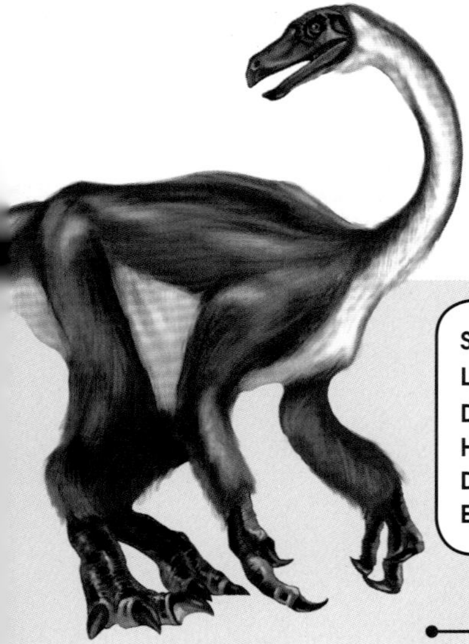

Falcarius is a Therizinosaurian and it shares its name with the Latin word for "sickle" due to the shape of its curved claws. Its diet, however, is unknown; while it had carnivore characteristics: a bipedal stance, claws and maybe even fur or feathers, it also had large hips and leaf-shaped teeth, which were herbivore traits.

Scientific name: Falcarius
Length: 12 feet
Diet: Herbivore, possibly omnivore
Habitat: Unknown
Discovered: North America
Era: Late Jurassic - Early Cretaceous

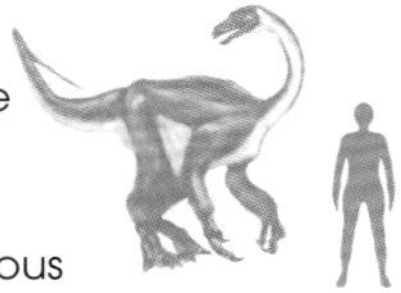

JONESING FOR THE JURASSIC

Tuojiangosaurus

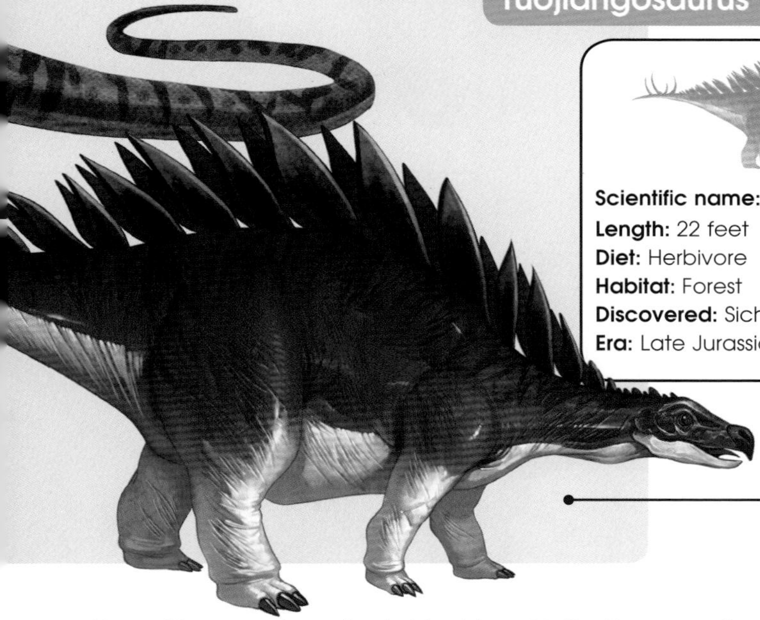

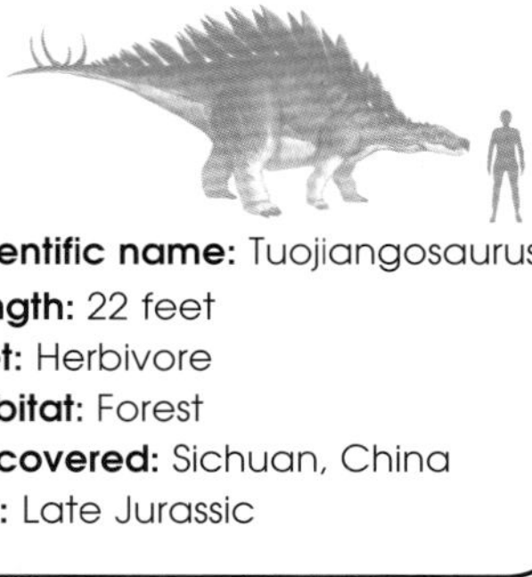

Scientific name: Tuojiangosaurus
Length: 22 feet
Diet: Herbivore
Habitat: Forest
Discovered: Sichuan, China
Era: Late Jurassic

Named because it was the first fossil found in the Tuo river in the Sichuan Province, China, Tuojiangosaurus was a typical stegosaurid except for the lack of certain vertebral spines for muscle attachment which likely prevented it from rearing up on its hind legs, and thus probably limited it to eating low-lying plants.

JONESING FOR THE JURASSIC

Yangchuanosaurus

A metriacanthosaurid theropod, two distinct species of Yangchuanosaurus have been discovered: Y. (Yangchuanosaurus) Shangyouensis (26 to 32 feet long) and Y. Magus (35 feet long). Its powerful tail probably comprised half its body weight, and its brain was large compared to its body, which suggests that it at least had some notable intelligence.

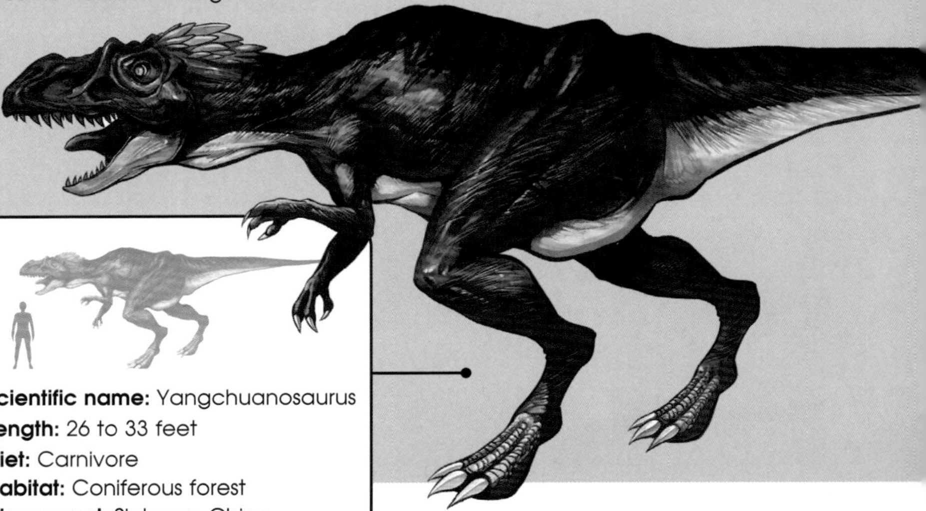

Scientific name: Yangchuanosaurus
Length: 26 to 33 feet
Diet: Carnivore
Habitat: Coniferous forest
Discovered: Sichuan, China
Era: Late Jurassic

JONESING FOR THE JURASSIC

Juravenator

Scientific name: Juravenator
Length: 2 feet
Diet: Carnivore
Habitat: Unknown
Discovered: Europe
Era: Late Jurassic

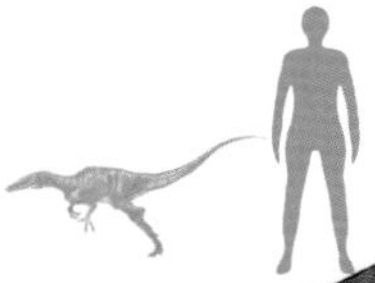

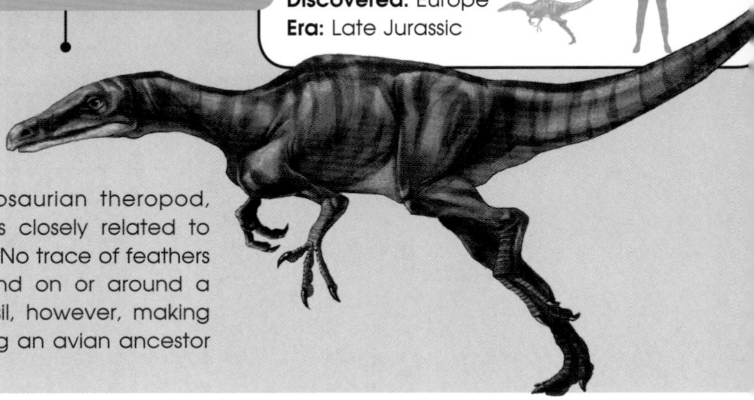

A small coelurosaurian theropod, Juravenator was closely related to Sinosauropteryx. No trace of feathers have been found on or around a Juravenator fossil, however, making claims of it being an avian ancestor dubious at best.

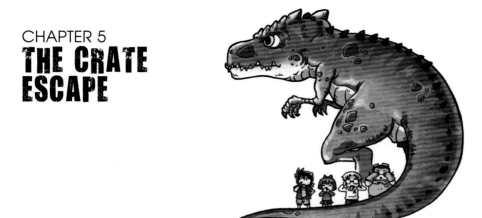

CHAPTER 5

THE CRATE ESCAPE

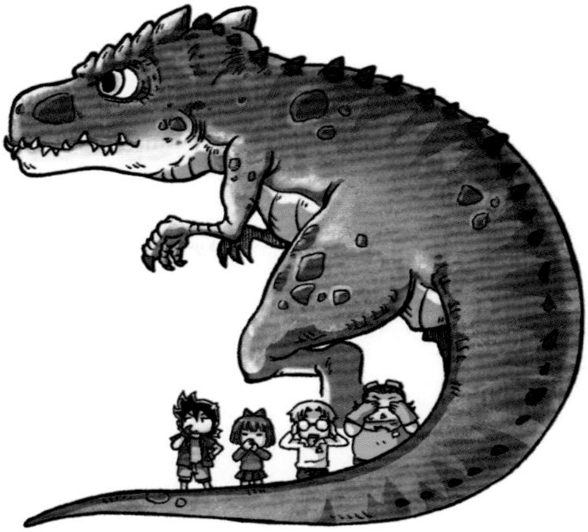

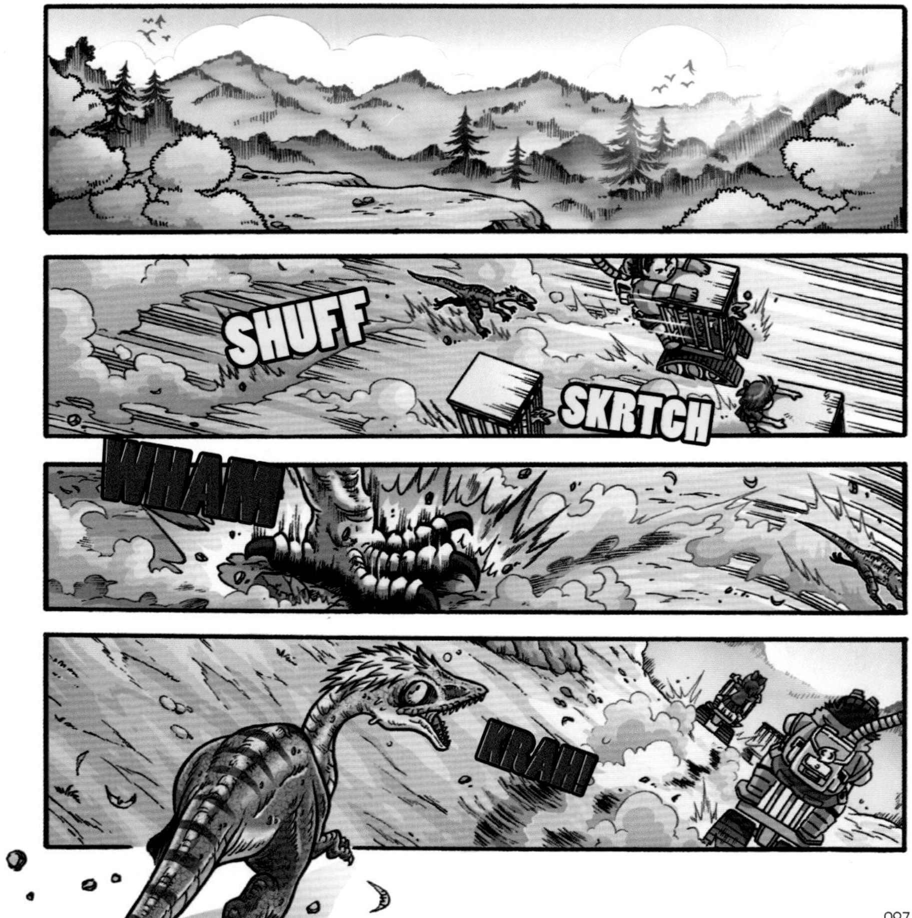
SHUFF
SKRTCH
WHAM
KRAH!

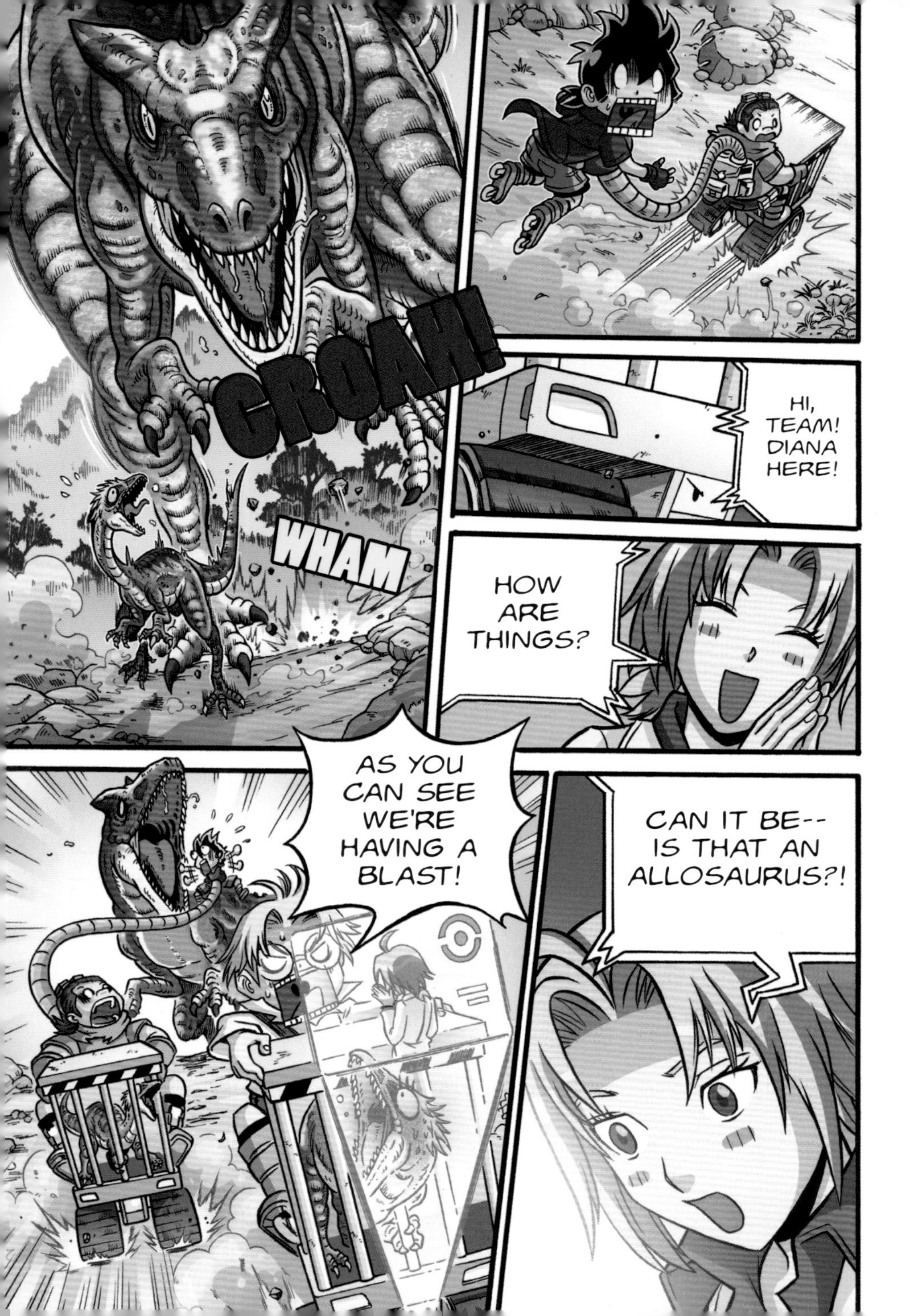
CROAH!
WHAM
HI, TEAM! DIANA HERE!
HOW ARE THINGS?
AS YOU CAN SEE WE'RE HAVING A BLAST!
CAN IT BE-- IS THAT AN ALLOSAURUS?!

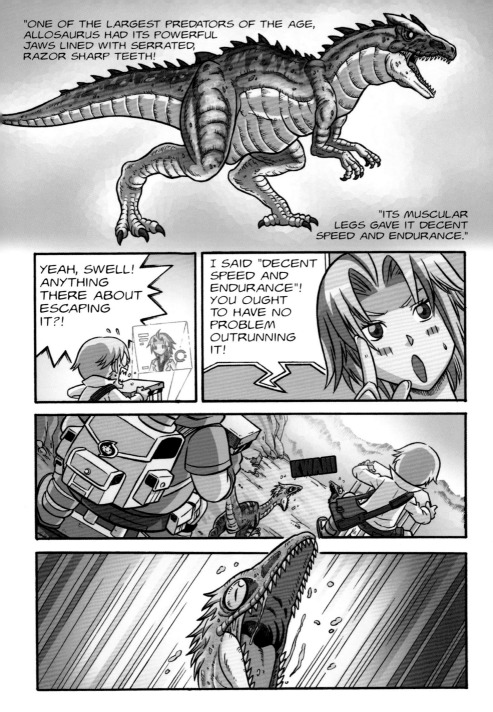

"ONE OF THE LARGEST PREDATORS OF THE AGE, ALLOSAURUS HAD ITS POWERFUL JAWS LINED WITH SERRATED, RAZOR SHARP TEETH!"

"ITS MUSCULAR LEGS GAVE IT DECENT SPEED AND ENDURANCE."

YEAH, SWELL! ANYTHING THERE ABOUT ESCAPING IT?!

I SAID "DECENT SPEED AND ENDURANCE"! YOU OUGHT TO HAVE NO PROBLEM OUTRUNNING IT!

KWAH!

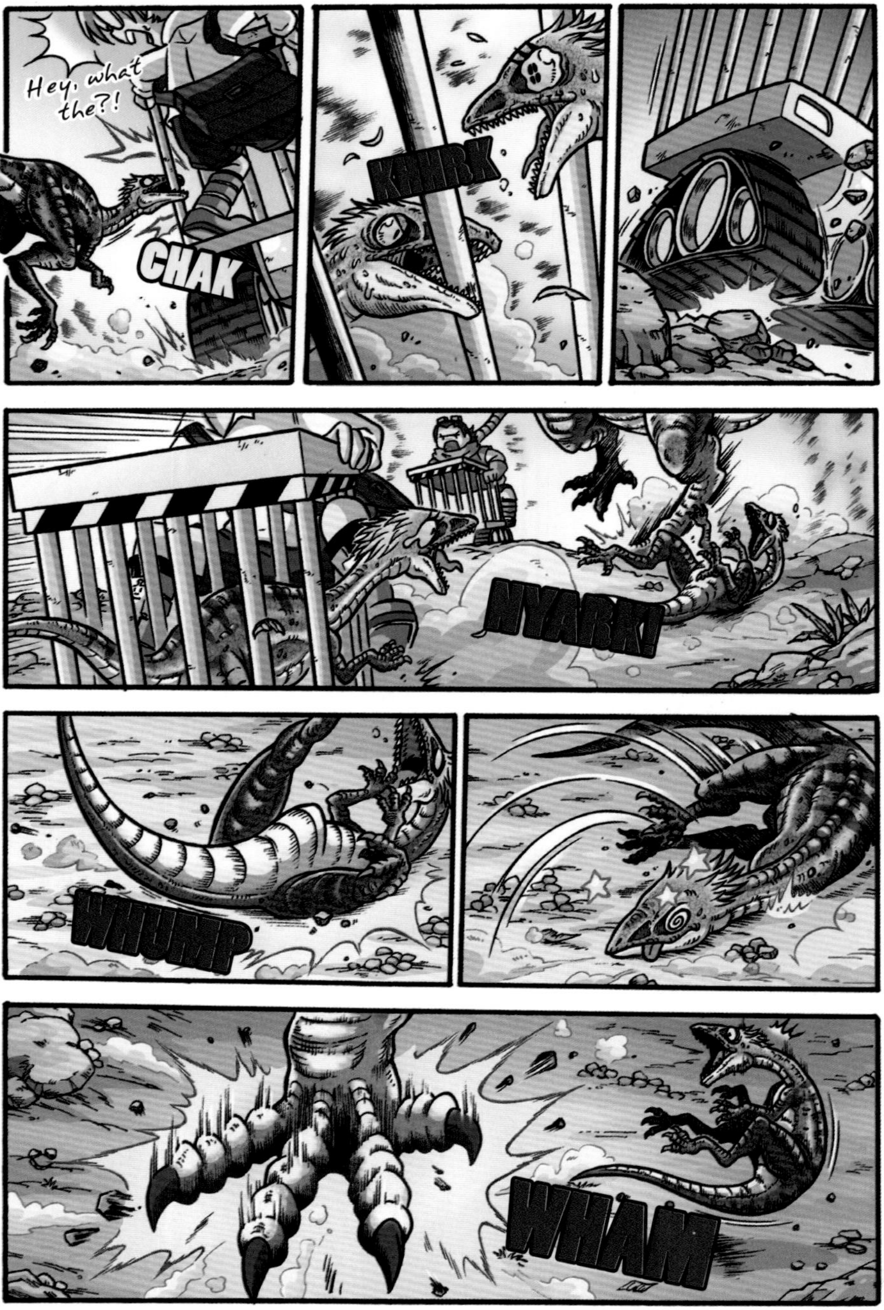
Hey, what the?!
CHAK
KHHRK
NYARK!
WHUMP
WHAM

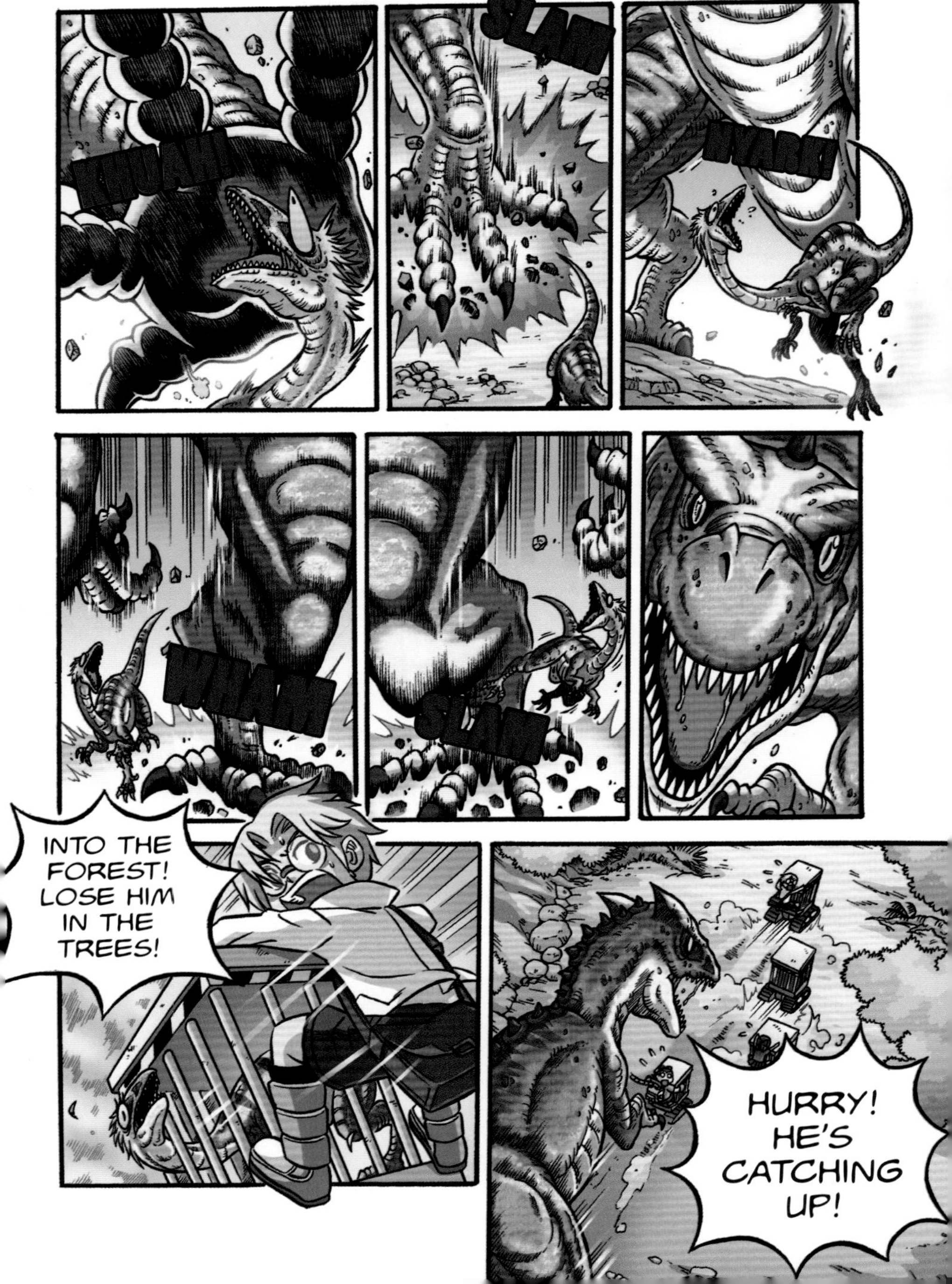
[redacted]
SLAM!
[redacted]
[redacted]
[redacted]
INTO THE FOREST! LOSE HIM IN THE TREES!
HURRY! HE'S CATCHING UP!

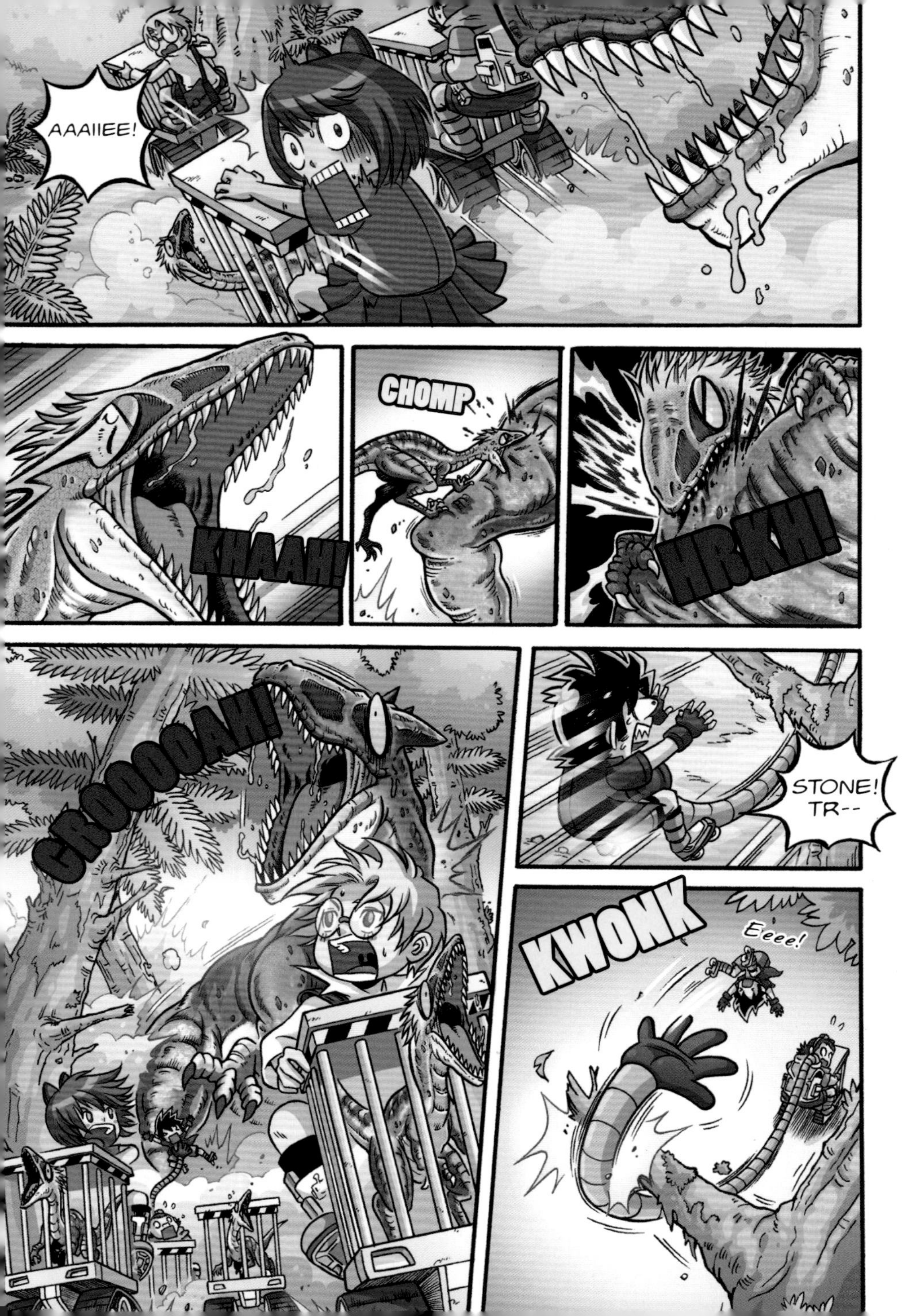
AAAIIEE!
KHAAH!
CHOMP
HRKH!
CROOOOAH!
STONE! TR--
KWONK
Eeee!

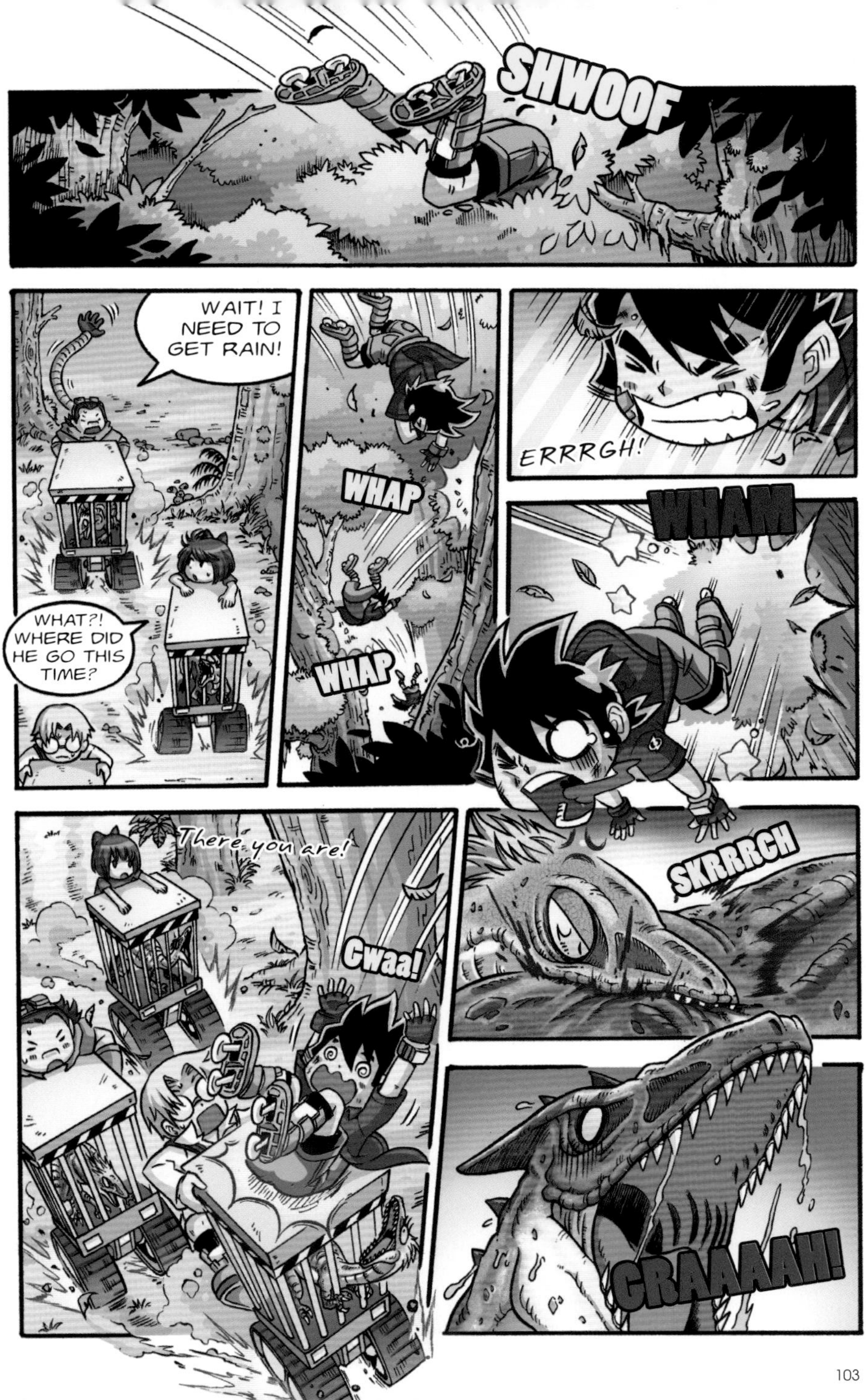
SHWOOF
WAIT! I NEED TO GET RAIN!
WHAT?! WHERE DID HE GO THIS TIME?
WHAP
WHAP
ERRRGH!
WHAM
There you are!
Gwaa!
SKRRRCH
GRAAAAH!

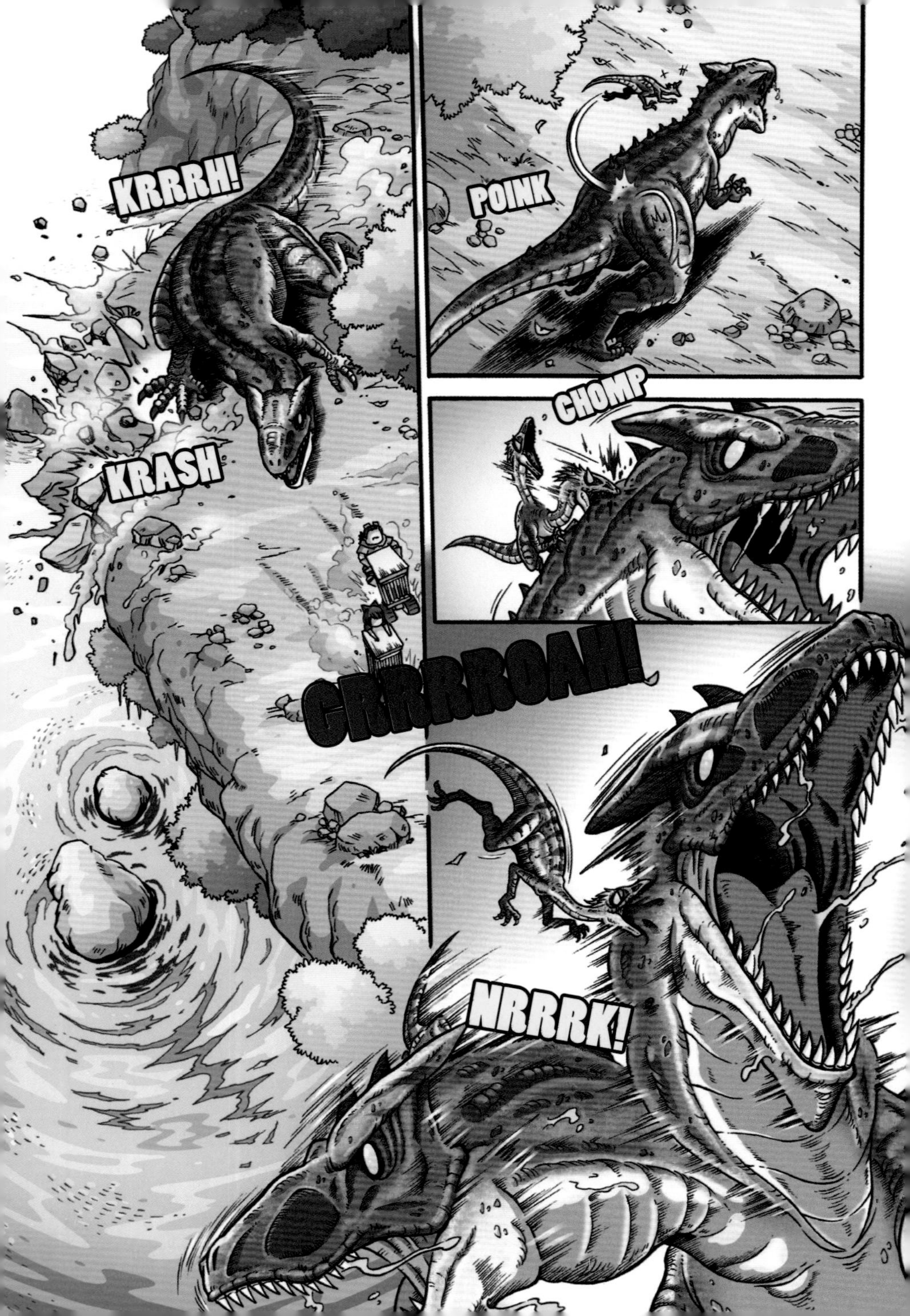
KRRRH!
KRASH
POINK
CHOMP
GRRRROAH!
NRRRK!

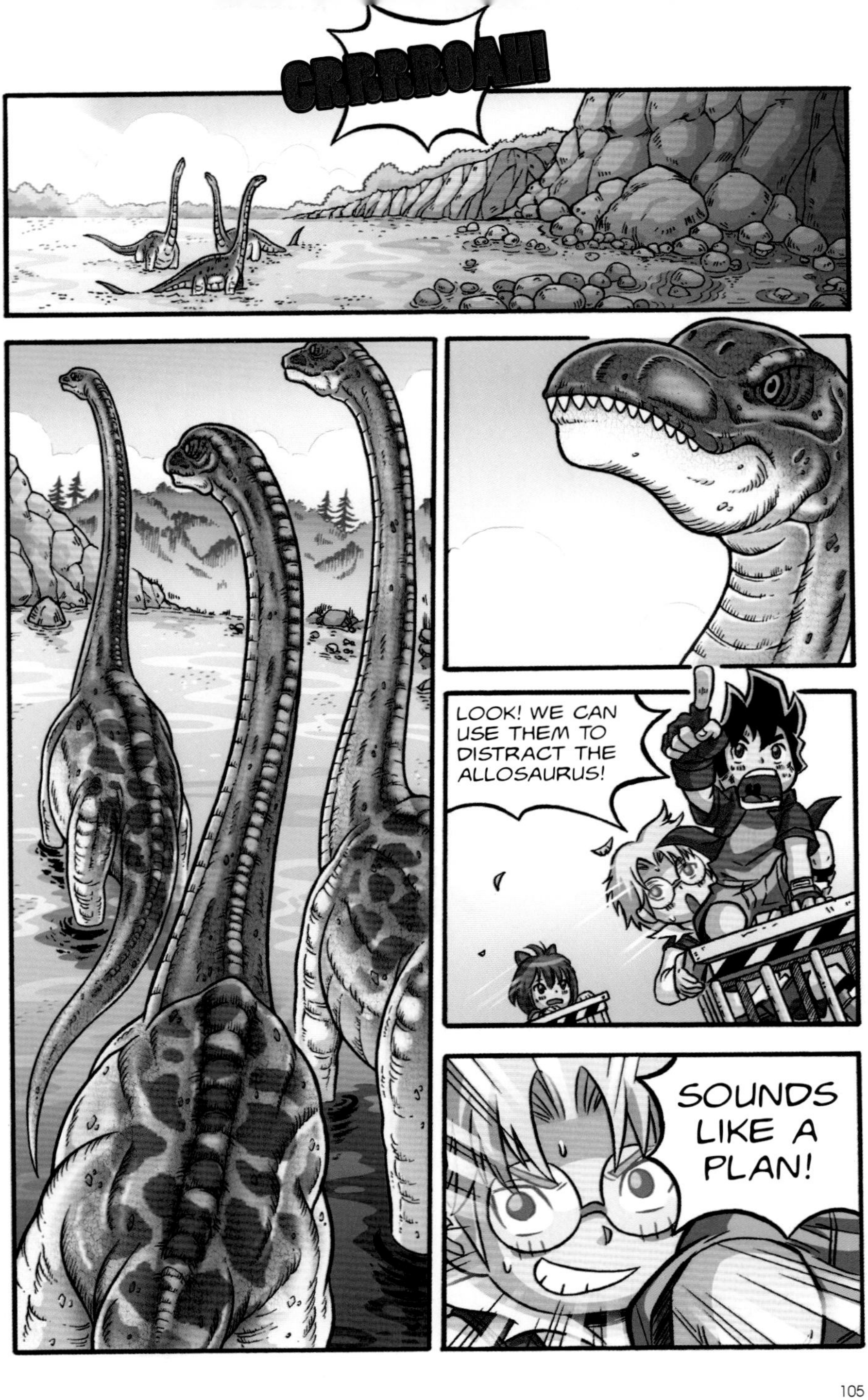
CRRRROAH!
LOOK! WE CAN USE THEM TO DISTRACT THE ALLOSAURUS!
SOUNDS LIKE A PLAN!

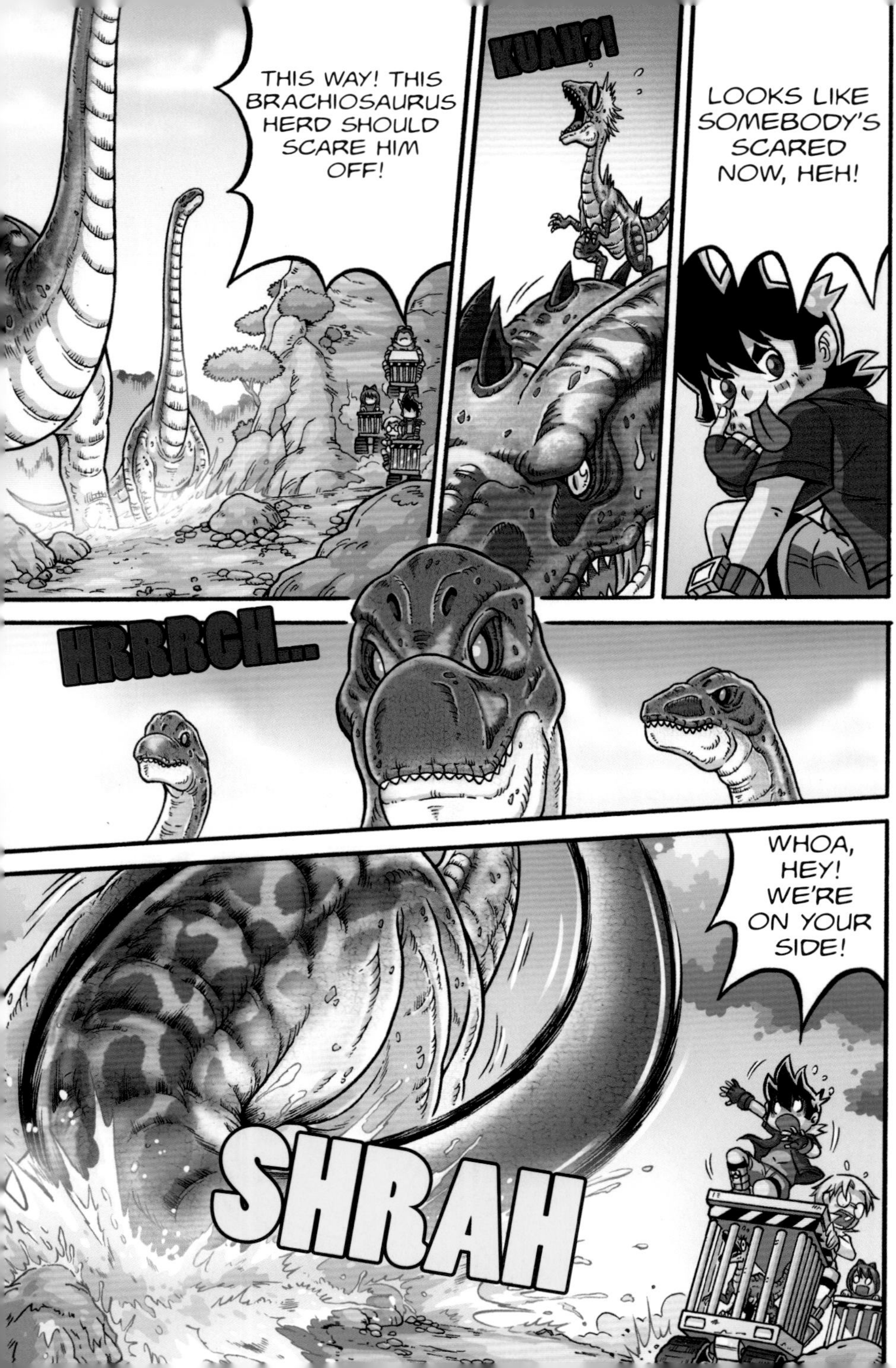
THIS WAY! THIS BRACHIOSAURUS HERD SHOULD SCARE HIM OFF!
KUAH?!
LOOKS LIKE SOMEBODY'S SCARED NOW, HEH!
HRRRCH...
WHOA, HEY! WE'RE ON YOUR SIDE!
SHRAH

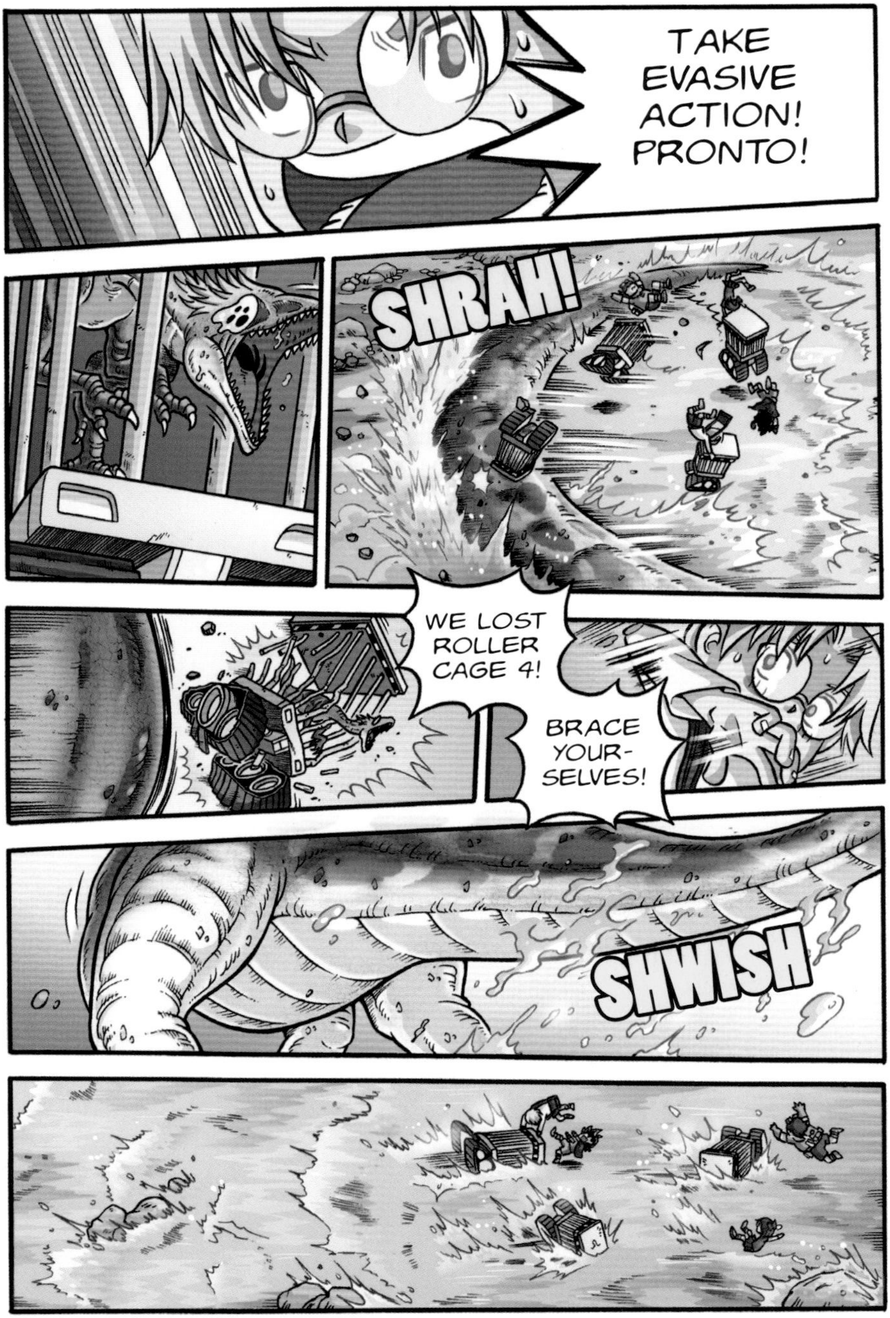
TAKE EVASIVE ACTION! PRONTO!
SHRAH!
WE LOST ROLLER CAGE 4!
BRACE YOUR-SELVES!
SHWISH

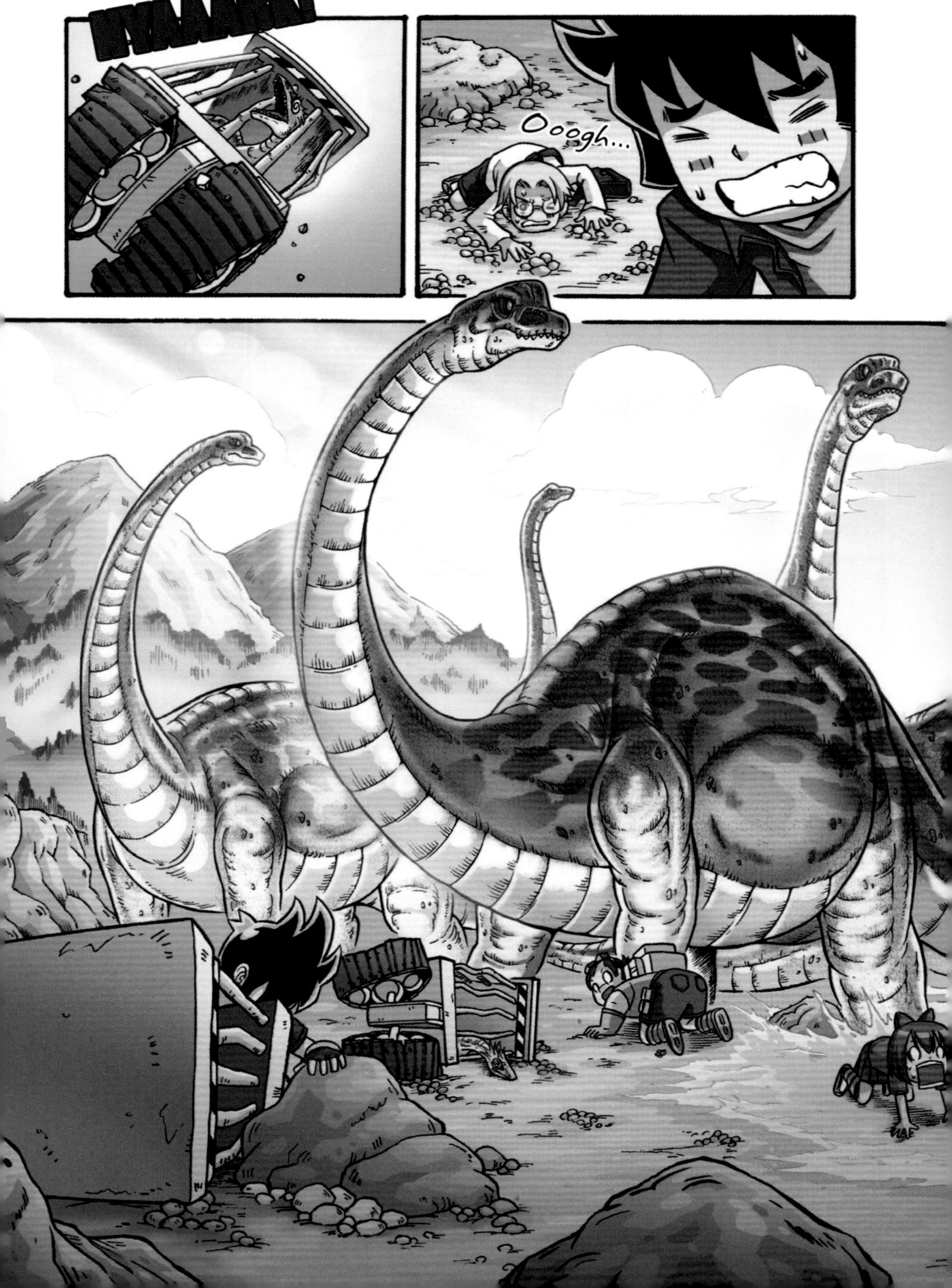

NYAAARK!
Ooogh...

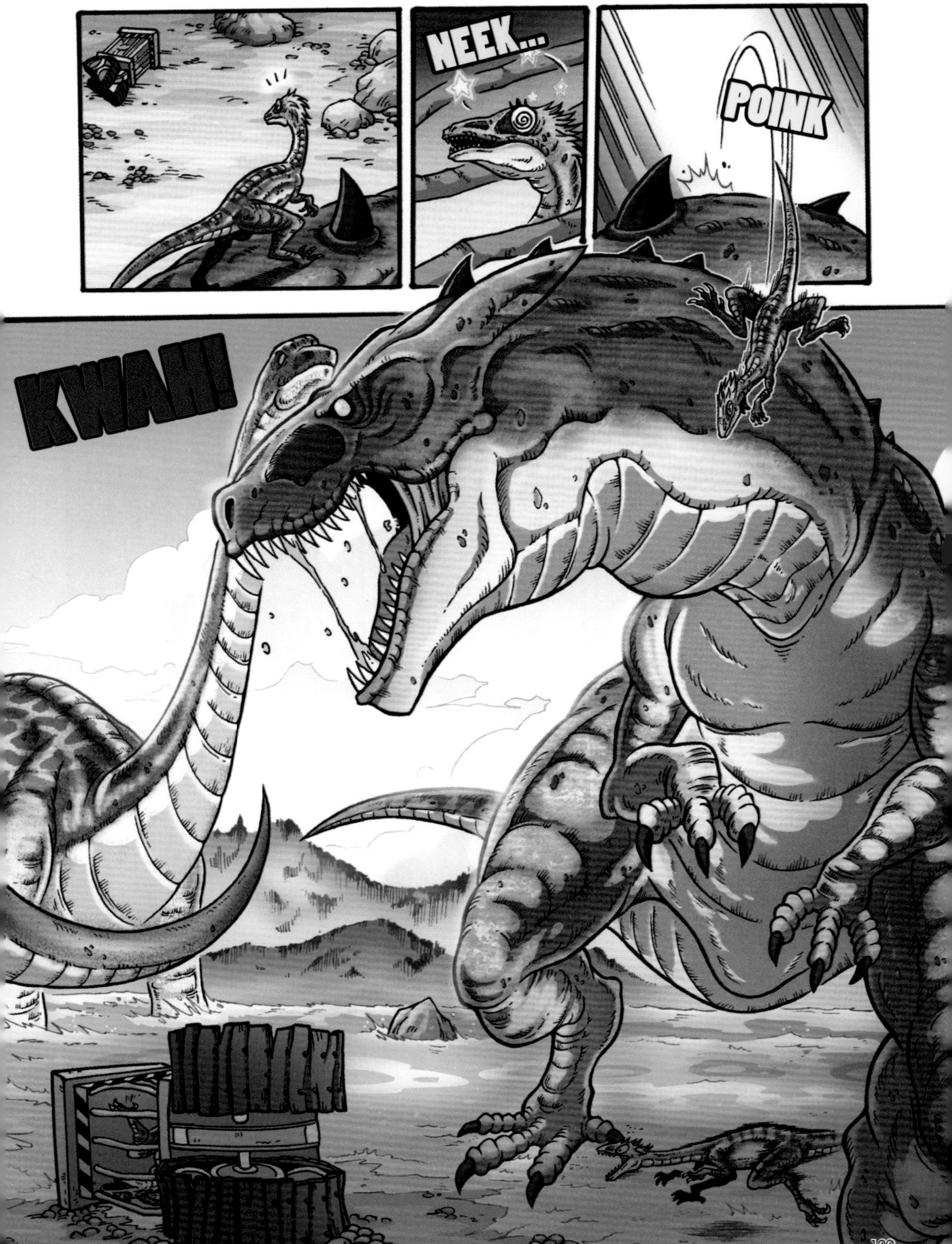
NEEK...
POINK
KWAH!

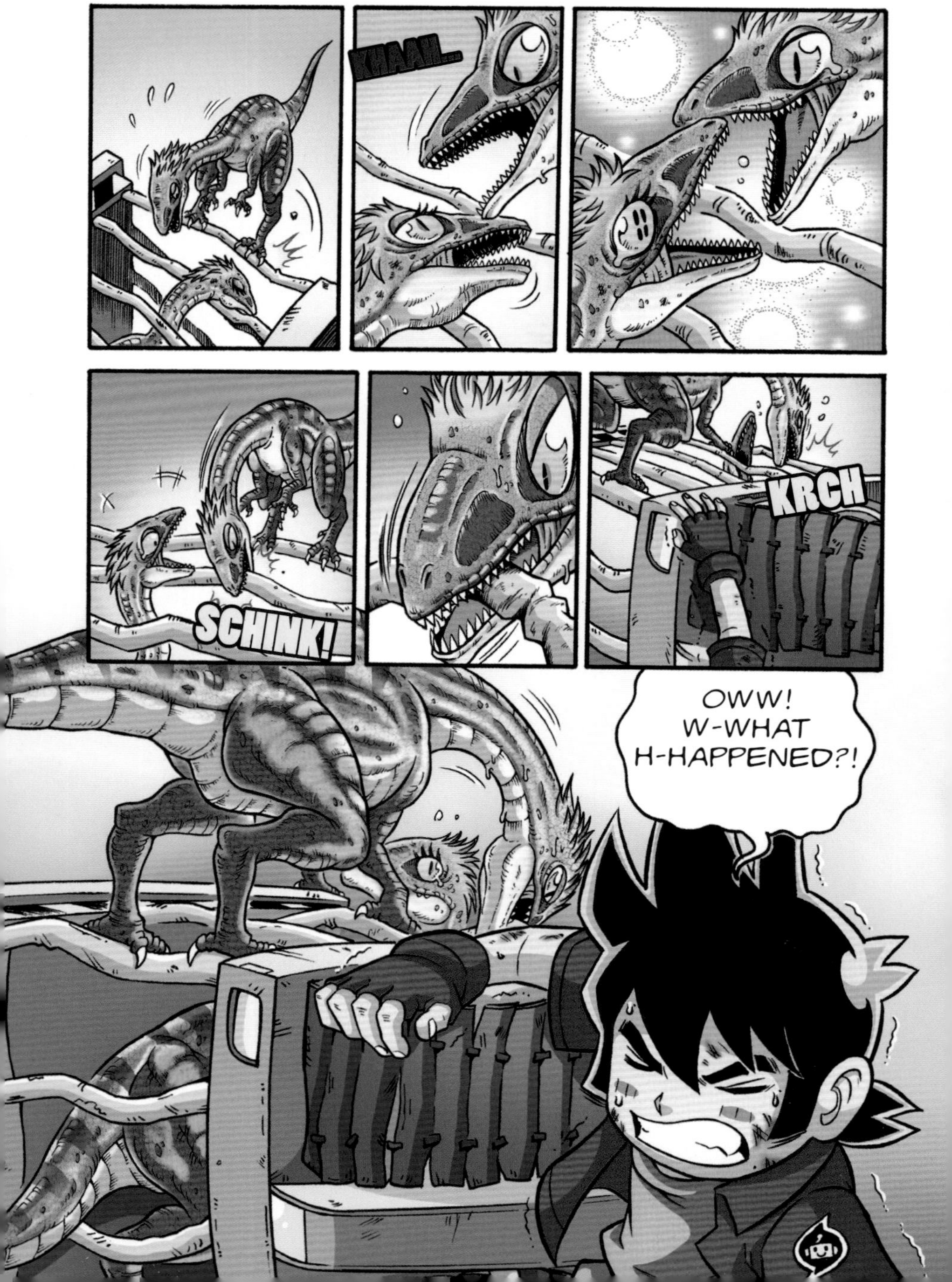
KHAAH...
SCHINK!
KRCH
OWW! W-WHAT H-HAPPENED?!

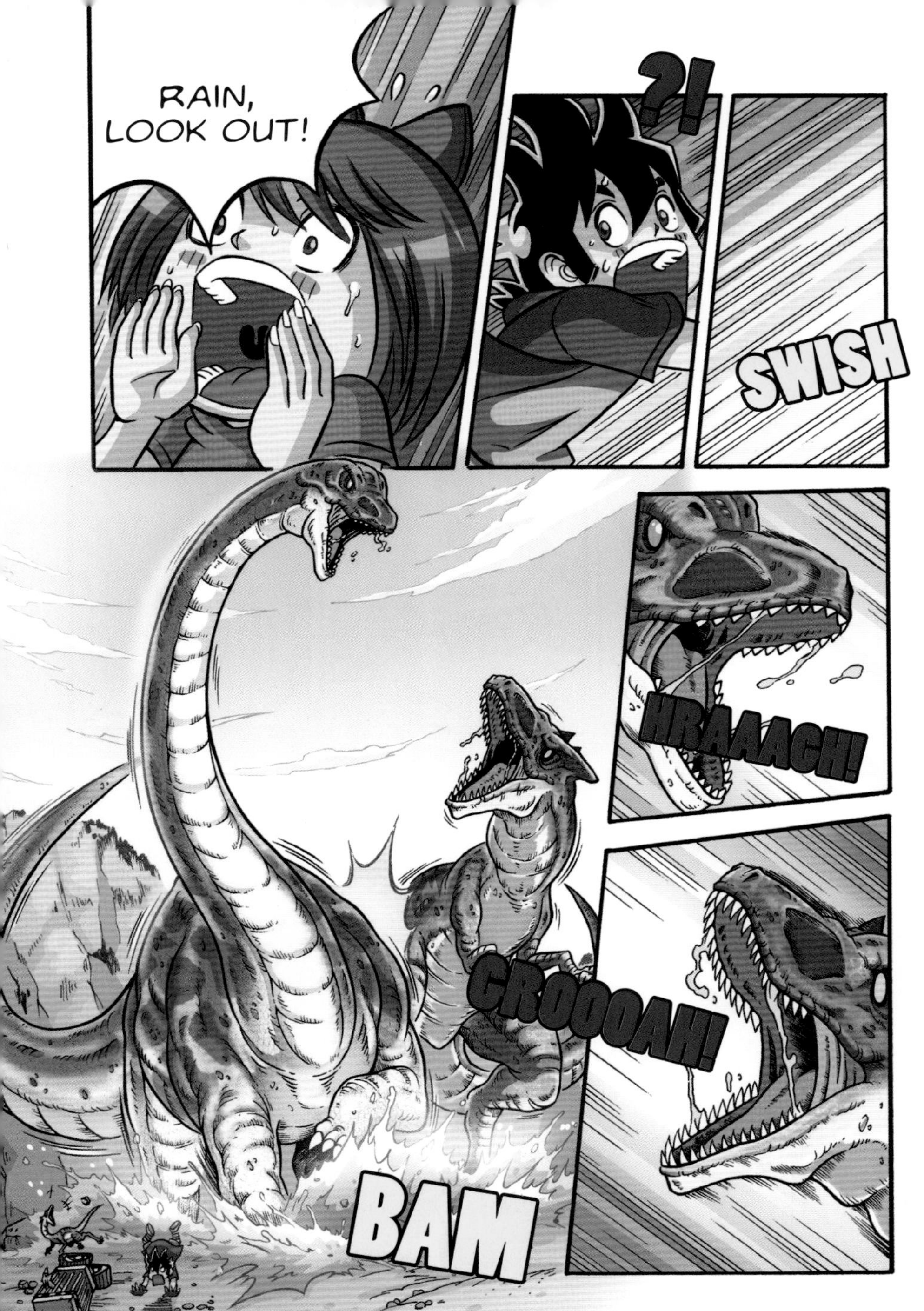
RAIN, LOOK OUT!
?!
SWISH
HRAAACH!
GROOOOAH!
BAM

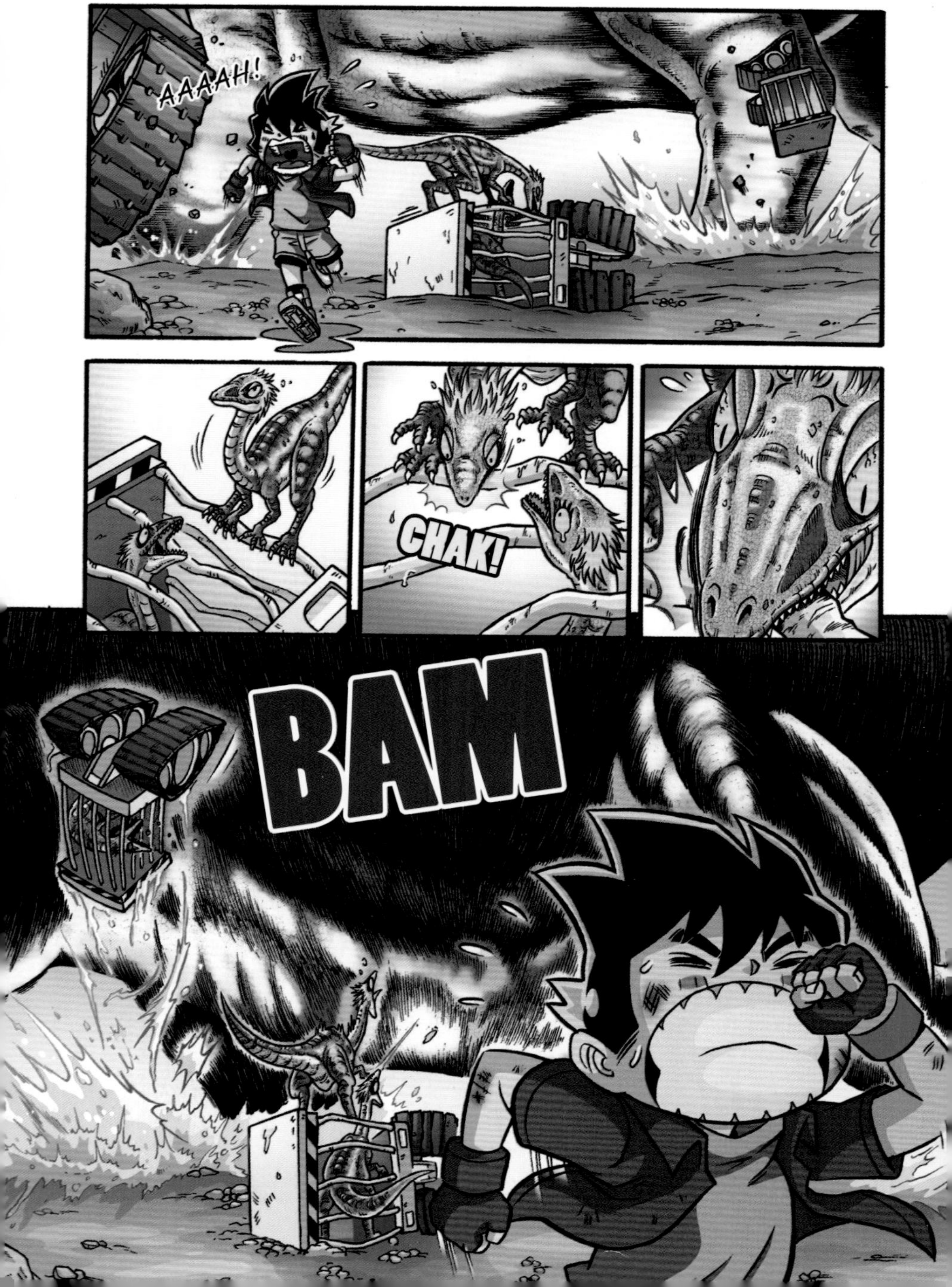
AAAAH!
CHAK!
BAM

JONESING FOR THE JURASSIC

Kentrosaurus

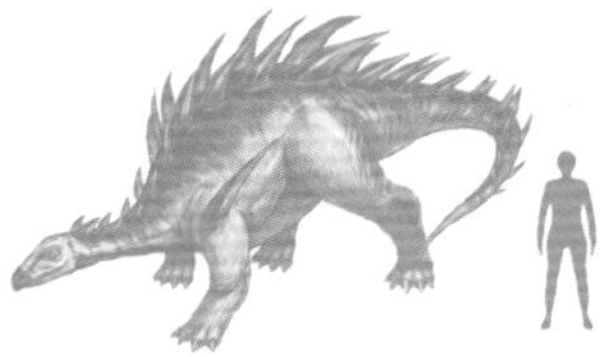

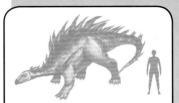

Scientific name: Kentrosaurus
Length: 14 feet
Diet: Herbivore
Habitat: Forests
Discovered: East Africa
Era: Late Jurassic

Closely related to Stegosaurus, Kentrosaurus was smaller in size. Despite a lack of Kentrosaurus skull fossils, experts believe it had a small brain, a low, elongated head, small cheek teeth and an upper rostral bone which formed a beak. Because of its relative size, it fed on low-lying plants.

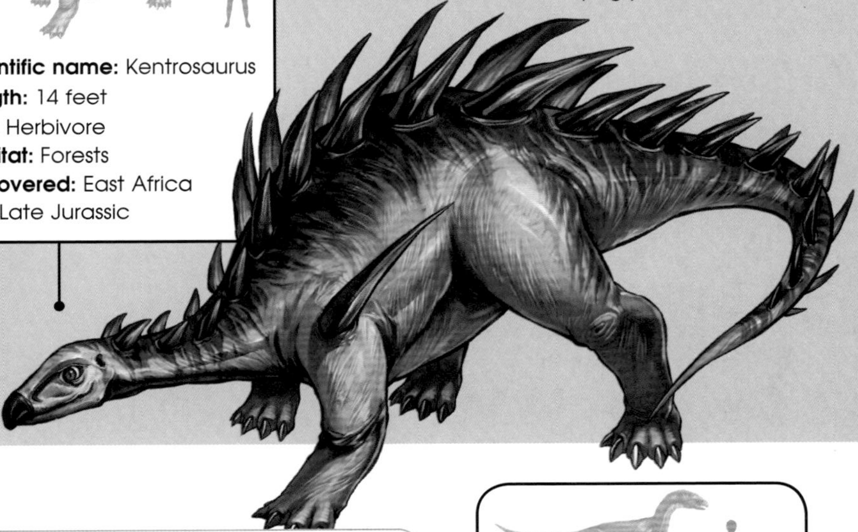

JONESING FOR THE JURASSIC

Dryosaurus

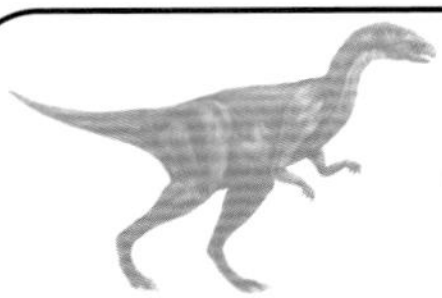

Scientific name: Dryosaurus
Length: 9 to 13 feet
Diet: Herbivore
Habitat: Woodlands
Discovered: North America, Tanzania
Era: Late Jurassic

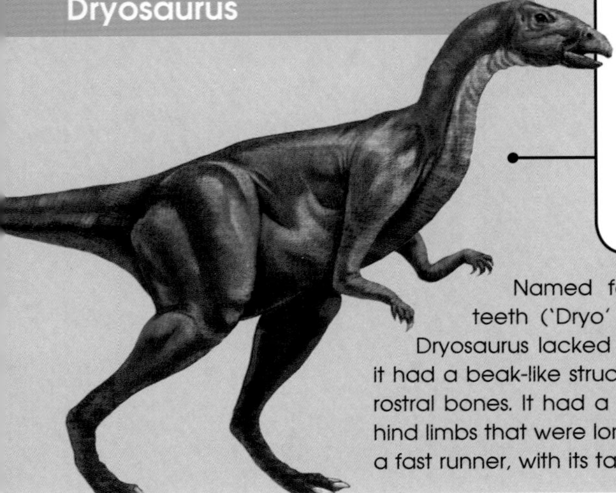

Named for its oak-leaf shaped cheek teeth ('Dryo' meaning 'oak' in Greek), the Dryosaurus lacked upper frontal teeth — instead, it had a beak-like structure formed by overdeveloped rostral bones. It had a lightweight body and powerful hind limbs that were longer than its forelimbs, making it a fast runner, with its tail helping keep balance.

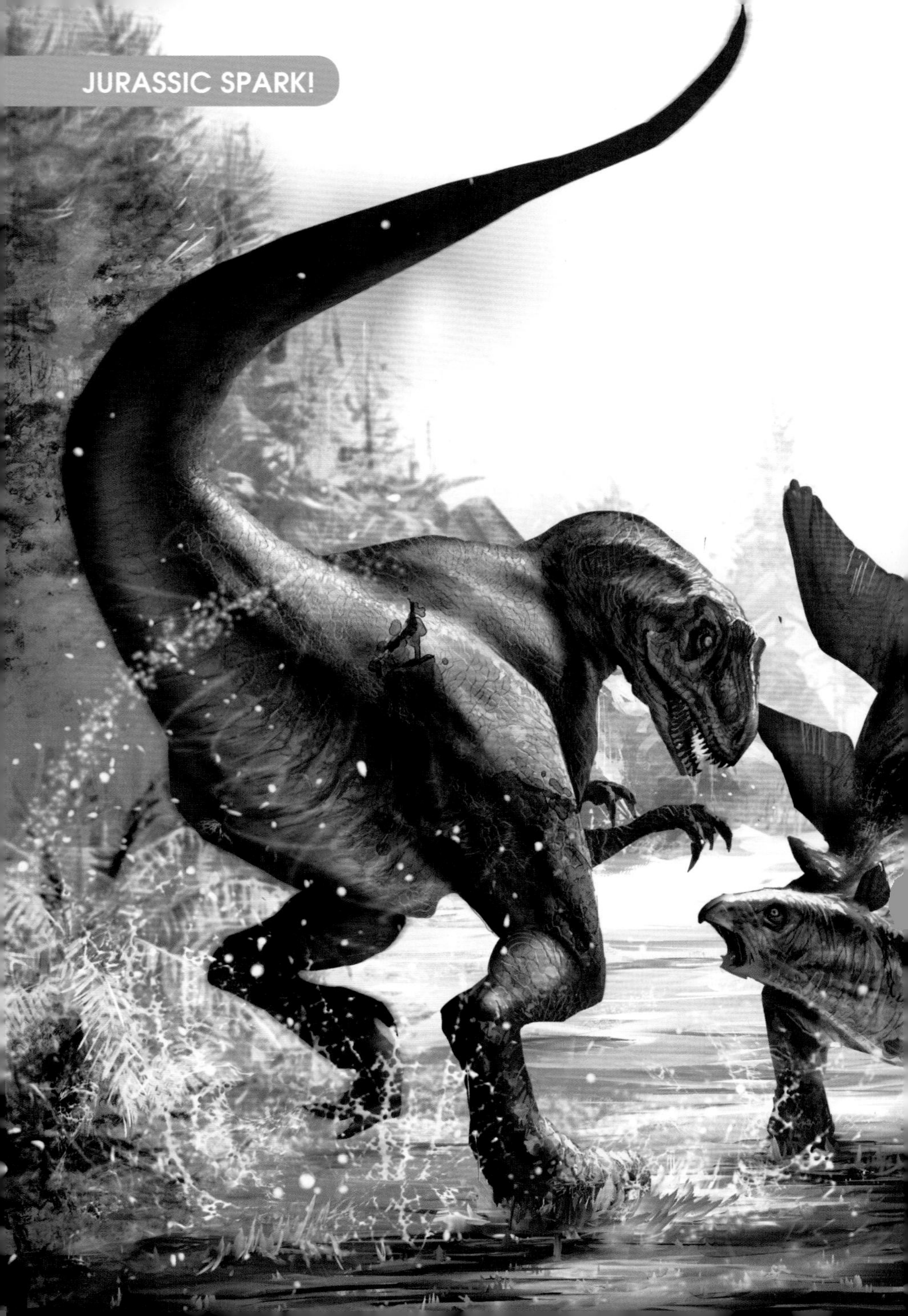

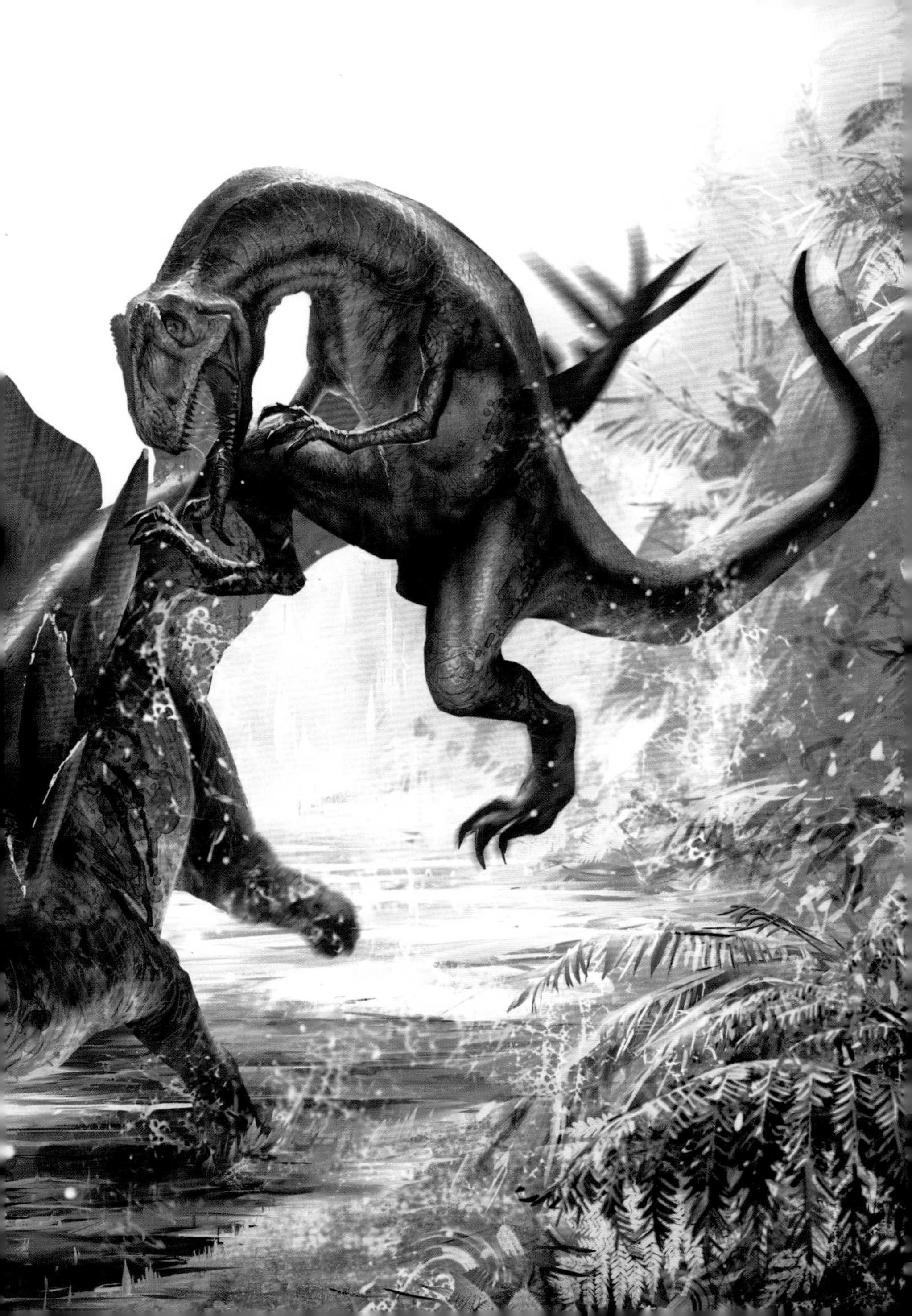

Though primitive birds may have had feathers, they were still mostly flightless. The next stage in bird evolution would involve losing most (if not all) of their teeth, followed by tail shortening. This was followed by their bones becoming hollow, enabling them to reduce body weight sufficiently facilitating actual flight. Stronger bones, especially in the ribs (to make up for being hollow) and flexible necks also helped.

The Iberomesornis was an early Ornithotoracine during the Cretaceous.

Archaeopteryx

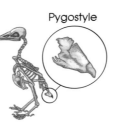

Confuciusornithidae

Enantiornithines

Ornithothoraces
(alula feathers)

Pygostyle bone

Pygostyle

Pygostylia
(Reduced and fused tail vertebrae)

Alula feathers

Alula feathers were early feathers found on Ornithothoraces that helped them maintain stability at low speeds; indeed, modern birds still have alula feathers for the same purpose. The Ornithothorace Enantiornithine had them, but it went extinct after the Cretaceous.

Shortening tails

Less than 25 vertebral bones; different from other manitoraptors. Loss of surplus bone weight facilitated flight.

Pygostyle

Confuciusornithidae and Ornithothoraces were a little more advanced than Archaeopteryx, as their 5 final vertebral bones fused together into a bony plate called the "pygostyle."

Alula feathers

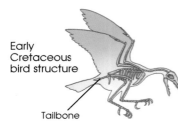

Early Cretaceous bird structure

Tailbone

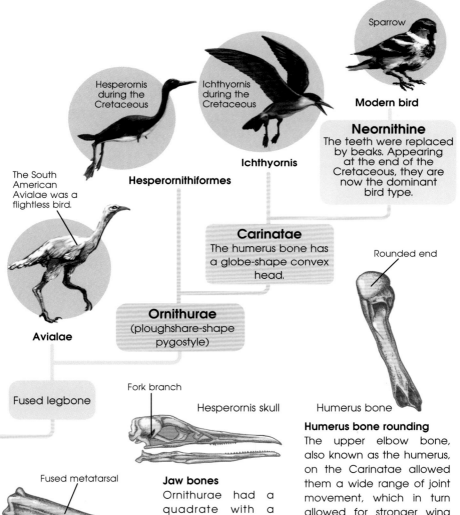

Sparrow

Hesperornis during the Cretaceous

Ichthyornis during the Cretaceous

Modern bird

Neornithine
The teeth were replaced by beaks. Appearing at the end of the Cretaceous, they are now the dominant bird type.

Ichthyornis

Hesperornithiformes

The South American Avialae was a flightless bird.

Carinatae
The humerus bone has a globe-shape convex head.

Rounded end

Ornithurae
(ploughshare-shape pygostyle)

Avialae

Fused legbone

Fork branch

Hesperornis skull

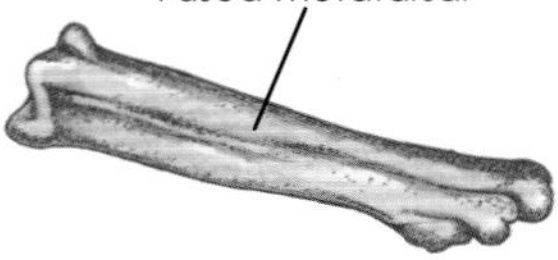

Humerus bone

Fused metatarsal

Humerus bone rounding
The upper elbow bone, also known as the humerus, on the Carinatae allowed them a wide range of joint movement, which in turn allowed for stronger wing movements.

Jaw bones
Ornithurae had a quadrate with a sharp orbital process. (A squarish bone with which the jaw articulates)

Fused legbones
The metatarsal bones of the Ornithurae had lengthened and fused into the tarsometatarsal, a foot bone.

JONESING FOR THE JURASSIC

Ornitholestes

With a heavily built skull and large eyes, Ornitholestes was an effective, intelligent hunter, and an extremely fast runner. Its excellent eyesight, allowed it to spot well-hidden prey. Its amazingly flexible forelimbs might have been used to grasp prey with both "hands" simultaneously.

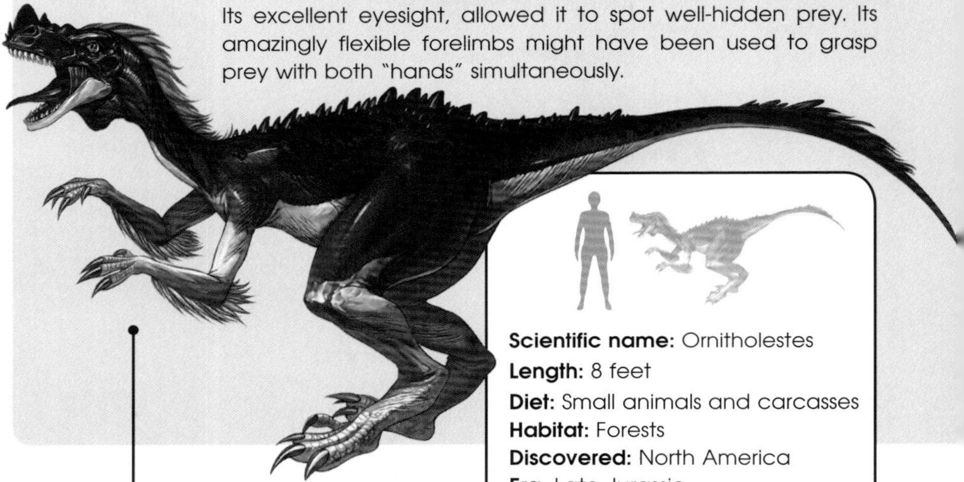

Scientific name: Ornitholestes
Length: 8 feet
Diet: Small animals and carcasses
Habitat: Forests
Discovered: North America
Era: Late Jurassic

JONESING FOR THE JURASSIC

Gasosaurus

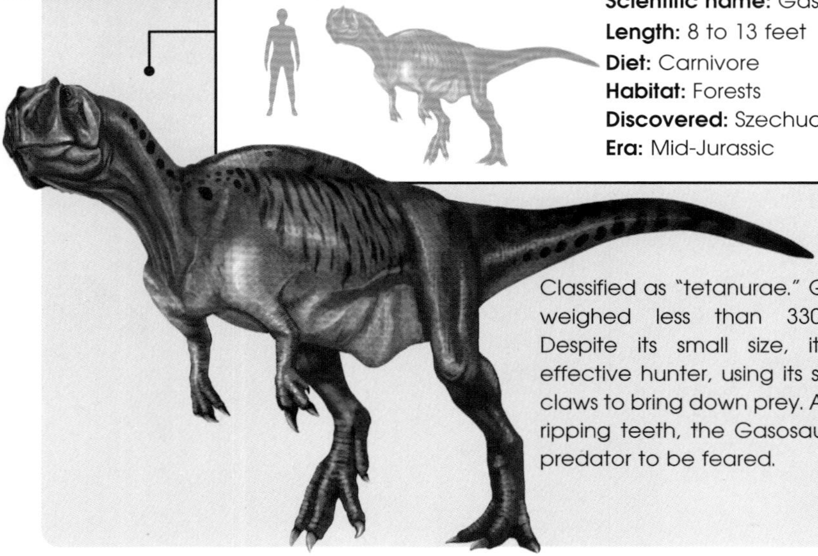

Scientific name: Gasosaurus
Length: 8 to 13 feet
Diet: Carnivore
Habitat: Forests
Discovered: Szechuan, China
Era: Mid-Jurassic

Classified as "tetanurae." Gasosaurus weighed less than 330 pounds. Despite its small size, it was an effective hunter, using its speed and claws to bring down prey. Armed with ripping teeth, the Gasosaurus was a predator to be feared.

CHAPTER 6

PATH-FLOUNDERS

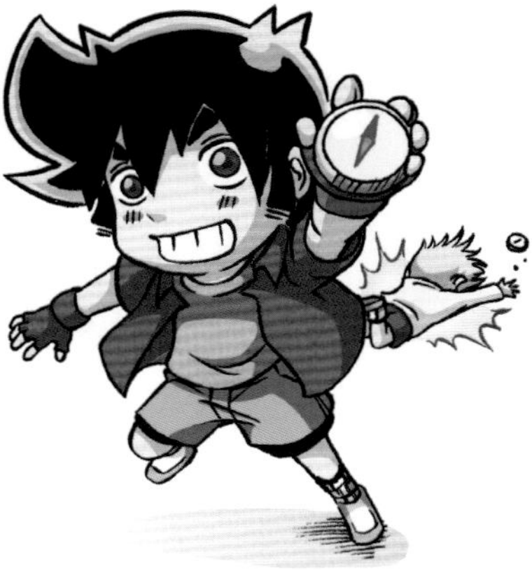

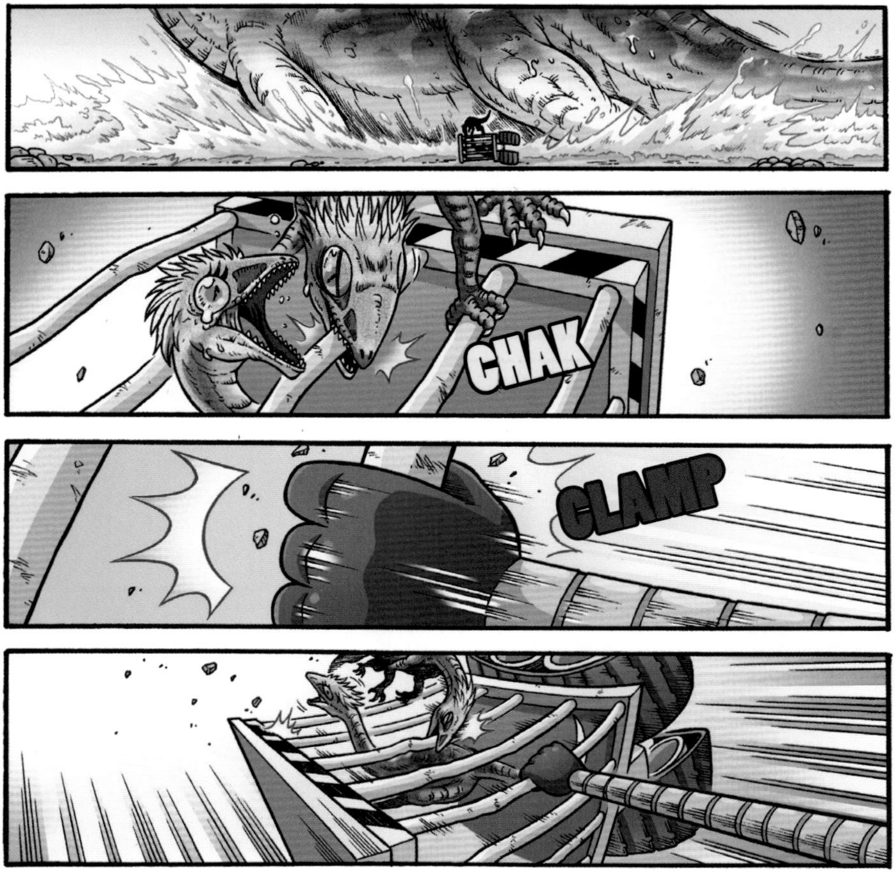
CHAK
CLAMP

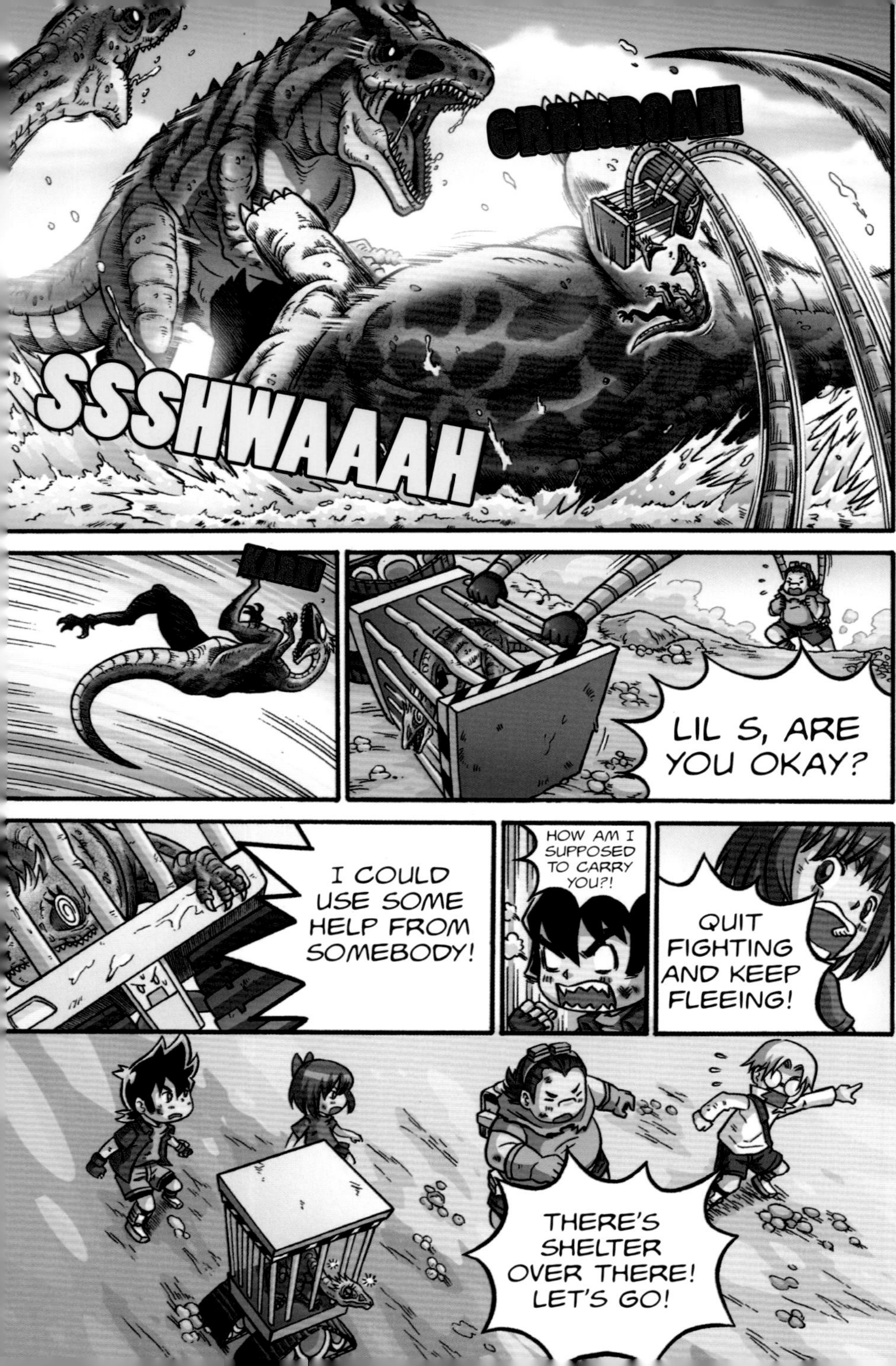
CRRRROAH!!
SSSHWAAAAH
LIL S, ARE YOU OKAY?
I COULD USE SOME HELP FROM SOMEBODY!
HOW AM I SUPPOSED TO CARRY YOU?!
QUIT FIGHTING AND KEEP FLEEING!
THERE'S SHELTER OVER THERE! LET'S GO!

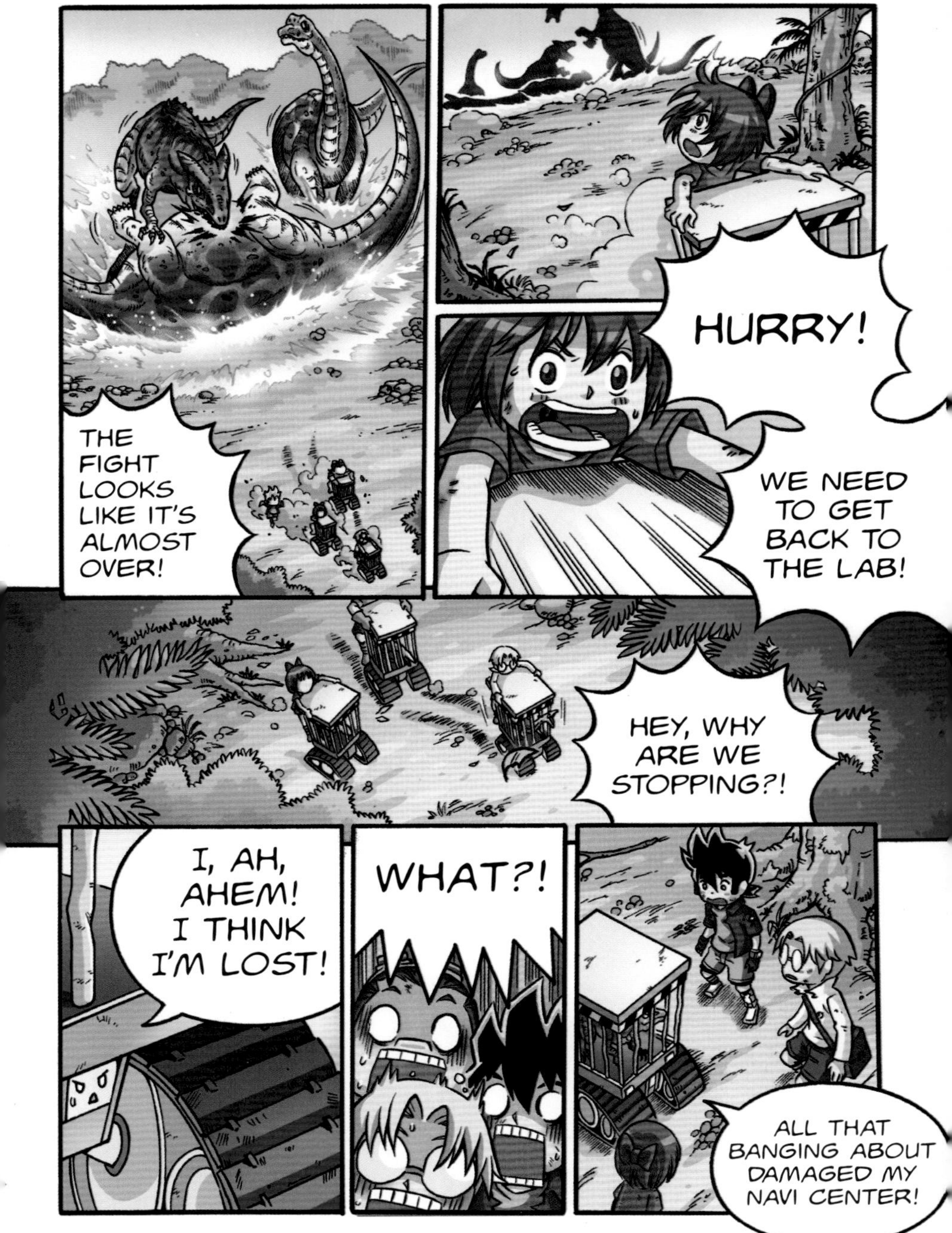
THE FIGHT LOOKS LIKE IT'S ALMOST OVER!
HURRY!
WE NEED TO GET BACK TO THE LAB!
HEY, WHY ARE WE STOPPING?!
I, AH, AHEM! I THINK I'M LOST!
WHAT?!
ALL THAT BANGING ABOUT DAMAGED MY NAVI CENTER!

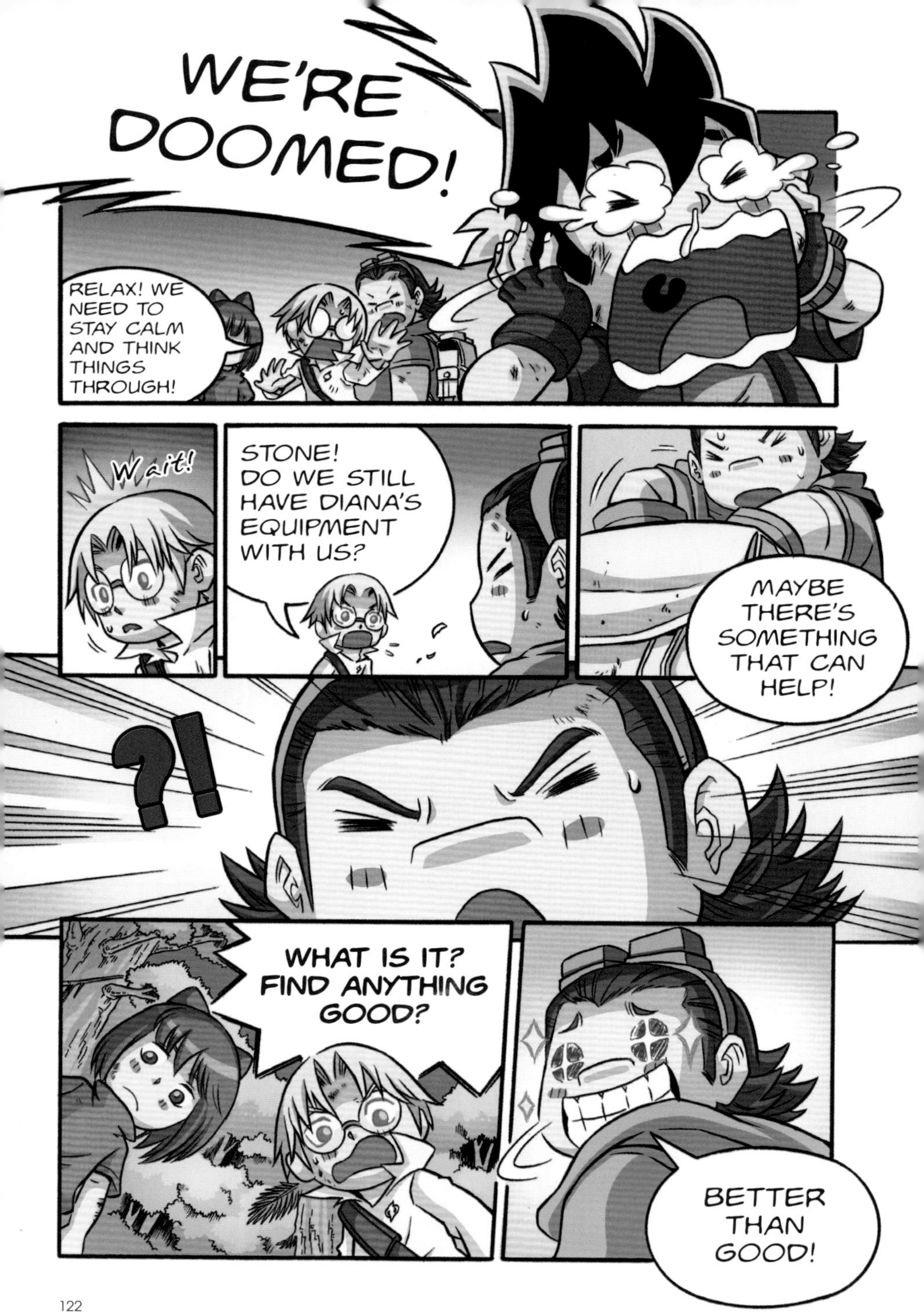
WE'RE DOOMED!
RELAX! WE NEED TO STAY CALM AND THINK THINGS THROUGH!
Wait!
STONE! DO WE STILL HAVE DIANA'S EQUIPMENT WITH US?
MAYBE THERE'S SOMETHING THAT CAN HELP!
?!
WHAT IS IT? FIND ANYTHING GOOD?
BETTER THAN GOOD!

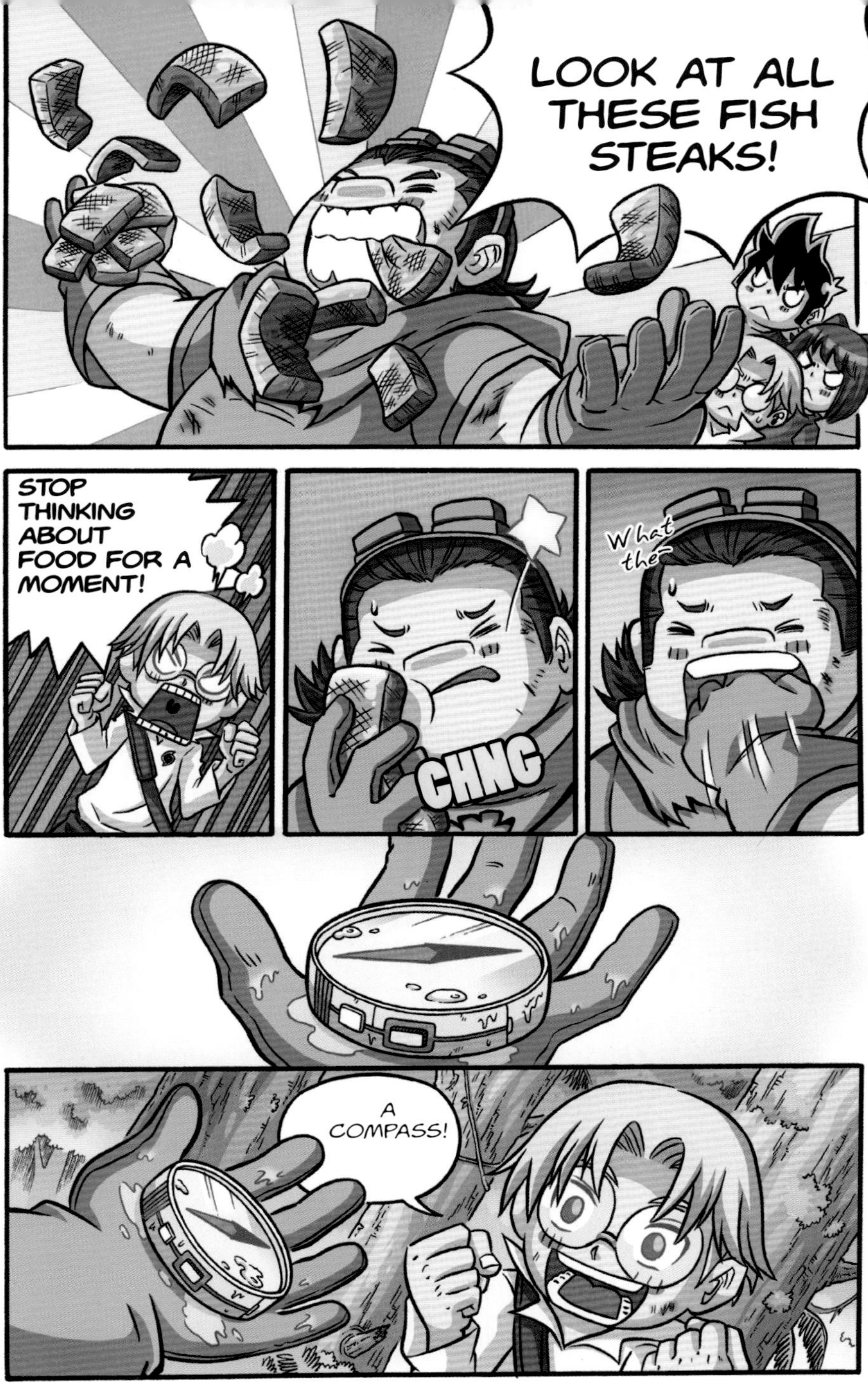
LOOK AT ALL THESE FISH STEAKS!
STOP THINKING ABOUT FOOD FOR A MOMENT!
CHNG
What the—
A COMPASS!

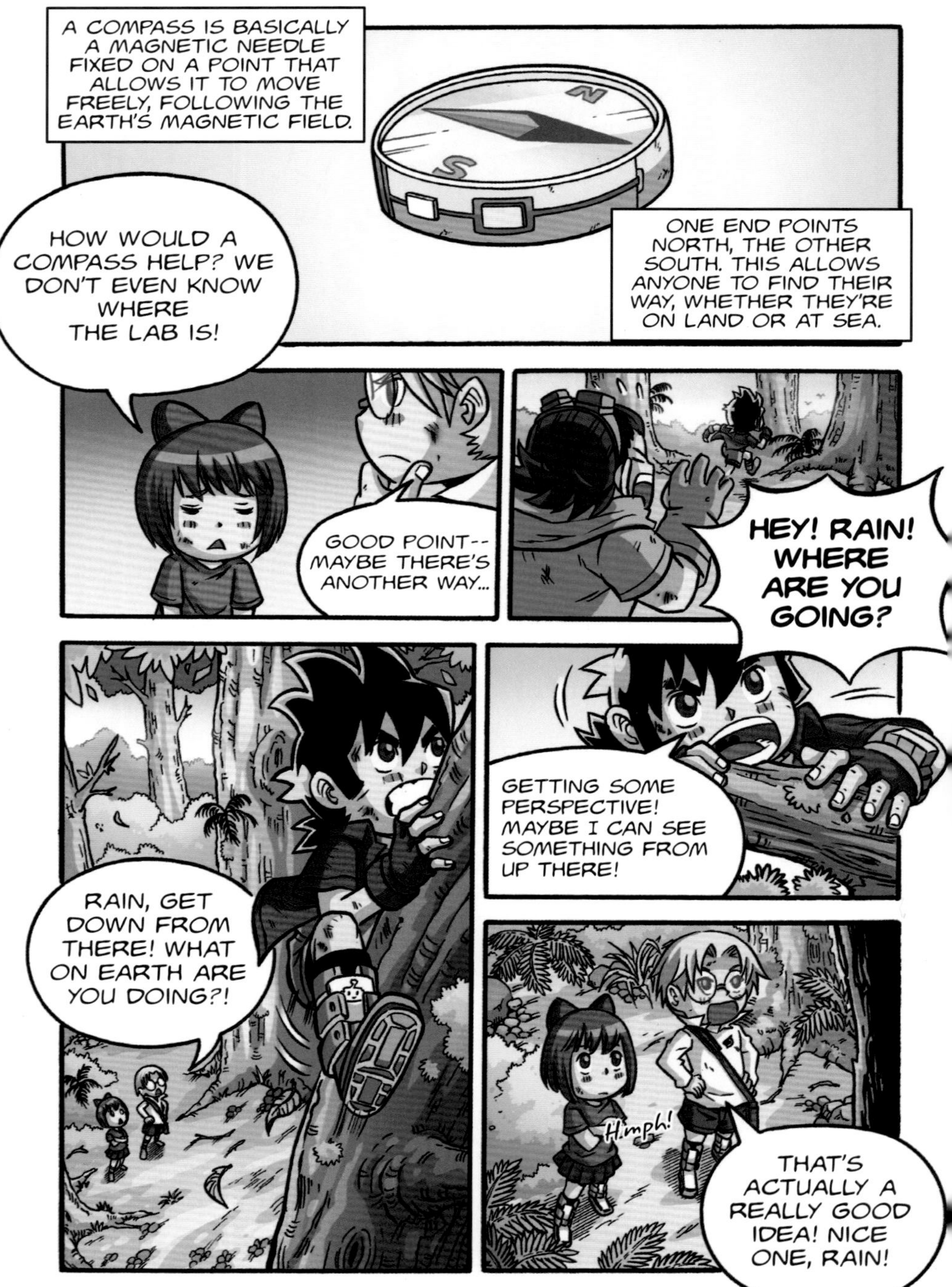
A COMPASS IS BASICALLY A MAGNETIC NEEDLE FIXED ON A POINT THAT ALLOWS IT TO MOVE FREELY, FOLLOWING THE EARTH'S MAGNETIC FIELD.
N
S
ONE END POINTS NORTH, THE OTHER SOUTH. THIS ALLOWS ANYONE TO FIND THEIR WAY, WHETHER THEY'RE ON LAND OR AT SEA.
HOW WOULD A COMPASS HELP? WE DON'T EVEN KNOW WHERE THE LAB IS!
GOOD POINT--MAYBE THERE'S ANOTHER WAY...
HEY! RAIN! WHERE ARE YOU GOING?
GETTING SOME PERSPECTIVE! MAYBE I CAN SEE SOMETHING FROM UP THERE!
RAIN, GET DOWN FROM THERE! WHAT ON EARTH ARE YOU DOING?!
Hmph!
THAT'S ACTUALLY A REALLY GOOD IDEA! NICE ONE, RAIN!

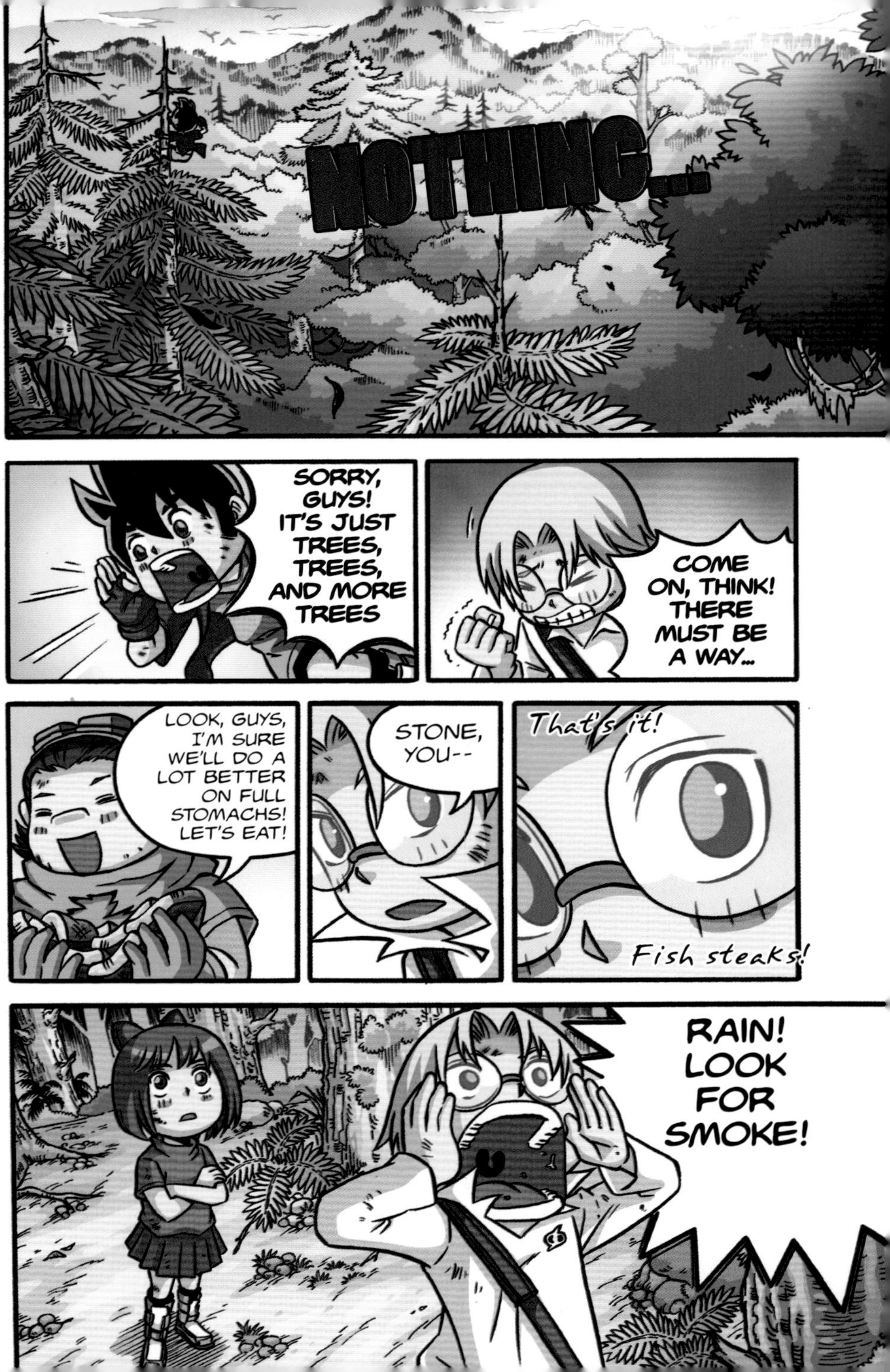
NOTHING...
SORRY, GUYS! IT'S JUST TREES, TREES, AND MORE TREES
COME ON, THINK! THERE MUST BE A WAY...
LOOK, GUYS, I'M SURE WE'LL DO A LOT BETTER ON FULL STOMACHS! LET'S EAT!
STONE, YOU--
That's it!
Fish steaks!
RAIN! LOOK FOR SMOKE!

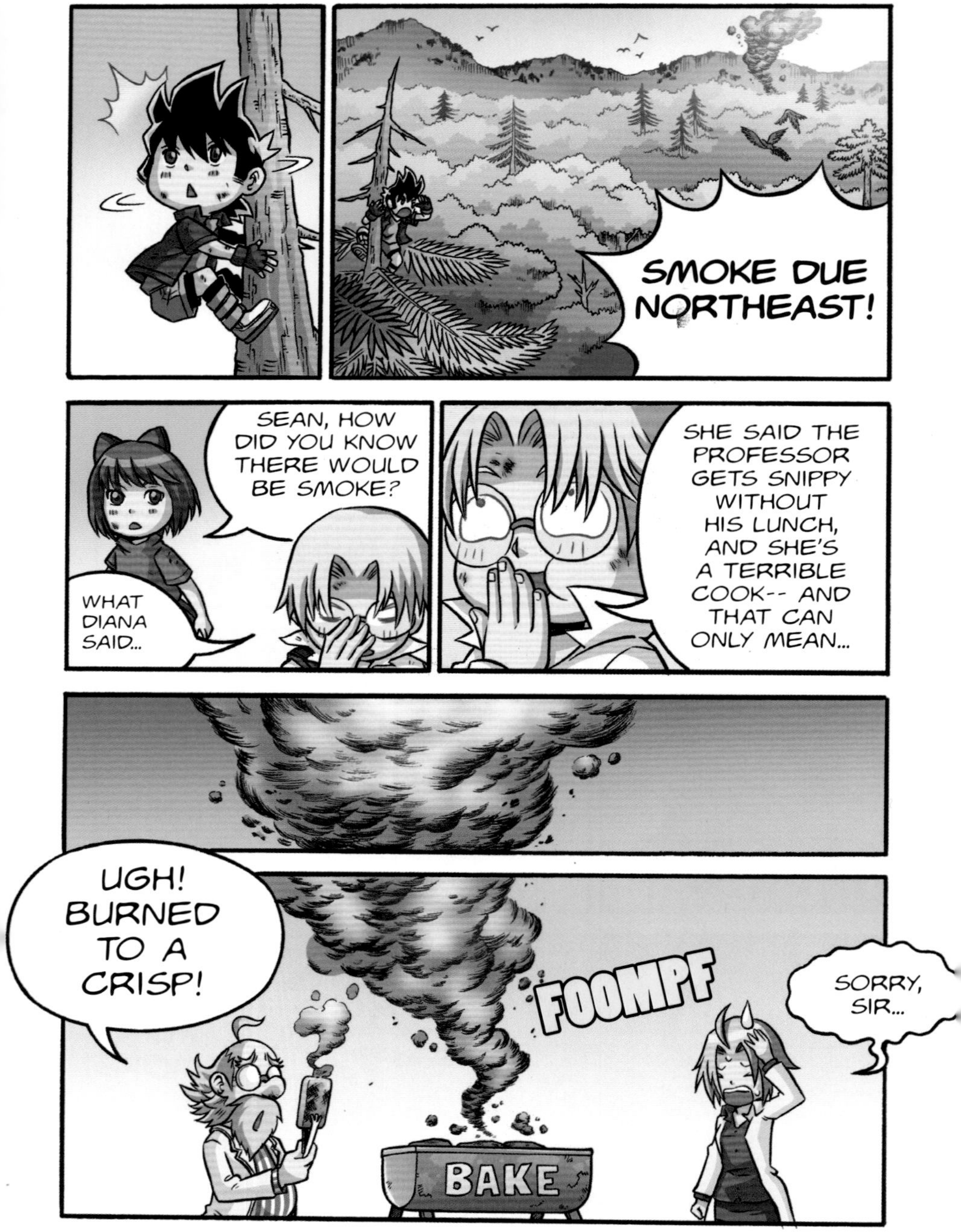
SMOKE DUE NORTHEAST!
SEAN, HOW DID YOU KNOW THERE WOULD BE SMOKE?
WHAT DIANA SAID...
SHE SAID THE PROFESSOR GETS SNIPPY WITHOUT HIS LUNCH, AND SHE'S A TERRIBLE COOK-- AND THAT CAN ONLY MEAN...
UGH! BURNED TO A CRISP!
FOOMPF
BAKE
SORRY, SIR...

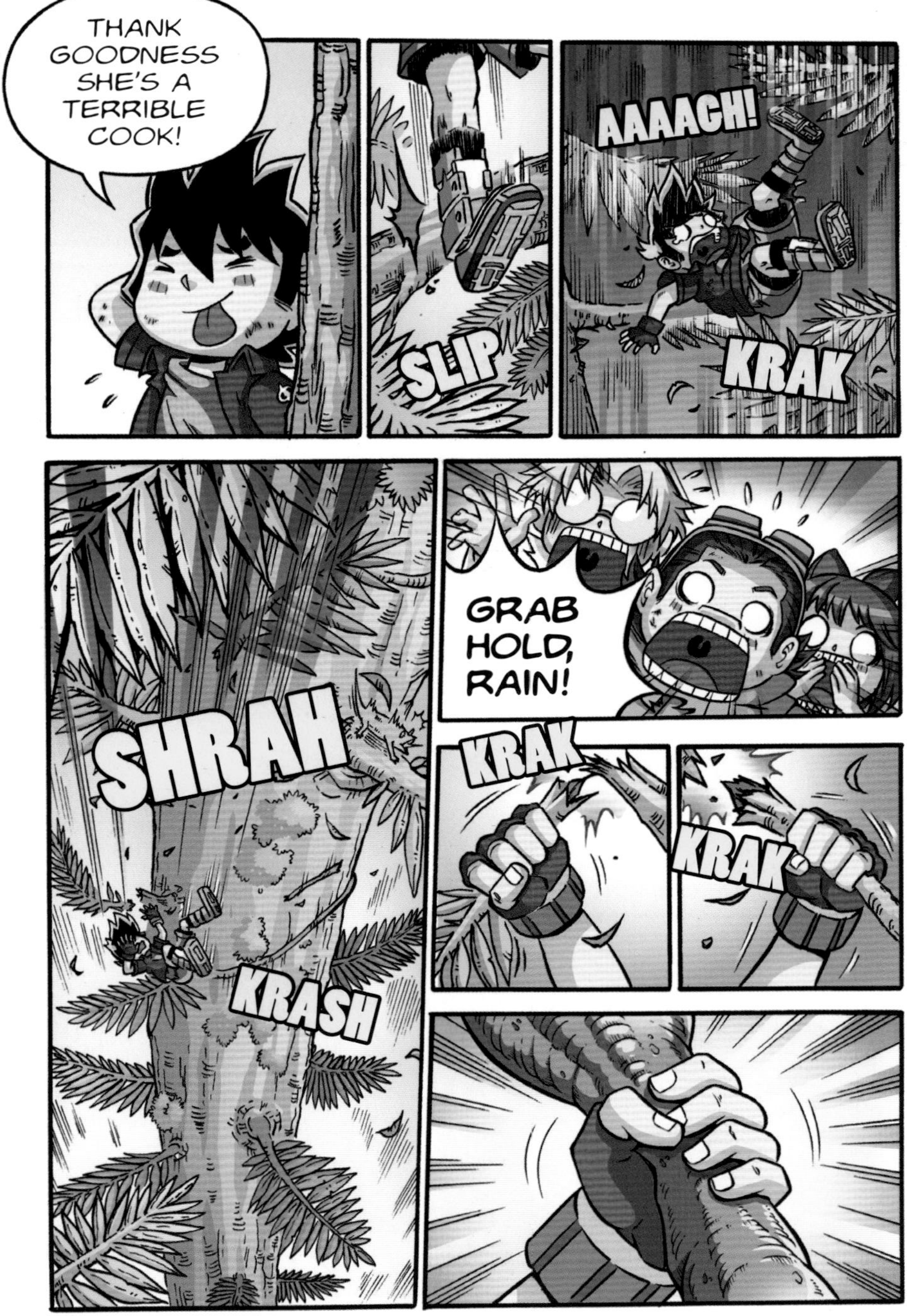
THANK GOODNESS SHE'S A TERRIBLE COOK!
SLIP
AAAACH!
KRAK
SHRAH
KRASH
GRAB HOLD, RAIN!
KRAK
KRAK

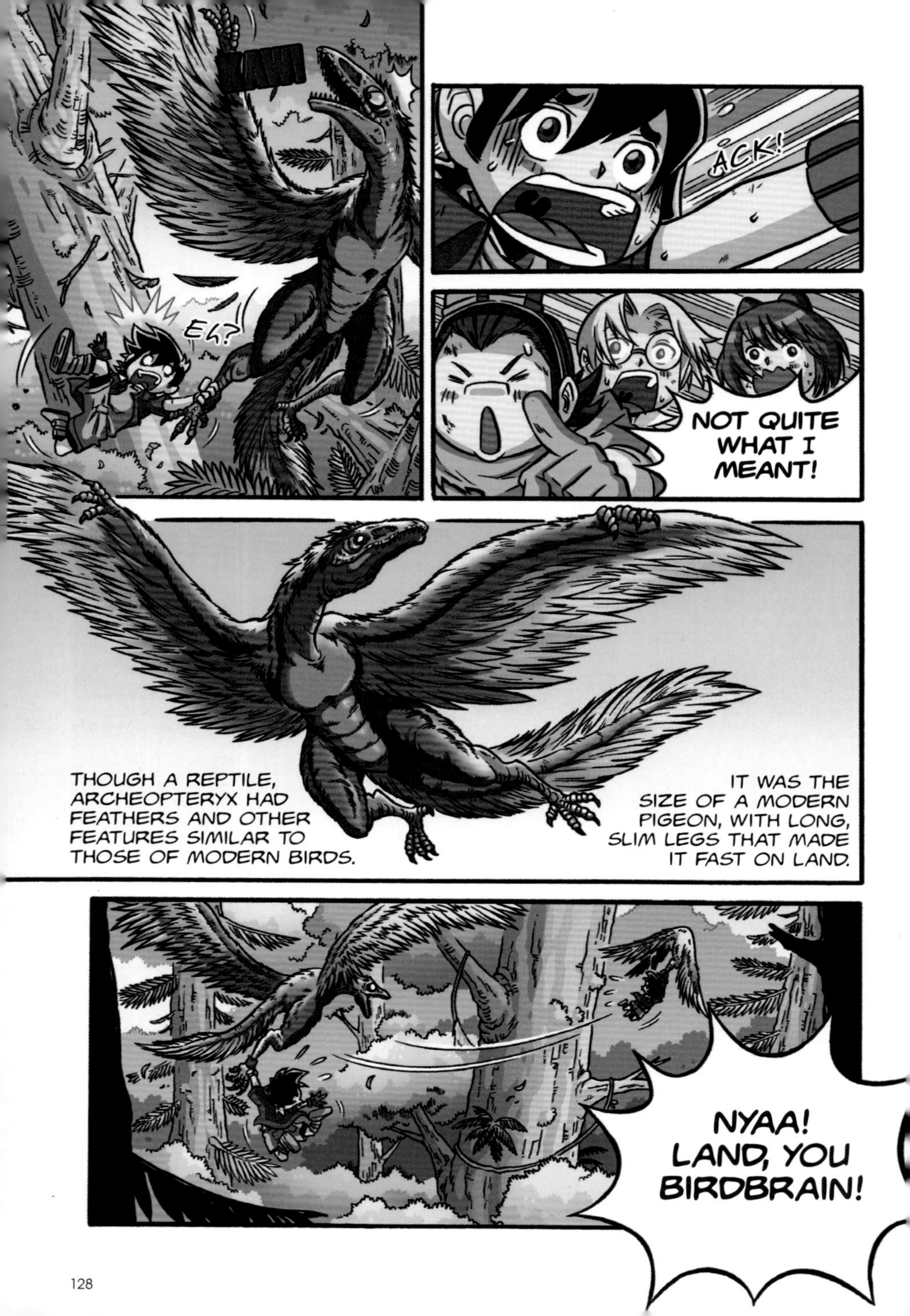
KAW!
EH?
ACK!
NOT QUITE WHAT I MEANT!
THOUGH A REPTILE, ARCHEOPTERYX HAD FEATHERS AND OTHER FEATURES SIMILAR TO THOSE OF MODERN BIRDS.
IT WAS THE SIZE OF A MODERN PIGEON, WITH LONG, SLIM LEGS THAT MADE IT FAST ON LAND.
NYAA! LAND, YOU BIRDBRAIN!

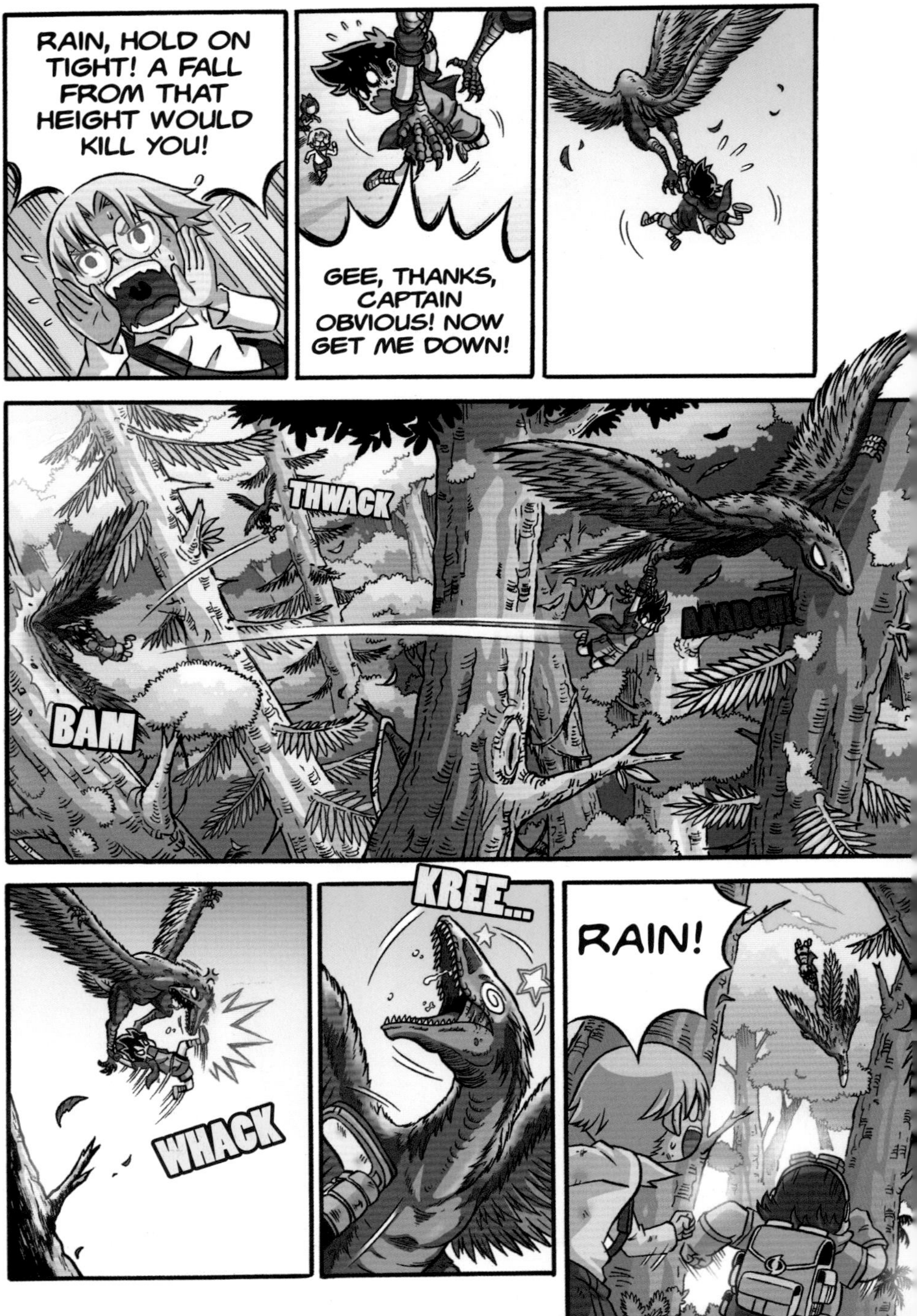
RAIN, HOLD ON TIGHT! A FALL FROM THAT HEIGHT WOULD KILL YOU!
GEE, THANKS, CAPTAIN OBVIOUS! NOW GET ME DOWN!
THWACK
AAARGH!
BAM
WHACK
KREE...
RAIN!

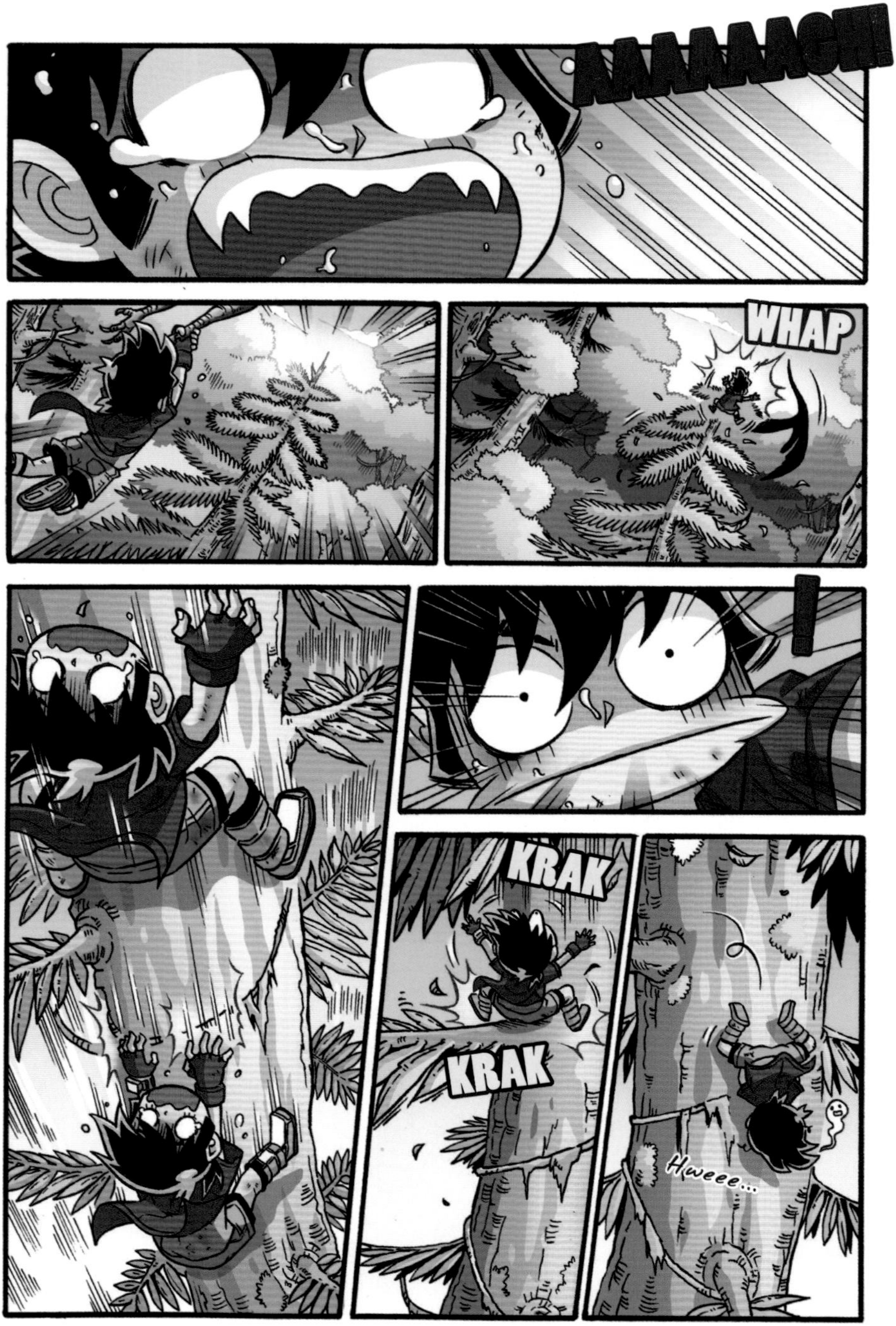
AAAAAAACH!!
WHAP
!
KRAK
KRAK
Hweee...

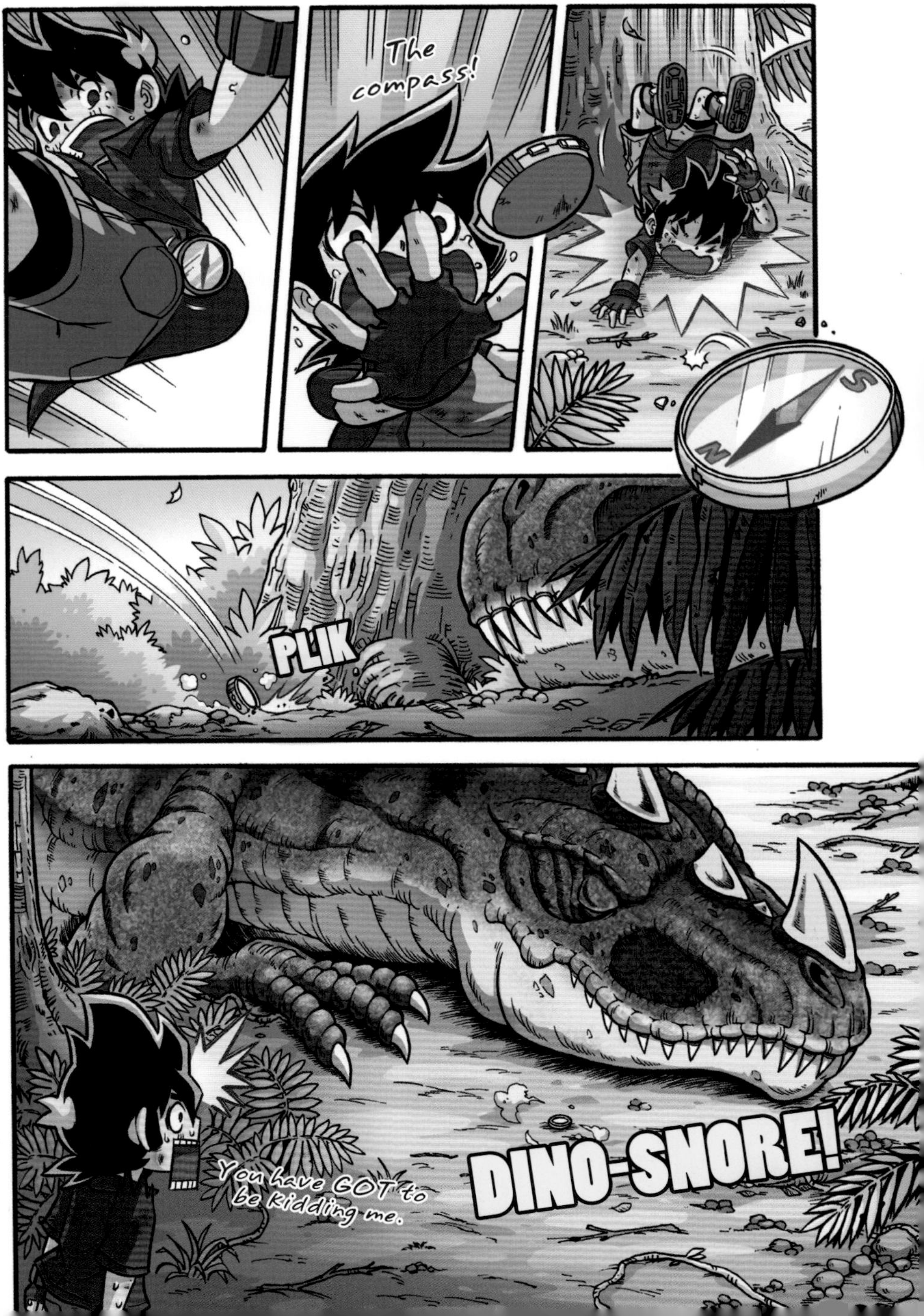
The compass!
PLIK
You have GOT to be kidding me.
DINO-SNORE!

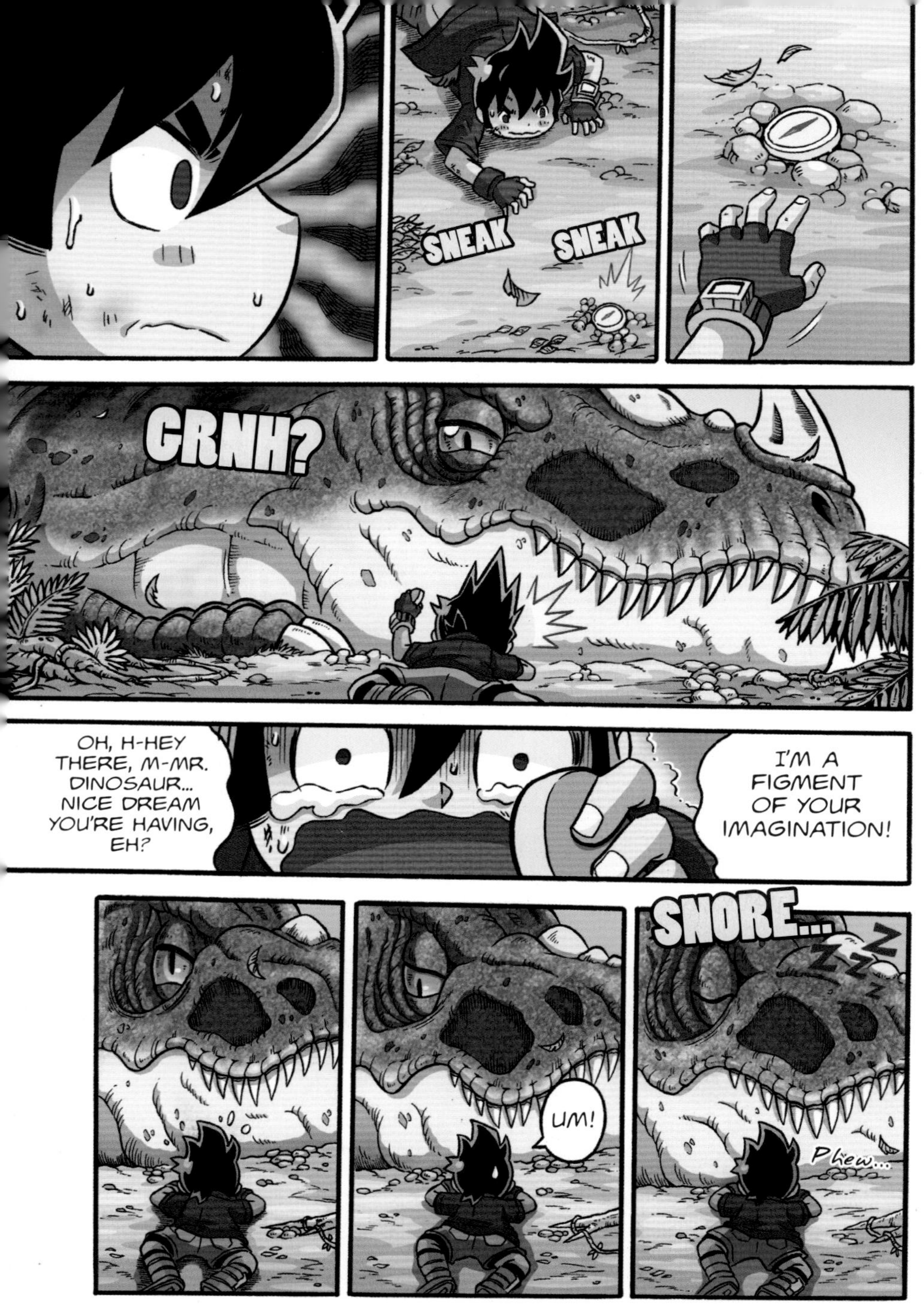
SNEAK
SNEAK
GRNH?
OH, H-HEY THERE, M-MR. DINOSAUR... NICE DREAM YOU'RE HAVING, EH?
I'M A FIGMENT OF YOUR IMAGINATION!
UM!
SNORE...
Phew...

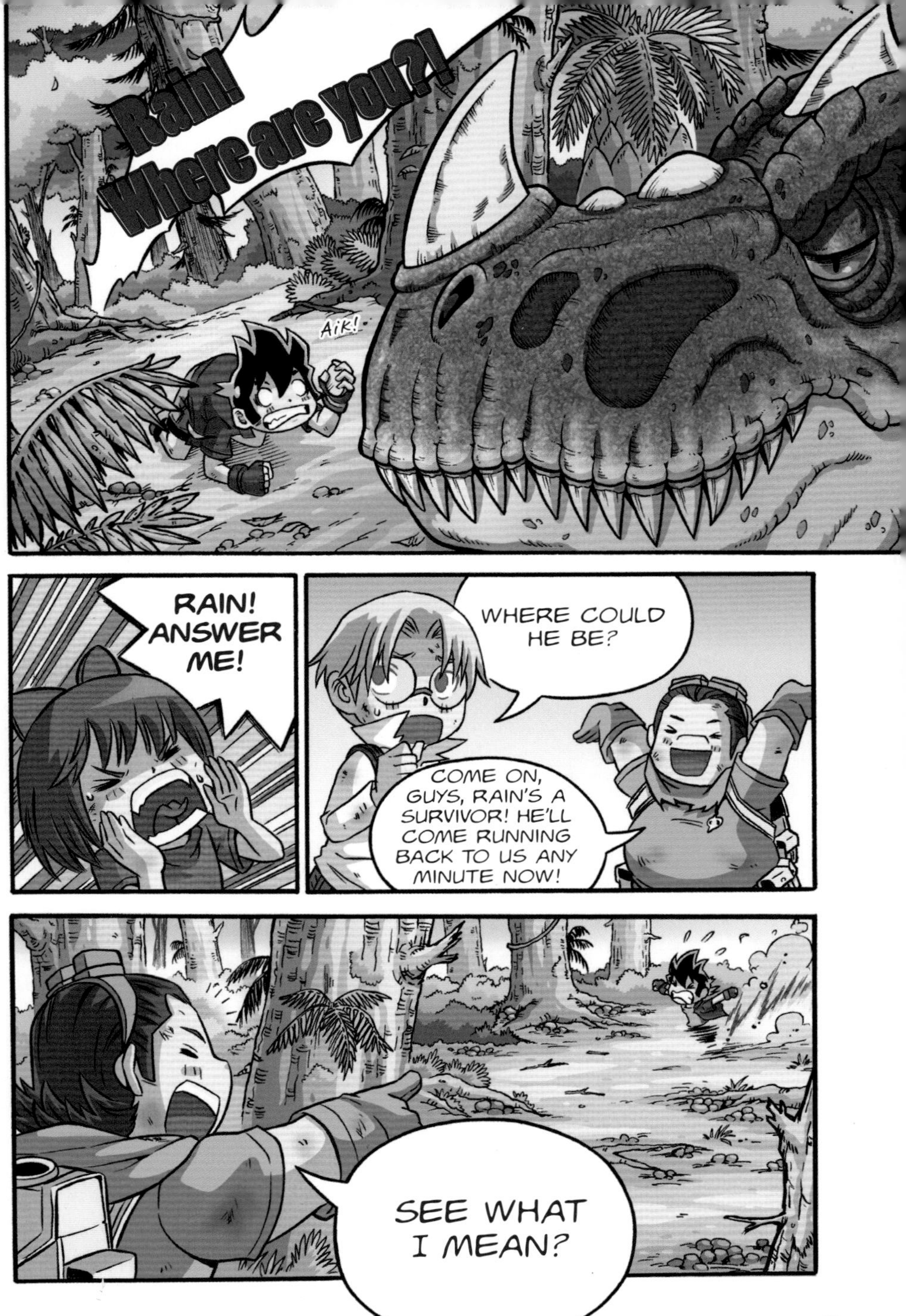

Rain! Where are you?!
AiK!
RAIN! ANSWER ME!
WHERE COULD HE BE?
COME ON, GUYS, RAIN'S A SURVIVOR! HE'LL COME RUNNING BACK TO US ANY MINUTE NOW!
SEE WHAT I MEAN?

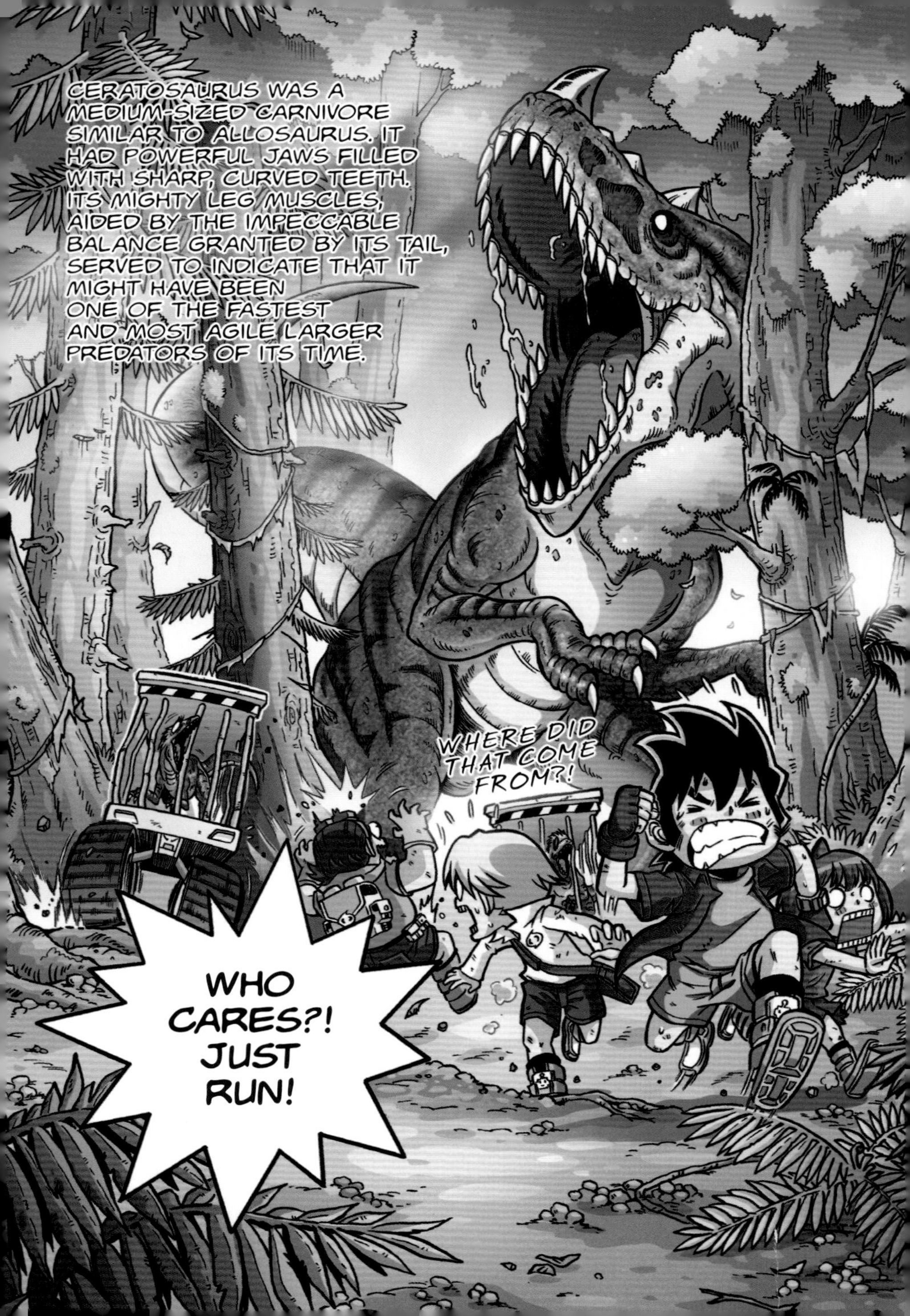
CERATOSAURUS WAS A MEDIUM-SIZED CARNIVORE SIMILAR TO ALLOSAURUS. IT HAD POWERFUL JAWS FILLED WITH SHARP, CURVED TEETH. ITS MIGHTY LEG MUSCLES, AIDED BY THE IMPECCABLE BALANCE GRANTED BY ITS TAIL, SERVED TO INDICATE THAT IT MIGHT HAVE BEEN ONE OF THE FASTEST AND MOST AGILE LARGER PREDATORS OF ITS TIME.
WHERE DID THAT COME FROM?!
WHO CARES?! JUST RUN!

What qualifies the Archaeopteryx as a primitive bird? Wings with both primary and secondary feathers

Scientific name: Archaeopteryx
Length: 2 feet
Diet: Carnivore
Habitat: Tropical areas
Discovered: Western Europe
Era: Late Jurassic

Crow-sized Archaeopteryx was covered in feathers and had plenty of birdlike features. Following its discovery in 1861, its status as one of the first primitive birds has never been challenged, and it is still the focus of much research. Due to its relatively small chest area, it has been debated extensively whether it could have accommodated chest muscles powerful enough for flight.

Taking wing; Dinosaur to bird evolution

In order to maintain stability, primitive bird bones slowly hollowed out and in some cases, even fused together. The chart below shows the specifics, but in general, chest bones and forelimbs became larger, bones hollowed out and tails became shorter and wider.

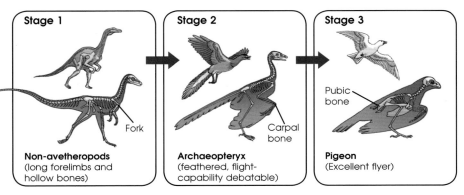

Stage 1

Fork

Non-avetheropods
(long forelimbs and hollow bones)

Stage 2

Carpal bone

Archaeopteryx
(feathered, flight-capability debatable)

Stage 3

Pubic bone

Pigeon
(Excellent flyer)

Archaeopteryx — not a bird?

In July 2011, examination of a "Xiaotingia zhengi" fossil by a team from the institute of Vertebrate Paleontology and Paleoanthropology (IVPP) in China raised doubts of the Archaeopteryx's "bird" status. Much of the paleontological community, however, were unconvinced.

JURASSIC SQUAWK!

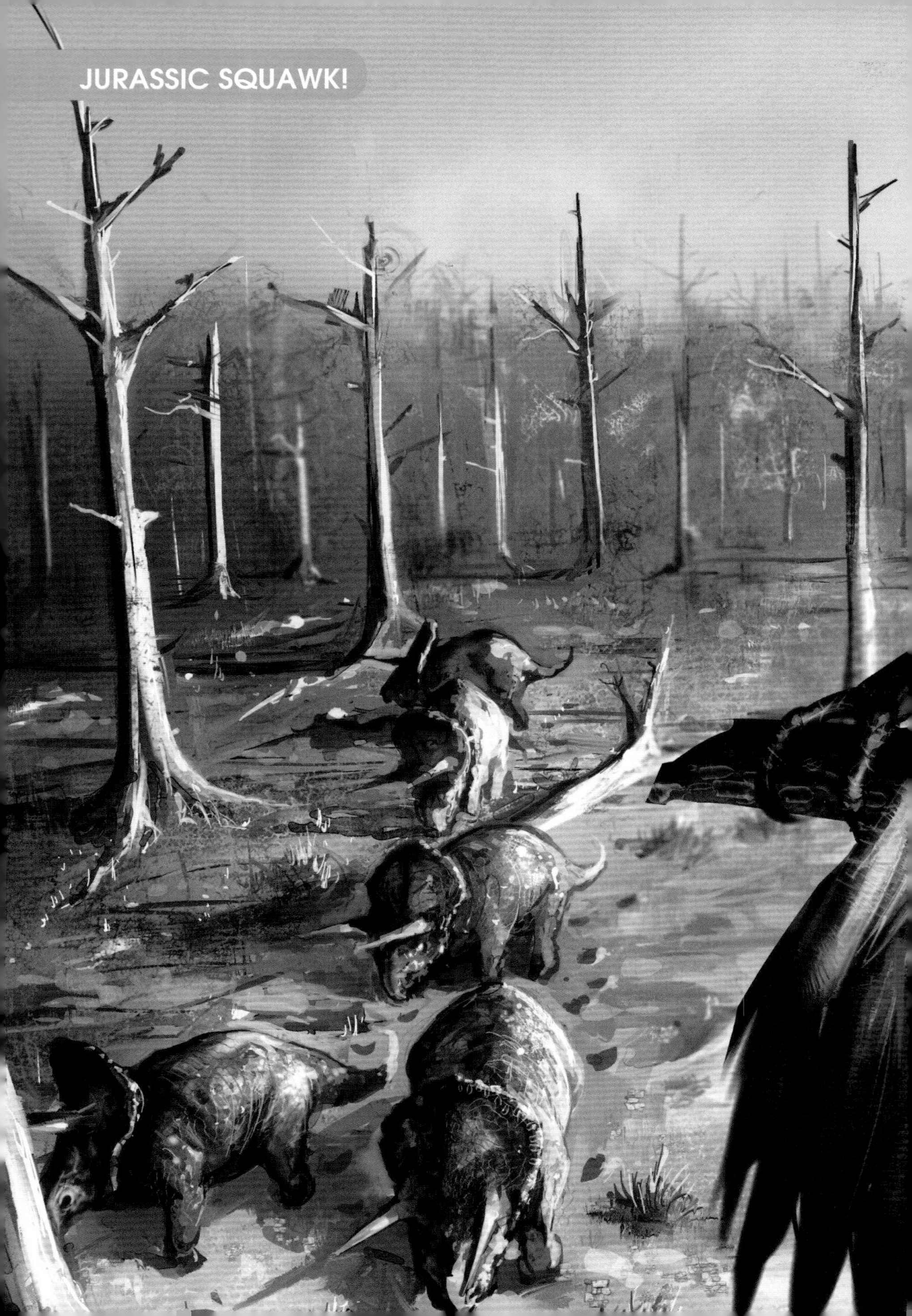

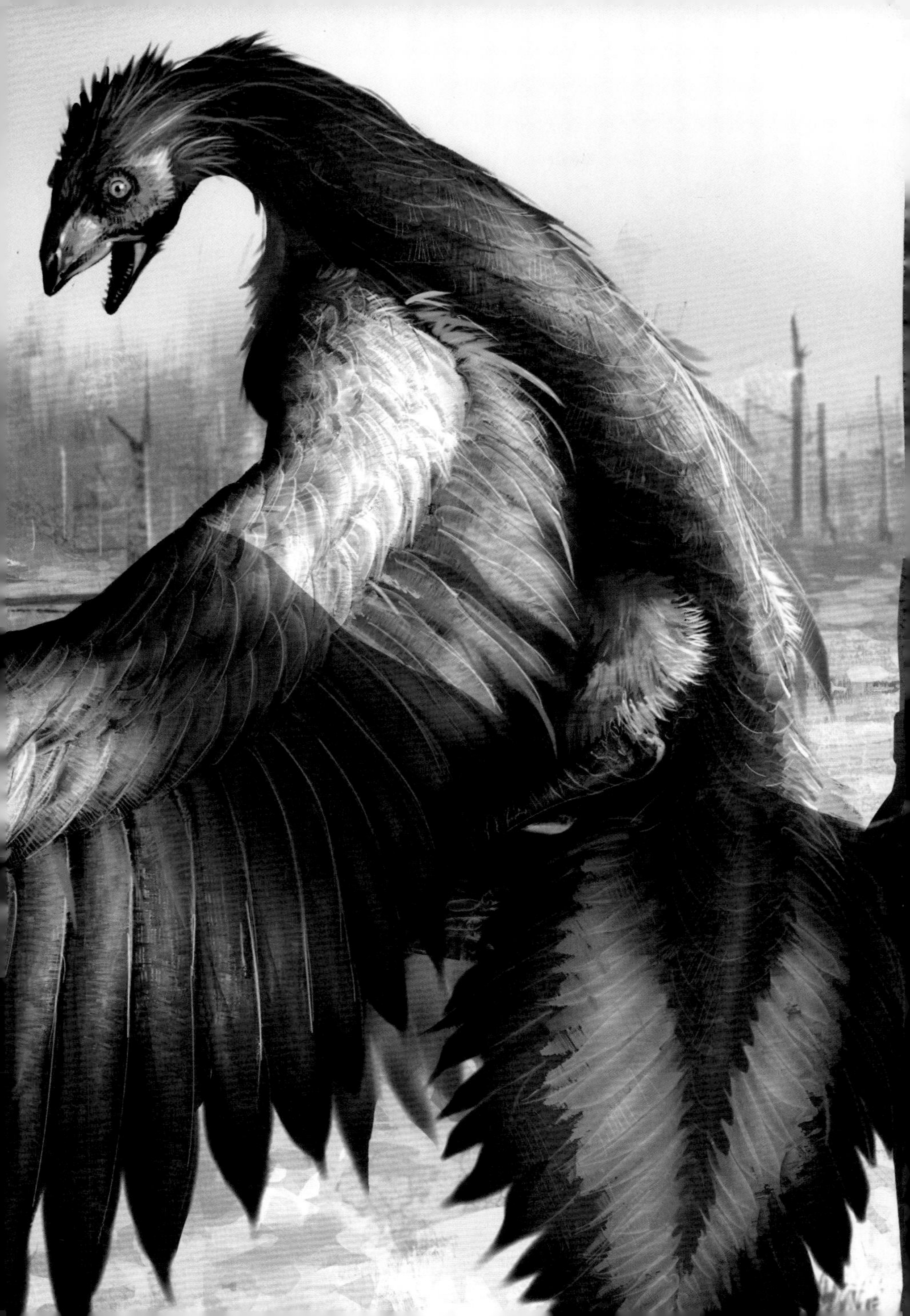

JONESING FOR THE JURASSIC

Thalassodromeus

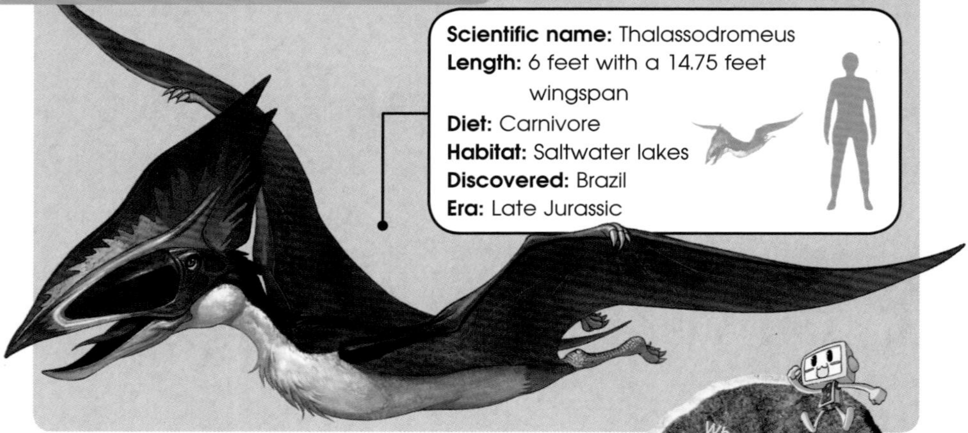

Scientific name: Thalassodromeus
Length: 6 feet with a 14.75 feet wingspan
Diet: Carnivore
Habitat: Saltwater lakes
Discovered: Brazil
Era: Late Jurassic

Thalassodromeus' unique traits include a knifelike "crown" 4.6 feet in length, which took up almost 75% of its head! The crown helped it steer, control body temperature and attract mates. It is believed that Thalassodromeus' diet consisted primarily of fish.

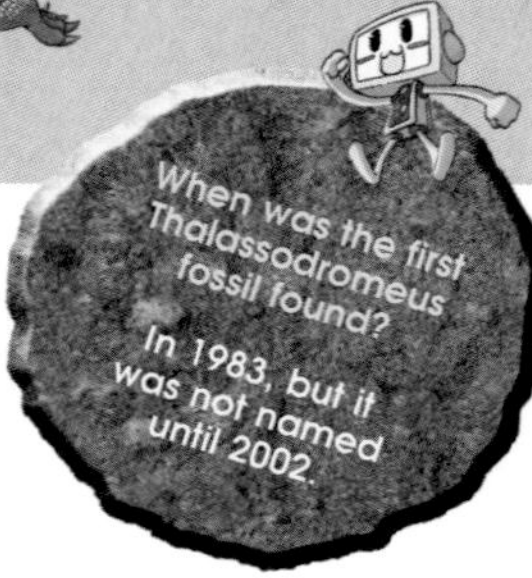
When was the first Thalassodromeus fossil found?
In 1983, but it was not named until 2002.

JONESING FOR THE JURASSIC

Anurognathus

Scientific name: Anurognathus
Length: 3.5 inches with a 19.5 inch wingspan
Diet: Insectivore
Habitat: Savannah
Discovered: Germany
Era: Late Jurassic

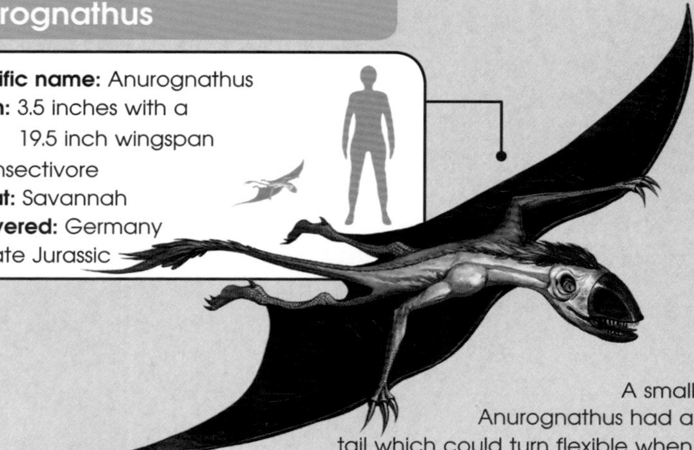

A small pterosaur, Anurognathus had a short, rigid tail which could turn flexible when hunting to increase maneuverability. Its many needle-like teeth came in handy for snaring insects, but its tiny, stubby head was one of the few features it did not share with "true" pterosaurs.

CHAPTER 7

FOOD FIGHT!

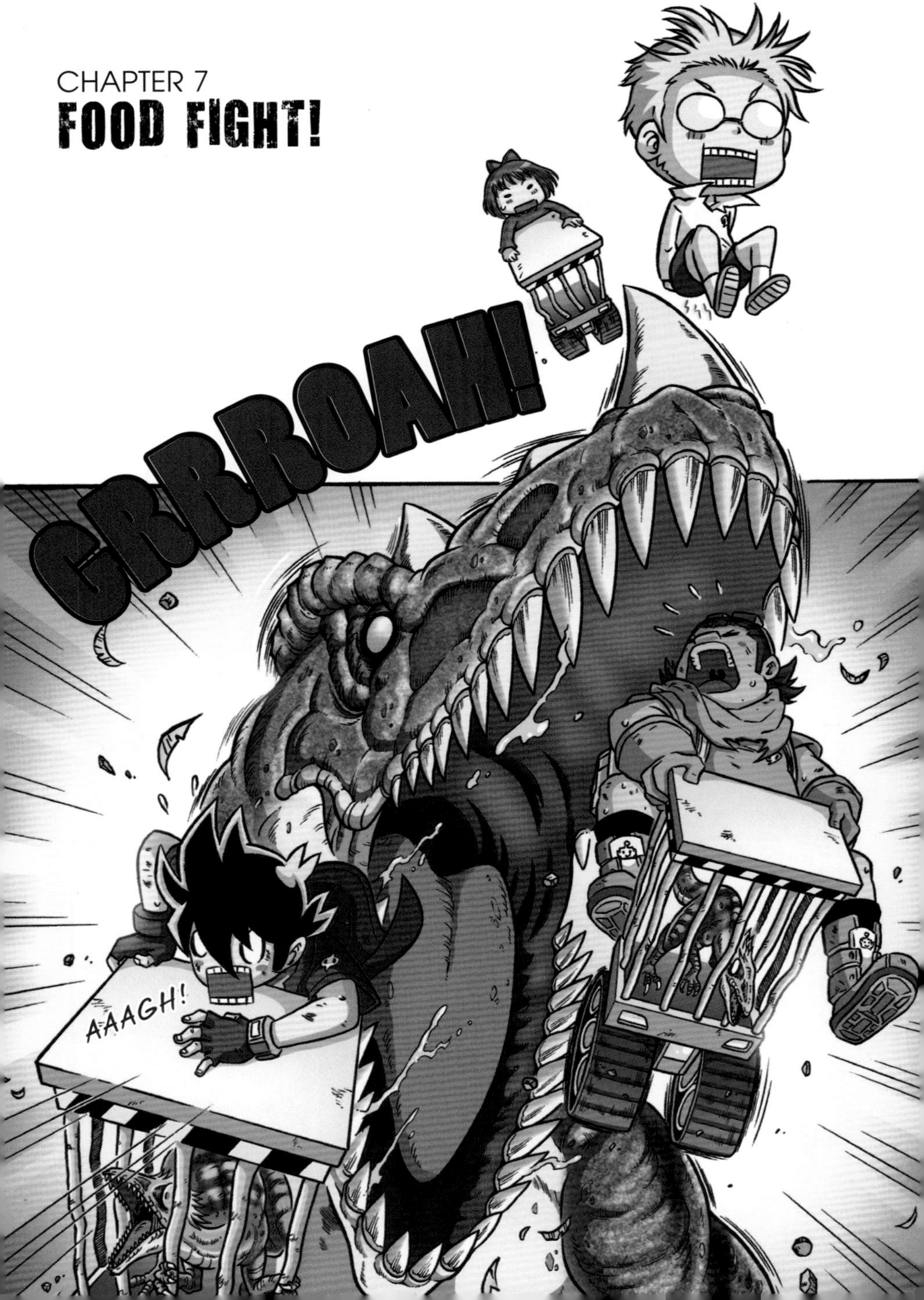
GRRROAH!
AAAGH!

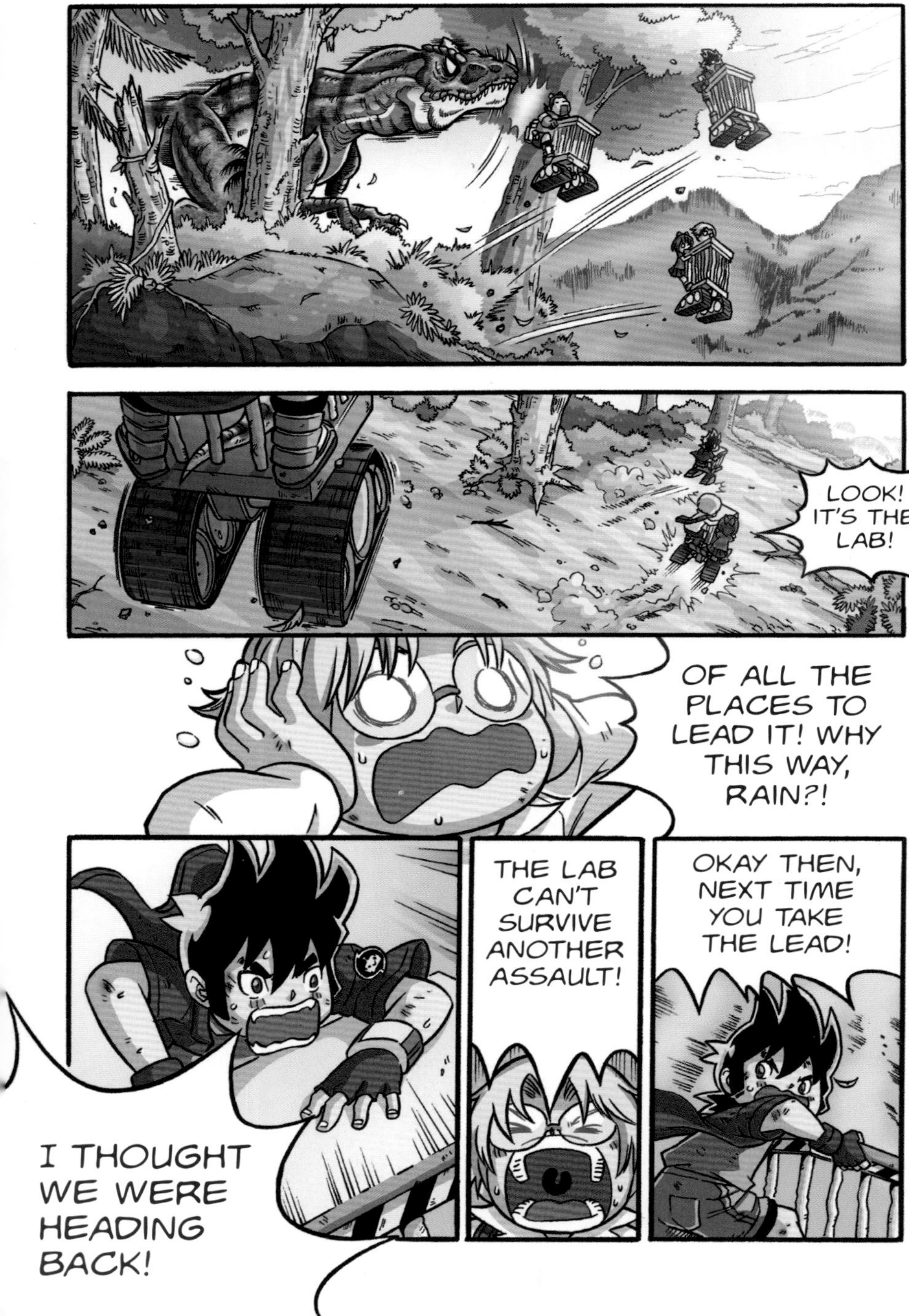
LOOK! IT'S THE LAB!
OF ALL THE PLACES TO LEAD IT! WHY THIS WAY, RAIN?!
I THOUGHT WE WERE HEADING BACK!
THE LAB CAN'T SURVIVE ANOTHER ASSAULT!
OKAY THEN, NEXT TIME YOU TAKE THE LEAD!

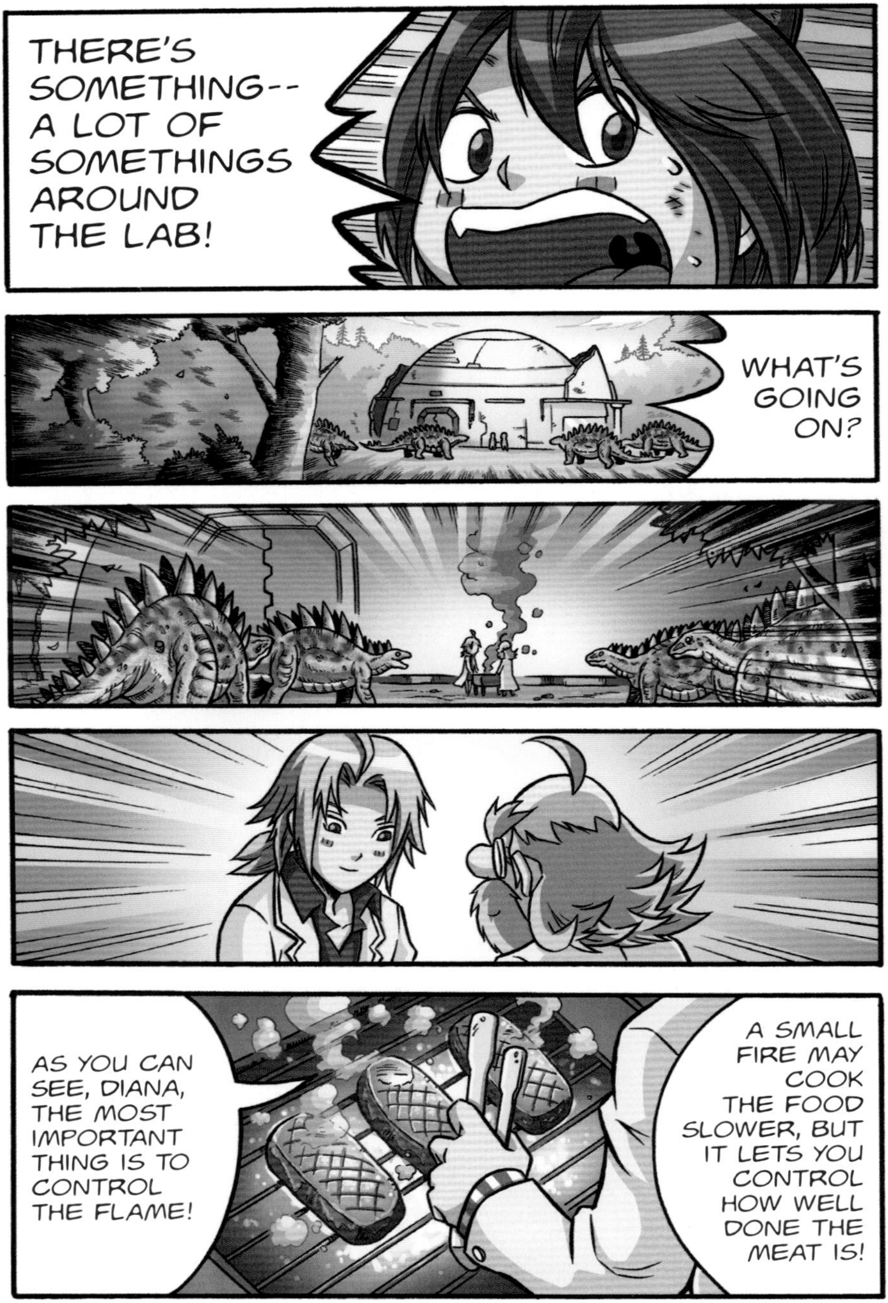
THERE'S SOMETHING-- A LOT OF SOMETHINGS AROUND THE LAB!
WHAT'S GOING ON?
AS YOU CAN SEE, DIANA, THE MOST IMPORTANT THING IS TO CONTROL THE FLAME!
A SMALL FIRE MAY COOK THE FOOD SLOWER, BUT IT LETS YOU CONTROL HOW WELL DONE THE MEAT IS!

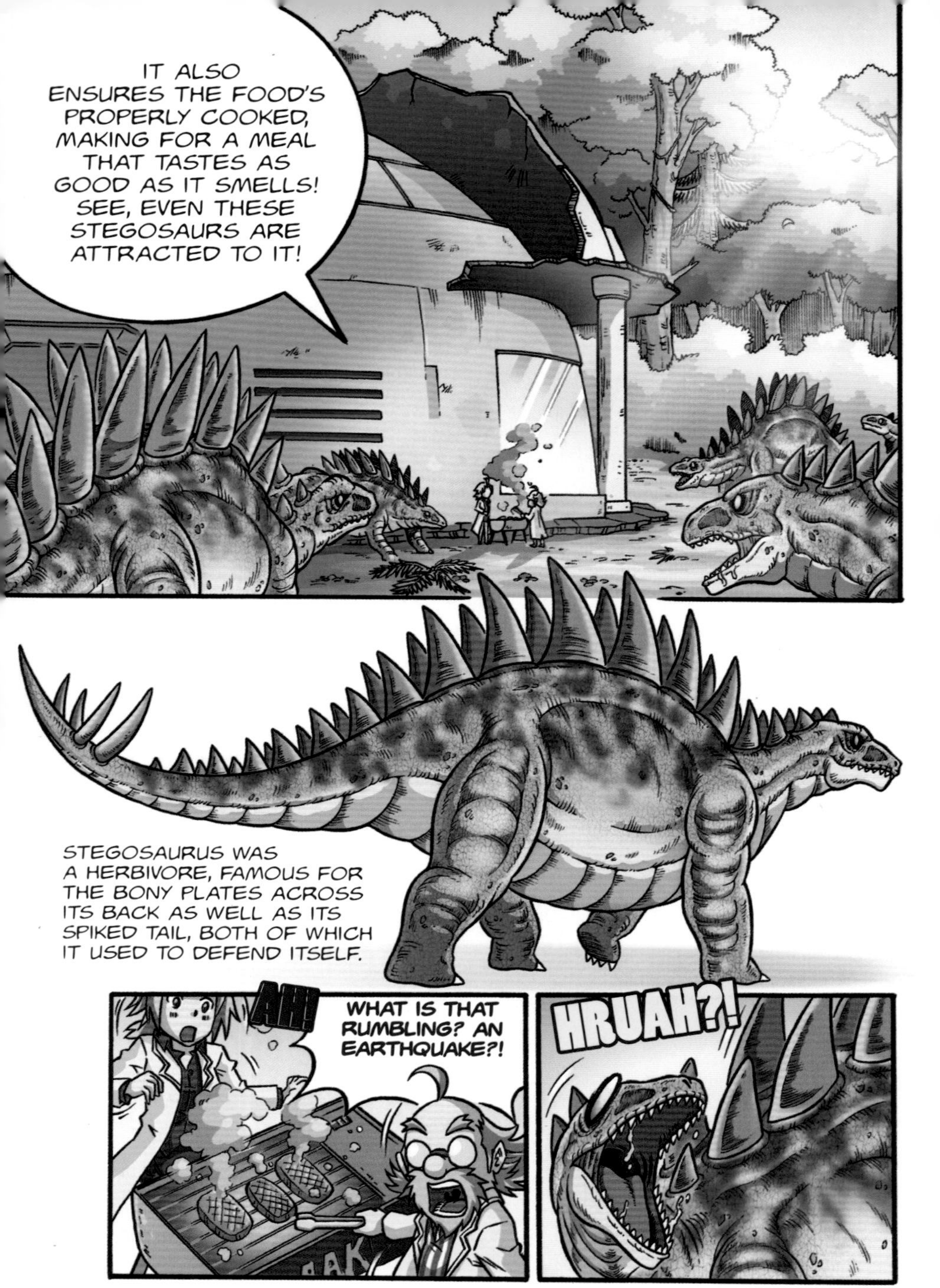
IT ALSO ENSURES THE FOOD'S PROPERLY COOKED, MAKING FOR A MEAL THAT TASTES AS GOOD AS IT SMELLS! SEE, EVEN THESE STEGOSAURS ARE ATTRACTED TO IT!
STEGOSAURUS WAS A HERBIVORE, FAMOUS FOR THE BONY PLATES ACROSS ITS BACK AS WELL AS ITS SPIKED TAIL, BOTH OF WHICH IT USED TO DEFEND ITSELF.
AH!
WHAT IS THAT RUMBLING? AN EARTHQUAKE?!
HRUAH?!

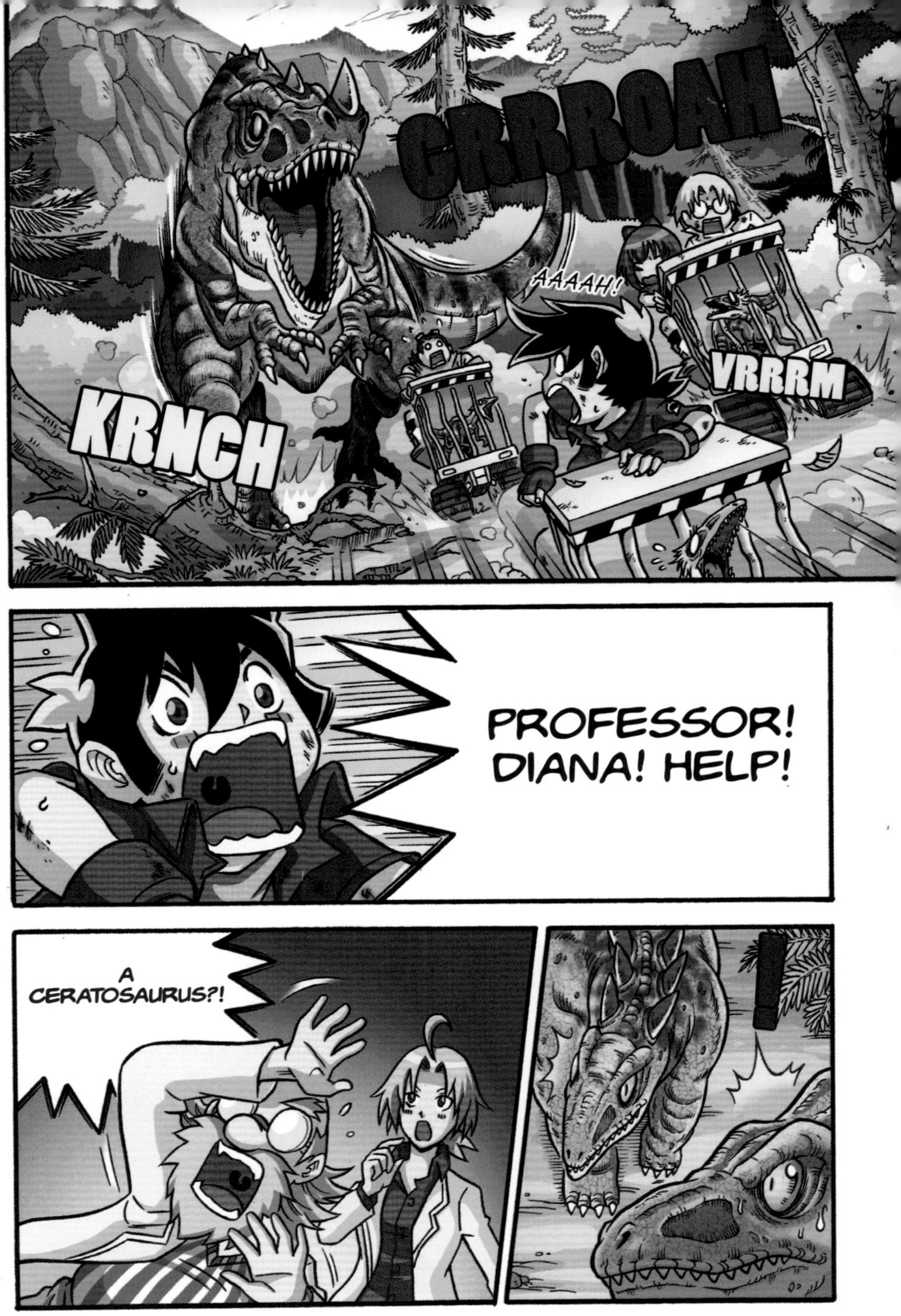
GRRROAH
AAAAH!
VRRRM
KRNCH
PROFESSOR! DIANA! HELP!
A CERATOSAURUS?!
!

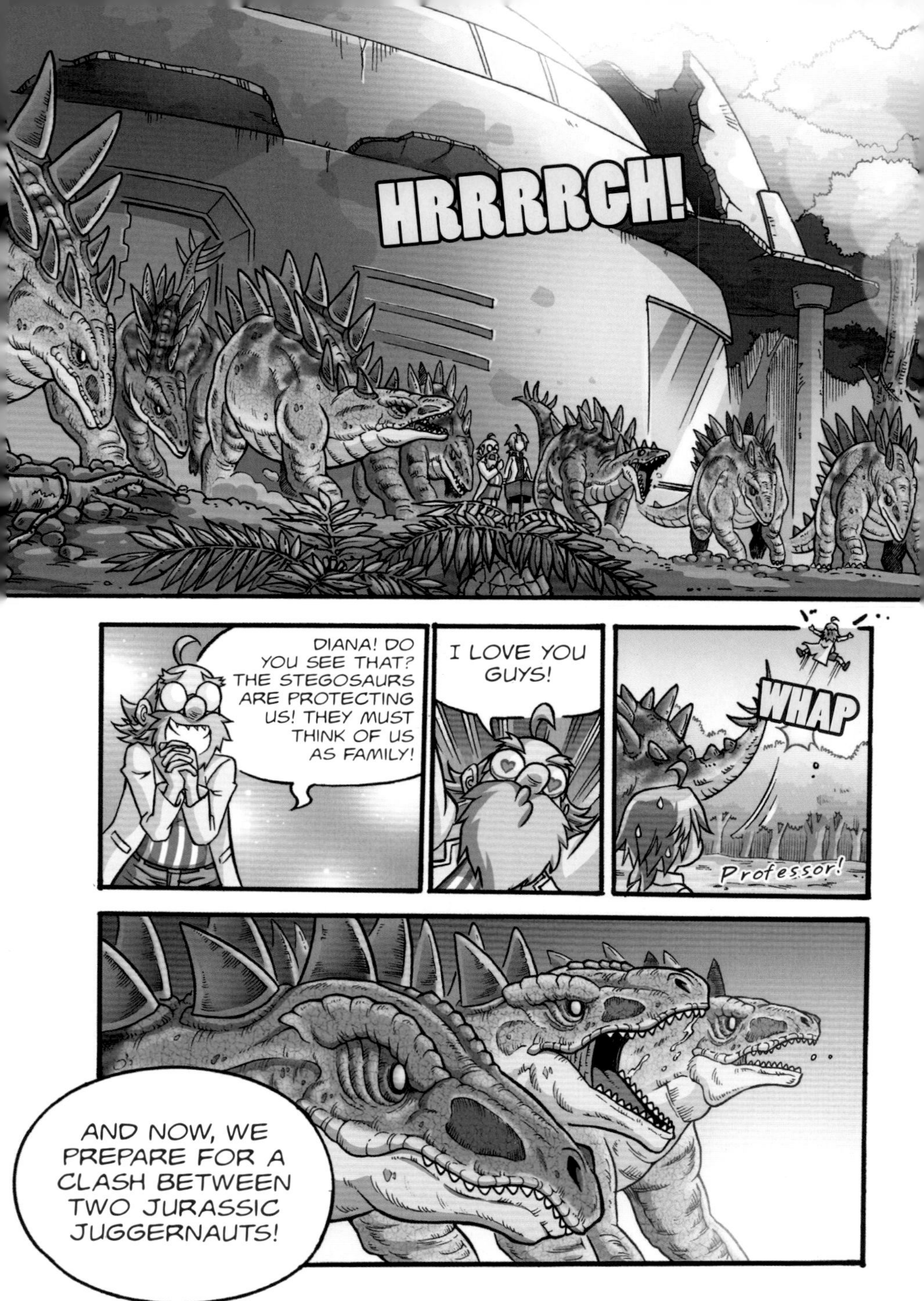
HRRRRCH!
DIANA! DO YOU SEE THAT? THE STEGOSAURS ARE PROTECTING US! THEY MUST THINK OF US AS FAMILY!
I LOVE YOU GUYS!
WHAP
Professor!
AND NOW, WE PREPARE FOR A CLASH BETWEEN TWO JURASSIC JUGGERNAUTS!

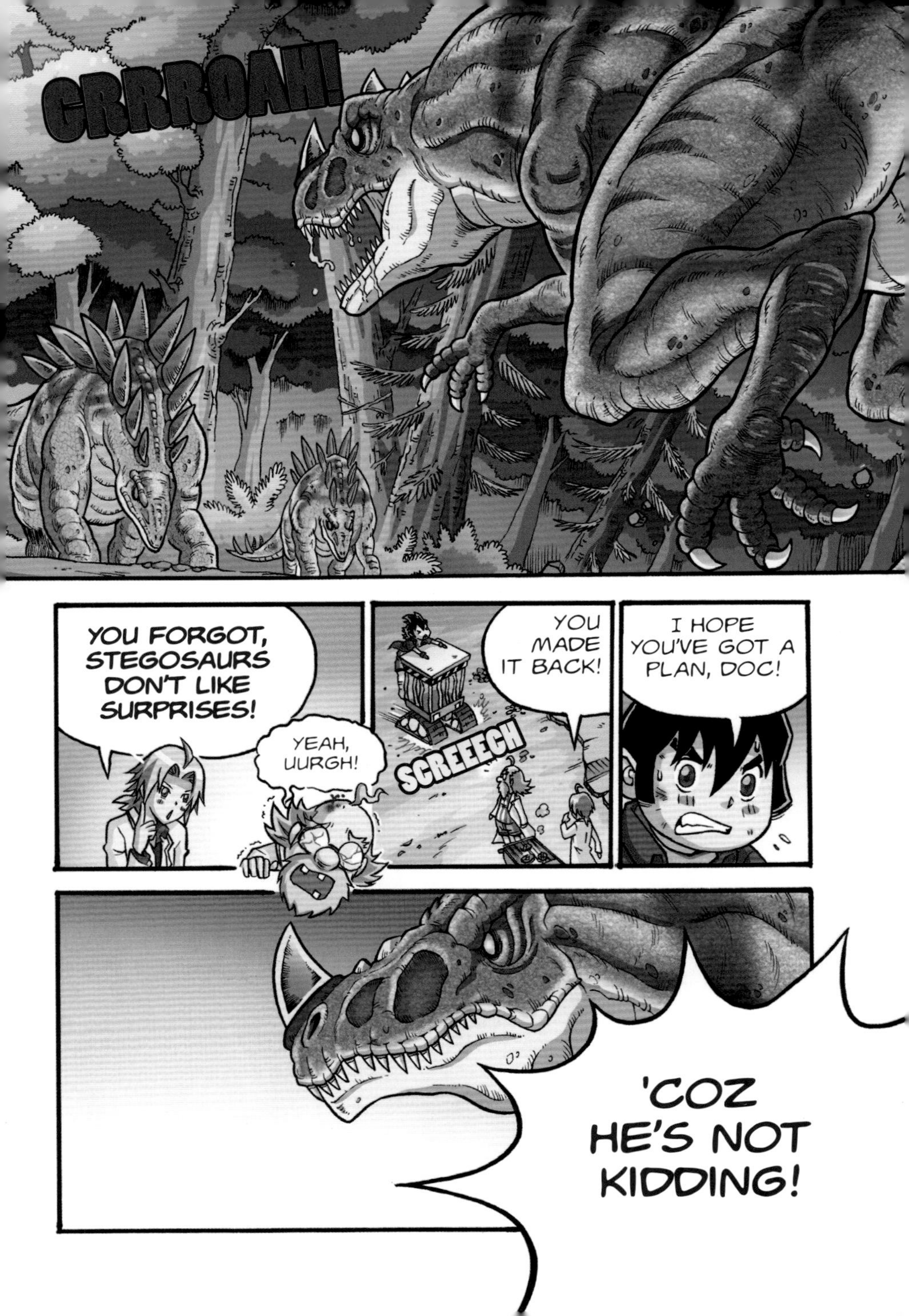

CRRROAH!
YOU FORGOT, STEGOSAURS DON'T LIKE SURPRISES!
YEAH, UURGH!
SCREEECH
YOU MADE IT BACK!
I HOPE YOU'VE GOT A PLAN, DOC!
'COZ HE'S NOT KIDDING!

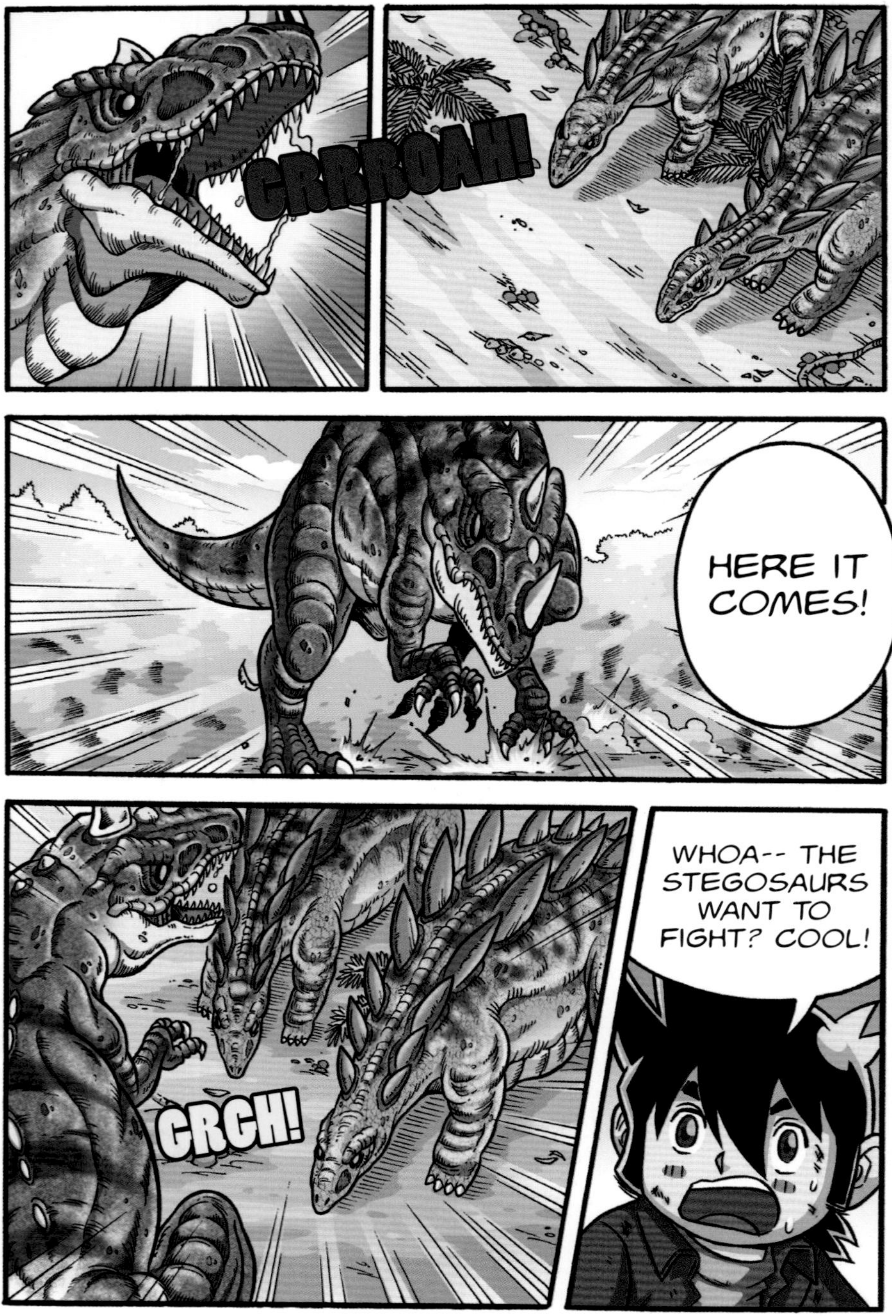
CRRROAH!
HERE IT COMES!
WHOA-- THE STEGOSAURS WANT TO FIGHT? COOL!
GRCH!

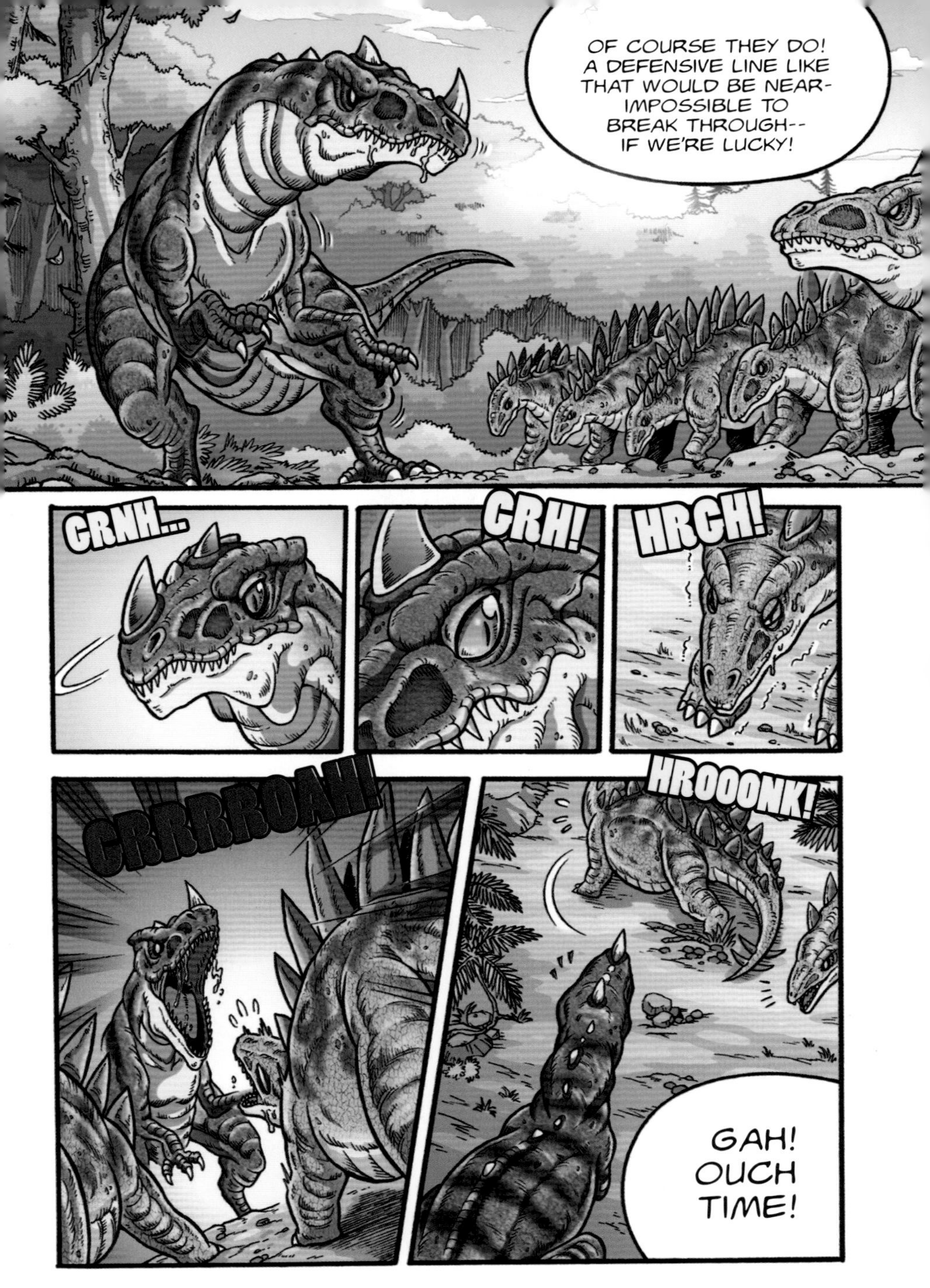
OF COURSE THEY DO! A DEFENSIVE LINE LIKE THAT WOULD BE NEAR-IMPOSSIBLE TO BREAK THROUGH-- IF WE'RE LUCKY!
CRNH...
CRH!
HRGH!
CRRRROAH!
HROOONK!
GAH! OUCH TIME!

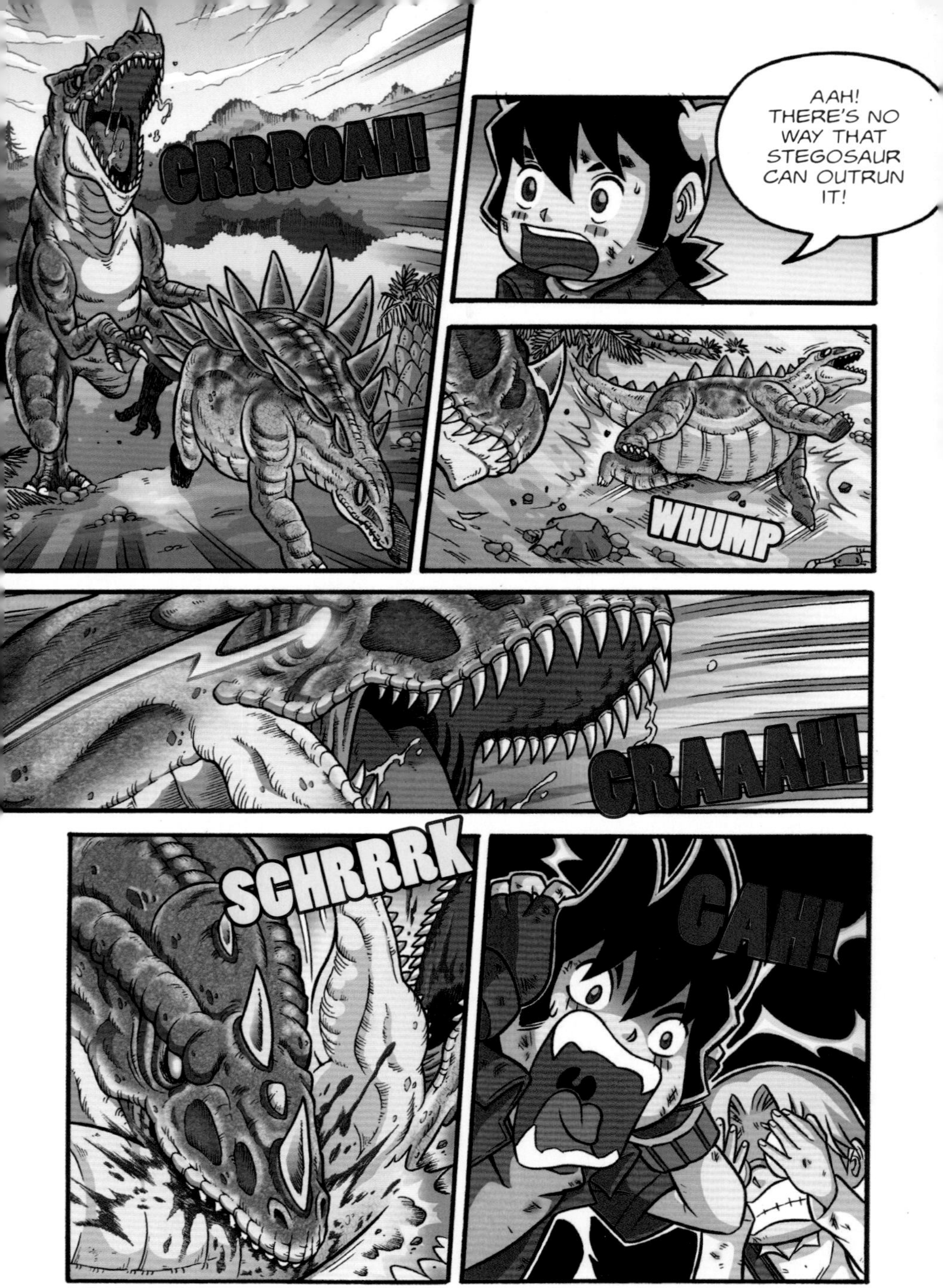
CRRROAH!
AAH! THERE'S NO WAY THAT STEGOSAUR CAN OUTRUN IT!
WHUMP
CRAAAH!
SCHRRRK
GAH!

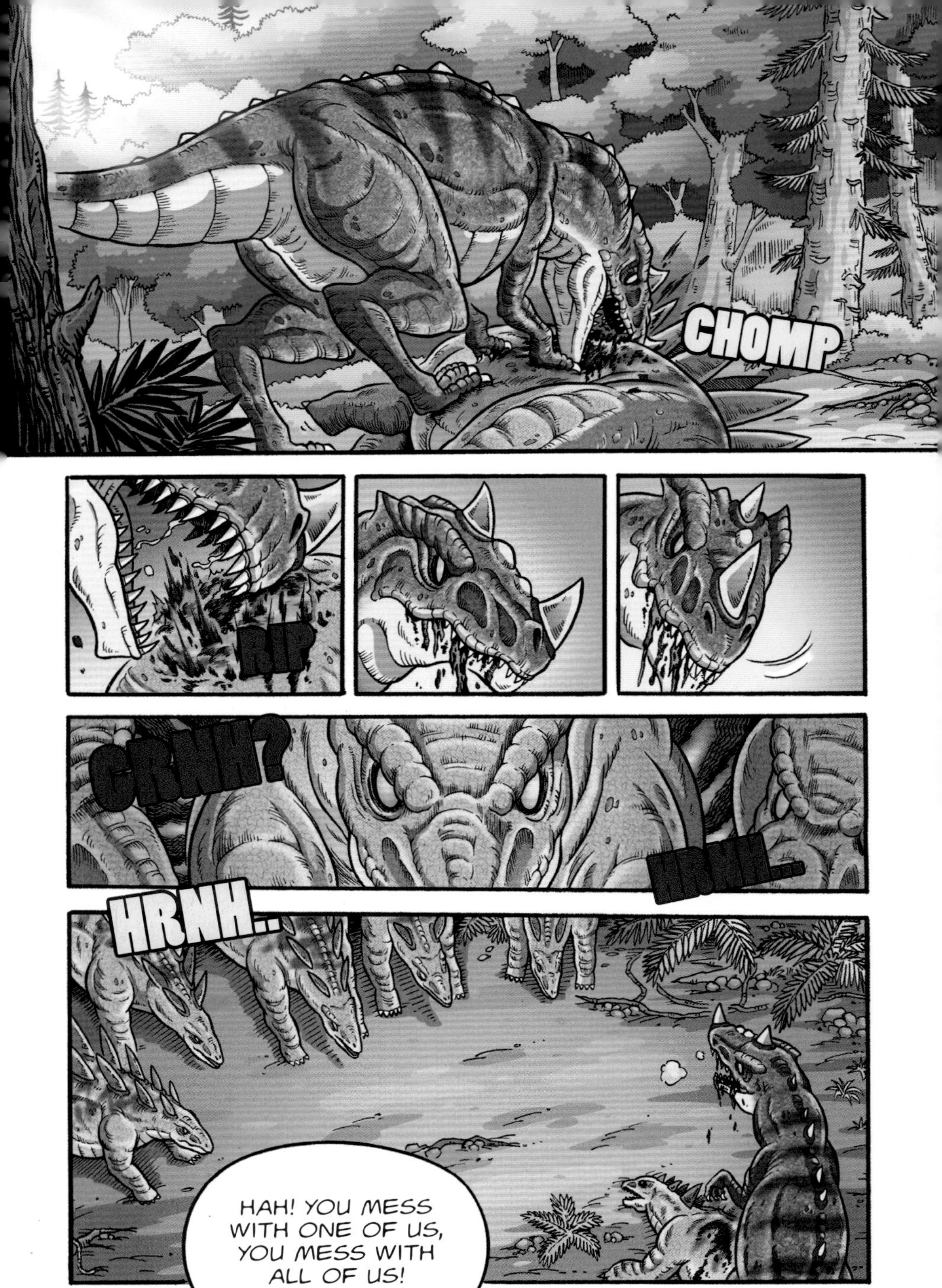
CHOMP
RIP
CRNH?
HRNH...
HRNH..
HAH! YOU MESS WITH ONE OF US, YOU MESS WITH ALL OF US!

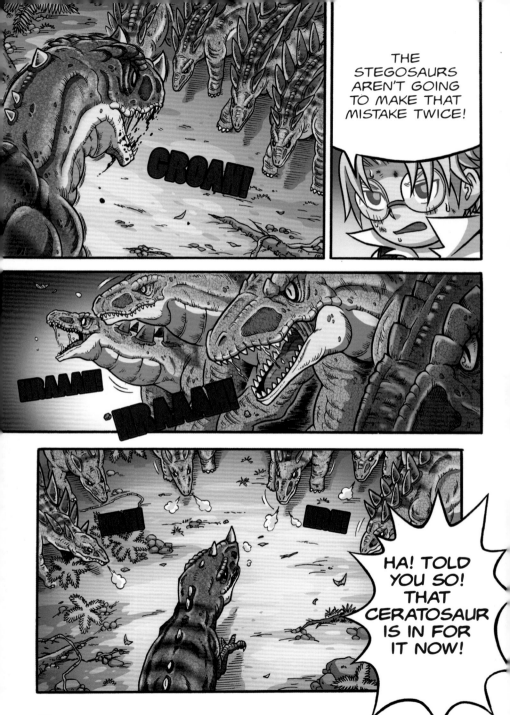

THE STEGOSAURS AREN'T GOING TO MAKE THAT MISTAKE TWICE!

CROAH!!

KRAAH!!

KRAAAH!!

HA! TOLD YOU SO! THAT CERATOSAUR IS IN FOR IT NOW!

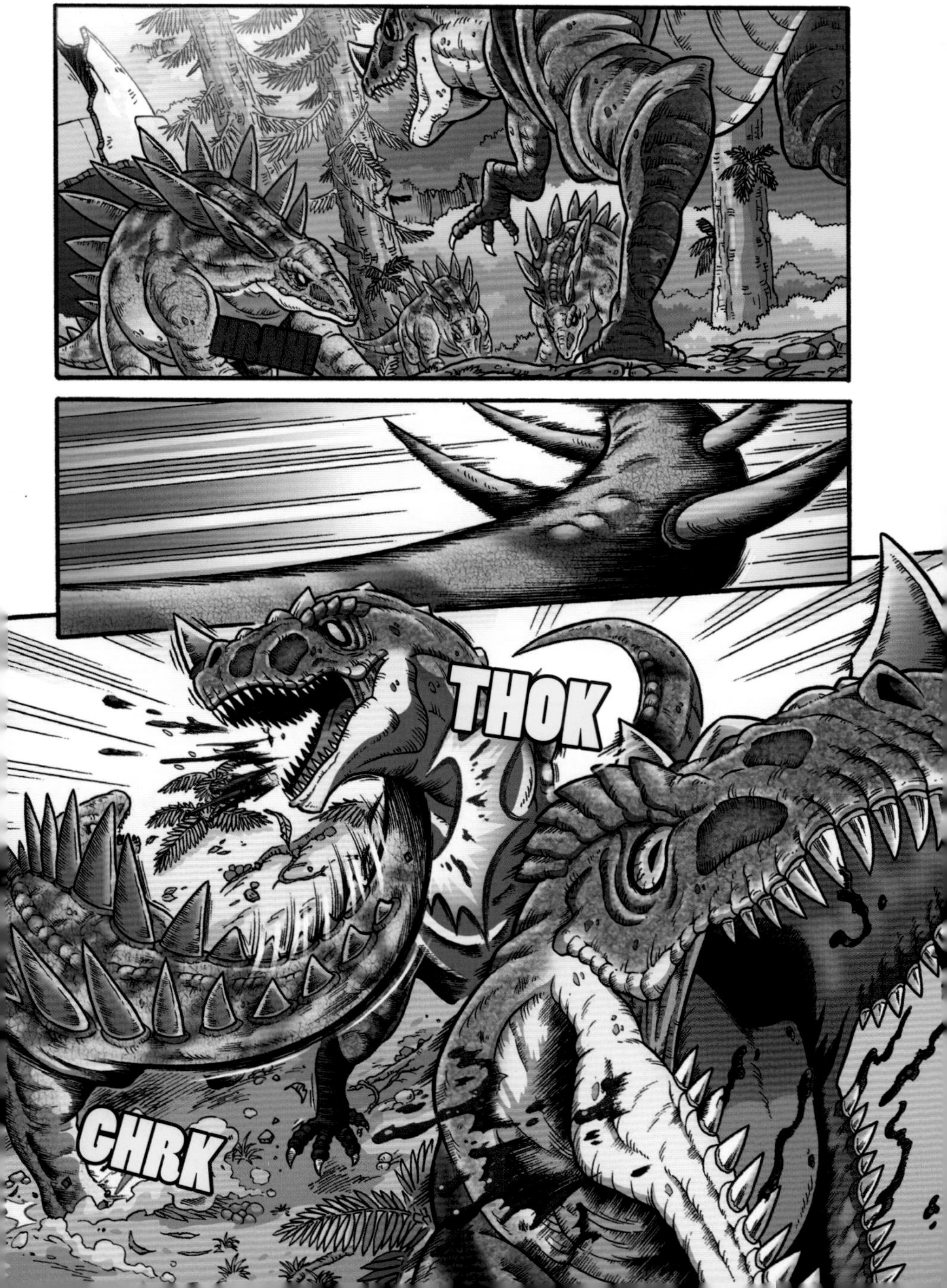
HRMM!
THOK
CHRK

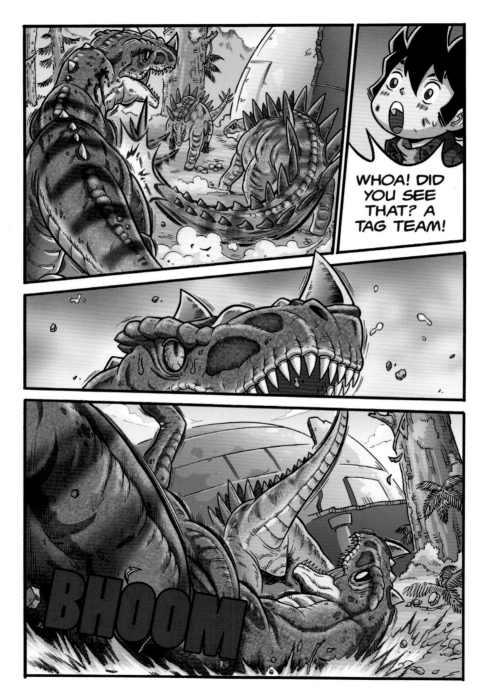

WHOA! DID YOU SEE THAT? A TAG TEAM!

BHOOM

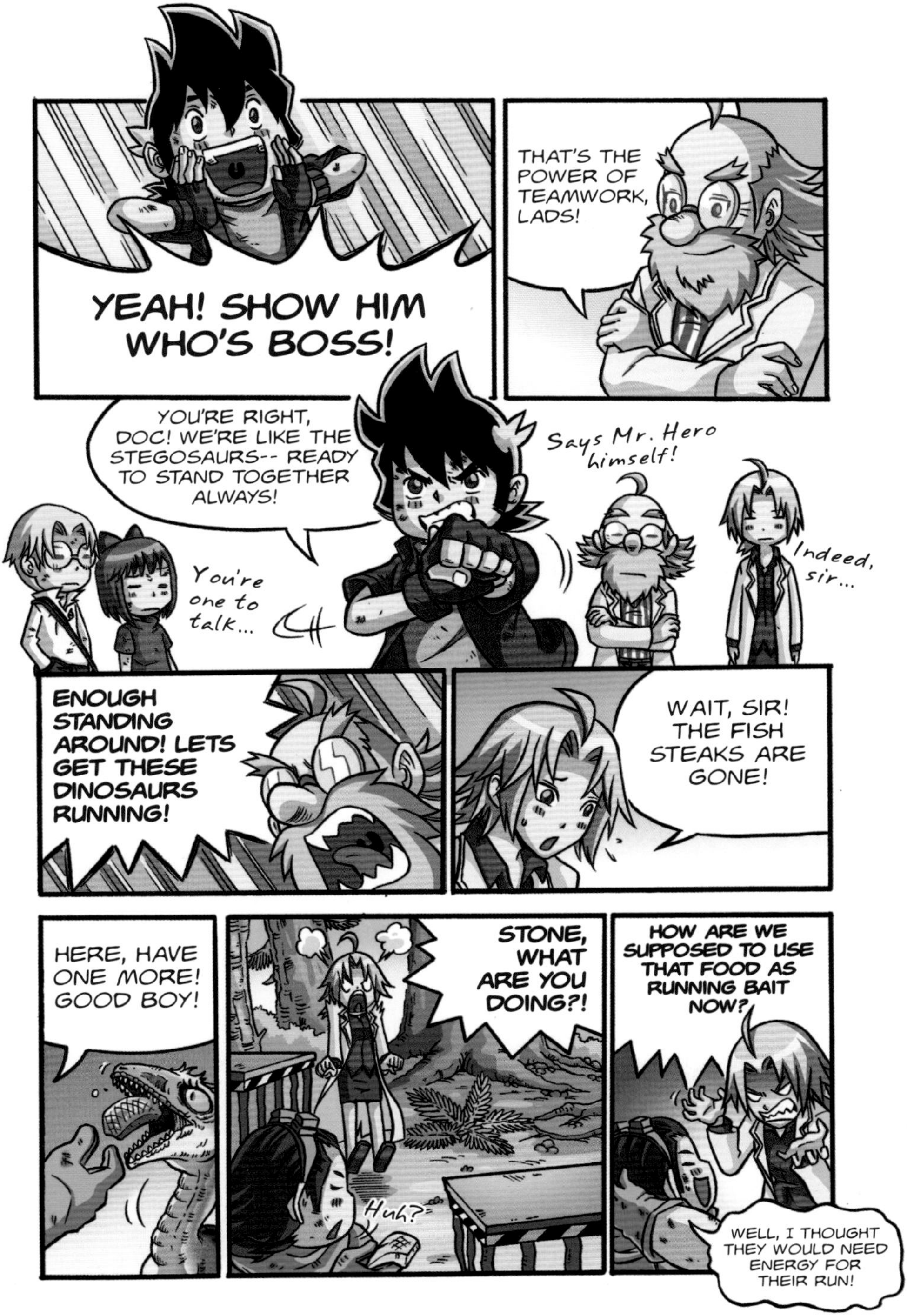

YEAH! SHOW HIM WHO'S BOSS!
THAT'S THE POWER OF TEAMWORK, LADS!
YOU'RE RIGHT, DOC! WE'RE LIKE THE STEGOSAURS-- READY TO STAND TOGETHER ALWAYS!
Says Mr. Hero himself!
Indeed, sir...
You're one to talk...
ENOUGH STANDING AROUND! LETS GET THESE DINOSAURS RUNNING!
WAIT, SIR! THE FISH STEAKS ARE GONE!
HERE, HAVE ONE MORE! GOOD BOY!
STONE, WHAT ARE YOU DOING?!
Huh?
HOW ARE WE SUPPOSED TO USE THAT FOOD AS RUNNING BAIT NOW?
WELL, I THOUGHT THEY WOULD NEED ENERGY FOR THEIR RUN!

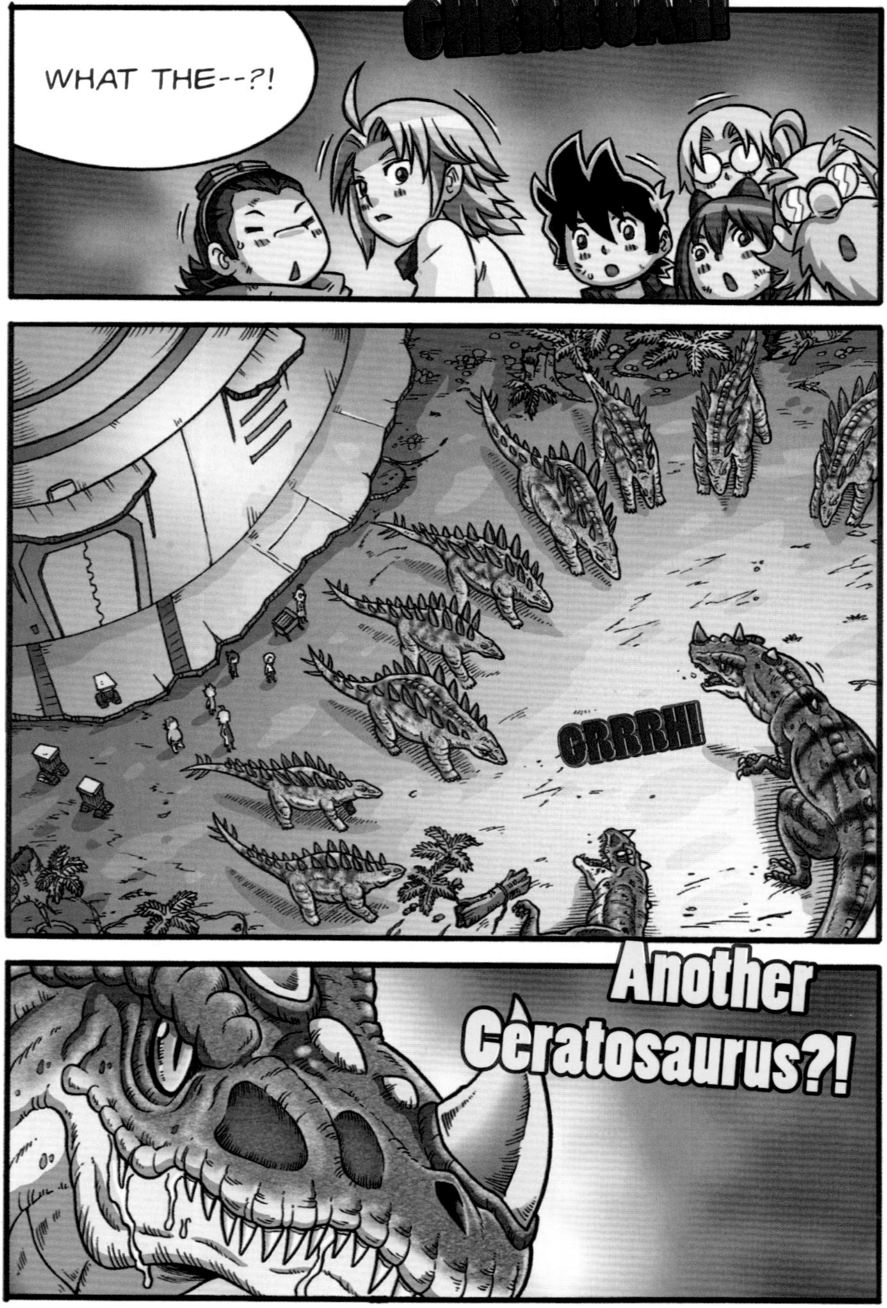
CHRRROAH!!
WHAT THE--?!
CRRRH!
Another Ceratosaurus?!

Stegosaurus

Scientific name: Stegosaurus
Length: 29 feet
Diet: Herbivore
Habitat: Open forests
Discovered: North America, Portugal, and Europe
Era: Late Jurassic

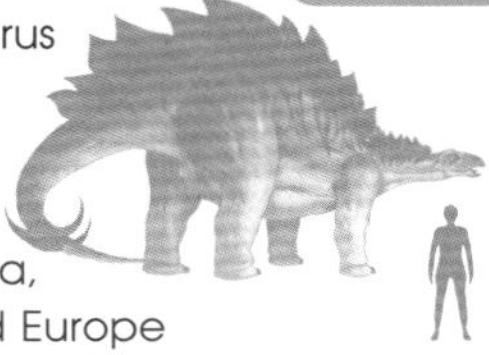

Quite possibly one of the most popular and well known dinosaurs, Stegosaurus was about the size of an average bus. It had bony spikes and 17 plates embedded in its back and tail. The spikes were most likely used for defence while the plates might have been defensive and/or decorative.

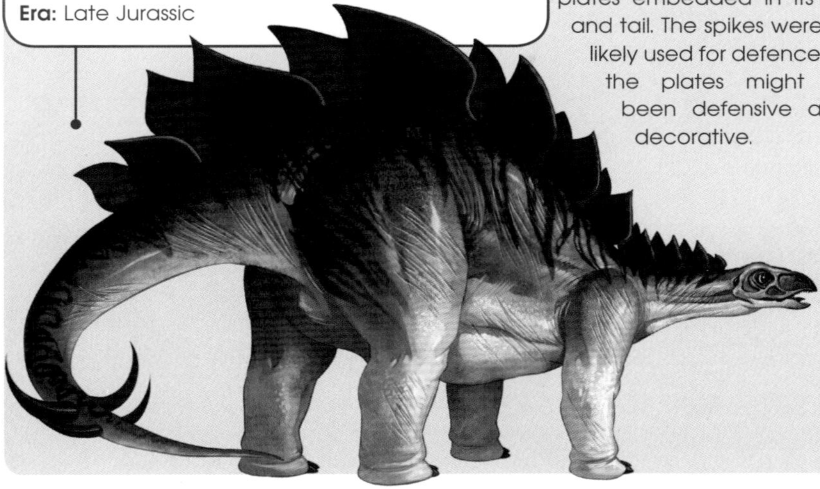

The Stegosaur's bony plates

The bony plates had blood vessels running through grooves, which has led recent research to suggest that they may have helped the Stegosaurus absorb heat when out in the open, and to cool down in the shade or rain.

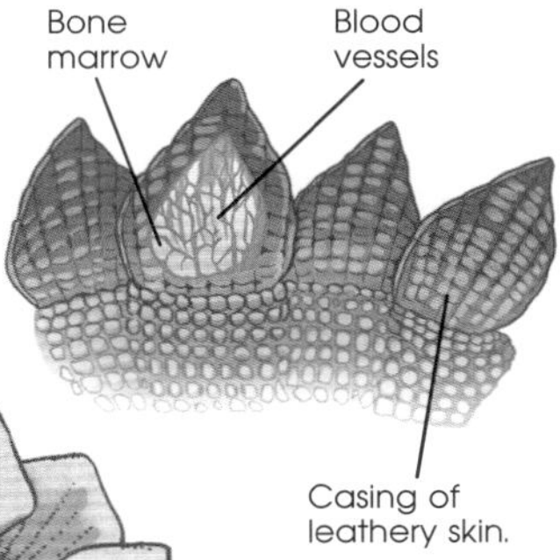
Bone marrow
Blood vessels
Casing of leathery skin.

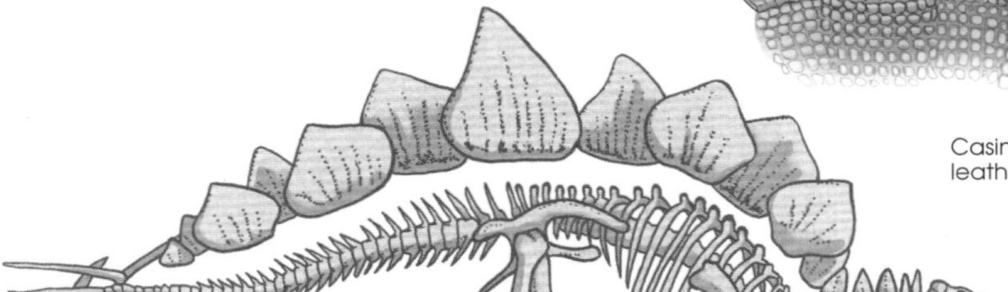

Studies show that an adult Stegosaurus might have had up to 17 plates and 4 tail spikes.

JONESING FOR THE JURASSIC

Camptosaurus

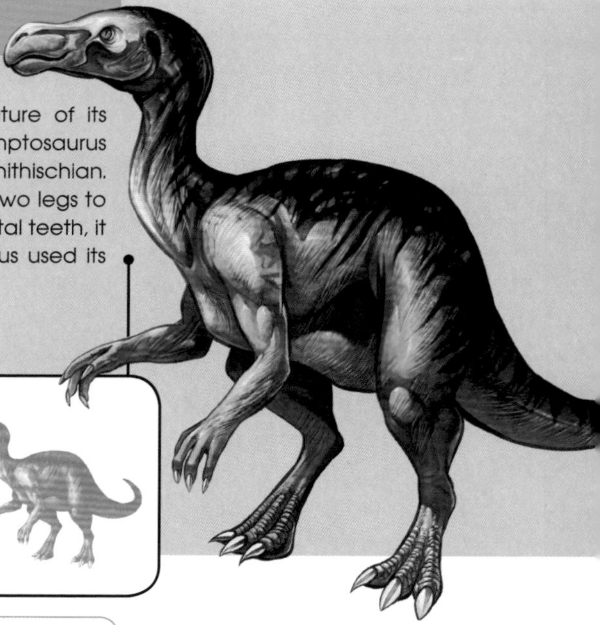

Named for the bowed curvature of its spine when on all fours, Camptosaurus was a plant-eating, beaked ornithischian. Feeding on all fours, it took to two legs to escape predators. Lacking frontal teeth, it was thought that Camptosaurus used its cheek teeth to chew food.

Scientific name: Camptosaurus
Length: 16.5 to 23 feet
Diet: Herbivore
Habitat: Forests
Discovered: Europe, North America
Era: Late Jurassic

JONESING FOR THE JURASSIC

Xuanhanosaurus

Xuanhanosaurus was a smaller predatory therapod that weighed around 551 pounds. Most theropods had short forelimbs, but its long, dexterous fingers, which, when combined with a large chest and powerful shoulders, might have meant that it used all four limbs, a rarity among carnivorous dinosaurs.

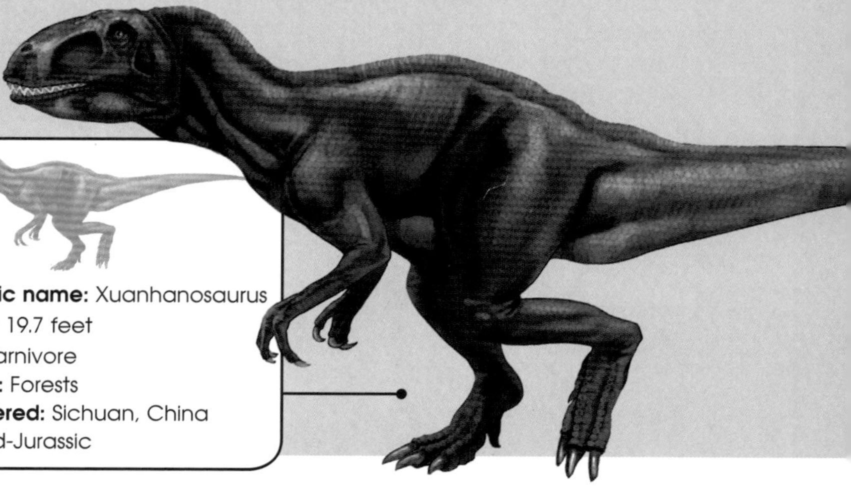

Scientific name: Xuanhanosaurus
Length: 19.7 feet
Diet: Carnivore
Habitat: Forests
Discovered: Sichuan, China
Era: Mid-Jurassic

CHAPTER 8

RACE AGAINST TIME!

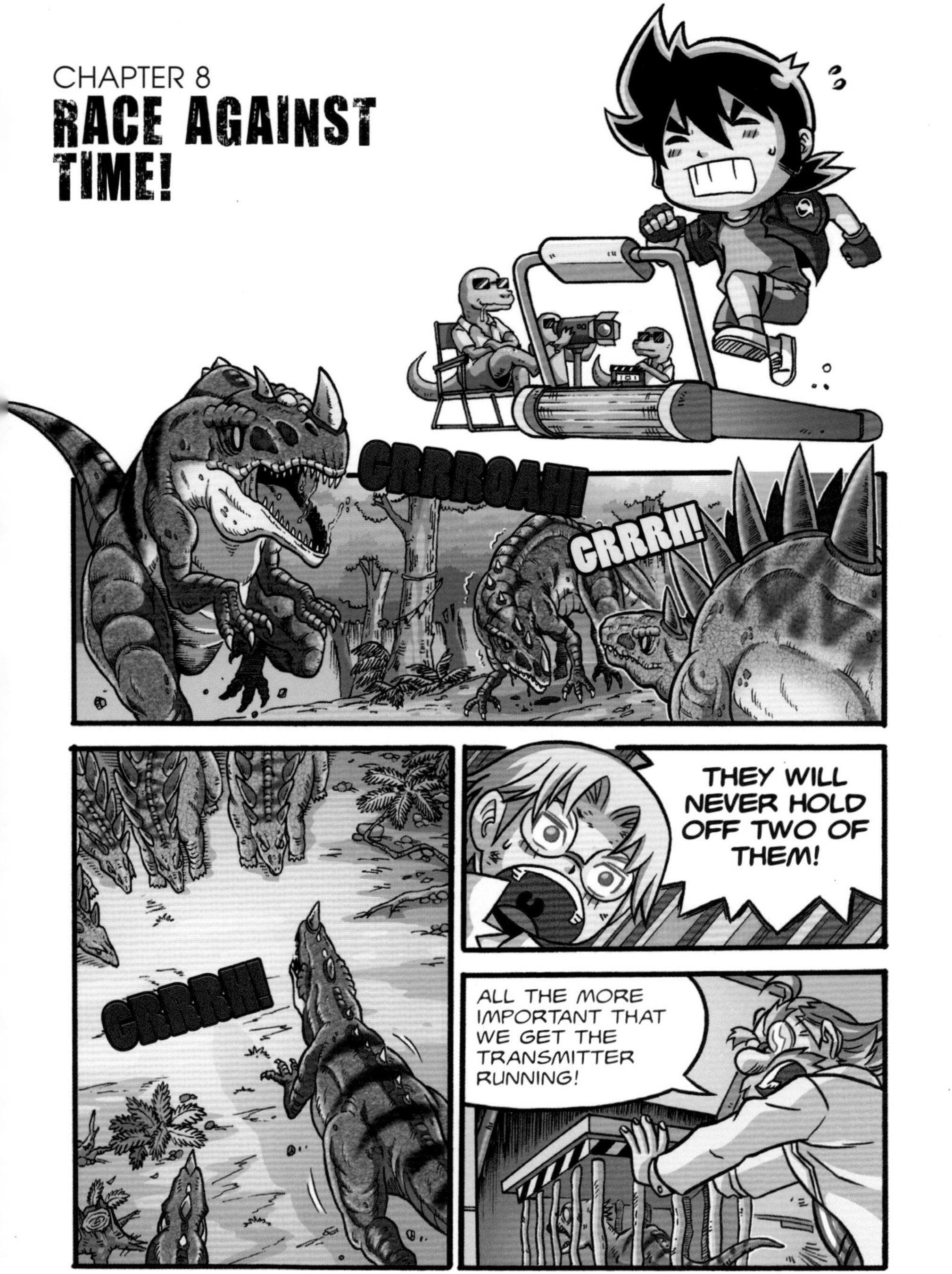
CRRROAH!
CRRRH!
CRRRH!
THEY WILL NEVER HOLD OFF TWO OF THEM!
ALL THE MORE IMPORTANT THAT WE GET THE TRANSMITTER RUNNING!

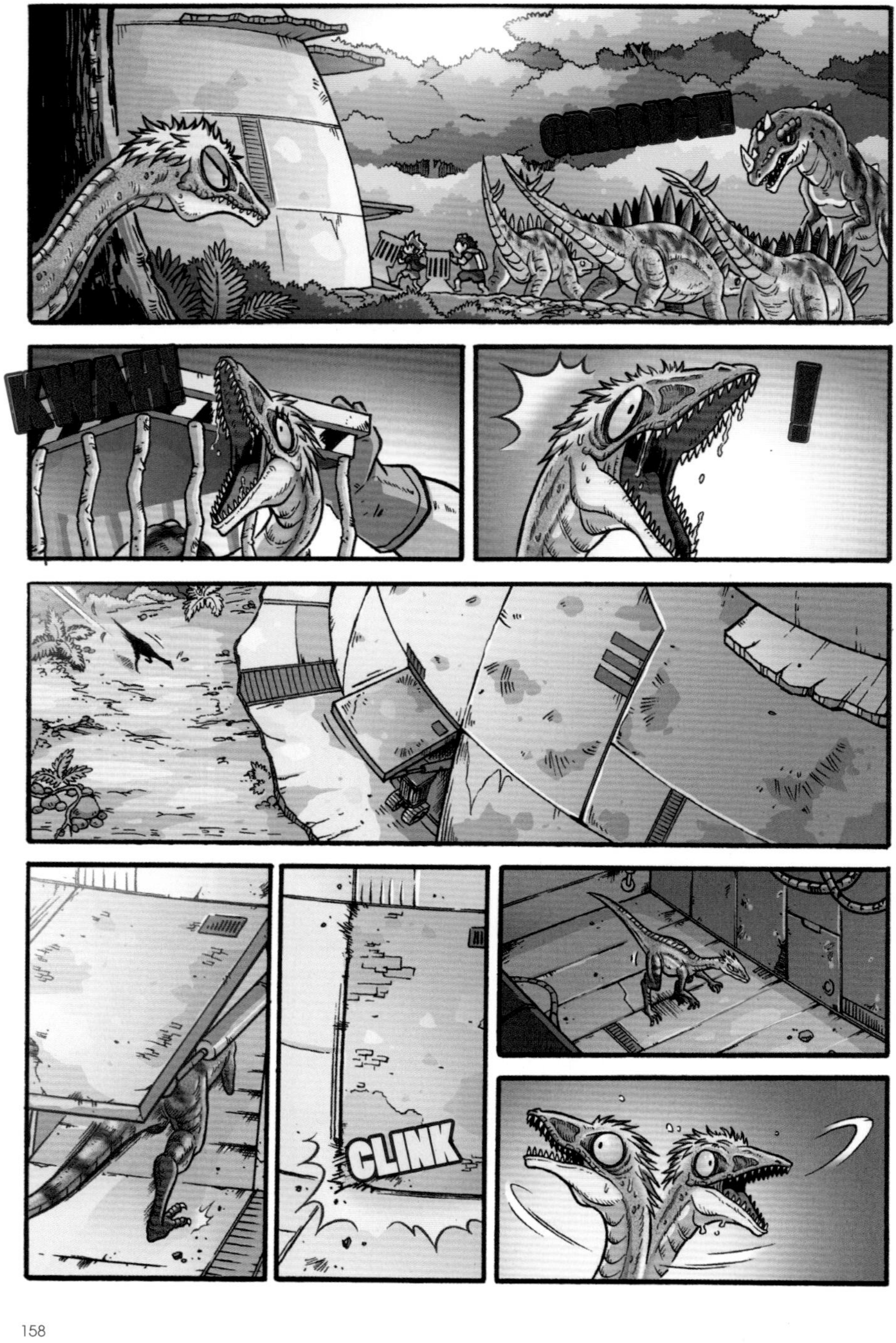

CRRUNCH!
KWAH!
!
CLINK

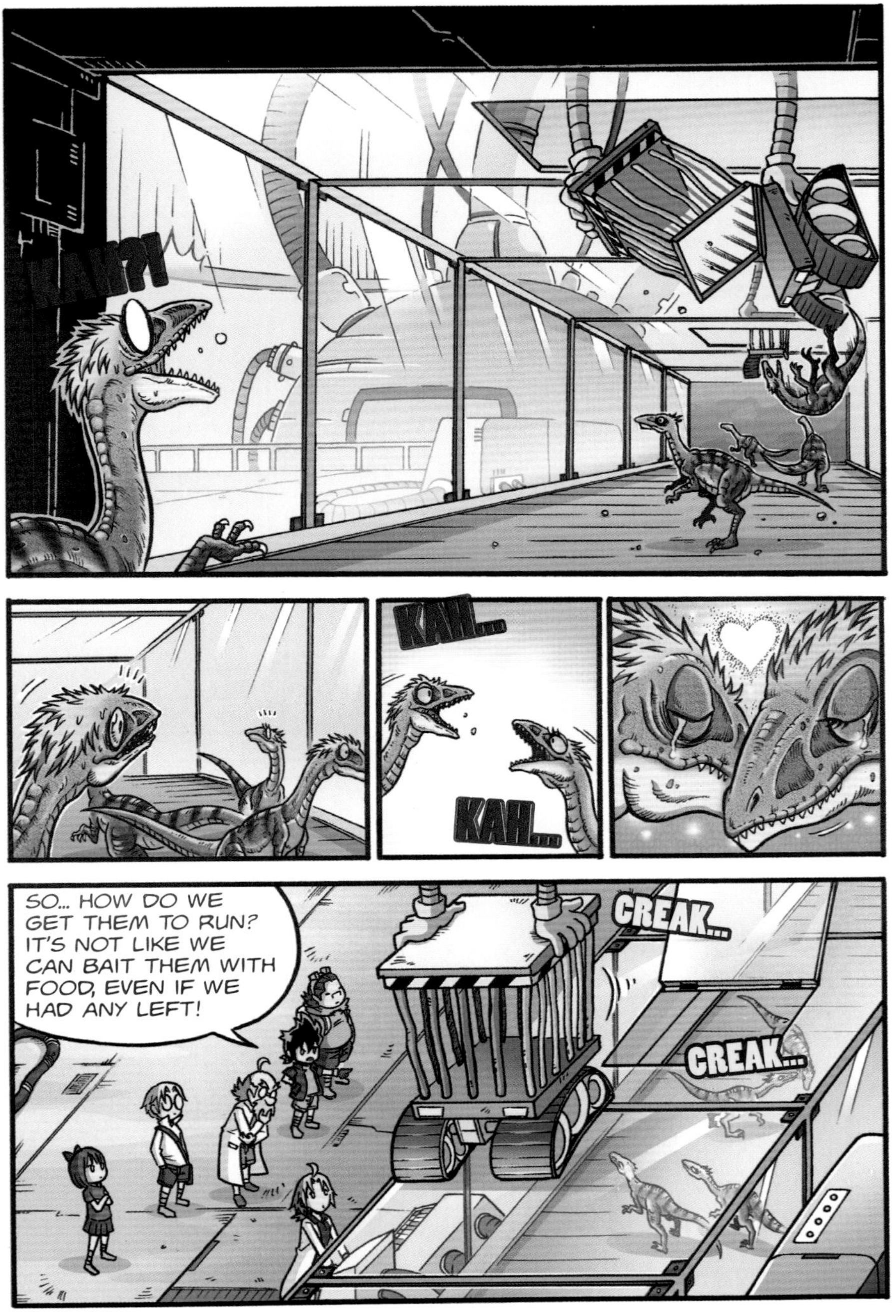
KAH?!
KAH...
KAH...
SO... HOW DO WE GET THEM TO RUN? IT'S NOT LIKE WE CAN BAIT THEM WITH FOOD, EVEN IF WE HAD ANY LEFT!
CREAK...
CREAK...

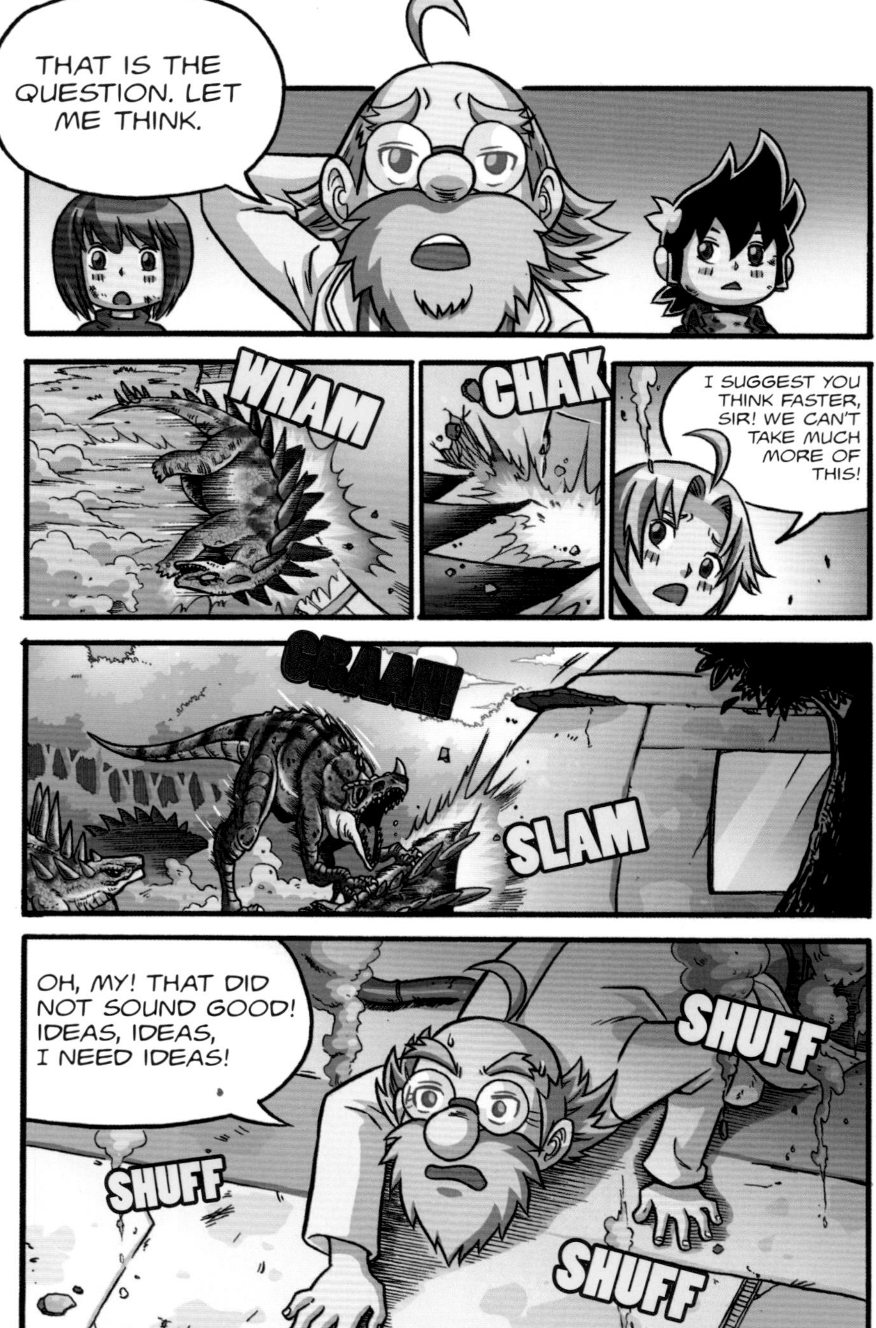
THAT IS THE QUESTION. LET ME THINK.
WHAM
CHAK
I SUGGEST YOU THINK FASTER, SIR! WE CAN'T TAKE MUCH MORE OF THIS!
SLAM
OH, MY! THAT DID NOT SOUND GOOD! IDEAS, IDEAS, I NEED IDEAS!
SHUFF
SHUFF
SHUFF

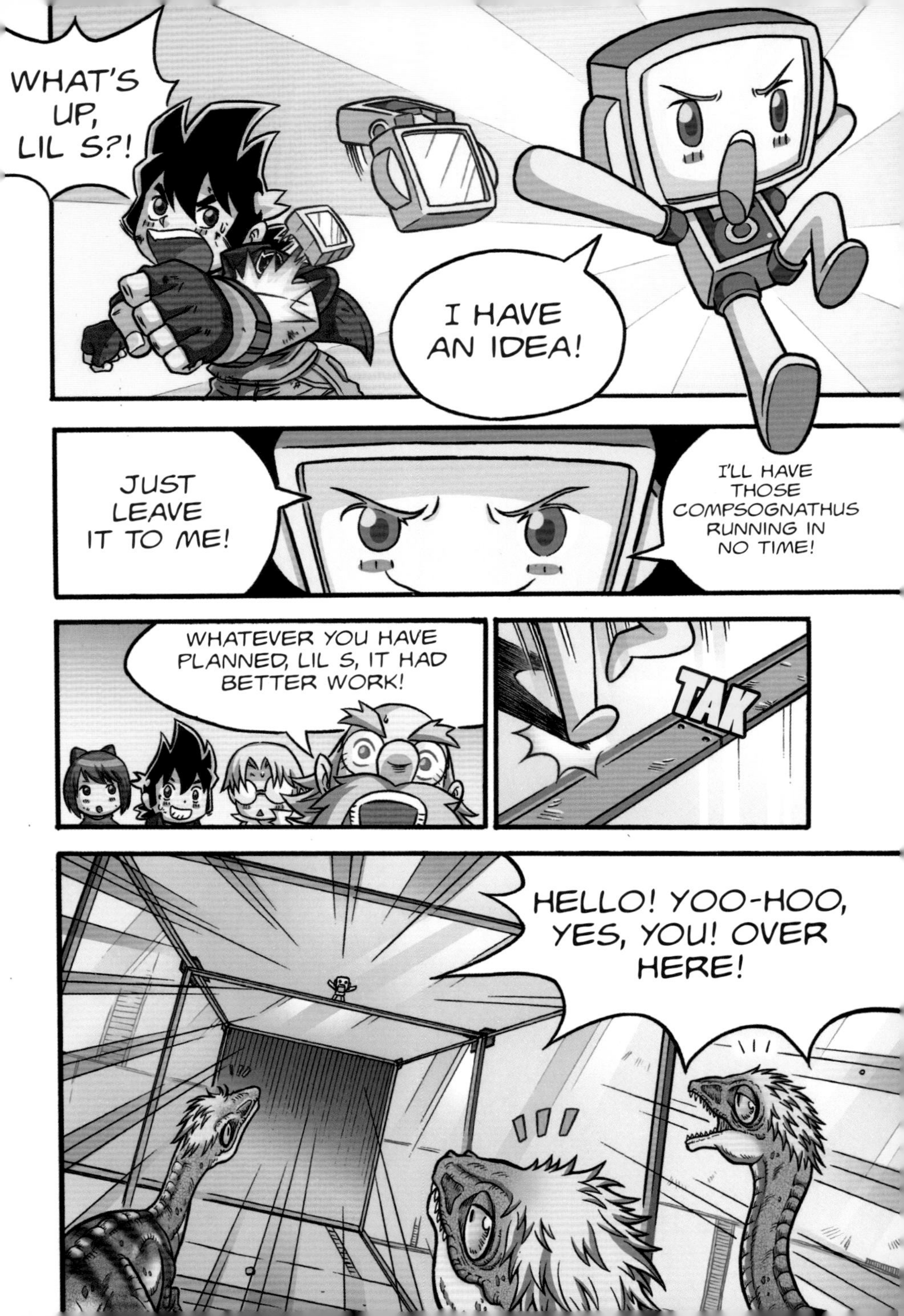
WHAT'S UP, LIL S?!
I HAVE AN IDEA!
JUST LEAVE IT TO ME!
I'LL HAVE THOSE COMPSOGNATHUS RUNNING IN NO TIME!
WHATEVER YOU HAVE PLANNED, LIL S, IT HAD BETTER WORK!
TAK
HELLO! YOO-HOO, YES, YOU! OVER HERE!

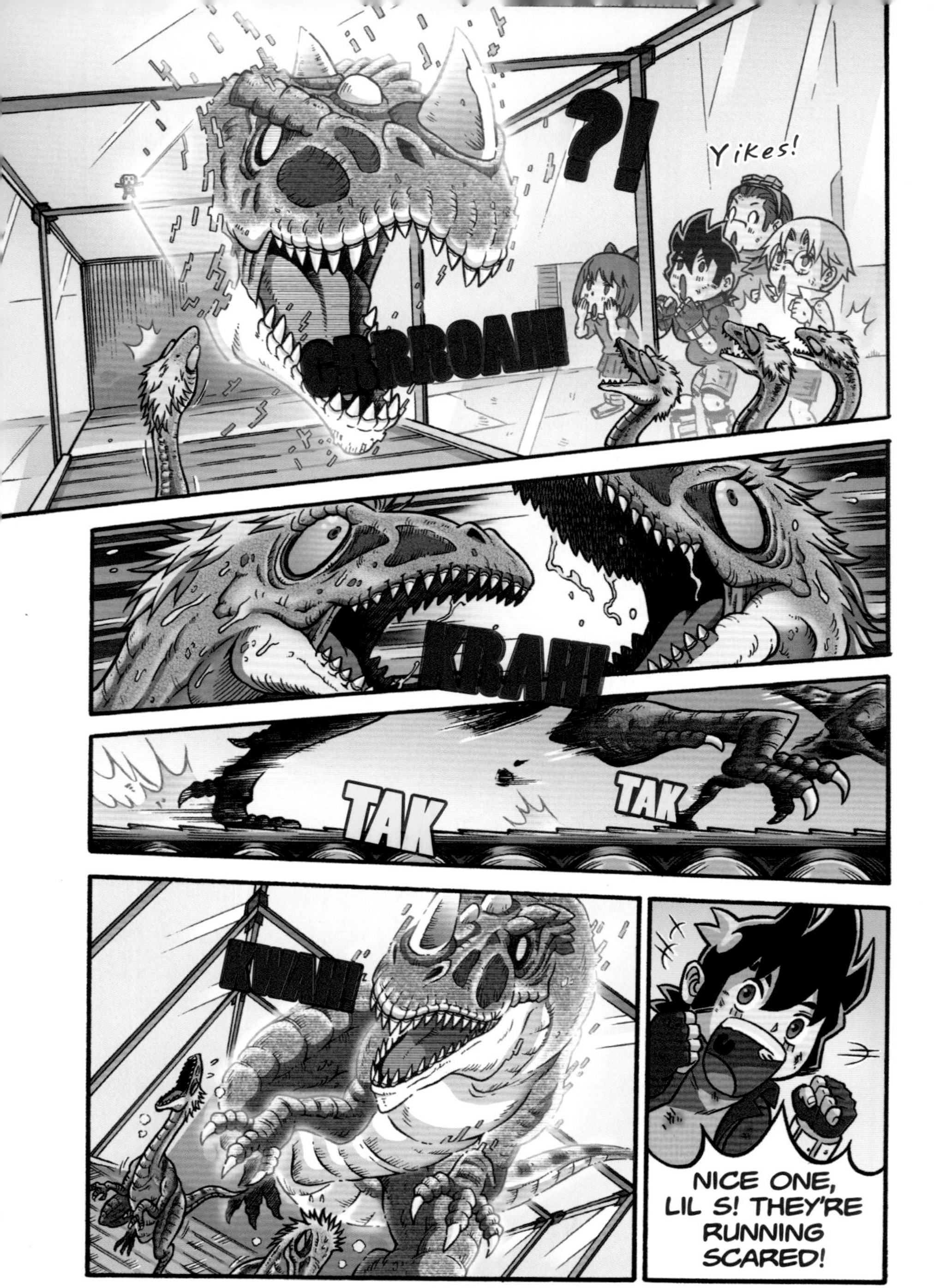
?!
Yikes!
GRRROAH!
KRAH!
TAK
TAK
KWAH!
NICE ONE, LIL S! THEY'RE RUNNING SCARED!

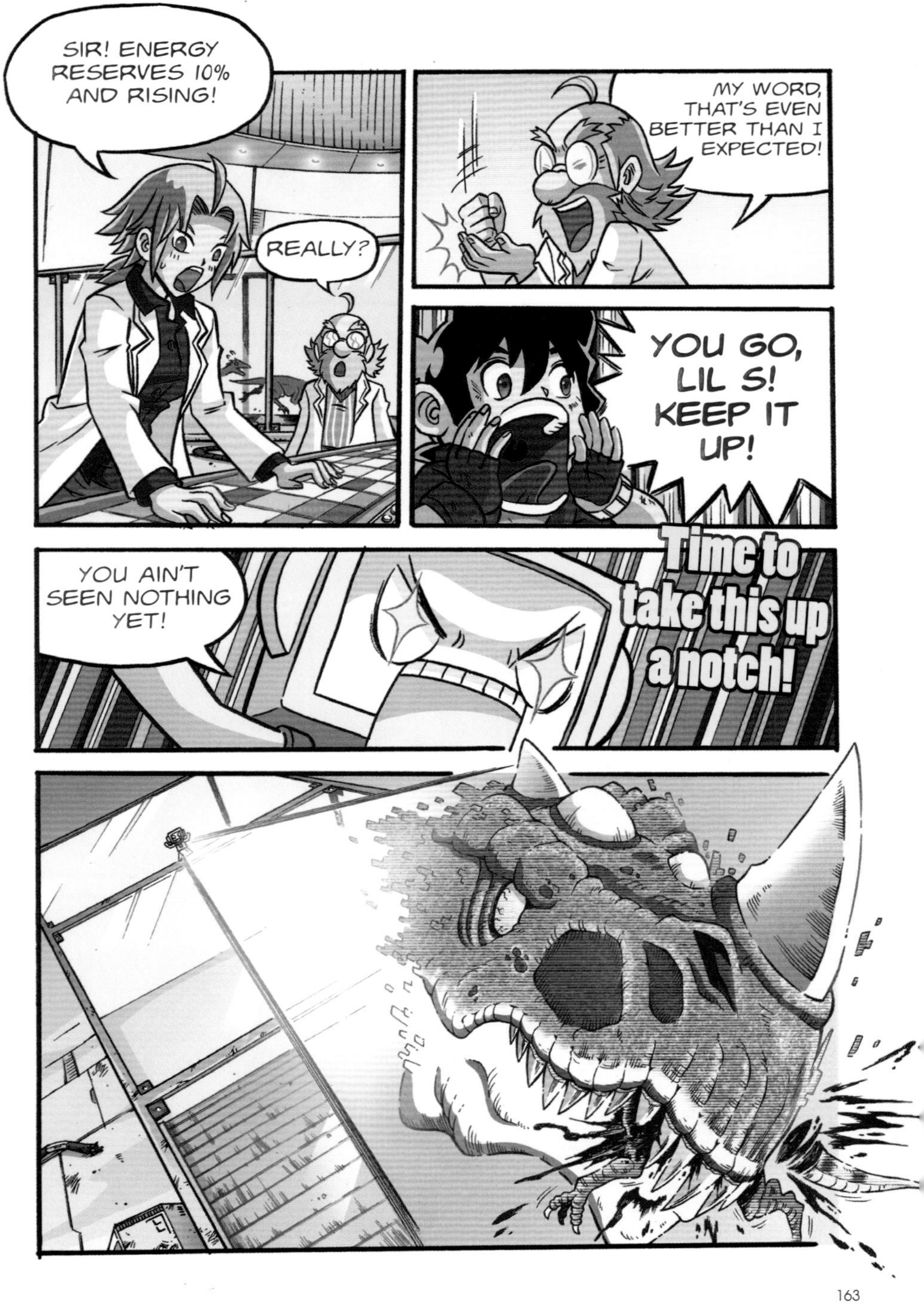
SIR! ENERGY RESERVES 10% AND RISING!
REALLY?
MY WORD, THAT'S EVEN BETTER THAN I EXPECTED!
YOU GO, LIL S! KEEP IT UP!
YOU AIN'T SEEN NOTHING YET!
Time to take this up a notch!

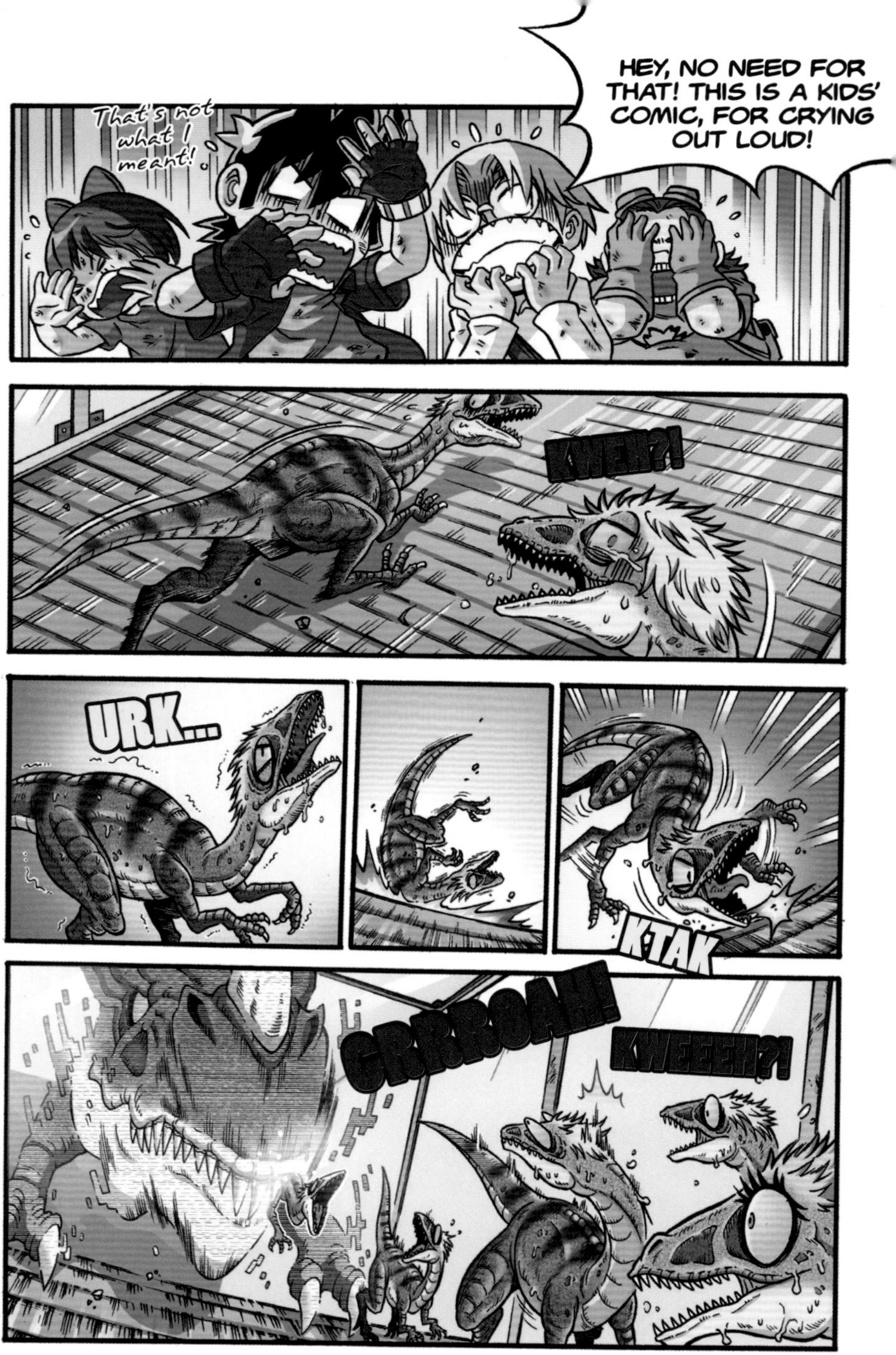
HEY, NO NEED FOR THAT! THIS IS A KIDS' COMIC, FOR CRYING OUT LOUD!
That's not what I meant!
KWEH?!
URK...
KTAK
GRRROAH!
KWEEEH?!

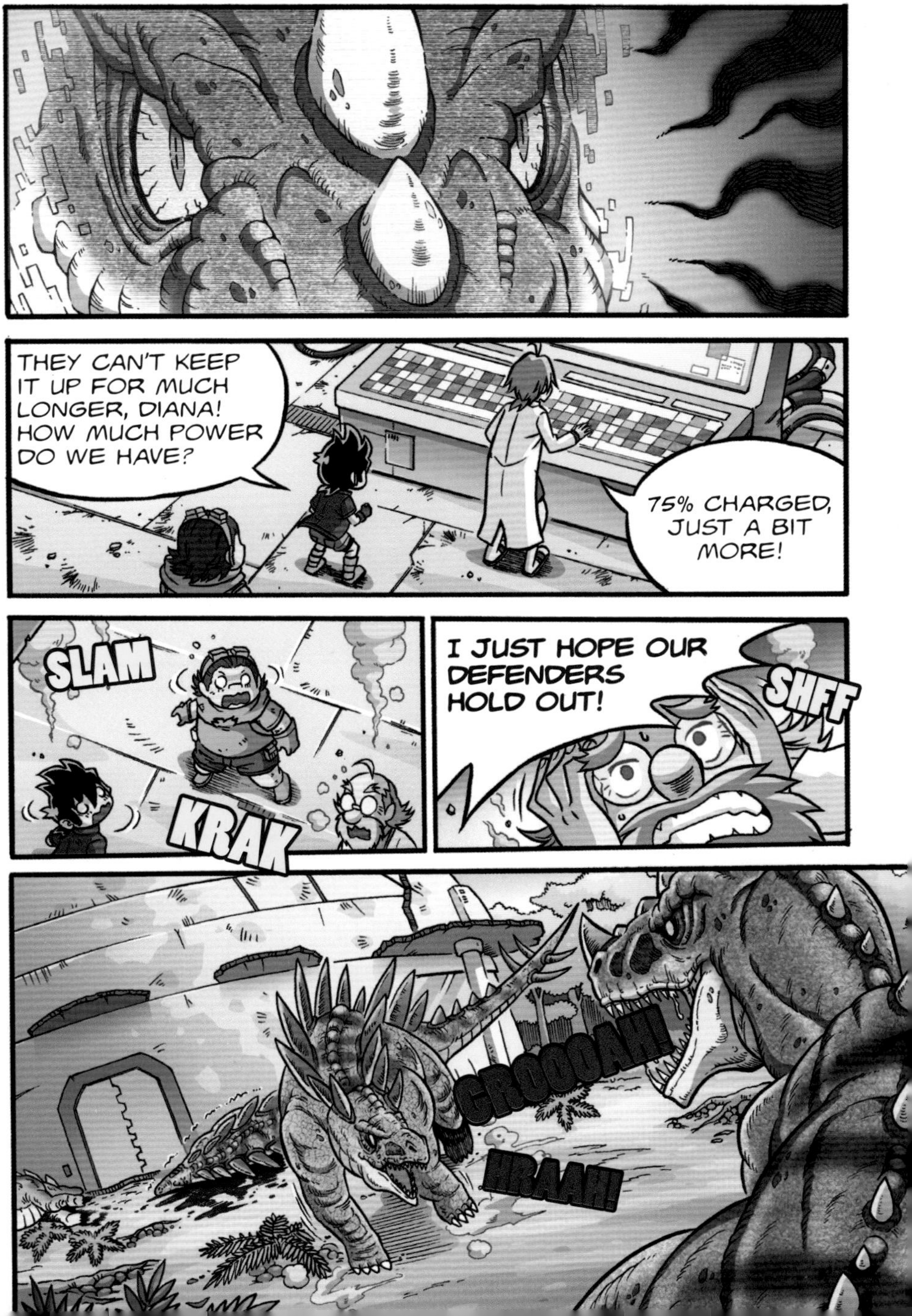

THEY CAN'T KEEP IT UP FOR MUCH LONGER, DIANA! HOW MUCH POWER DO WE HAVE?
75% CHARGED, JUST A BIT MORE!
SLAM
KRAK
I JUST HOPE OUR DEFENDERS HOLD OUT!
SHFF
CROOOAH!
HRAAH!

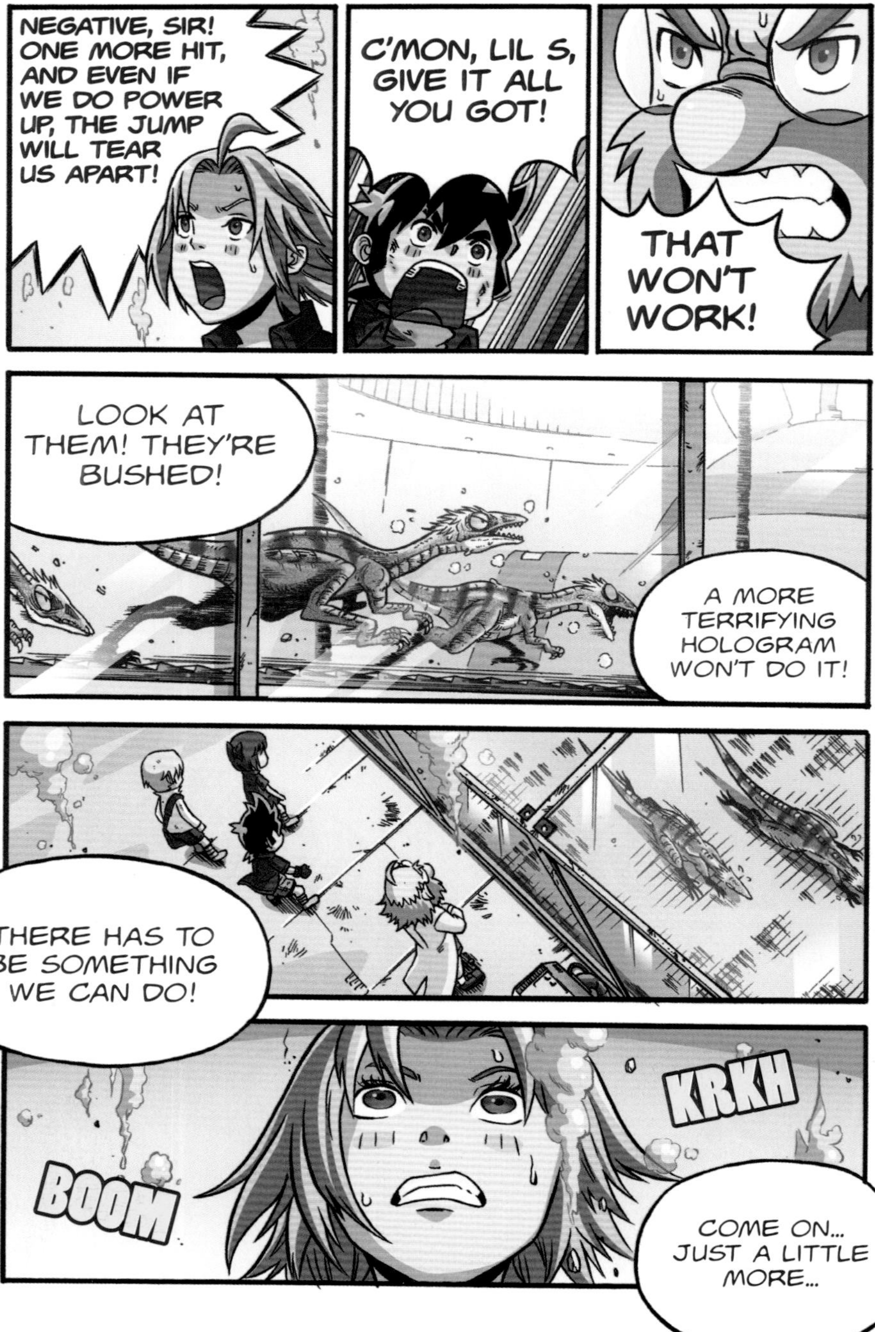
NEGATIVE, SIR! ONE MORE HIT, AND EVEN IF WE DO POWER UP, THE JUMP WILL TEAR US APART!
C'MON, LIL S, GIVE IT ALL YOU GOT!
THAT WON'T WORK!
LOOK AT THEM! THEY'RE BUSHED!
A MORE TERRIFYING HOLOGRAM WON'T DO IT!
THERE HAS TO BE SOMETHING WE CAN DO!
KRKH
BOOM
COME ON... JUST A LITTLE MORE...

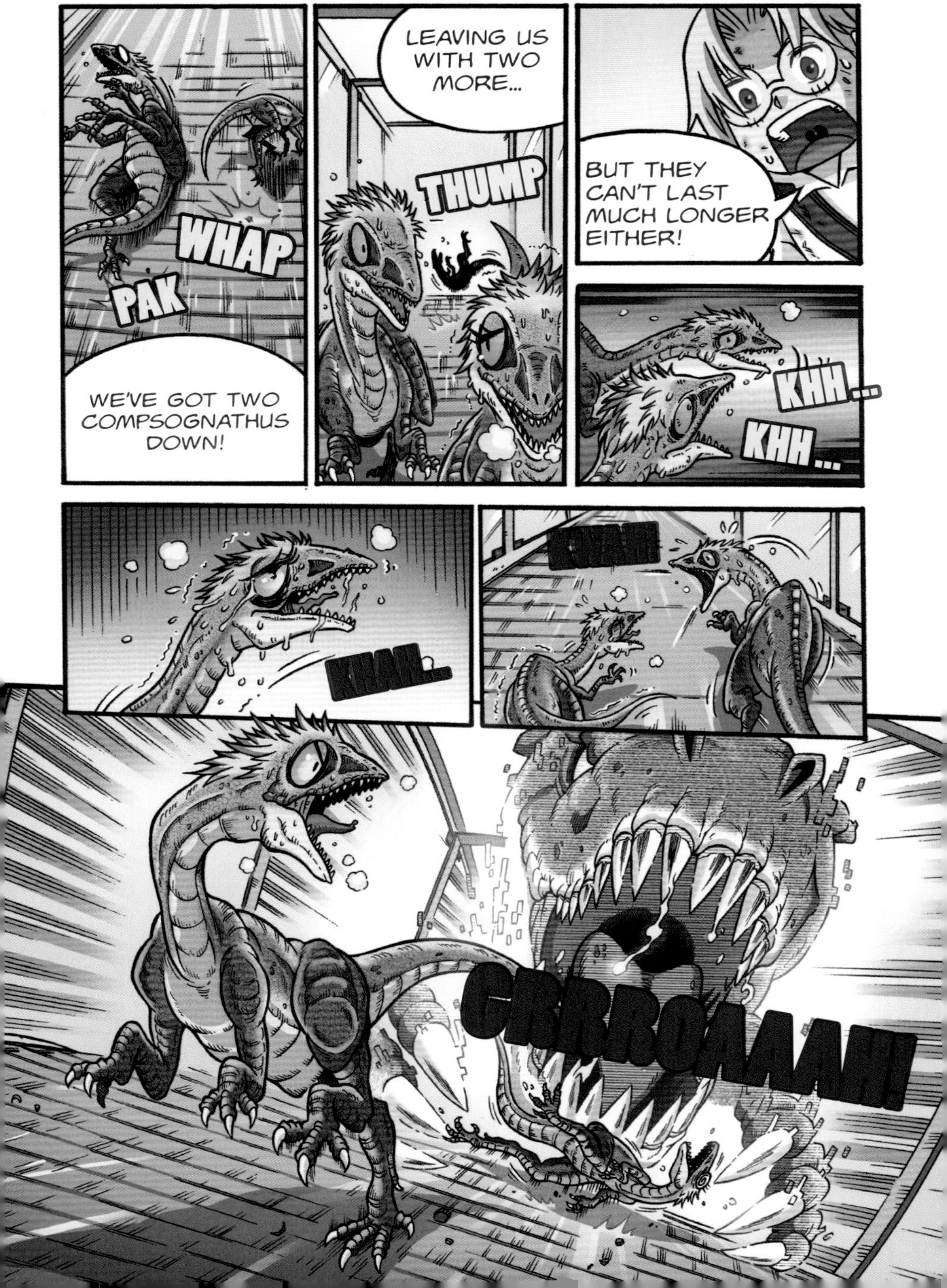
WHAP
PAK
WE'VE GOT TWO COMPSOGNATHUS DOWN!
LEAVING US WITH TWO MORE...
THUMP
BUT THEY CAN'T LAST MUCH LONGER EITHER!
KHH...
KHH...
CRRROAAAH!

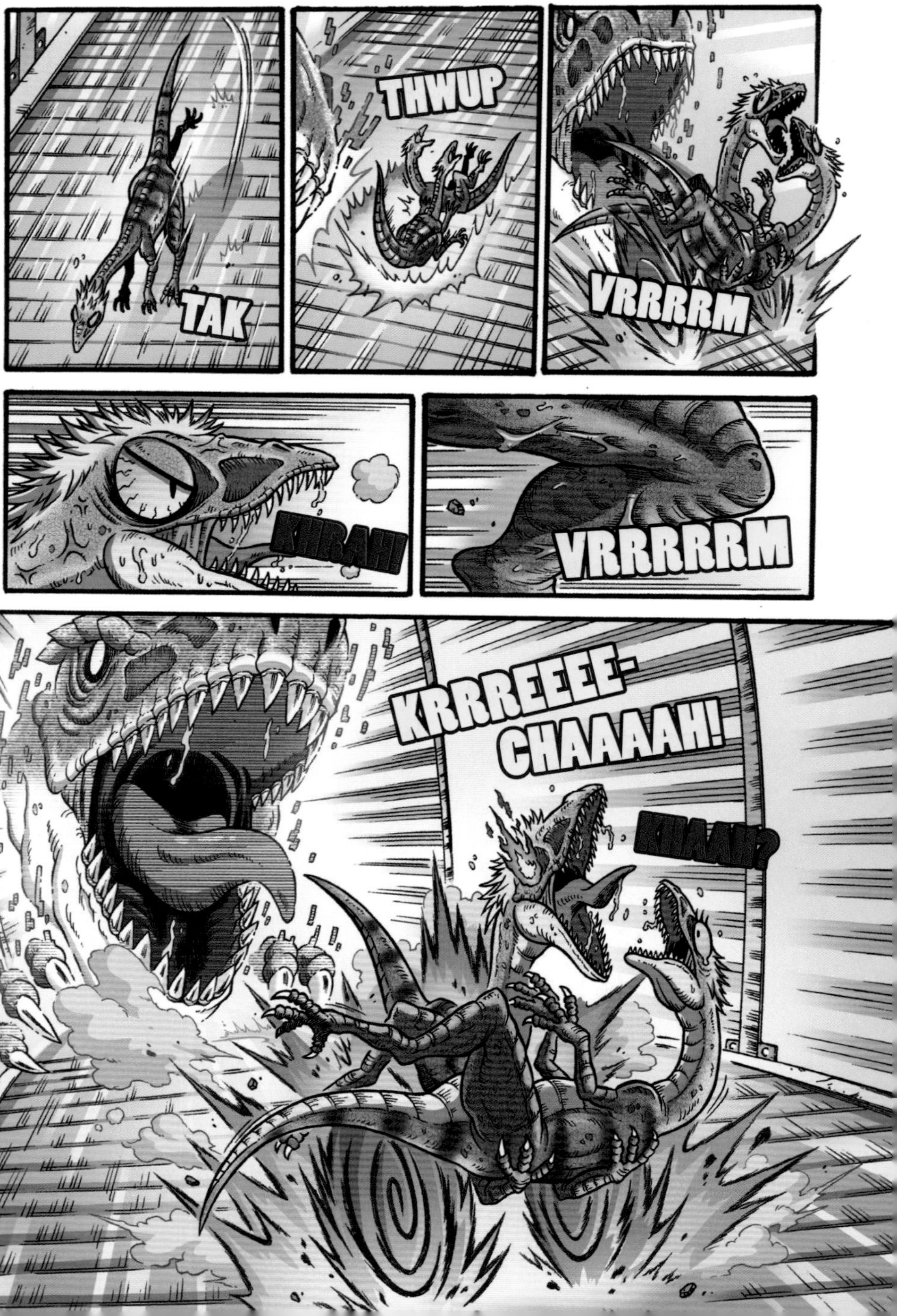
TAK
THWUP
VRRRRM
KHRAH!
VRRRRRM
KRRREEEE-
CHAAAAH!
KHAAH?

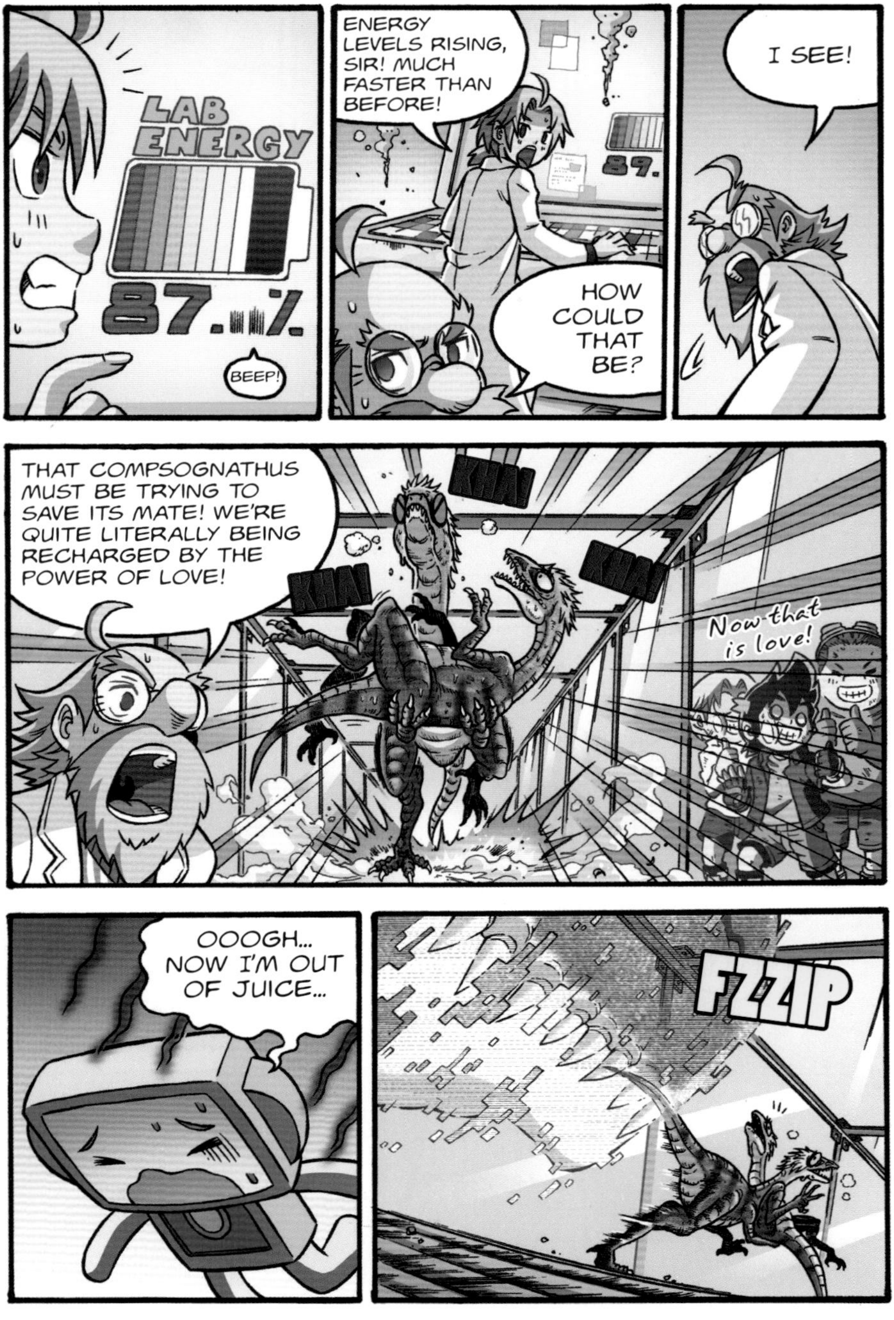
LAB ENERGY
87.%
BEEP!
ENERGY LEVELS RISING, SIR! MUCH FASTER THAN BEFORE!
HOW COULD THAT BE?
I SEE!
THAT COMPSOGNATHUS MUST BE TRYING TO SAVE ITS MATE! WE'RE QUITE LITERALLY BEING RECHARGED BY THE POWER OF LOVE!
KHA!
KHA!
KHA!
Now that is love!
OOOGH... NOW I'M OUT OF JUICE...
FZZIP

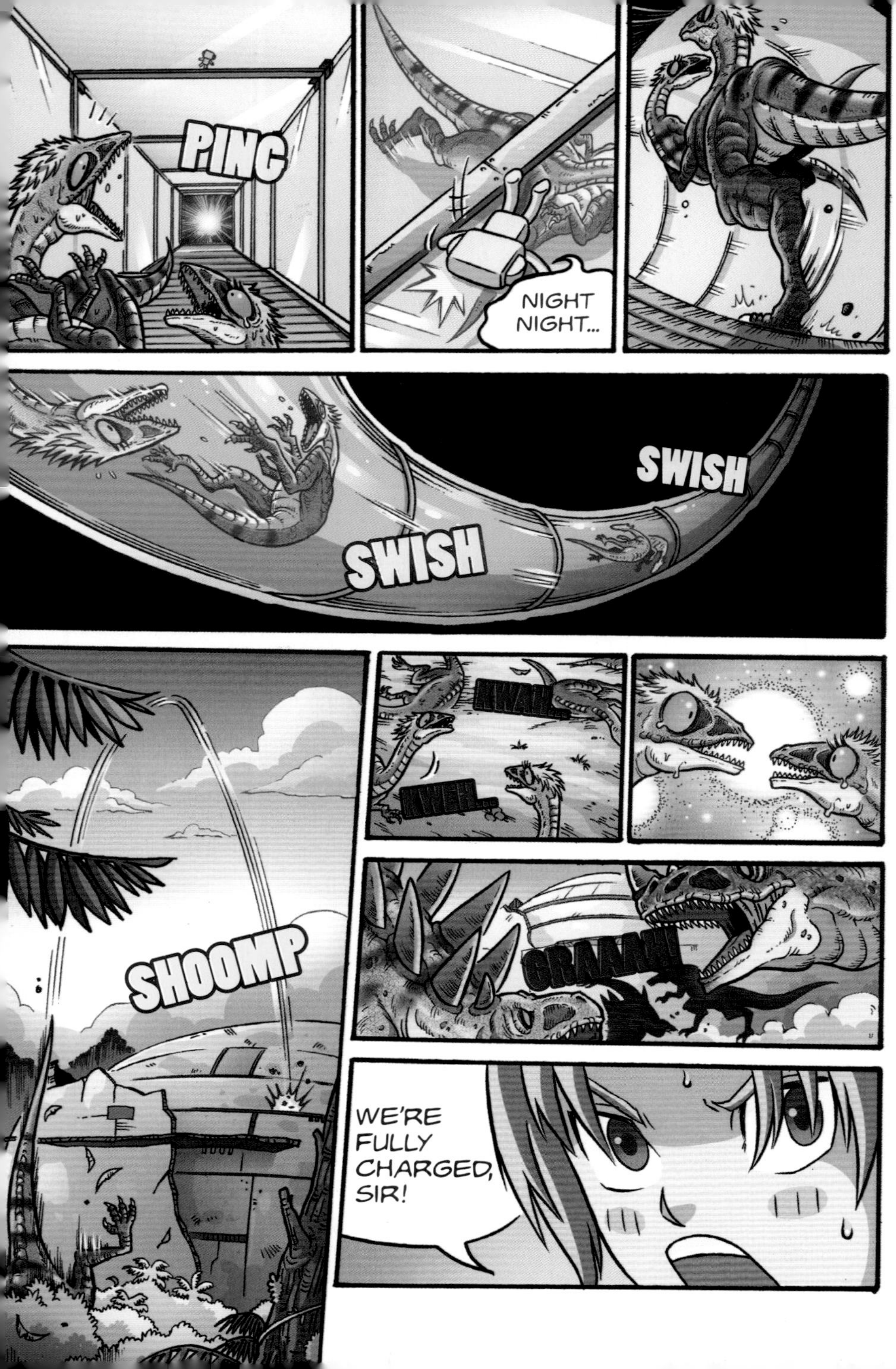
PING
NIGHT NIGHT...
SWISH
SWISH
SHOOMP
KWAH...
KWEH...
WE'RE FULLY CHARGED, SIR!

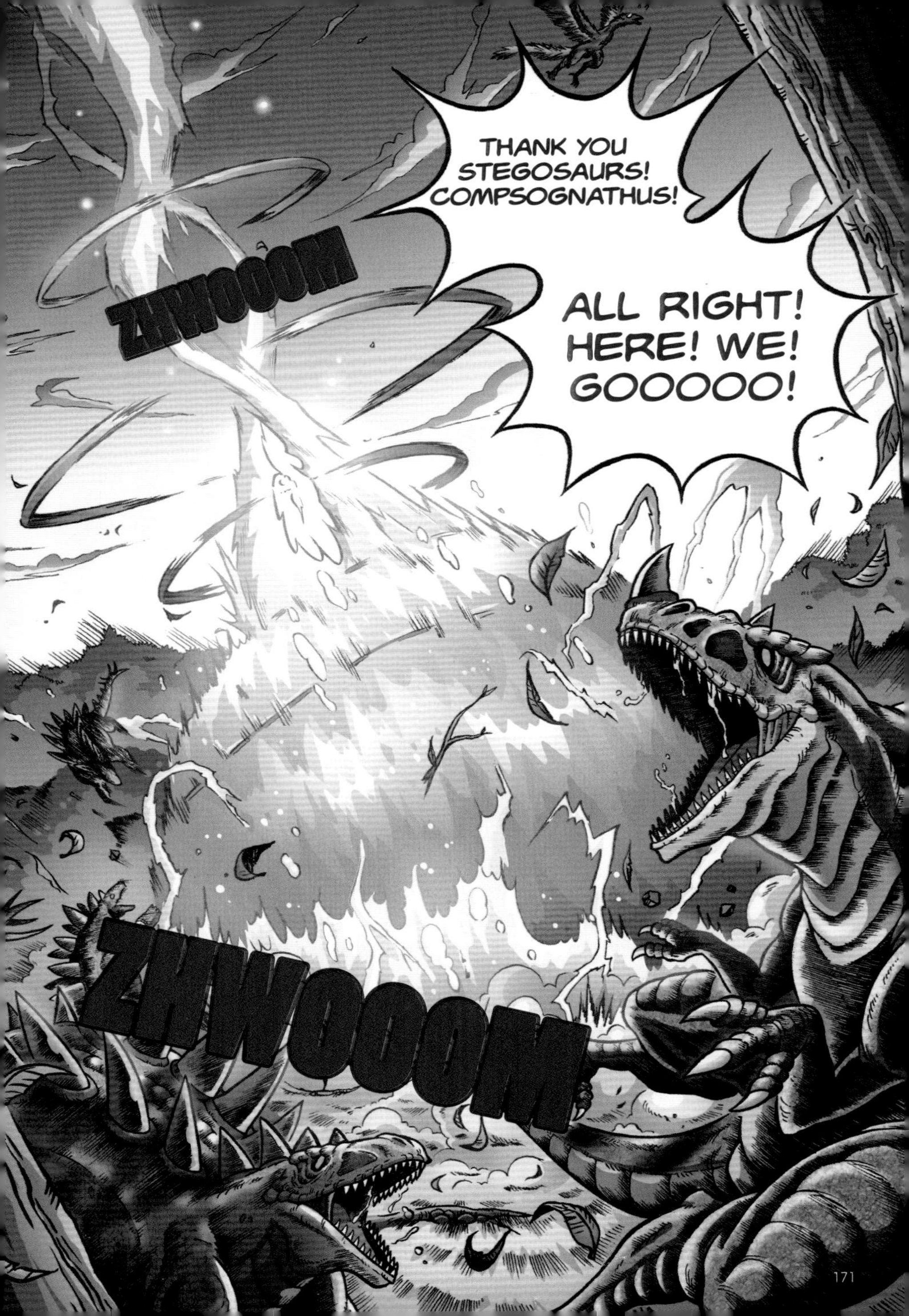
THANK YOU STEGOSAURS! COMPSOGNATHUS!
ZHWOOOM
ALL RIGHT! HERE! WE! GOOOOO!
ZHWOOOM

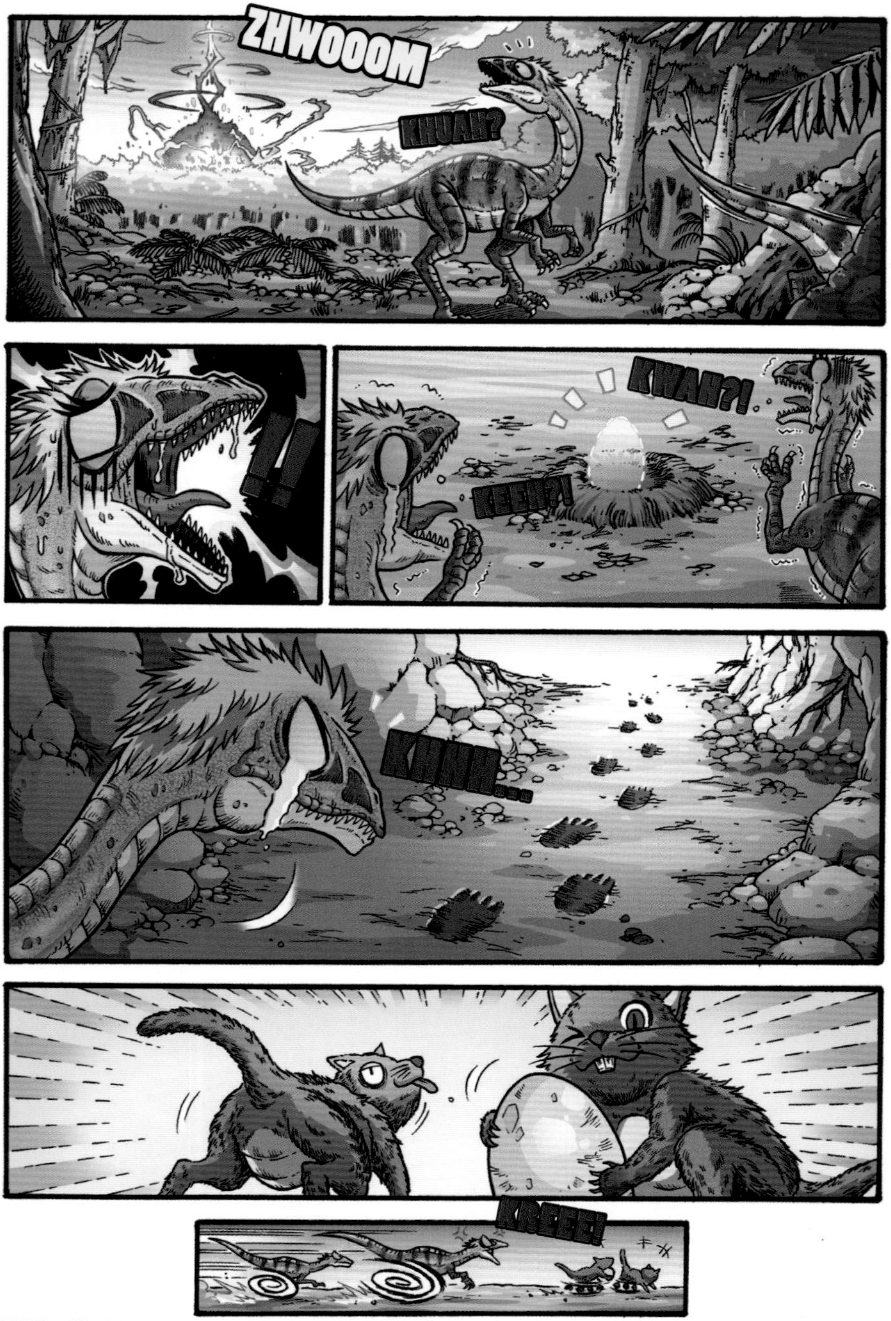
ZHWOOOM
KHUAH?
!!
KWAH?!
KEEH?!
KHHH...
KREEE!

SEE YOU IN DINOSAUR EXPLORERS #7!

Ceratosaurus

Scientific name: Ceratosaurus
Length: 19.7 feet
Diet: Carnivore
Habitat: Forests
Discovered: North America
Era: Late Jurassic

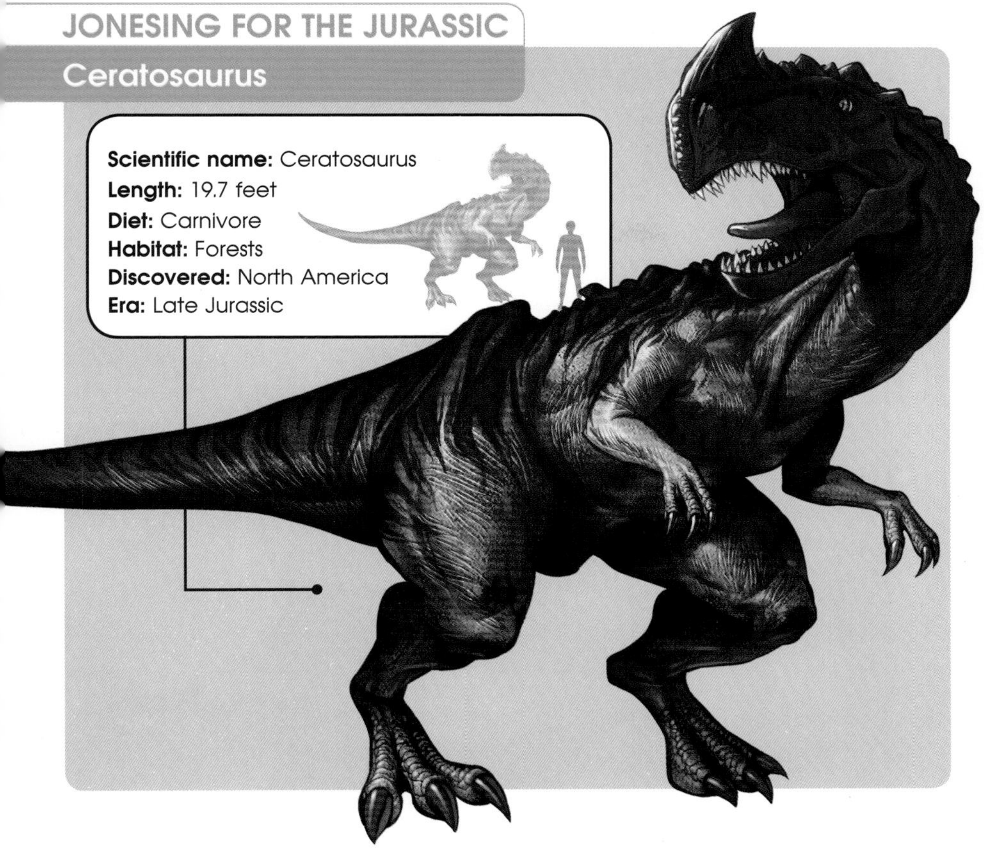

A typical theropod, Ceratosaurus' unique feature was its large blade-like nasal horn, and a pair of hornlets above its eyes. The horns were too short to do harm and as such were thought to be purely cosmetic, to attract mates. Due to its relatively small size, and flattened crocodilie-like tail, experts think that the Ceratosaurus might have been amphibious.

Unique theropod skull features

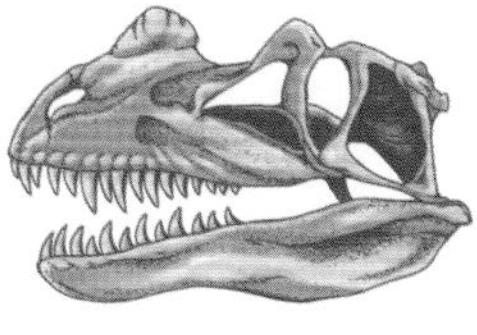

Ceratosaurus
Large horn on the nose, smaller "hornlets" above the eyes.

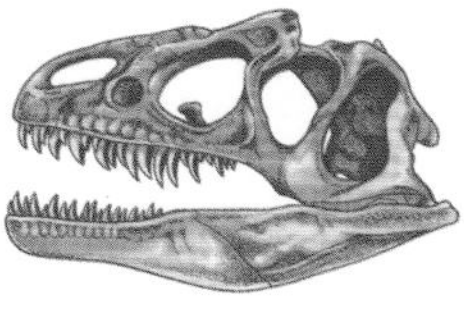

Allosaurus
Bony horn ridges above the eyes.

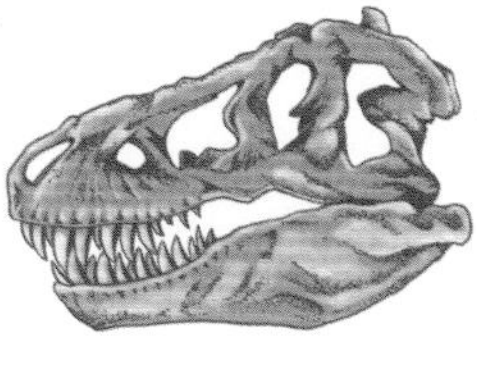

Tyrannosaurus
Small bony ridges above the eyes.

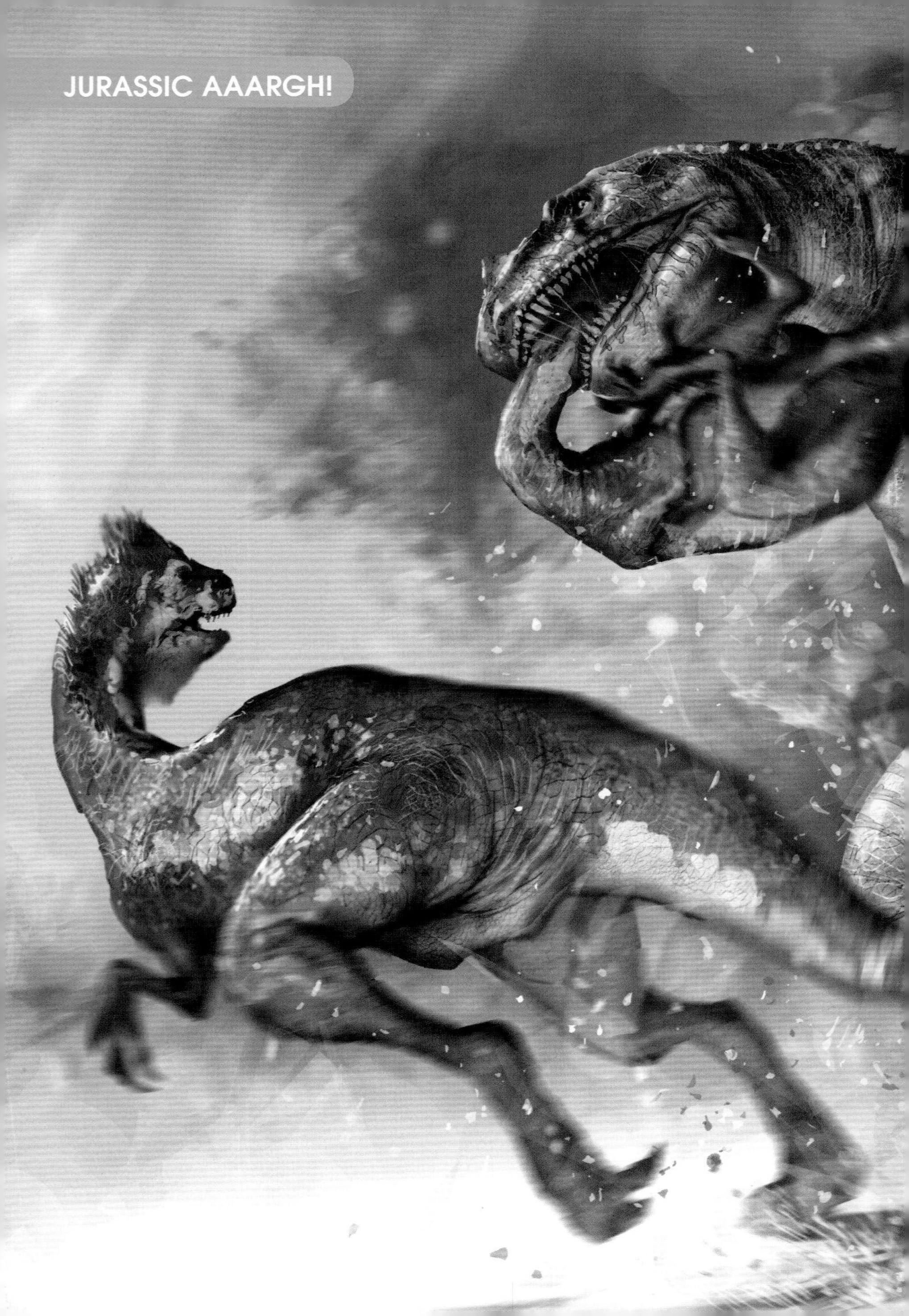

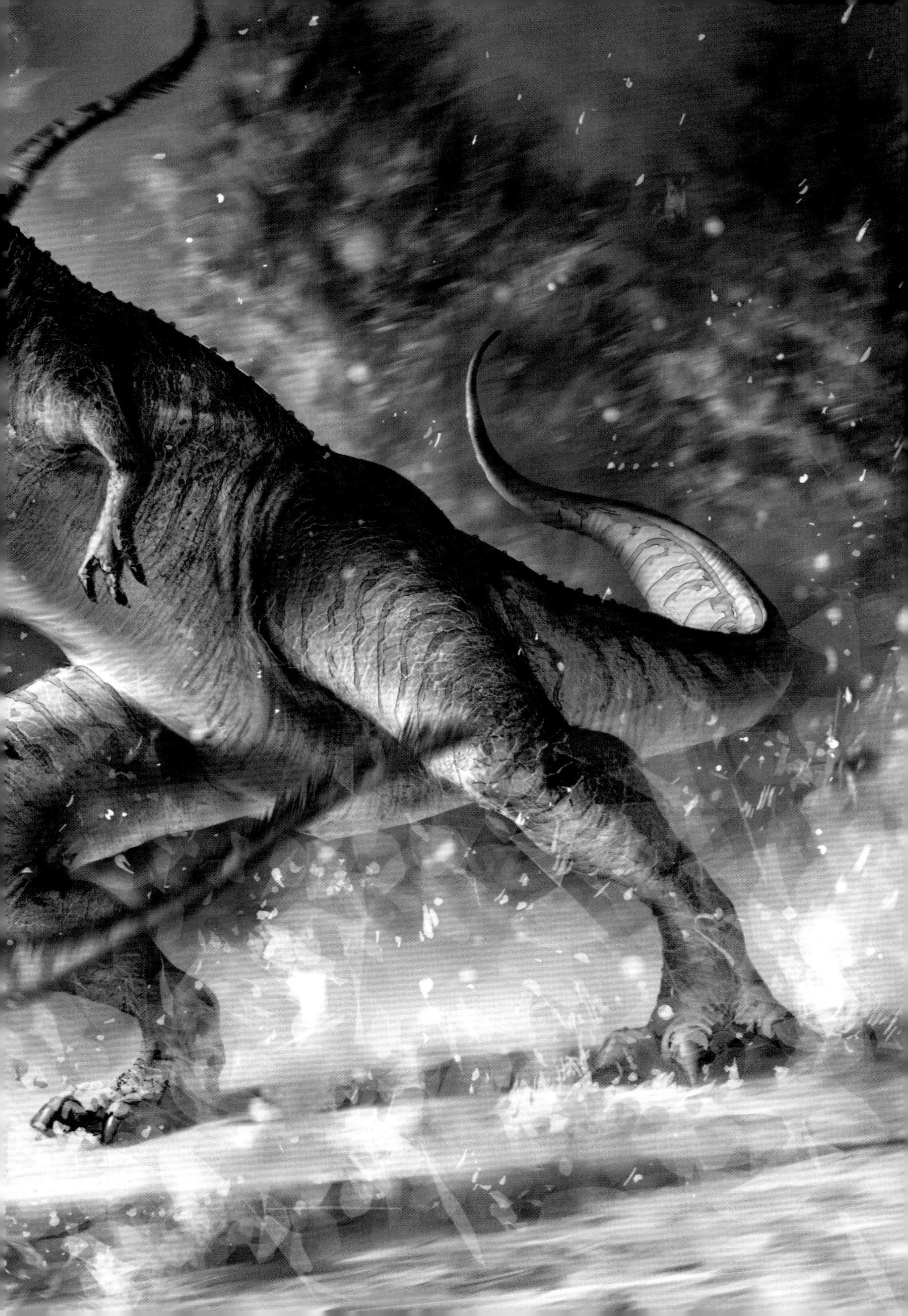

WATCH OUT FOR PAPERCUTZ™

Welcome to the scary, science-filled sixth DINOSAUR EXPLORERS graphic novel by Redcode and Albbie, writers, and Air Team, artists, from Papercutz, those post-historic people dedicated to publishing great graphic novels for all ages. I'm Jim Salicrup, Editor-in-Chief and longtime Flinstones fan, here with some exciting Papercutz publishing news—so exciting, it was even in the New York Times! So exciting, I'm going to tell you all about it right now...

Papercutz has managed to get the North American rights to publish perhaps the most successful comics series in the world—ASTERIX! Now some of you may not have heard of this Asterix fella, so let's take a quick journey in the Papercutz Particle Transmitter...

We're back in the year 50 BC in the ancient country of Gaul, located where France, Belgium, and the Southern Netherlands are today. All of Gaul has been conquered by the Romans... well, not all of it. One tiny village, inhabited by indomitable Gauls, resists the invaders again and again. That doesn't make it easy for the garrisons of Roman soldiers surrounding the village in fortified camps.

So, how's it possible that a small village can hold its own against the mighty Roman Empire? The answer is this guy...

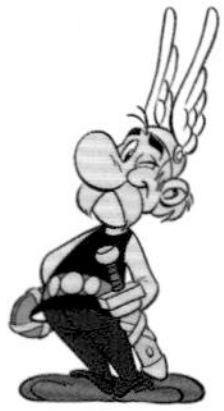

This is **Asterix**. A shrewd, little warrior of keen intellect... and superhuman strength. Asterix gets his superhuman strength from a magic potion. But he's not alone.

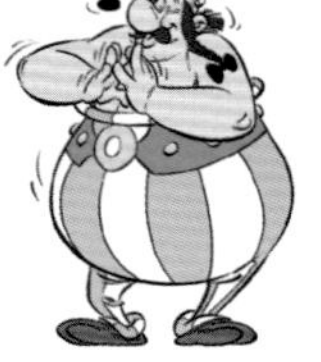

Obelix is Asterix's best friend. He too has superhuman strength. He's a menhir (tall, upright stone monuments) deliveryman, he loves eating wild boar and getting into brawls. Obelix is always ready to drop everything to go off on a new adventure with Asterix.

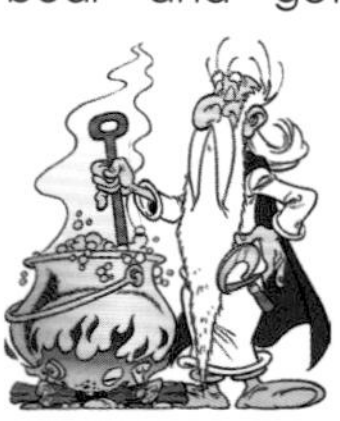

Panoramix, the village's venerable Druid, gathers mistletoe and prepares magic potions. His greatest success is the power potion. When a villager drinks this magical elixir he or she is temporarily granted super-strength. And that's just one of the Druid's potions! And now you know why this small village can survive, despite seemingly impossible odds. While we're here, we may as well meet a few other Gauls...

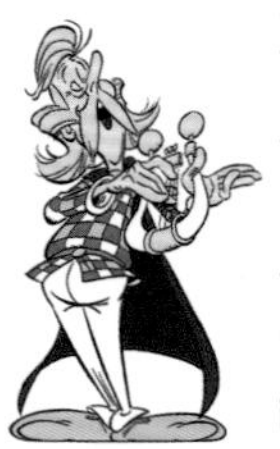

Cacofonix is the bard—the village poet. Opinions about his talents are divided: he thinks he's awesome, everybody else think he's awful, but when he doesn't say anything, he's a cheerful companion and well-liked...

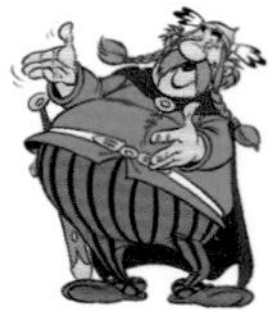

Fisticuffix, finally, is the village's chief. Majestic, courageous, and irritable, the old warrior is respected by his men and feared by his enemies. Fisticuffix has only one fear: that the sky will fall on his head but, as he says himself, "That'll be the day!"

There are plenty more characters around here, but you've met enough for now. It's time we get back to the palatial Papercutz offices, and wrap this up. Now, where did we park that Particle Transmitter...? Oh, there it is!

We're back, and we hope you enjoyed this trip back in time, even if there weren't any dinosaurs to explore in 50 BC. For more information about ASTERIX and his upcoming Papercutz graphic novels, just go to papercutz.com. As for Rain and the rest of the gang, not to mention tons of prehistoric creatures, they'll be back soon in DINOSAUR EXPLORERS #7 "Cretaceous Craziness." We're sure you won't want to miss it!

Thanks, JIM

STAY IN TOUCH!

EMAIL: salicrup@papercutz.com
WEB: www.papercutz.com
TWITTER: @papercutzgn
INSTAGRAM: @papercutzgn
FACEBOOK: PAPERCUTZGRAPHICNOVELS
FANMAIL: Papercutz, 160 Broadway, Suite 700, East Wing, New York, NY 10038

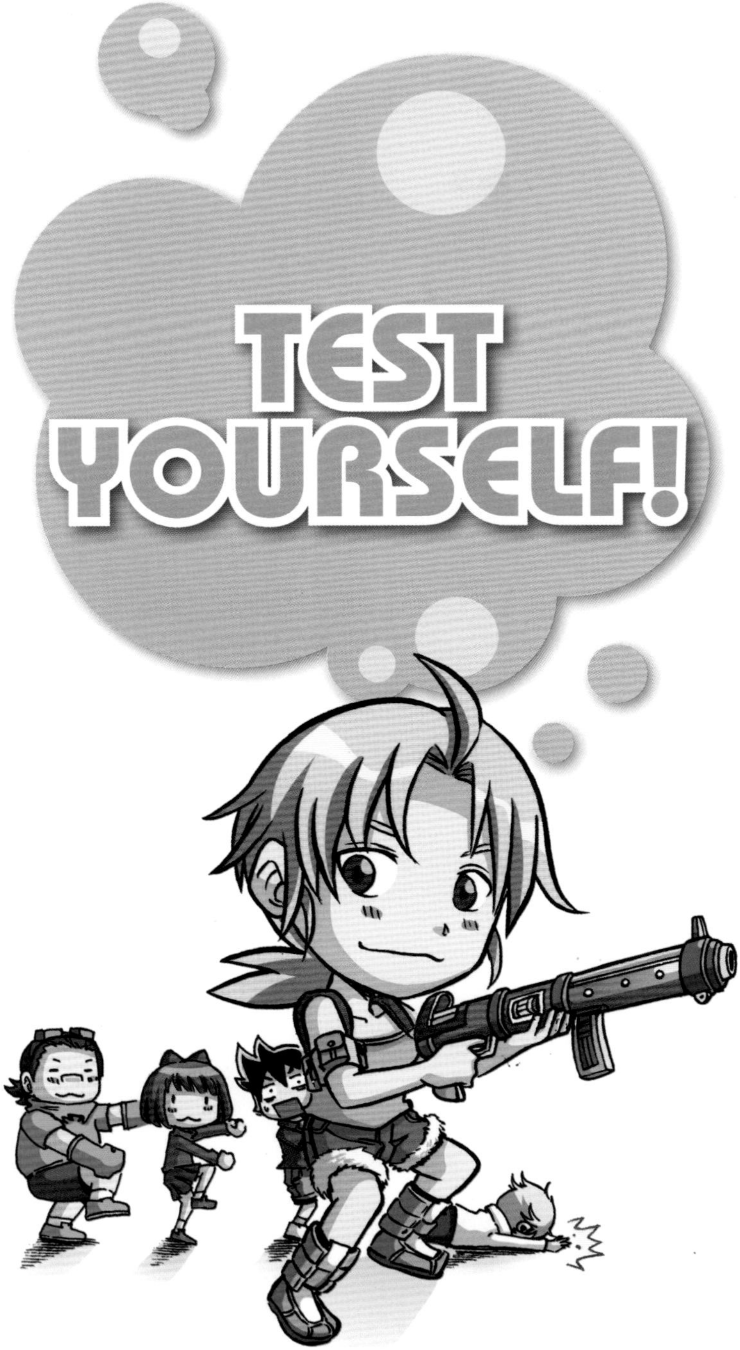
TEST YOURSELF!

ABOUT THE JURASSIC...

01 **How long would a 98.5 feet sauropod's intestines be?**

A - 98.5 feet

B - 262 feet

C - more than 328 feet

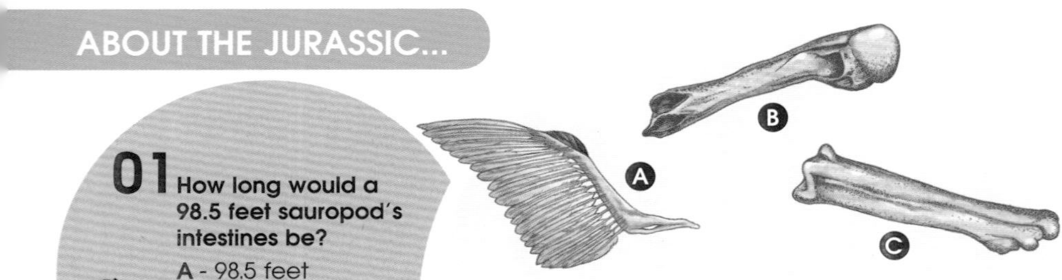

A
B
C

02 **Which of these adaptations, enabled birds to be more agile?**

03 **Which of these was once known as "Brontosaurus"?**

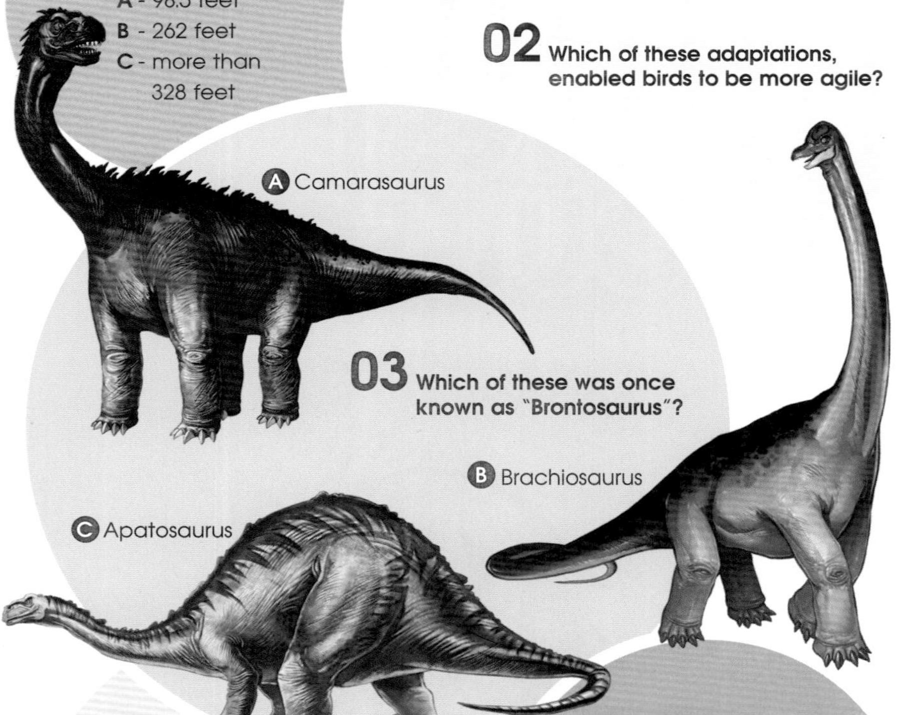

A Camarasaurus
B Brachiosaurus
C Apatosaurus

04 **Which part of the Stegosaurus is shown in this picture?**

A - Leathery skin

B - Blood vessels

C - Teeth

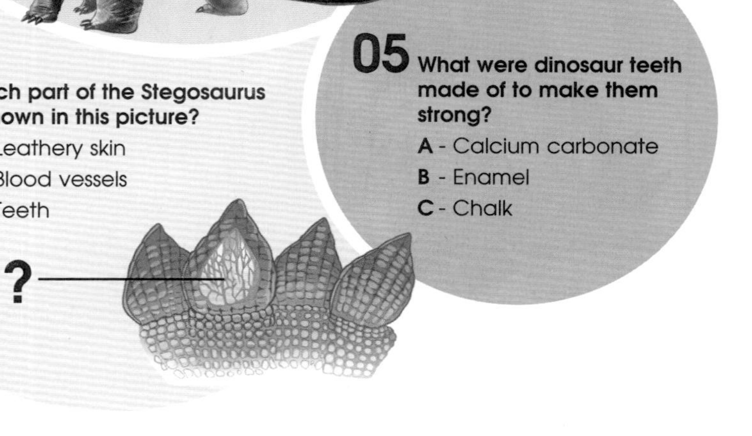

?

05 **What were dinosaur teeth made of to make them strong?**

A - Calcium carbonate

B - Enamel

C - Chalk

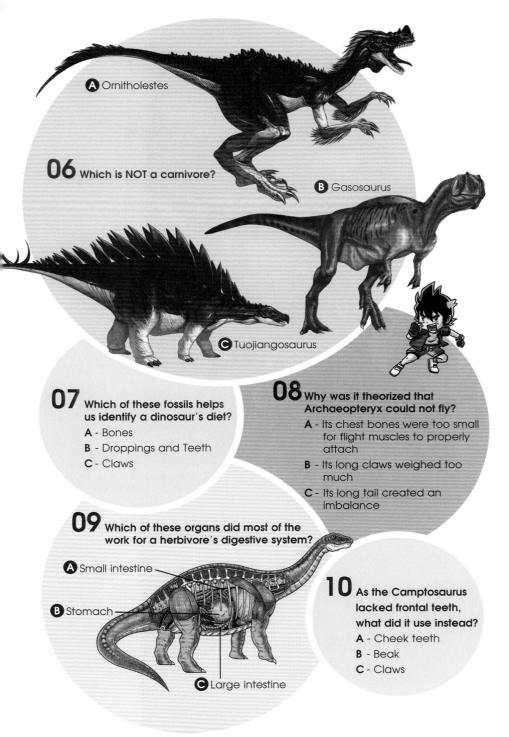

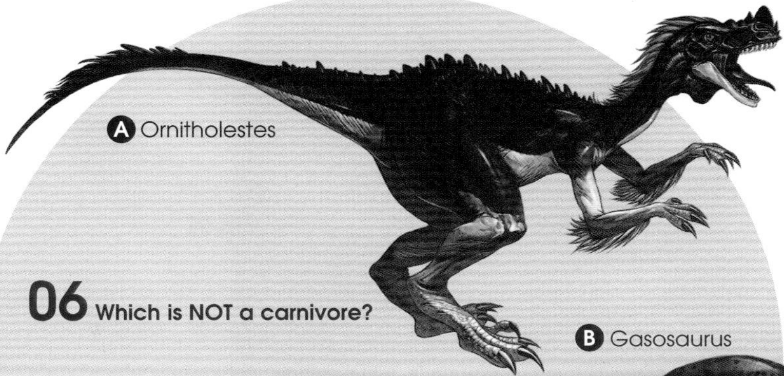
A Ornitholestes

06 Which is NOT a carnivore?

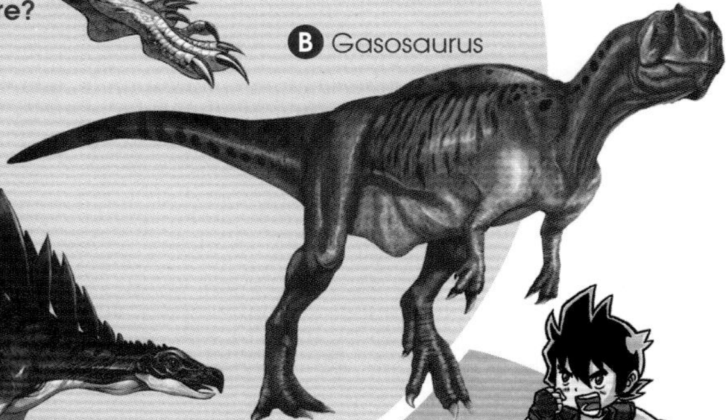
B Gasosaurus

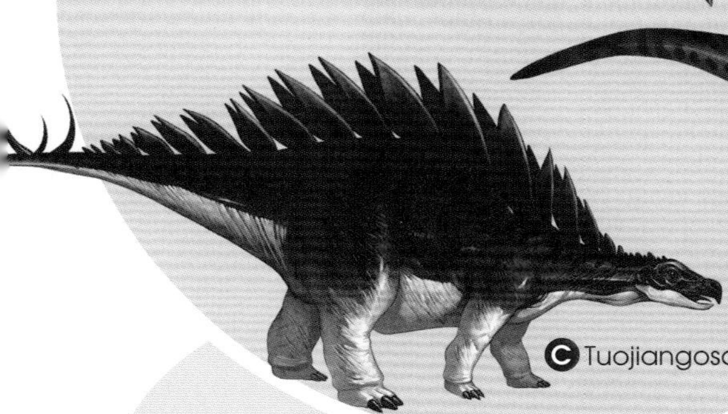
C Tuojiangosaurus

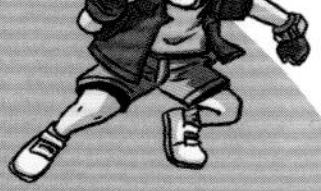

07 Which of these fossils helps us identify a dinosaur's diet?

A - Bones

B - Droppings and Teeth

C - Claws

08 Why was it theorized that Archaeopteryx could not fly?

A - Its chest bones were too small for flight muscles to properly attach

B - Its long claws weighed too much

C - Its long tail created an imbalance

09 Which of these organs did most of the work for a herbivore's digestive system?

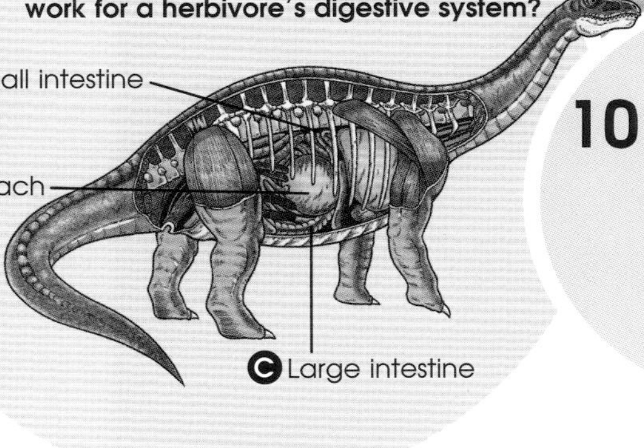
A Small intestine
B Stomach
C Large intestine

10 As the Camptosaurus lacked frontal teeth, what did it use instead?

A - Cheek teeth

B - Beak

C - Claws

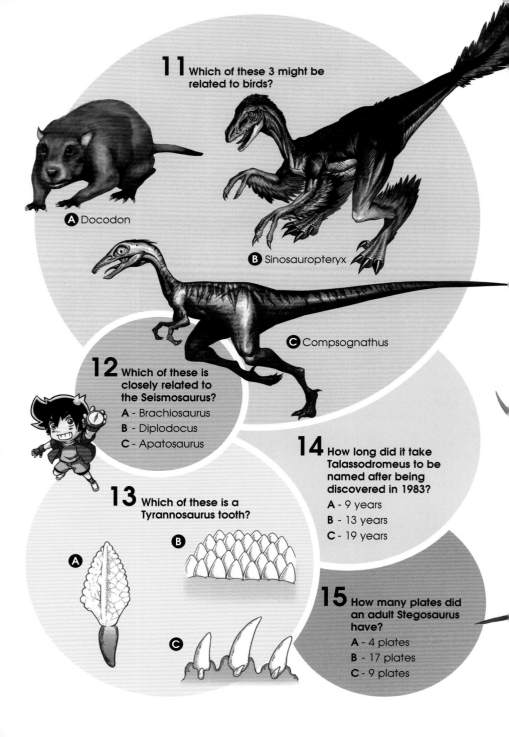

11 Which of these 3 might be related to birds?

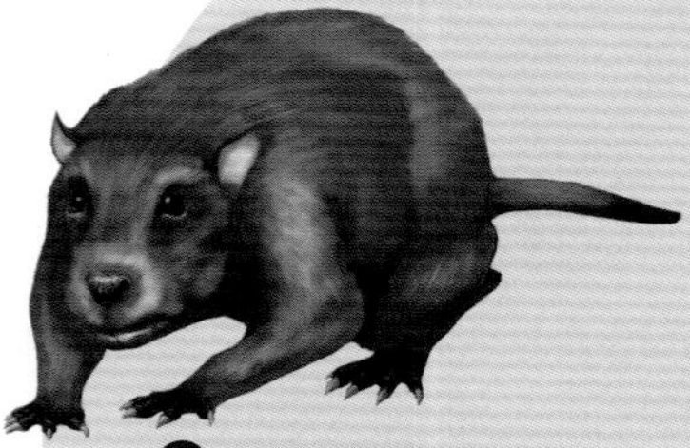

A Docodon

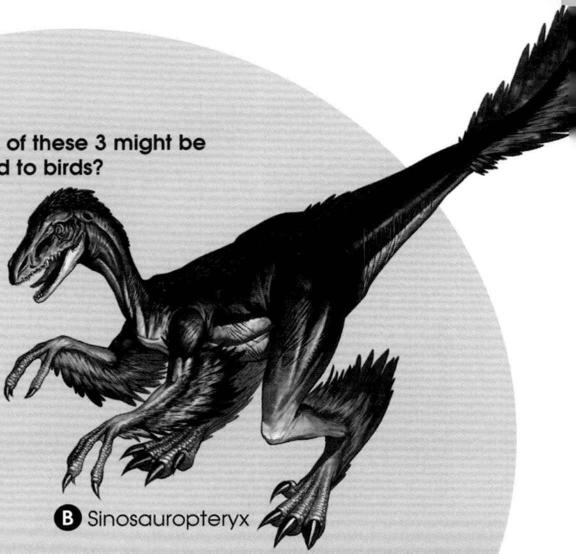

B Sinosauropteryx

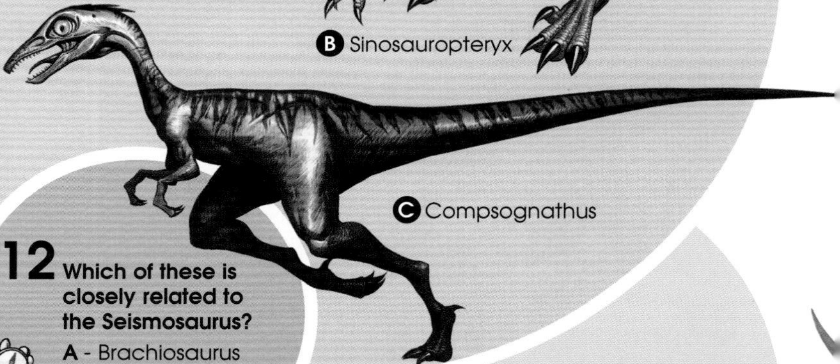

C Compsognathus

12 Which of these is closely related to the Seismosaurus?

A - Brachiosaurus

B - Diplodocus

C - Apatosaurus

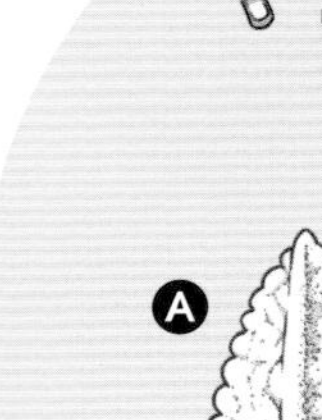

13 Which of these is a Tyrannosaurus tooth?

A

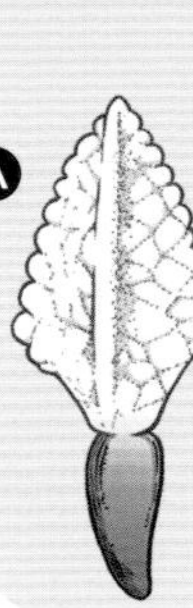

B

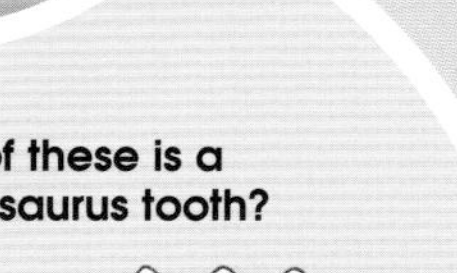

C

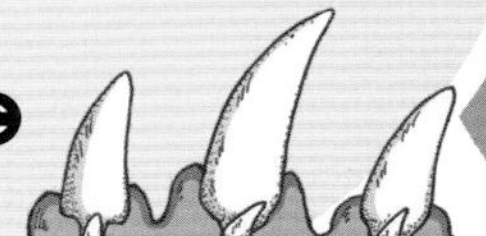

14 How long did it take Talassodromeus to be named after being discovered in 1983?

A - 9 years

B - 13 years

C - 19 years

15 How many plates did an adult Stegosaurus have?

A - 4 plates

B - 17 plates

C - 9 plates

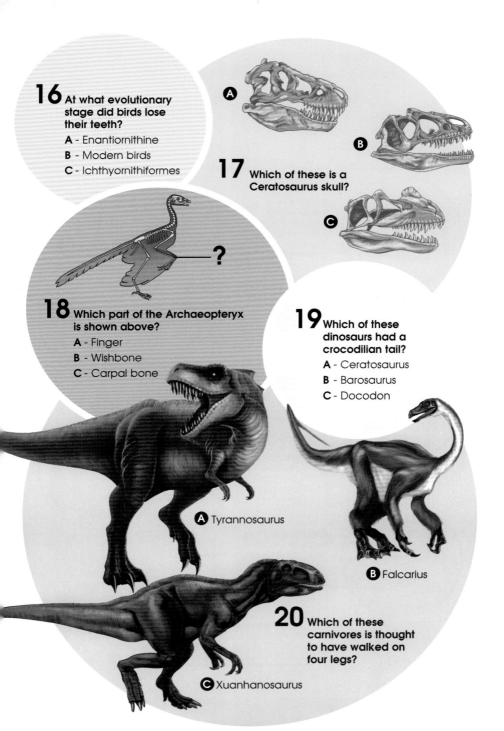

16 At what evolutionary stage did birds lose their teeth?

A - Enantiornithine
B - Modern birds
C - Ichthyornithiformes

A

B

17 Which of these is a Ceratosaurus skull?

C

?

18 Which part of the Archaeopteryx is shown above?

A - Finger
B - Wishbone
C - Carpal bone

19 Which of these dinosaurs had a crocodilian tail?

A - Ceratosaurus
B - Barosaurus
C - Docodon

A Tyrannosaurus

B Falcarius

20 Which of these carnivores is thought to have walked on four legs?

C Xuanhanosaurus

ANSWERS

01 C	02 B	03 C	04 B	05 B
06 C	07 B	08 A	09 C	10 A
11 B	12 B	13 C	14 C	15 B
16 B	17 C	18 C	19 A	20 C

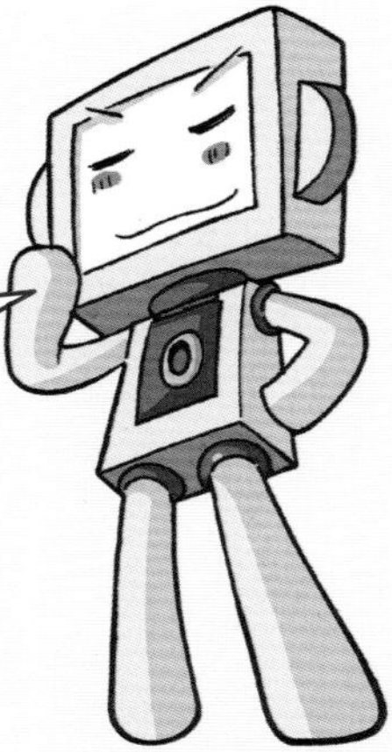

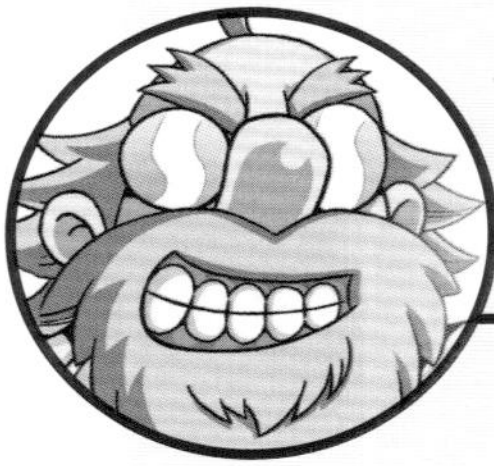

All correct?

Congrats! You're as smart as I am! I think.

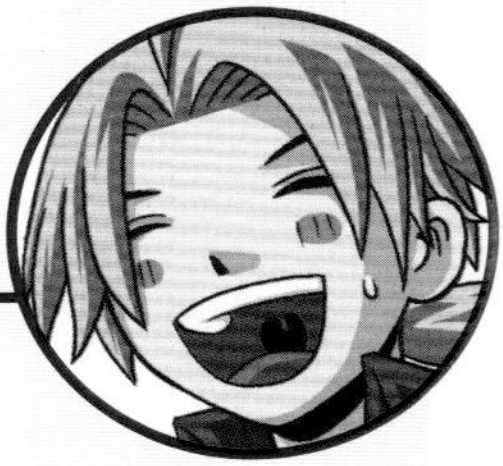

16 – 19 correct?

I'm actually smarter than the Doctor! Don't tell anyone!

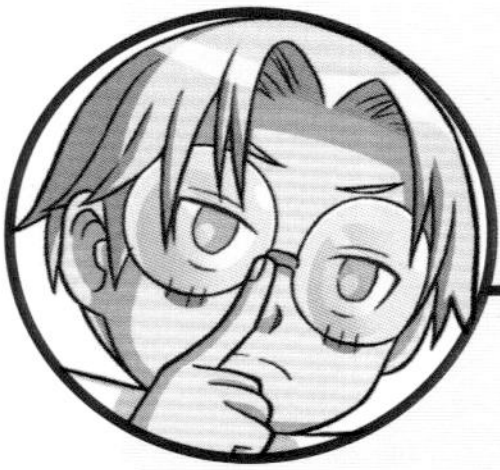

12 – 15 correct?

Don't just take in knowledge — apply it to real life!

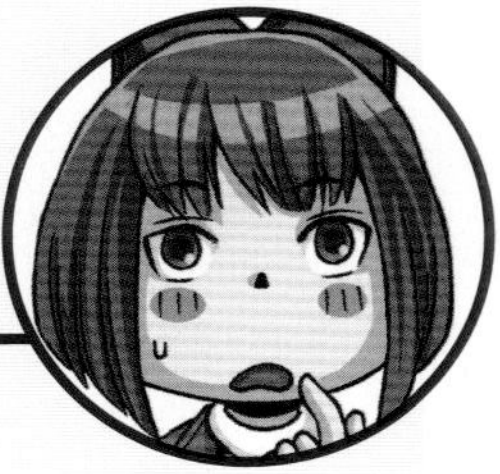

8 – 11 correct?

What? You're smarter than me? Impossible!

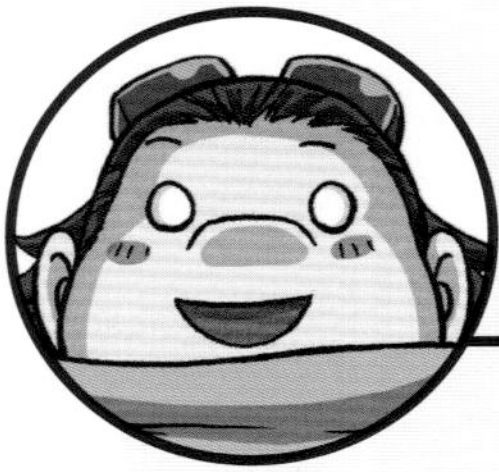

4 – 7 correct?

Huh, looks like we both can use some work! Let's go to the library! Studying's better with friends!

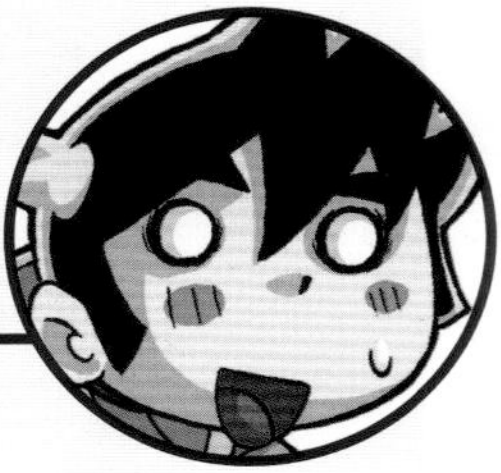

0 – 3 correct?

Don't worry, you're as S-M-R-T smart as me!

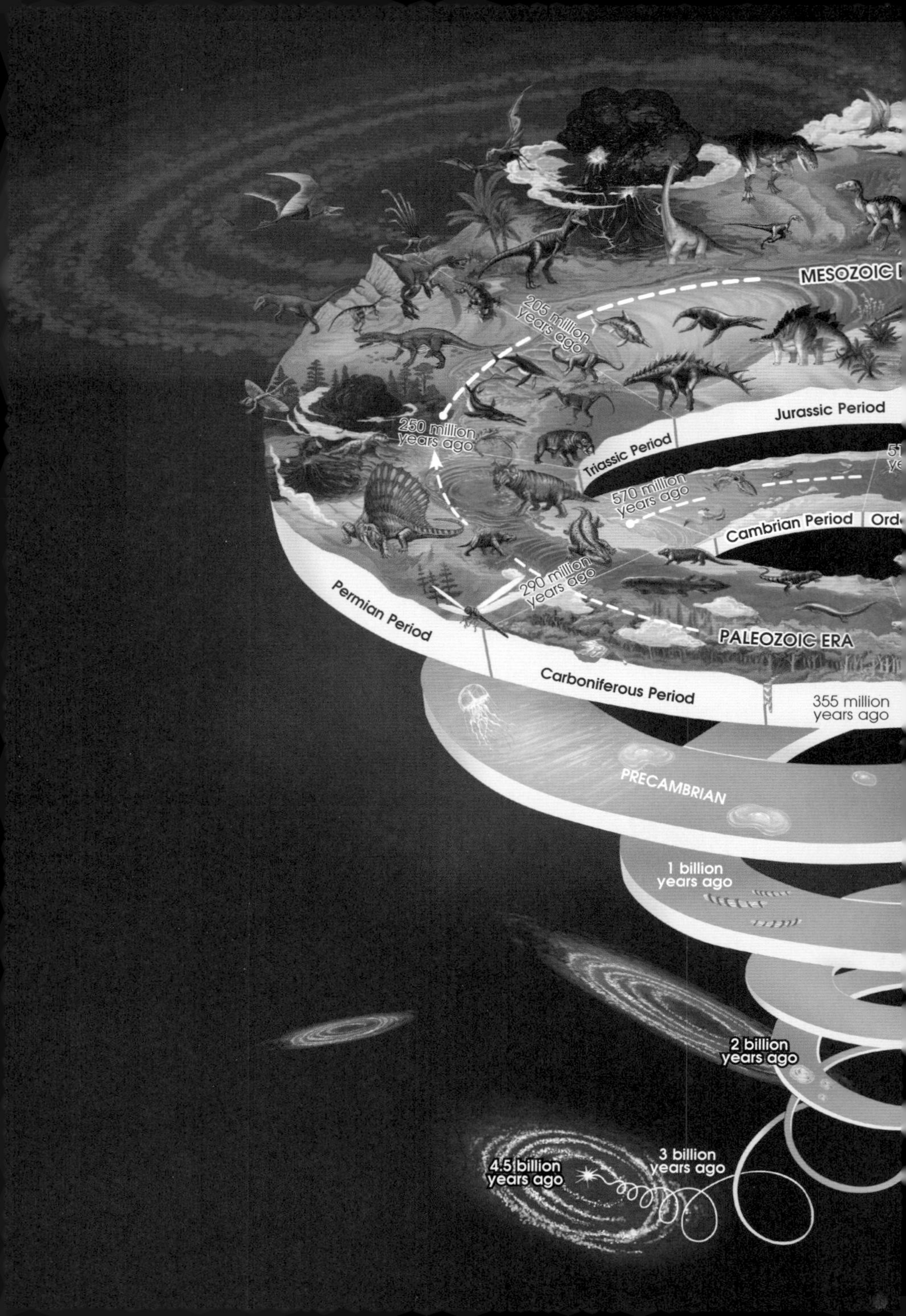
MESOZOIC
205 million years ago
250 million years ago
Triassic Period
Jurassic Period
570 million years ago
Cambrian Period
290 million years ago
Permian Period
PALEOZOIC ERA
Carboniferous Period
355 million years ago
PRECAMBRIAN
1 billion years ago
2 billion years ago
3 billion years ago
4.5 billion years ago